Lucifer Rising

by
Sharon Bowers

JUSTICE HOUSE PUBLISHING

Tacoma, Washington
www.justicehouse.com

Lucifer Rising

by
Sharon Bowers

JUSTICE HOUSE PUBLISHING

Tacoma, Washington
www.justicehouse.com

ISBN: 0-9677687-2-1
This printing January 2000
2 3 4 5 6 7 8 9

PRINTED IN CANADA

For KG...

Because I promised you the first one, so many years ago...

Acknowledgements

Many thanks belong to people whose names I don't know.
Who sent words of encouragement for absolutely no reason.
I'm still floored by the power of it all. Thank you.

For those whose names I do know... Thanks belong to the "It's All Fiction" girls— who let me get away with saying that far too many times. To Chris, for listening to me rant and rave— not to mention designing my book cover. To Cris, whose support during this whole thing was invaluable. To Claire, for her generosity, her patience, her willingness to go there a million times listening to me talk.

And to my mother and father— for pretending never to be shocked by it all.

*Special thanks go to Susan L. Because she believed in the book before I did. Because she wouldn't let me get away with **not** writing it. I wish you only the best.*

Sharon Bowers
September 1999

Thus says the Lord God: "You were the seal of perfection, full of wisdom and perfect in beauty. You were in Eden, the garden of God... You were the anointed cherub who covers; I established you; you were on the holy mountain of God; you walked back and forth in the midst of fiery stones. You were perfect in your ways from the day you were created till iniquity was found in you... You became filled with violence within, and you sinned; therefore I cast you as a profane thing out of the mountain of God; and I destroyed you...

Ezekiel 28:12

Chapter 1

There was one advantage to wearing the black hat in the government's modern dress version of cowboys and Indians, Jude Lucien thought as she smoothly shifted her new Porsche Boxster and slid easily out of the congested Miami traffic. *You get all the cool toys.* The car was right off the lot, paid for with the hard-earned dollars of some Colombian drug dealers that she had shanghaied a few weeks ago. They were amateurs anyway, a group of yahoos just off the plane, trying to hustle their way into the business with a few kilos of blow and some Glock 9mms. *Obviously they didn't understand the organized part of organized crime.* Jude snorted in memory of the men who first thought they could bluster their way through a meeting with her, and then—when that didn't work—bully her into making a deal with them by waving their guns around. One man choked to death after she crushed his larynx with a well-placed jab; the other had fallen to his knees in appeal when he saw his friend's fate. A swift bullet to the head had ended his pleas for mercy. Fortunately for him, the Colombians' supplier was a man of greater vision who had smoothly transferred his allegiance—and his product—to Jude's operation.

It's some bizarre Darwinian mutation, she mused as she hit the long stretch of ocean highway on her way home. *Survival of the most ruthless.*

Worthiness no longer has a place... it all comes down to ability to do what has to be done. And those bastards weren't able to. Her roiling thoughts were at odds with the panoramic vista to her right— long stretches of exotic houses bordering an impossibly blue ocean— and more in line with the bloody demise of the sun on her left. Jagged, red-gold tendrils streaked the twilight sky, giving way on the evening's stage to the unnatural vibrancy of the Neon City. Her Miami only really came alive once the night had ascended, when people seemed mistakenly to believe that their transgressions were, if not invalid, then at least invisible. In a way, Jude was like the gatekeeper of their debauchery. Certainly whenever she entered a room, her presence evoked primal memories of the seven deadly sins in those who watched her.

Jude Lucien was barely past her thirtieth birthday, but there was a timeless sense of assurance in the way she moved. She was tall and sleek, with a polished veneer of civility that still couldn't conceal the truculent energy that was her essence. Confronted with the hard planes of her cheekbones, the inky fullness of her black hair, and the seductive indigo of her eyes; most people were generally rendered speechless. The smart ones, however, never forgot about the cunning mind that whirred incessantly behind those baby blues.

"Presentation is everything..." Jude vaguely remembered her mother once saying. Although time had rendered both her mother and most of her pronouncements meaningless, whenever Jude rose to a social occasion, she was inevitably reminded of her mother's incessant harangues on the subject. Shalimar, incense, and the relentless cadence of her mother's voice raised in anger or prayer were pretty much the only remembrances remaining from Jude's childhood. They were also the very things that she left far behind when she had last walked out of the ramshackle slum her mother called a boardinghouse. Fifteen years later, the lectures on manners, breeding, and appearance that she had done her best to ignore now served the dark woman well. Jude could sit a table with royal elegance, discuss fine art and literature knowledgeably, and wear couture gowns so well it would make a model weep with jealousy. Unfortunately it was all in the service of a bloody and dark business that would have chilled her mother's unknowing soul.

To call Jude *just* a drug dealer would be about as accurate and all-encompassing as calling da Vinci *just* a painter. Her long fingers reached all over the world, and they were dipped not just in the honey pots of the drug trade, but also in gun running and gambling as well as assorted other legitimate businesses. For reasons baffling to her competitors, Jude drew the line at peddling human flesh. *"I don't begrudge anyone his or her pleasures,"* she said on the subject. *"But quite frankly the idea of my people providing a girl to some fat, old man so he can shove his dick up her ass does not appeal to me."*

Once the dark, golden prodigy of the Drug Enforcement Agency, Jude was now biting with a vengeance the hand that used to feed her. They had plucked her from the streets, where she was a wild child rapidly making a name for herself in murky corridors, and submerged her in a world of liquid decadence and powdered highs. They had changed her name and given her a badge that wouldn't protect her in the circles where she traveled. However, the unique skills that Jude brought to her new life could not be taught in any academy. Something in her had always responded to the maleficent call of those she was obligated to hunt, making her the perfect undercover agent. In a world where one misstep meant an instant and irreversible retribution, she had thrived—snaring increasingly larger prizes and turning them obediently over to her DEA masters. Somewhere along the line, something went complexly—horrifically— wrong.

◻ ◻ ◻

"The Seraph of Death?" Jack Lucas looked incredulously at the small, golden-haired woman who stood before him. "What the fuck is a seraph?" He ran a hand through his ill-cut shaggy, gray hair. "Is that some new AIDS strain?"

The woman tapped her foot impatiently at his tirade and waited for her editor to calm down. "A seraph is an angel, Lucas. That's all."

"Then why the fuck don't you say 'The Angel of Death?' This is the Miami *Herald*, Liz, half your readership doesn't speak English too well, let alone know what a fucking seraph is."

Liz Gardener winced every time Lucas said *fuck*—which was a lot. So much so that the newsroom editor asked her once if she had some sort of nervous condition. "I can't call her the Angel of Death because that makes her sound like a half-baked sidekick to Jack Kevorkian. Seraph is more menacing, don't you think?" Clear green eyes gleamed in excitement over her subject. Liz had been on the beat only a year or so, and she hadn't yet lost her enthusiasm. She also had a real gift for the language that made someone like Lucas—who had been very much a plain *who-what-when-where* reporter—ache with both pride and envy.

Lucas flung himself dramatically back in his chair and appraised his star pupil. "Menacing? Yeah, babe, it's menacing. But read the fucking article. Alleged this—alleged that—rehashing the trial—which was over a year ago. And she was fucking acquitted! All you got is menacing. Where're your sources? I know you got 'em, cause you ain't been running around this last month making shit up."

Liz squirmed uncomfortably in her chair. She knew the article was weak, but her hands had been tied. "My sources won't talk on the record and the DEA files are sealed. Security issues—they say." She snorted dismissively. "We'd have to go to court in order to get them opened, and that would blow my plan right out of the water anyway."

"Waitaminute!" Lucas held out a hand. "One: you want me to run a story like this without at least two credible, named sources? You know better than that. Two: what do you mean 'your plan?'"

Liz grinned brilliantly at her boss. The story had been a lure to get the editor interested. She knew there was way more to this than just a simple article, and she fully intended to get the whole thing. "Lucas, you know as well as I do—there's something big here. It's got everything—drugs, murder, corrupt law enforcement. And a beautiful woman at the center of it all."

"The story was last year, Liz." He folded his arms, but Liz could tell by the way his eyes never left hers that he was hooked. Usually when Lucas had made up his mind, he dismissed his petitioner by returning to the insurmountable piles on his desk. Liz ascribed to the theory that there were two major forms of organization—files and piles. Lucas—God bless his irascible, tiny heart—was a piler. She glanced around the mountains of paper surrounding her and bit back a sigh. The electronic age had yet to touch her boss.

"The trial yeah, sure. But—"

"Stop right there."

"But—"

Lucas made a grunting noise and held out a meaty hand. He grabbed his coffee cup, refilled it from a pot that Liz knew had to be six hours old, and sat back down. "Now—start from the beginning. Sell it to me, Liz—and maybe we can work something out."

Liz grinned again and ran small hands through her own honey-blond hair. She was closer to thirty than twenty but still got carded at dance clubs and liquor stores. Her lithe body was kept trim with regular workouts, and she had become quite a proficient kickboxer. In her line of work, it had come in handy a couple of times. Her ready smile and piercing green eyes seemed to work their way into a person's soul and make them want to tell her their story. That was also something that came in handy in her line of work.

She had been at the *Herald* for about a year, having come there from a small paper in Arlington, Virginia. The daughter of a diplomat, she had shunned the family name and worked her own way through college, penning romance novels to pay her tuition to George Washington University. Though she readily admitted that it was an unusual way to work through school, she had been telling stories since before she could remember. It seemed a natural way to turn something her parents had always discounted into a profitable enterprise.

She had studied political science and international relations, thinking that perhaps she had a future as a congressional aide or lobbyist. Liz was good with people and knew, from a youth spent observing the dinner parties and cocktail hours her parents hosted, that often the most powerful people in a room were the ones who worked behind the scenes. She had no desire to wield that power, but she was fascinated by those who did. That was how she ended up in journalism. It wasn't the *what* that intrigued her, but rather the *who* and—most importantly—the *why*. That, in a nutshell, was the reason she had been mesmerized by the story of Jude Lucien's high fall from grace.

She had just arrived at the *Herald* when the ex-DEA agent had been brought to trial on charges of murder, conspiracy to murder, and assorted other drug-related wrongdoings. Liz had been a desk jockey in the newsroom and could only follow the trial from a distance, but she was hypnotized by the face of the woman who silently stared back into the cameras. Even the grainy newspaper photos splashed across the front page of the *Herald* couldn't hide the surreal beauty of the defendant, or her preternatural calm.

Liz couldn't explain it, but Jude Lucien's reckless disregard of moral and legal boundaries fascinated her. More than anything, she found herself almost needing to know this woman—to get behind the enigmatic half-smile and the penetrating eyes—so she could understand the darkness that seemed to emanate from even her very image.

She watched from the sidelines as, piece by piece, the state's case began to crumble around the reddened ears of State's Attorney Mark Brugetti. Witnesses mysteriously recanted their statements, files disappeared, and to top it all off—the DEA became totally non-cooperative, declaring that opening their files to the state would jeopardize other on-going operations. The state's case now stood on the testimony of one convicted felon who was at the scene—dubious ground to say the least. But what had delivered the *coup de grace* to the case against Jude was the ex-agent's testimony itself. It had cost Liz a week of dinners with the insufferable bore of a man who had the courthouse beat—not to mention a nightly struggle with him at the door afterwards—but she had managed to snag a *Herald* press pass for the days of Lucien's testimony.

There was an atmosphere of controlled chaos at the courthouse. Lucien's attorneys had stated repeatedly throughout the proceedings that Jude fully intended to defend her name on the stand, but common wisdom dismissed that as courthouse steps posturing. No lawyers in their right minds would allow their defendant on the stand with so many accusations against her. As the foundations of the state's case had been slowly whittled away, it had seemed suicide to let Lucien testify, because it would open her up to questions that no one else had come forward to answer.

She had taken the stand nonetheless, coolly regal in a sleek black suit that Liz immediately pegged as an Armani instinctively knowing Lucien would never settle for any designer knock-offs. The reporter marveled at the smoldering aura that surrounded the ex-agent as the dark woman calmly swore to tell the truth, the whole truth, and nothing but the truth, so help her, God. Her lead attorney, a photogenic young woman who nevertheless paled in comparison to her client, began a series of routine questions that in no way, shape, or form surprised anyone.

The prosecutor had been impatiently waiting for his turn throughout the defense's questioning. As soon as Lucien's attorney said, "Your witness," Brugetti jumped to his feet and stalked over to where Lucien silently regarded him from the stand.

It was also the moment everyone else in the courthouse had been anticipating. All around her, Liz could hear the quickened breathing of the people assembled in the stuffy room.

Brugetti dispensed with formalities and stared at the defendant with unconcealed hostility. "You had quite a long career with the DEA, Ms. Lucien. Longer than most agents," he began innocuously. He paused for a moment—Liz could see he was waiting to see if the dark woman would take the bait. Clearly, however, Lucien wasn't about to answer anything other than a direct question. Finally he prompted, "Didn't you?"

"I believe you have the paperwork in front of you, Mr. Brugetti. But yes, I did have a fairly long career with the agency."

"You were an undercover agent, correct?"

Lucien shifted slightly in her seat and re-crossed her long legs, leaning back in her chair. The conservative, well-cut ensemble did nothing to hide the ripple of muscles in her body as she moved. Liz saw the slight smile that played upon the ex-agent's lips as she observed the others watching her. Lucien looked for all the world like some lazy jungle cat sunning itself on a tree. Certainly not like a woman on trial for her life. "Yes," she answered the attorney absently.

"Which means you consorted repeatedly and for long periods of time with drug dealers and their associates, and were quite successful in convincing those people you were 'one of them.' Correct?"

"That would seem to be the definition of 'undercover.'"

"Tell me, Ms. Lucien, how did you manage to be so convincing? For instance, did you ever take drugs with these men?"

Liz groaned mentally. This guy was just too stupid for words. He was drawing attention to all the things Lucien had done on behalf of the government, at their instructions, rather than what the agent had done once she left the organization.

"If you're asking me if I inhaled, Mr. Brugetti, the answer is yes." A rakish smile lit her features, inviting others in the courtroom into the joke. "But it was when I was sixteen and hiding out in the backyard of Eddie Fazini's house. His parents were away for the weekend, and he raided his brother Tommy's stash. Unfortunately, Tommy caught and beat the tar out of us. So I feel I've paid my debt to society on that particular count." A brief ripple of laughter coursed its way through the courtroom—touching everyone, Liz noticed, including the jurors. "These days alcohol is my drug of choice," she finished.

"So you're saying you've never done drugs either in your capacity as a DEA agent or as a private citizen?" He looked skeptically at her.

"Alcohol is a drug," she corrected him. "But when you're in a room full of paranoid cokehead dealers, having a glass of bourbon in your hand is a whole lot better than a snort of blow up your nose. Call it the lesser of two evils." The harsh cut of her words drew everyone's attention to the danger that Lucien had placed herself in repeatedly at the government's behest. Liz looked at Brugetti and almost felt sorry for the ungainly man. He was baring his own jugular for the kill, and she knew Jude Lucien would not let the chance slip by.

Brugetti, however, continued gamely on. "Jack Taylor testified that he saw you snort cocaine with the members of what was then—called the Massala Cartel and later that he saw men—at your instructions—ambush and murder these people. And that you personally murdered Enrico Massala, even though he was working with the DEA at the time."

"I'm aware of the allegations Mr. Brugetti. I was in the courtroom at the time."

"And how would you address these accusations, Ms. Lucien? That you were responsible for so much carnage?" he asked smugly.

The brief flash of annoyance was clearly visible as it darted across the dark woman's features. Lucien arched a questioning eyebrow at Brugetti before speaking, "Let me be frank. I served the DEA for more years than I care to remember. And during that time, I participated in over 500 arrests that resulted in over 400 convictions and the removal from circulation of hundreds of kilos of cocaine and other substances with an estimated street value in the millions. Hell, probably into the billions. My job every day was to take drugs off the street and put bad guys in jail. What you, or Mr. Taylor, failed to bring up during his 'eye-witness' testimony, was that he was one of those bad guys. So you better call him back up here and ask him if he remembered witnessing this 'carnage' before or after I hauled his sorry carcass off to prison. Do you get me?"

The press gallery had erupted—along with the rest of the courtroom. And although Brugetti had sputtered on through the rest of his cross-examination, the fight had effectively been stripped from him. The trial continued, but the conclusion was forgone in most people's minds. Jude Lucien would be acquitted.

What Liz always remembered the most, however, was that the accused had never denied any of the charges from the stand.

◻ ◻ ◻

Steam fogged the oval mirror as Jude stepped through the shower door. Swiping the condensation away with a thick towel and then using it to briskly absorb the water running down her lean body, she was confronted with a slightly hazy reflection. The face that stared back at her in the mirror was smooth and unlined by the tensions of her profession. Never one to contemplate the favors granted to her by the genetic lottery, Jude bent over, grabbing a professional-grade blow dryer and applying it to thick hanks of black hair. Half an hour later, she efficiently brushed the dark strands out of her face and then daubed the tiniest bit of mascara on her lashes. Sliding her lithe body into a soft, black leather skirt, she tucked in a burgundy silk camisole and zipped up the side. Glancing in the mirror one last time as she stepped into her shoes, she bit back a long sigh. "Show time," she whispered to the reflection.

I am not looking forward to this...

The evening was to be fairly routine—if anything in Jude's tumultuous life could be called that. A simple preliminary meeting between herself and the new head of the Massala Cartel. Dinner and drinks between two business associates.

Yeah, right... Then why don't normal Fortune 500 companies have pat-downs before the CEO's shake hands?

It had taken years since the death of Enrico Massala for the family to regroup after Jude's devastating raid. Ultimately the man who emerged as the new leader—a distant cousin named Romair—was a more progressive thinker who said he had no desire to further antagonize the woman personally responsible for taking half his family's business.

Jude, being a pragmatist, accepted the invitation to sit down. The six months immediately following the Massala Massacre—as the papers called it—had not been pleasant ones for her. She had been forced to leave the country for a while, and still outraged members of the Cartel had come after her. She had taken down more than one gun-for-hire that they had purchased. Only one had come seriously close to harming her, but it irritated Jude to have to carry a piece everywhere she went.

Makes going to the gym damn hard...

The Cartel had been less outraged and more inclined to deal when they learned their precious Rico had been working the Feds for a deal for himself, at the expense of everyone else. Eventually a détente had been called so everyone could get back to the business of making money. *Then that idiot Brugetti almost ruined everything. He should have just taken the Agency's advice and dropped the damn case.* Jude didn't think much about the trial these days. In fact, no one did. Not with the OJ circus that took place right after, and the Oklahoma bombers' trials after that. *Nope... I'm old news.* And that was just the way she liked it. Plenty of people still stared at Jude—they couldn't help it—but very few of them knew who she was. Or what she was capable of.

The sleek little car edged its way down the curving driveway of Jude's oceanfront home. Night had taken the bite off the summer's heat, and the briny scent of seawater filled Jude's lungs. Breaking at the road's edge, she breathed deeply, enjoying the peaceful silence and half-wishing she was sitting on her deck—guitar and bourbon within easy reach, with nothing more on her mind than deciding whether or not to make the short trek to the water's edge. But there were deals to be made this night, and she had business to conduct. Throwing the car into gear, she shoved away her idle musings and hurled herself into the darkness' comforting arms.

◻ ◻ ◻

Across the city another woman was getting ready for a night on the town. But unlike Jude, Liz Gardener was most anxious to get her evening underway. One of her contacts—a fringe player in the vast network of

Jude's employees—had finally come through and told the reporter that Jude was having dinner at *Monde*, one of the nicer restaurants in town.

As the months went by and the furor over the trial died down, Liz was nevertheless still intrigued by the dark woman's mysterious presence. With her drive and determination, Liz didn't stay on the desk for long and was soon working her way through the crime beat. It was the most hectic of all the city assignments, having to be on call for reports that came out of the station house. Over the months she had learned to sleep to the soothing lullaby of the police scanner. However it gave the honey-haired woman the perfect opportunity to develop contacts who would be a link to Lucien. She kept her ears open for any other murmurs about her activities but, until recently, had come up with nothing.

Then, about a month ago, she finally found someone who confirmed that not only had Lucien never left the business but that something big involving the ex-agent was about to go down. That was when Liz started putting together her plan. Granted, most of the details hadn't been worked out, but Liz could no longer fight the almost overwhelming urge to do something about her obsession with the stranger.

"If she's eating at the restaurant that means she's not seriously working—at most she's entertaining associates. And that means she'll probably end up at the Club later," Her snitch earnestly explained. *"Show up there around midnight and tell the guy at the door that Eddie recommended the place. That'll get you through the front door and away from the mobs out front."*

Now Liz studied her wardrobe dubiously. While she enjoyed the occasional night out dancing, places like the Club were not frequent stops on her social circuit. She knew it by reputation as one of the city's most exclusive nightspots with well-tailored patrons, great music, and a waiting line a mile long. The question facing Liz now was an eternal one.

What on earth do I wear?

She didn't have the faintest idea of how to go about garnering Jude Lucien's attention; and if by some miracle she did, what she would do once that happened. Lucas had been skeptical of her plan but told her he had enough faith in his protégé to give her free rein in this venture.

More likely he thinks I'll never get close to her in a million years, so it will be a moot issue. He's probably right. But at least I can say I tried. Maybe then I can finally let all this go.

Liz's fair brows knit together as she burrowed in the depths of her closet, finally emerging triumphantly with the delicate Vera Wang dress her mother had given her. It had been a bribe to attend one of the countless inaugural balls her parents had been obliged to appear. Liz had managed to duck all of them except one; and, fortunately, she still had the dress.

"Gotta hand it to Mom," she said to herself as the dress slithered over her body and melded to her supple curves. "The old lady's got great taste." She pirouetted smoothly, examining the dress from all sides. It was a rich emerald green, with a daring scoop that ran the length of her back, and a teasing slit up the side. It was a bit risqué for an inaugural ball—her father had taken one look at her in it and almost had an apoplectic fit—but it was perfect for an evening at a place like the Club. The dress would manage to make her fit in, while simultaneously setting her apart from the rest of the crowd. She had wondered what her mother had in mind when she had picked out the dress for her only daughter. More likely than not, she thought Liz was running out of time to make a "suitable" match. *Right,* Liz snickered at the idea. *We all know that's not going to happen.* Liz's "life choices," as her brother called them, were not a popular subject for discussion in the Gardener household—particularly in an election year. So it was with a sigh of relief for both Liz and her family that she took the job with the *Herald.*

She sighed and shook the cobweb of memories from her thoughts. Running her hands along the length of her trim body and looking at herself in the mirror, Liz felt an unfamiliar burn in her stomach. She didn't know if it was a flare of anticipation for the chase or for just the chance of finally meeting the woman who had occupied most of her waking moments—and not a few of her sleeping ones—for quite a long time.

❑ ❑ ❑

"Gentlemen," Jude nodded graciously at Romair Massala. He had a pair of thickset bodyguards Jude only thought of as *Muscle.* When the first one made a move as if to pat her down, Jude merely arched a severe brow and fixed him with an arctic winter stare. The Muscle backed down and flicked a questioning glance at his boss who waved him away. Jude clearly was not carrying. The slim leather skirt and silk top left no room for concealment. She had deliberately foregone a jacket for that simple reason—to show that she was wasn't afraid of them.

The maitre d' swept over and seated Jude and Massala. He then promptly led the Muscle to a comfortable table that was nearby, but not near enough so they could overhear the conversation. They were plainly irritated by this latest development, and Jude hid her amusement behind a careful perusal of her menu. They had been seated at her usual table, a cozy corner arrangement where she could see the entire restaurant. Jude settled into her chair, observing Romair as he surreptitiously glanced around at his surroundings. "You're traveling alone this evening?" he inquired solicitously. "Surely a woman as beautiful as yourself wouldn't be wandering about...unescorted?"

He wants to know where my Muscle is. "Why shouldn't I? I don't much enjoy traveling with an entourage," she replied placidly. "But perhaps you know something I don't. Do you think I have reason to be concerned?" Jude examined her opponent across the table. Without a doubt, Romair Massala was a handsome man. With shrewd brown eyes and a thick, unruly mass of black hair, he exuded a boyish vitality as well as a cunning awareness. He had arrived from the outer ranks of the Cartel's lieutenants—a distant cousin toiling away in obscurity until Jude's raid had created a vacuum of power within the family.

"Ms. Lucien—may I call you Jude?" He nodded in thanks when Jude gestured her acquiescence. "Jude, I'm a direct man. And I think you respect directness. I must admit I am a little concerned. There has been a lot of bad blood between the Massalas and your organization. In fact, there are some who still think we owe you a blood debt—despite our recent understandings. I'm sure you've heard the mutterings. I'd think that would be very...disturbing...for you."

Jude sighed heavily and shook her head. *Damn.... Why do they always try this?* "You're right, Romair, I do respect directness. So I'll try and be equally direct with you. You're very young and very ambitious—I can appreciate that—but you haven't done your homework." She paused and took a healthy sip of her wine before continuing. "If you had, you'd know that I own this restaurant." She indicated two waiters standing promptly at attention not six feet away, "And that those men are not waiters, but employees of mine." Jude offered him a brilliant smile that lit up the pale blue in her eyes and was an ironic contrast to the threatening growl in her voice. "I heard you were very bright, Romair. Please don't disappoint me this early in our relationship." The smile left her eyes and was replaced with a caliginous stare that seemed more suited to some medieval torture room than a well-lit, expensive French restaurant. "Don't try to intimidate me, Romair. Your goons and your guns don't frighten me. Whatever damage you think you can inflict, I can return tenfold. Do we understand each other?" She leaned back in her chair and relaxed in feral contemplation of her prey.

There was an enormous pause during which Romair Massala could have done a thousand things—nine hundred and ninety nine of which would have gotten him killed, if not this night, then another. But Romair was indeed a smart man. He inclined his head to his dinner partner, tacitly acknowledging that his bluff had been called. "Of course, Jude. I was merely speaking hypothetically."

"As was I, Romair." She granted him another smile, this one not laced with malicious promise. "Now, can I recommend something from the menu? Or would you prefer to hear the specials?"

⫐ ⫐ ⫐

Apparently Eddie's recommendation didn't carry as much weight as my snitch thought it did, Liz thought disgustedly a few hours later. *A solid half an hour of flirting and I barely make it into the bloody bar. Why the hell didn't he tell me there was a VIP Room? If she's anywhere, that's where she is, not down here in the meat-market with the trolls.*

The small reporter had been talked up, felt up, and was now fed up with the calculated chaos of the Club. Music pulsed from every possible point in the place, beating against the rhythm of her own heart. The air was thick with the smell of designer colognes, cigars, and cigarettes of shaky legal standing. Liz fought not to gag as a particularly pungent wave of Calvin Klein's latest aromatic effort swept by her. She turned back to the bartender—with whom she had developed a strong rapport over the last two hours—and furrowed her brows. Paying attention to people—bartenders, waiters, doormen—that others walked right by without noticing had more than once given her the information she needed to break a story. "Hit me again, Barnes," she said, sliding her glass across the slickly polished black mica bar.

Barnes grinned cheerfully at the honey-haired woman. "Excuse me for asking, but this doesn't really seem like your kind of place, if you know what I mean."

Liz cocked her head and regarded the bartender archly. "Is that the current way of asking 'What's a nice girl like you doing in a place like this?'"

"Nothing wrong with being a nice girl." Barnes shrugged, pushing wisps of mahogany hair out of her face. "I used to be one myself, before I started working here," she finished with another winning grin.

"Even nice girls get restless sometimes," Liz muttered, more to herself than anything, but the bartender's keen ears picked up the statement.

"I know what you mean." Barnes nodded her agreement. "Lotta people looking for a lotta things here." She glanced around at the bar as she expertly mingled gin and tonic into a perfect blend. Twisting a lime rind into a tiny curl, she presented the drink to Liz with a flourish. "There you go."

"Thanks," Liz replied, handing over a bill. "We all are searching for something, aren't we?'

"That's the truth," the bartender answered easily. "And I see those pretty green eyes of yours wandering all over this place. So, what is it you're looking for?" A slightly suggestive pause rested between them— nothing too intimidating—just something for both women to enjoy. "Just a little trouble?"

Liz smiled and started to offer a teasing reply when a graceful form flickered in her peripheral vision. Jerking her head around abruptly, she caught a long flash of tanned legs as they mounted the winding staircase. Her eyes trailed up their length—over the supple leather skirt, up the narrow waist, across the breadth of silk-clad shoulders, through the dusky length of inky black hair—until they landed hard against two sapphire chips that glittered darkly back at her.

The reporter felt her breath catch and her heart lurch, and she let out a tiny gasp of recognition. Barnes quickly followed her line of sight and shook her head warily. "Oh no, lady. Believe me, you don't want that much trouble."

◻ ◻ ◻

Jude wasn't sure just what it was that made her turn and look over the roiling crowd below her. Normally she just made her way straight up to the VIP Room and ignored the seething mass of bodies on the main dance floor. But for some reason, tonight her eyes were drawn to a sliver of warm light trailing down on a honey-haired woman at the corner of the main bar.

There she met eyes that gazed into her own without hesitation. Even at a distance, their shimmering jade hue was unmistakable, and Jude fancied she could see golden flecks in them. For an endless moment, they submitted quietly to each other's survey, ignoring the flowing bodies around them, until Romair tapped at the dark woman's shoulder, breaking her budding connection with the other woman.

She snapped her head around to the Argentinean, not bothering to conceal the irritation from her tone. "Why don't you gentlemen go ahead without me? I need to check on a few things downstairs. Just tell Sasha that you're my guests and she'll take care of you."

The Muscle stared at her suspiciously, but Romair nodded agreeably. "Sure, Jude. We'll see you upstairs." He smiled at her conspiratorially and leaned closer. "I don't blame you. She's quite a beauty." He gestured slightly in the direction where the slim woman had been standing.

Jude dismissed him with a brief nod and swiftly returned her eyes to the corner of the bar. "Damn..." she muttered when she saw the space had been filled by a group of boisterous young Turks waving martini glasses wildly in the air. Suppressing a slightly disappointed sigh, she began scanning the room for a trace of the stranger when another tap at her shoulder drew her attention once again from the dance floor.

Irrationally infuriated by her new business partner's repeated distractions, Jude whirled around...and fell right back into the malachite swirls of the stranger's eyes. Up close, she could see that golden flecks were indeed sprinkled across her irises, and there was a disarming openness in the woman's glance that made Jude feel oddly like she was being entrusted with something precious.

She let her eyes roam over the rest of the slender figure before her, taking in the fiery highlights of the honey hair, the defined shoulders, and the devastating curves underneath that dress which—had Jude still been a practicing Catholic—would have sent her scurrying for the nearest confessional.

Slowly the blue gaze made its way back to the woman's face and the wide smile that was waiting for her there. "Hi," the stranger said softly. "Have you heard all those stories about how seeing someone across a crowded room could change your life?"

A lazy smirk curled around the edges of Jude's mouth as she nodded. "Do you really think any of those stories are true?"

"Well," the small woman replied, "I have a sneaking suspicion that if you go ahead and introduce yourself, we'll find out soon enough."

Chapter 2

I can't believe I just said that. Liz mentally slapped herself upside the head, but Jude merely smiled in answer—the dark highlights of her eyes dancing—and guided her up the winding staircase, ushering her into the VIP Room.

Immediately Liz was struck by the difference between this room and the main floor downstairs. It was like they were in two entirely different worlds. Instead of boring a hole into her consciousness with its relentless pounding, the music up here was a mournfully seductive purr seeping slowly into her bloodstream. The frenetic lightshow illuminating the best poses of the spastic dancers downstairs was gone, replaced by a warm bronze glow that cast a heroic glamour over everyone in the room—especially the woman in front of her. Liz glanced quickly around, although all she really wanted to do was wallow in the decadent vision that was Jude Lucien herself. "So...this is where the big girls go," she muttered to herself. Jude's answering snicker tickled the edges of her hearing, and she turned back to her hostess. "You haven't introduced yourself." She smiled. "Or is it you'd rather I just go on thinking of you as some tall, dark, and stunning stranger?"

A part of Liz was an eternal voyeur—watching everyone, even herself, as they went through life. It was part of why she was such a great reporter.

That part stood back now in stunned disbelief at the words that fell effortlessly from her lips. *It's gotta be the dress talking,* Liz silently considered, wondering where on earth all this witty repartee was coming from.

Whatever it was...it seemed to be working, for Jude's attention was riveted firmly on their play, and she seemed oblivious to the inquisitive looks flashed their way. The women made a striking pair, dark and light linked together in quiet conversation, and unaware of the way their bodies visually complemented each other.

"I don't know," Jude teased in reply. "When a beautiful woman walks up to me and says she's going to change my life...it's a big decision. What do you think I should do?"

Liz pretended to consider the question for a moment then smiled knowingly at her new companion. "I think you should go for it."

"Worth the risk, huh?" An elegantly curved brow arched reflectively, as if appraising what Liz had to offer.

"I think so," she bantered easily. *Oh yeah...gotta be the dress.* Liz was suddenly aware of just how much of her skin was being offered up to Jude's sauntering gaze. Noting the appreciative glimmer in the flickering blue, she fervently hoped the dim lighting camouflaged the warm blush she felt rising in her cheeks. "But I guess it all depends on how much of a risk you're willing to take."

An intrigued flare arced in Lucien's eyes as she grinned wolfishly at the smaller woman, and Liz felt a tiny shiver of anticipation at what was happening between them. "Never let it be said that I'm not a gambling woman. So allow me to properly introduce myself. My name is Jude Lucien." She offered a graceful hand to Liz.

Score one for the home team, Liz thought exultantly as she took Jude's hand, surprised at its unexpected warmth. But then again, Liz considered, everything she had learned about this woman involved heat— from the violence that cloaked the dark woman in its unmistakable colors, to the smoldering glow that lit her restless eyes. *It's a wonder her touch doesn't burn,* she mused and was surprised to feel her thoughts slipping recklessly of their own accord to other circumstances that might involve this woman's touch. She knew the game was well underway, but she willfully ignored her growing suspicion that the rules had somehow dramatically changed.

Jude's growling voice jerked her abruptly back to reality. "I'm not working tonight, Sasha," she was saying to a slim woman dressed totally in white. The severe cut of the suit threw the high planes of the woman's face into sharp relief, its color emphasizing the warm caramel glow of her skin.

The stranger continued on as if Jude hadn't spoken. "There's a problem—"

"That's why I pay you so much, Sash," Jude replied with a grin, absently flicking a stray ringlet of the woman's curly dark hair across her slender shoulders. "So you can handle the problems. Now go earn your salary."

"Ookkaayy," Sasha drew out the word in a singing breath. "I see you've got your hands full." She sent a knowing glance over to Liz, who quietly bristled at the implication. "Aren't you even going to ask about Massala?" the woman inquired softly.

Liz's ears perked up at the mention of the Cartel's name; but she kept on her face a slightly attentive, yet ultimately bored, expression. Years of being a diplomat's daughter had taught her when it was best to look like one of the wall decorations. Beneath the placid exterior however, her mind raced. *Massala... that's got to be the major move I've been hearing about.*

Jude tossed a lazy glance at a corner booth where the trio of men sat lowering a round of empty glasses onto a table already crowded with them. "Looks like you've got them comfortably settled. Just make sure they have a good time—"

"And keep them out of your hair," Sasha finished. "I know the drill." There was a familiar air between the two women, but Liz detected a faint hint of resentment in the slim woman's voice. *Almost as if she's jealous.* Liz had no doubt that Jude's romantic history was as turbulent as the rest of her life seemed to be. Judging from her behavior, this woman had very likely been a part of it. Sasha nodded to another booth, discreetly tucked away in a dim corner. "Your table's ready."

"Thanks, querida." Jude dismissed the woman with a casual pat on her shoulder and returned her attention to Liz. "I'm sorry for the interruption. You were saying...?" Her voice conveniently trailed off, deftly allowing the other woman the option of continuing their play or retreating to safer ground.

"I was saying, I'm pleased to meet you, Jude. My name is Elizabeth Peterson," Liz had decided earlier to use her first and middle names, instead of her last name. If Lucien got a wild hair and decided to check her out, the last thing Liz wanted was the drug dealer discovering that she was a reporter. Because the name was also the pseudonym she had used during her romance novelist days, it would bear up reasonably well under scrutiny.

"Well, Elizabeth...if I may...?" she arched a quiet brow asking for permission as she gestured to her table. "Why don't you have a seat and I'll get us something to drink?"

"Absolutely." Liz allowed herself to be seated at the corner booth and enjoyed the view of her companion's long legs as she strode away. The dark richness of the leather skirt clung deliciously to the curve of Jude's hips, and Liz found herself again contemplating Jude in a decidedly unprofessional light. Something in the back of her mind muttered a low warning about the dangers of getting entangled with this particular woman—but it was lost in the rich echo of the dark woman's vibrant laugh ringing in her ears.

◻ ◻ ◻

Elizabeth Peterson, huh? Jude snickered to herself as she reached the bar. *She's got to be the first woman I've met in a year who actually has a last name.* She shook her head in amusement. "Hey Parker," she called the bartender over. "Hand me the downstairs phone." Two seconds later she had Elizabeth's drink order from a rather stunned Barnes. "Gin and tonic and a bourbon on the rocks," she told Parker, who rushed to fill the order.

It wasn't often Jude showed up at the Club, and her employees were a little in awe of the dark woman they called *El Diablo* behind her back. Jude spent far less time here in the evenings than she used to. In the bad old days she had cut an erotic swath through the population of the Club. There had been a seemingly endless supply of beautiful bodies offered to her; and she had ravenously fed on their passion, discarding each of them when they mistakenly believed that their presence in her bed gave them purchase on her life.

The bodies were still offered these days; but unfailingly, Jude graciously declined them with a charming smile or a teasing remark. In fact, she realized with a start, it had been more than a year since anyone had moved her enough to pursue them. *Maybe that's why I'm so attracted to this woman...hormones,* she considered, but found herself almost wishing to discover some other reason. Elizabeth Peterson was undeniably beautiful—the lissome body outlined by that damned dress left no doubt about that—but there was a spark in her jade eyes that called to Jude. *We'll see,* she promised herself, returning to the honey-haired woman at her table.

"Here you go." Jude slid easily into the intimate booth beside Elizabeth. "Gin and tonic."

Her companion looked confused. "How did—I didn't tell—"

"I have my sources." Jude laughed as narrowed green eyes focused on her. "Actually I just called downstairs and asked. Seems you made quite an impression on Barnes," she teased.

"Who?" Elizabeth cocked her head. "Oh, the bartender. She was really nice."

The dark woman arched a contemplative brow at the woman beside her. "You know, she has quite a reputation as a charmer around here. She'll break your heart if you give her a chance."

"Oh? Are you saying you won't?" Elizabeth shot back at her with a gleam in her eye. "You look like the type who would have quite a fierce reputation herself."

Ooh...she wants to play. "I've found it's best not to believe everything you see. Sometimes circumstances have a way of... changing what the truth is," she replied. "Besides, you said you were going to change *my* life. So I believe it should be my place to ask *your* intentions."

"I know, I know... what's a nice girl like me doing in a place like this?" Elizabeth shook her head. "Barnes asked me that. Why does everyone ask me that?"

"Maybe you look like a nice girl," Jude offered.

"But I thought you didn't believe everything you saw," the smaller woman taunted.

"I never said I *believed* you were a nice girl. Merely that you looked like one."

"Oh." A beautiful flush warmed Elizabeth's features as she played with the lime perched on the edge of her glass.

Jude smiled in delight at her response. The young blonde was absolutely charming. "Besides, I've never see you here before, and I own the place. So I know most of the regulars. What brings you out this evening?"

The honey-haired woman shrugged her shoulders softly, drawing Jude's attention to the quiet ripple of muscles in her arms and neck. "I'm not sure really. I was just kind of restless. Like if I stayed where I was for one more second I'd go crazy."

"I know what you mean," Jude said, swallowing the last of her drink and enjoying the sting of the liquor as it seared its way down her throat. A passing waitress picked up her glass and returned silently with another. Jude nodded at the girl briefly before beginning her story. "There was this crazy old lady who lived down the street from me when I was growing up. Everybody called her Aunt Betty. Don't know why. She was always shouting at the kids, telling us she could read our fortunes and tell us our futures. Most of the adults kept us away from her. But... funny thing was...the older I got, the more sense Aunt Betty began to make. The adults just didn't want us to hear the things she had to say. One of the things I remember the most was something she called 'The Night Crawl.'"

"The Night Crawl?" Elizabeth echoed and sipped her own gin and tonic somewhat more sedately.

Jude nodded. "Betty always said that it was the thing that makes you sweat when it isn't hot. It makes your dogs twitchy and your girlfriends mean, and it sends you out into the night looking for something you don't have. She would say that it's what sends nice girls like you to places like this."

"So..." Elizabeth asked with a small smile. "You think I'm suffering from the Night Crawl?"

Glittering sapphires arrogantly roamed Elizabeth's svelte form once more. "Oh yeah," Jude drawled.

In the ensuing silence, both women became vividly aware of the mutual seduction that was taking place. A kinetic attraction between their bodies and minds sparked, and a flint of arousal kindled a slow flame in Jude's belly.

"What do you suggest I do about it?" Elizabeth murmured, her voice dropping slightly.

I can think of one or two things to start with, Jude's unruly thoughts offered. Aloud, she said nothing and took a long sip of her drink. The intimate tone of the smaller woman's words sent the fire rocketing deep between Jude's legs. The dark woman was totally unprepared for her body's instant reaction to this stranger, and she needed just a second to collect herself. Her impulse was to continue their sensual banter and indulge in the pleasures that were implicit in their conversation, but something that wanted to know more about the clever woman sitting across the table held her back.

Elizabeth must have sensed the conflict flickering behind Jude's eyes, for her expression immediately softened, and she placed a gentle hand on the older woman's arm. "I'm sorry—I was just teasing—I don't know what's gotten into me—"

Jude covered the slim fingers with her own. "Don't be sorry," she interrupted. "It's just...been a long time," she said, surprising herself with her candor. "I don't want it all to go too fast." She finished, with a brilliant smile.

An answering grin lit up Elizabeth's face. "Me either. I guess we did skip some of the preliminaries."

"That's an understatement," the dark woman commented wryly. The shared laughter that followed effectively dissipated the thick sexual tension that had built between them. Now that their attraction had been acknowledged, an easy air settled over the table, allowing Jude relax into a more leisurely pace. "You already know that I own the Club, but what about you? How do you occupy your days?"

"I'm a writer."

It wasn't a surprising revelation to Jude by any means, if only because during their short acquaintance Elizabeth had more than proven herself verbally adroit. "What sort of writer?"

"A romance novelist, actually," she replied, a sheepish grin on her face.

Jude's eyebrow leapt skyward. *Now that's a surprise.* Her brows furrowed. She didn't know why but she was...*disappointed*...somehow. "Really?"

Elizabeth shrugged. "It's paid the bills pretty well, but now I'm getting out of it. I finally have a chance to write something that I really care about. Something important." Excitement shone in her clear green eyes, and Jude couldn't help but smile.

"Can I ask what your new book is about?" Seeing her companion frown at the question, Jude quickly retreated. "It's okay. You don't have to tell me about it if you don't want to."

"No...it's okay." Elizabeth squeezed Jude's hand softly, causing them both to realize that their fingers were still intertwined. Neither woman made a move to untangle them now. "I'm just superstitious, that's all."

"Afraid you'll jinx the muse?" she teased. Jude had known a lot of agents back in her DEA days who had rituals they followed before a big bust, talismans they carried when they were undercover—different things to protect them from the unknown dangers lurking in the shadows. She guessed writers must have similar habits. For her part, Jude had no such superstitions, firmly believing that she made her own luck, and no charm could protect her quite as well as her instincts and the Sig Sauer P220 that accompanied her most everywhere she went.

"I guess." Elizabeth shrugged, clearly embarrassed.

Jude leaned down next to the small woman's ear and whispered, "You blush beautifully, you know." Smiling at the deepening flush that suffused her companion's pale features, she continued, "I think I could watch you all night."

The honey-haired woman cocked her head questioningly. "I thought we were slowing down."

"Slowing down, yes. Stopping, no." Jude grinned rakishly. "There's a difference."

"I see," she nodded, a playful light creeping into her gaze. "In that case—"

Her words were abruptly halted by a looming shadow over their table. Jude scowled before looking up to see Romair Massala's handsome face beaming down at her. Quickly masking her irritation, she smiled back at him and gracefully excused herself to Elizabeth with a muttered apology.

"I hate to interrupt your conversation, Jude," the tall man purred. "But I'm afraid I have to be going."

"But it's early," Jude demurred, although she could have cared less. All she wanted to do was return to the alluring woman at the table. After a brief, quiet struggle, her business instincts won out. "And your men looked like they were having such a good time."

He laughed quietly. "Indeed we all were. I do, however, have a wife waiting anxiously back home."

"Anxiously?" Jude quirked an eyebrow. She remembered something in the dossier on Massala that mentioned a wife in Buenos Aires, but she was surprised that he had brought her to the States.

"Ah, my sweet Paola worries still, even though we have been together for 10 years now. I am a very lucky man."

"Congratulations," the dark woman complimented him, storing the information away for future reference and grimly promising herself to have a *word* with whomever prepared her dossier. A man devoted to his wife was a different man from one who kept his spouse tucked far, far away. He could either be a more vulnerable or more dangerous adversary depending on the circumstances, and Jude needed to know which it would be. "We should all be so lucky," she finished.

"Ah, but my dear Jude, why do I think you would miss the hunt more than you would relish the joy?" His eyes glittered darkly as he nodded to the table where Elizabeth sat. "There's a wildness in you that refuses to be tamed, and I do not envy the task before the one who tries to do so."

A shiver darted through Jude's long frame at the Argentinean's words, feeding into the banked arousal Elizabeth had inspired, flushing her whole body with its warmth. "That's pretty mystical for a man who envisions himself leading his Family into the new millennium."

"I come from an old line of gypsies. We can't help what we see. Perhaps one day I'll be able to tell you what I see when I look at you." Taking her hand in his own, he graciously brought her knuckles to his lips and placed a delicate kiss there. The gesture—which would have seemed awkward or pretentious in another man—was instead imbued with a courtly air of respect that surprised the dark woman. She expected many things of Romair Massala, but this wasn't one of them. For the first time, she began to wonder if she had underestimated her new business partner.

"I'm not sure I want to know, Romair." The words were meant to be teasing, but somehow, they came out gently serious.

"I think you already do know," came the equally serious reply. "You just won't let yourself see."

She laughed quietly to relieve the tension in her gut. "There you go again, getting mystical." This time the teasing note was firmly in place as she reined in the extraordinary sensations caroming around her body.

He smiled in response, willing to let the conversation go. "Forgive me—it is my heritage, after all. I have enjoyed meeting you, Jude Lucien. Perhaps the bad blood will soon be washed away with this new understanding between us. I hope you feel the same."

The small smile that played along Jude's lips was genuine as she inclined her head slightly in agreement. "Perhaps so, Romair. I look forward to speaking with you again soon. Thank you." Aware of the Muscle hovering just in the edges of her peripheral vision, she guided him to the door and handed him off safely to her assistant's capable hands. "Sasha will see to your car, gentlemen. Perhaps we'll be seeing you again soon?" Although she stood with the men and made small talk while Sasha handled the details of their departure, Jude's mind raced with thoughts of the honey-haired woman waiting for her patiently in the corner.

❐   ❐   ❐

So that's Massala, Liz ruminated over this new player, watching Jude speaking intently with the olive-skinned man. *They said the Cartel would never recover from the Massacre. Looks like they were wrong. I wonder if the DEA knows about this.* While one part of her mind mulled over the possible reasons for Romair Massala and Jude Lucien to be meeting, the other part was distinctly aware of the havoc the dark woman was wreaking on her senses.

Ever since she had laid eyes on Jude, her brain and her libido had been warring with each other over her true intentions. *I had to get her attention,* she justified the wisp of a dress she was wearing and the tantalizing display of flesh it offered to Jude. *I just didn't know it would work quite so well....And of course she's going to think that I'm...I mean... Why else do people come alone to bars?* A searing heat scorched through her veins, warming places that were already far too warm for her safety.

Oh god...I'm in trouble here...Big, big trouble, she admitted to herself, knowing where they were headed. Where they had been headed since the first exchange between them.

Her plans were rapidly spinning out of control, and Liz didn't know which was worse—the fact that they were out of control, or the realization that she just didn't care. *I can do this...I can do this,* she chanted silently, watching the sleek form of the woman across the room even as she realized she was on the verge of breaching every ethic she had ever had. *I can do this...*she chanted one more time before giving it up. *Yeah...right...that's why I'm sitting here wearing a couture gown that shows more than it hides and freaking out that I'm about to go to bed with the most beautiful woman I've ever seen...who just happens to be the subject of the article I'm working on...but I can't stop it from happening because quite frankly I don't want to.*

Liz wasn't a stranger to impulsive passions, but the times—being what they were—weren't exactly safe for acting out one's raw desires. So she found herself living mostly in her head, contemplating long-legged beauties and sweet-smelling coeds from afar and—with her storyteller's talent—rendering them complicit in her pleasure. Over the last few months, the photographic image of Jude Lucien had become as familiar as her own reflection, and her dreamscape had played host to more than one fantasy involving the dark woman...

...touching, tasting, feeling...those hands, so graceful...that she had never really been able to consider before. She could easily imagine those hands reaching for her, drawing her in tightly...and those long arms surrounding her...quietly powerful....She could almost feel her legs wrapping around the tall woman's waist....And that laughter, wonderfully rich and textured with a thousand innuendoes....That deep voice calling to her, calling out her name...Elizabeth...Elizabeth...

"Elizabeth?"

Liz jerked out of her reverie to confront a very flesh-and-blood Jude Lucien standing before her. Yet another rush of heat bloomed across her face, this time not stopping there, but descending to points well south. "Sorry," she mumbled, gratefully accepting the cold glass her companion held out to her.

"You were really out of it there." The dark woman smiled. "What were you thinking about?"

Liz's eyes widened, and for just a moment she considered giving everything up—the story, the masquerade, all of it—to have an honest shot with this woman and see if the extraordinary sensations coursing through her were caused by the thrill of the hunt or the magnificent woman beside her. *That's really what I'm talking about here....Dammit...I like her...I didn't expect that.* A last vestige of professional responsibility kept her from throwing off the charade's cloak. It was the same part of her that prompted the next question. "I was just wondering who that man was. He's awfully handsome." She put a taunting edge into the last statement, implying equal parts curiosity and pique that her new admirer would leave her so terribly alone.

The lazy flicker of Jude's eyes told Liz that her mission had been accomplished. "He's just a business associate." She dismissed Massala with a wave of an elegant hand.

"That's all?"

"Well, if you're that interested, I could give you his number," she drawled, leaning back in her seat with negligent ease. "But his wife might object. Tell me, do all tall, dark strangers inspire your curiosity?" she questioned with a puckish smile. "Am I merely one of a dozen strangers that have caught your fancy?" Her voice dropped an octave, becoming a tantalizing growl that instantly redefined the meaning of erotic for Liz for all time. "You walk in here with your golden hair and your green cat's eyes...wearing a body that's a sin in any religion you care to name...with a smile that's pure honey and so sweet that I can almost taste it from here....What chance do I stand?" Jude leaned in a little closer and closed her eyes, inhaling softly, as if to steal some of the smaller woman's precious essence. It was a line meant to seduce...and it worked marvelously on Liz as her heart pumped the furious blood to flood her face. She knew her response was clearly visible to the dark woman, and that knowledge sent a tingling awareness to her breasts and a tiny shiver darting between her thighs.

Liz swallowed hard, her throat distinctly dry. "That's quite an image you conjured up." She managed to inject a light tease into her voice. "You make me sound like a hell of a seductress."

"Are you?" Jude asked, the cobalt shards of her eyes glittering.

"No more so than you are," she replied evenly, responding to the challenge in the dark woman's words. Thinking to herself, *Okay...two can play this particular game....And I'd bet you a million dollars, Ms. Lucien, that I'm better at it than you are.* Words were, after all, her stock in trade. "But if I were, this would be the part where I tell you that you smell like leather and the night, and your eyes promise things forbidden to ordinary people. And if you were a character in one of my books, you'd arrive in a storm full of thunder and lightning, and I'd dress you in black. Then later, I'd undress you and spend long passages on the shape of your mouth, the stretch of your legs, the breadth of your shoulders." She paused for a moment for dramatic effect, then asked quietly. "Is that what you imagine I'd say?" A hypnotic tension enveloped the women, and the rest of the room receded even further from their consciousness. Liz knew her plans were demolished beyond any recall; but she didn't care, couldn't care right now about anything but the game that was playing out between them.

Amazingly, Jude folded first, acceding with a slow nod of her head and a rueful half-smile. Liz released the breath she didn't know she'd been holding and smiled in response. "Now," the smaller woman continued in a more normal tone. "Can we drop the games and get real?"

A genuine laugh rumbled from the dark woman's throat, and Liz noted with shock that the hand Jude ran through her onyx hair was slightly trembling. Unfolding her length from their booth, Jude stood and offered Liz a now rock-steady hand. "Come on," she commanded softly.

Unhesitatingly the smaller woman curled her fingers in Jude's and asked, "Where are we going?"

"Someplace where we can be real."

◫ ◫ ◫

The brushed metal of the Boxster glimmered platinum in the moonlight, and the neon flashed off its surface. The night was free of the humid dampness that crowded the air during the daylight hours, and people seemed to move easier and freer under the moon's benevolent gaze. Their exit from the Club was interminably delayed by all those who stopped the pair with a greeting for Jude. Everyone, it seemed to Liz, wanted the dark woman's acknowledgment, as if it were a benediction on their night's revelries. Indeed, Jude was hailed by some of the patrons with the reverence befitting a high priest. She was their brooding savior who brought them release from a mundane existence with her nightclub, her drugs, and her own mercurial presence.

"Do you actually know all those people?" Liz asked when they were finally tucked into the car and safely speeding away from the thronging crowd.

"More or less," Jude answered cryptically.

Holding her own hair back with a hand and angling her body so that she was facing the driver more than the windshield, Liz studied the smooth profile of the woman beside her. While the planes of Jude's face were undeniably classic, the ironic contrast between the woman's full lips and the strong cut of her jaw refused to let her features settle into a complacent beauty. Rather, Jude's face was a challenging one—much like the woman herself. The reporter's glance was drawn down the bronze length of a strong arm to watch the play of lithe muscles in Jude's forearm as she shifted gears. Graceful fingers were wrapped around the gearshift, stroking the leather absently as she drove. Another kiss of arousal fired Liz's body, forcing her to shift in the seat's easy embrace.

The movement drew Jude's eyes from the road to her passenger, and Liz realized she had been caught staring. "You okay?" Jude asked.

"Just wondering where we're going. We seem to be headed out of the city."

"I have a house on the beach. I thought it might be a little easier to talk there. But if there's somewhere else you'd rather go..."

"No," Liz assured her. "Not at all." She turned away from her companion and inhaled deeply, relishing the salty air that invaded her lungs. *Okay...I've picked a hell of a time to get awkward and shy on her, haven't I?* But Jude seemed to not mind her silence, in fact she seemed comforted by it, smiling quietly to herself as she piloted the car deftly through the darkness.

A right turn down what looked like a deserted road took them up a winding drive, and the breath rushed from the reporter's body at her first glance of what Jude called her "beach house."

"Oh wow..." she whispered, taking in the smooth, elegant lines of the house that looked for all the world like it had been birthed right there on the peak's edge. It was all clean shapes and glass, with just the right combination of sharp angles and gentle curves. The whitewashed walls seemed to pulse with a silver sheen in the moonlight.

"You like it?" Jude murmured in her ear, standing directly behind her.

"It's magnificent...but it's familiar...somehow..." The lines of the house teased her memory, and Liz closed her eyes briefly to concentrate before popping them back open to feast upon the house.

The dark woman snickered at the comment. "I'll give you a hint. I read *The Fountainhead* way too many times."

"Frank Lloyd Wright!" Liz snapped her fingers. "Did he design this?" she asked in amazement.

"I wish," Jude chuckled. "No...but the architect who did was guided in part by Wright's principles. Would you like a tour?"

"Actually..." Liz realized that as beautiful as the house was, it didn't begin to compare to the woman standing beside her. "I'd love a walk on the beach. Maybe the tour after?"

"That, we can do." Jude smiled widely and gestured to her right. "There's a pathway here that leads down to the beach. But you might want to take off your shoes. Dolce & Gabbana pumps don't really mix well with sand," she teased, slipping off her own shoes and tossing them on the deck as they passed. Liz swiftly followed suit, relishing the soft feel of the grains between her toes.

"God, I haven't done this in so long," she muttered. "It feels too good." The roar of the ocean was a soothing contrast to the noise of the Club, and for the second time that night, Liz was struck by just how comfortable Jude seemed to be in silence. She glanced once more at the marvelous place that was Jude's home. "That's an awfully big house for one person. Do you live alone?"

They strolled along for a few more moments, until Liz thought Jude was just going to let the question rest unanswered. At last, Jude nodded towards her house and smiled. "When I decided I wanted to build a house, I wandered into this architect's office with no idea of what I wanted. Well, that's not exactly true," Jude chuckled ruefully. "I brought a paperback copy of *The Fountainhead* into the architect's office and said I wanted something that Howard Roark would have designed. She laughed at me and then sat me down in front of some books."

"Let me guess, Frank Lloyd Wright?"

Jude nodded. "I had no idea Roark was based on a real man. But when I saw his designs, I knew I wanted something like that. She taught me that Wright believed each line of a building should have a reason for existing—and I realized that's what I loved the most about them. His buildings were so *clean*—and that was the reason why. So I hired the architect and told her that the only limitation she had was that I wanted a house that looked like it belonged here. I'd owned this land for years before I was ready to build on it. I used to come here just so I could look up and see all the constellations....To wonder what it would be like to live in the sky." She smirked at her own exuberance and shrugged. "This place is my pitiful attempt to recreate that feeling."

She can't stand the idea of being closed in. The idea rocketed across Liz's tumultuous thoughts. Continuing their walk up the beach, the waves tickled at their bare feet, and an easy calm settled over the two women. "So, I guess that means you do live alone," Liz ventured.

"Actually I share the place with someone," Jude admitted. "Three someones as a matter of fact."

Pale brows shot up to dangerous heights as Liz fought to control her surprise. *Then what the hell was she doing to me in the Club?* Nothing she had found linked Jude to anyone, either romantically or familially, so the small reporter was at a loss.

Jude's shrill whistle pierced the quiet air and soon two loping, four-legged creatures emerged from the dimness. "Liz, meet Agamemnon and Clytemnestra." The tall woman knelt at the edge of the surf to greet the white dogs as they bounded joyfully to their mistress. "Come here, guys. Say hello to our guest." Obediently the dogs trotted over to Liz, one snuffling at her suspiciously. "Clytemnestra—" Jude warned.

The dog cast a baleful glance at her mistress, then, matching her mate, sat down and promptly offered a paw to a delighted Liz. "Thank you." The smaller woman took the paw, shaking it gravely. She copied the movement with Agamemnon, who was much more amenable to the whole process, even sticking his nose out for Liz to scratch. For her part, Clytemnestra snorted and trotted back to Jude.

"This one's a bit of a snob," Jude explained, ruffling the dog's coat affectionately. "But once you win her over, she's yours for life. Aggie, though...he loves everybody."

Agamemnon had apparently decided that he liked the way this small human scratched, because now he was enthusiastically thrusting his head into Liz's lap for more petting. "These are Akitas, right?" Liz asked, rubbing Aggie's ears.

"Right," Jude grinned. "Be careful he doesn't bowl you over. Sometimes he's kinda klutzy."

"Okay...I'm gonna ask. You said you shared the place with three someones. Here are two of your *someones*. Do I want to know where number three is? Or should I just rephrase my question and ask if you live with any other people?"

The dark woman chuckled. "You mean *people*...Oh," she dismissed the idea with a wave. "Nah, just me and the dogs. There's one more... Pete...but he stays mostly in the house."

"Pete?" Liz asked. "You have two Akitas with classical Greek names and a third dog named *Pete*?"

"Wait until you see him." She laughed and shook her head, "I don't think poor Pete could carry around a heavy name like Clytemnestra here."

Deciding that her sibling had had enough fun with the strange person, Clytemnestra nudged Aggie away from the small woman and bounded down the beach, Aggie fast on her heels. In the distance, the two women could hear the dogs faintly barking over the sound of the surf. Jude smiled at Liz as they resumed their stroll, this time back towards the house.

"So, you live with three dogs in a magical house, drive a fast car, and own a trendy nightclub. You sound just like the kind of woman my mother warned me about," Liz bantered.

"Your mother warned you about women?" Jude inquired archly. "How progressive."

"I was doing a little creative transference. I am a writer you know."

"Ah...I see. Would this be the part in your novel where you say 'Thanks for the drinks, but I have a really early meeting in the morning. Could you please call me a cab?'" She stopped and turned to Liz, her dark hair haloed by the lights shimmering from the house above.

Only the stark outlines of Jude's face were visible in the moonlight, but Liz felt as though every feature was already burned into her memory. Hesitantly she brushed the backs of her fingers across the graceful plane of the dark woman's cheek. "No, this is the part where I ask you to kiss me before I lose my nerve."

She felt the muscles of Jude's cheek flex into a smile as the taller woman murmured, "I thought we were slowing down."

Liz grinned in reply. "Slowing down, yes. Stopping, no," she replied, echoing Jude's earlier comment.

"Well then, I think that can be arranged." Jude leaned down slowly, bringing her lips close to Liz. Their faces hovered a fraction of an inch apart—each woman taking in the delicious scent of the other—and Liz knew that no matter what ultimately happened between them, the serenade of the waves and the cool mist of the sea spray against her skin would forever evoke this single perfect moment. Instinctively Liz's lips parted to receive the kiss, but instead of the gentle softness of the dark woman's lips, she heard a sharp *crack!* like thunder, and a white-hot pain blossomed in her left side. Jude hurled her to the ground, flinging herself alongside. "What the—"

"Stay down!" She could hear Jude hissing in her ear through the fuzzy whiteness descending upon her. "I'm not sure where they're shooting from, but they should have a harder time seeing us now." Jude's voice was a hollow echo ringing from within her head, but the words weren't making a whole lot of sense to the honey-haired woman.

"Uh...Jude?" It came out as a wheezing whisper.

The faintness of her voice must have clued Jude into what was happening, because her eyes raked over the smaller woman, stopping abruptly when she saw a black stain spreading across the thin material. "Oh shit—Elizabeth, you've been shot."

The last thing Liz thought before her consciousness mercifully released her from the pain was.....*She didn't kiss me.*

Chapter 3

Bleeding its rays into the rolling surf, the sun made an ostentatious debut over the horizon's edge, ignored by one of its most devoted viewers. So many times Jude had witnessed the magnificent sight now filling the floor-to-ceiling windows of her bedroom, but today she was focused on the still, silent form of Elizabeth Peterson. Although she had very much intended to see the dawn with the honey-haired woman in her bed....*This wasn't quite what I had in mind,* she thought wryly, her half-smile twisting into a grimace as she regarded the woman in her bed.

"She'll be as good as new. Not even a scar," the sweat suit-clad figure assured her, stripping off latex gloves and tossing them into his bag. "The bullet grazed her side, that's all. All that blood was from the flesh wound. No serious damage, but she'll be sore as hell for about a week. Try not to let her move around too much, so she doesn't tear out the stitches. I'll come back and take them out in about a week or so."

"Thanks, Stephen." Jude pulled a plain envelope from her back pocket and handed it over to the doctor. She didn't comment on the envelope's contents—ten thousand dollars in crisp new hundred dollar bills—just as the doctor hadn't commented on the bleeding woman that Jude's call had roused him from a narcotic-induced haze to treat.

Stephen Ryan had had a nodding Country Club acquaintance with Jude Lucien during her undercover days with the DEA. Of course, he hadn't known she was an undercover agent—that nasty little surprise had been revealed to him during a bust that had cost him his license to practice medicine. He had cursed the dark woman's soul up one side and down the other. In one fell swoop, she had stripped him of his reputation, his livelihood, and—most importantly—of all the trappings that livelihood had allowed him. Since then, however, he had learned to forgive and forget...

When Jude Lucien re-entered his life, Stephen had been reduced to selling medical supplies to pay for his miserable existence and the drugs that allowed him to forget all the wretchedness that had befallen him. Four in the morning and pouring down rain, he opened his crummy tenement door to a blood-soaked apparition that nevertheless possessed the most haunting eyes he had ever seen. Eyes that he had never been able to forget in the four years since they had exiled him to this personal Ninth Circle of Hell. "You..." he stammered.

"I need you..." The voice was as silken as it had been on the tennis courts—as it had been the day she busted him. And now...only six steps ahead of the police herself and shot to boot...the bitch had the temerity to smile at him just like they were at some goddamned cocktail party. "One bullet passed right through....The other one is in my leg...you're going to have to get out."

Bolstered by his injected courage, he told her, "I'm not going to do shit," and attempted to slam the door in her face.

His dramatic gesture was stopped abruptly as she thrust her wounded arm against the flimsy plywood and tossed it back open. "Yes, you are," she continued calmly, limping into his living room/bedroom/kitchen. "Because I'm going to pay you $50,000 dollars in cash." Smiling coldly as his eyes went wide. "And if you do a good enough job and keep your fucking mouth shut....I'll make sure you never end up in another place like this again."

It was a siren song to his heroin-addled brain—and he didn't know if she were an angel come to save him or a devil here to complete his damnation. Quite frankly, he didn't care. He had learned that they called her the Archangel on the streets because of her terrible vengeance, and her tumble from the mount had filled them all with a sort of giddy relief. Now she was one of them, but not...Even in his torpor, Stephen realized that the woman in his room was something more terrible, more dangerous than the worst horror from his nightmares—mostly because she seemed like an answered prayer.

"You're bleeding on my couch," he said stupidly.

"And I'm going to keep bleeding until you take this fucking bullet out and stitch me up," she snarled at him, the growl of her voice the only sign of the pain he knew she had to be feeling.

"Or I could just call the police and let them sort this out." Greed made him wonder if he could get more money out of her. He should have noticed the warning glint in her eyes, the unmistakable signs that her temper was burning short, but the drugs had rendered the details of her facial expression blurred, the azure glitter dulled.

She shook her head wearily at him. "No, you're not." She pulled an evil-looking gun from a previously unnoticed holster. "I was hoping we could do this in a business-like fashion, but if I have to..."

"No, no," the unlicensed doctor assured her, quite convinced that she could hold the gun to his head while a bullet was being pulled from her body. "We can. I'm sorry. Let me go get my kit..."

Moments later he had sliced a gaping hole in her leather pants and was staring at the supple muscle where the bullet was embedded. "You want a hit for this?" He offered her his rig.

She arched a sardonic brow at him. "I don't fuck with that shit," she snapped.

"This is gonna hurt then. I don't have any other painkillers." The scalpel sliced cleanly in the rent flesh, opening up a gash wide enough for the forceps to slip in. He saw her face go white with the strain of fighting the pain. "Go ahead and scream," he counseled her. "People do it around here all the time." He laughed mirthlessly. "Maybe they'll think I'm getting lucky."

A blood-curdling howl was wrenched from the dealer's lungs as the forceps found their target and dislodged the bullet from its resting place with a sickening squelch.

"Almost..." he crooned as a lover would to his paramour. Grasping a firmer hold on the tiny projectile, he maneuvered it out of the dark woman's flesh. "There...little sucker, isn't it? Good old Smith & Wesson 38. Just be glad they weren't using hollow points."

Jude shuddered at the thought. "Let's hear it for local law enforcement. They couldn't hit the broad side of a skyscraper. I'm glad I didn't have to put any of them down."

Stephen blanched at her mocking words. "You were shooting at cops?" Not wanting any of the heat a dead policeman would bring to his door. He was afraid of Jude Lucien, but—after the short stint he had already done—he was afraid of prison more.

She looked at him blankly. "Who do you think I was shooting at? Besides," she added with a grimace as he swabbed the wound with antiseptic and began to stitch it closed. "If they had been the Cartel, I'd be dead right now."

"Why is that?" he muttered absently, intent on making his stitches even and neat.

"They have better aim." Jude chuckled with gallows humor. She watched him work a moment in silence, and he became aware of the faint coriander scent of her skin mixed in with the metallic tang of blood. "Nice stitching," she commented as he finished up.

"Where's the one that went right through?" he asked. The mellow high was beginning to wear off as the adrenaline of practicing his craft kicked in.

"Here," she said, indicating her left bicep. "Just needs cleaning and stitching."

"I'm surprised you didn't insist on doing this one yourself," he commented dryly.

Jude grinned toothily at him. "I'm a lefty. Or I would have."

Stephen just shook his head and looked at the shreds of her linen shirt. "You know it will hurt a lot less if I just unbutton the shirt and take it off your shoulders."

"Whatever," she shrugged, deftly sliding the buttons loose and slipping the shirt off her torso.

The smack had long ago rung any impulse of desire from his system, but his long years of studying the human physique made him cast an appreciative glance over Jude's bronze skin. She was flesh and blood— the wounds attested to that—but still the dealer's body seemed crafted into some sort of torturing perfection that made his marrow ache to look at her.

"You done?" she prompted him.

"Yeah, you'll live."

"You have any antibiotics?"

"No, but I can get you some in the morning."

"You think I'm staying here tonight?" The cold tone of voice clearly told him that particular idea was ludicrous.

"I don't think you should be walking on that leg."

"I'll be the judge of that." She stood shakily, bracing her weight on her one good leg and closing her eyes as a wave of pain washed across

her strained face. Slowly she opened them, mastering the agony in front of him. A hissing breath expelled from her mouth, and she smirked at his disbelieving eyes. "Get the antibiotics and I'll have the 50K here in the morning? Got it?"

"Uh...How am I supposed to pay for these antibiotics?"

"How do you pay for this?" She tossed his rig at him. "Same way, Sparky."

He nodded, at a loss. Suddenly he didn't want her to leave. Her presence, while sinister, was also sickly reassuring, as if he knew that nothing more wicked could befall him while in her company. "Don't you want a shirt or something? I mean, yours is soaked."

Jude cocked an eyebrow at him, glancing dubiously around the room. "I don't know," she demurred. "Kind of goes with the ripped leather pants, don't you think?"

"Here." He scrambled over to the rickety dresser in the corner and pulled out a black linen shirt, a relic from his better days. "Take this," thrusting it into her hands before she could refuse. "You could probably wear my jeans, but it would probably hurt more to take the leather off right now. Do you have anything for the pain at home?"

She nodded tightly, slipping the shirt gingerly over her wounded arm. "How do I look?" she mocked.

Stephen found himself smiling back. She really was a beautiful woman, despite the blood and grime covering her face, despite the chaos she had visited on his life. "Like a million bucks," he replied sincerely.

"Well," she snorted derisively. "At least like 50K, right?"

That had been the beginning. A day later, a leather satchel arrived in the company of a slender woman with skin the color of rich toffee. "You have something for me, I believe?"

He handed over the antibiotics, and she had relinquished the satchel without further comment. Two days later a note with instructions directing him to a deserted warehouse arrived, where he found another "patient" waiting for him.

Stephen had never looked back. True to her word, Jude sent him a steady stream of people who needed medical services but could do without the officious eyes of a hospital staff. The joy of being a doctor again—if only in this rather doubtful sense—seemed to lessen his need for the narcotic, and he climbed out of the worst of the sloth of his dependency. The smack was now mostly an old friend; lulling other, newer aches that his acquaintance with Jude also inspired.

She had never again come to him injured, even during the worst of the Massala trouble. And this phone call was the first he'd had from her in over a year. These days he usually dealt with that cold bitch, Sasha, who looked at him like he was a piece of...

"A week, huh?" Jude's question knocked him out of his odd nostalgia. Her eyes were worried as she once more surveyed the woman on the bed.

"She'll be fine, I promise. Here, give her two every four hours if the pain is bad. And this should keep away any infection." He tossed two bottles at her that she deftly caught.

"You're a little more prepared these days, eh?" she teased, holding them up.

"A little. Now show me to the door of this monster of a house and let me get some sleep," he replied.

▢ ▢ ▢

*Ow ow ow ow ow ow...*Liz found herself unfortunately returned to consciousness by the prodding pain in her side. She remembered with vivid clarity the spicy scent of Jude's skin filling her nostrils, anticipating the faint brush of the tall woman's lips as they began their descent upon her mouth, and then...*nothing*...except this hot pain.

*Somebody shot me...*the reporter shuddered, trying to wrap her mind around the undeniable realization. *Which means somebody was shooting at Jude....Did they...?* Her tumultuous thoughts were stilled by the sight of the dark woman gliding into the room, obviously whole and unharmed. She had changed into a loose, button-down shirt and a worn, faded pair of Levi's that did almost as much justice to her lithe form as the leather skirt did. Her feet were bare, padding softly on the thick burgundy carpet. *Burgundy carpet...? Either this is the swankiest hospital I've never seen... or we ain't in one.*

"Hi there," Jude said softly. "Glad to see you're still among the living."

"Not as glad as I am," Liz rasped hoarsely.

"Have some water," Jude carefully handed her a heavy crystal drinking glass. "Not too much," she cautioned as Liz eagerly drank down the liquid, assuaging the dry itch in her throat. The cold water hit her stomach hard, almost coming back up and causing her to gag. "Easy..." Jude's hands were cool against her clammy skin, soothing her with a tenderness that Liz had never imagined the dark woman possessing. "Take these for the pain. They'll help," she said, guiding her to swallow two pills and then nestling the small woman back into the pillows.

"Thanks," Liz nodded as the dizziness did indeed subside. "Um... Jude?" she asked, her eyes darting around the room, taking in the majestic ocean panorama in front of her and the quietly elegant furnishings of the room. "This isn't a hospital, is it?"

"No," the dark woman chuckled, sitting the mug and the pill bottle back on the bedside table. "This is my bedroom."

Confused, Liz asked, "Why didn't you take me to a hospital?"

Jude pursed her lips, as if contemplating how to answer the injured woman. Finally she drew a deep breath and sighed. "Because they have to report gunshot wounds."

"Right. That's how they catch the bad guys."

A rueful smile crept over Jude's full lips as she nodded. "I know. But that's the problem, you see." She blinked, looking away from Liz and studying the now fully risen sun flooding the room with its warmth. "They consider me one of the bad guys, Elizabeth. And honestly, I can't afford the attention right now."

Liz's green eyes grew wide, registering the dark woman's brutal honesty with a shock. She had expected evasions, excuses about how there wasn't time to get her to a hospital. Anything but the truth. *Hmm... What do I say now?*

Quiet blue was focused on her once more. "Your wound isn't too serious. I mean, as far as gunshot wounds go. It just grazed your side. You'll be sore for a few days, but other than that, you're okay."

"I knew that, you know," Liz said quietly.

Puzzled by the non sequitur, Jude raised a questioning brow.

"That you're one of the bad guys. Or at least that you *were* one of the bad guys."

Now azure eyes paled in surprise. "What do you mean?" she asked suspiciously.

It was the reporter's turn to smile ruefully. She decided that a fair amount of honesty would be her best tactic. It also eased her growing sense of guilt about lying to this woman. The feeling had started in the Club, when she realized how real the attraction between them was, and it had only increased as she learned more about Jude. "Come on...For a while there you weren't exactly keeping a low profile. Weren't you on the cover of *Time* with some sort of 'Mafia Goddess' headline?"

"*Newsweek*," Jude answered faintly, rubbing the bridge of her nose. "Is that why you approached me?" she asked, a new hardness in her expression. "Looking for a thrill?"

"No," Liz hastily assured her. "No," she repeated, this time more softly and shaking her head. "Your name sounded familiar, but it wasn't until we'd come out here that I made the connection. You weren't exactly

forthcoming about what you did for a living, and this house isn't cheap."
And neither are your clothes, your car, or your purebred dogs.

Liz wasn't sure, but she swore that Jude looked...*relieved? Nah...
can't be...*at her words. Still, the dark woman nodded in apparent
acceptance of her explanation. She turned as if to go, then paced back to
Liz's bedside. "You knew? And you still wanted me to..." Her words
trailed off uncertainly.

"Kiss me?" A smile that the honey-haired woman couldn't control
ran loose across her face and was reflected in Jude's answering grin.
"Boy, did I. I hope I haven't lost my chance forever."

Jude didn't respond to the gentle banter. Instead she turned again as
if to go, then returned to Liz's bedside once more. "The doctor said you
should take it easy for the next few days...and...I'd feel much better if
you'd recuperate here. Think of it as a free vacation. You could write,
watch the ocean, and relax." She paused for a moment to study Liz's
startled face. "Of course you'd be free to come and go as you like..." she
assured the smaller woman.

"Why?" Liz asked simply.

The honey-haired woman could see lightning flashes of thought
jagging behind Jude's eyes. After a silent internal debate, she finally
answered, "Because I need a few days to make sure that none of this
follows you."

That stark truth was evident in the stabbing pain in Liz's side, searing
home the reality of the deadly game she was playing with Jude Lucien.
Bloodshed was an inevitable consequence of the life this woman led, and
Liz had just invited herself to the party. The people who had come after
Jude wouldn't care about an incidental casualty like Liz. *So why does
she?* "You can do that? Make sure they don't come back after me?"

"They probably wouldn't at any rate. As far as they're concerned
you're just some woman I picked up at the bar. But I'd like to be sure,"
Jude answered tonelessly. A heavy silence rested between them as Liz
fidgeted with the thick coverlet and Jude studied the ocean vista. Cool
indigo returned their solemn gaze to her. "I...I like you, Elizabeth. I'd
hate for...anything bad...to happen to you. Especially because of me."
Then a tiny grin tugged at the corners of her mouth. "And I'd like another
shot at that kiss thing," she added softly, teasingly.

A quiet chuckle rose up in Liz's throat, growing in strength as she
watched the smile break fully over the dark woman's face. "Ah...your
true intentions revealed at last."

"You're right. All of this was one big set-up to get you into my bed," Jude replied dryly.

I could have told you that you didn't have to go to all the trouble, Liz's thoughts retorted. Aloud, she said, "Well, I hate to criticize, but don't you think that this is just a little overdone?" She indicated her prone position. "I mean your objectives have been achieved: I'm flat on my back and—" She lifted up the covers and glanced underneath, "Yup, I'm naked." *I'm naked?*

Jude smiled at the furious blush on Liz's fair features. "I didn't peek. Well, much..." She held up her hands to ward off the menacing glare tossed her way. "Hey, I couldn't help it. I had to get your dress off to see the wound." She paused, then added mischievously, "It wasn't my fault you weren't wearing any underwear."

"Hey!" Liz protested. "It's not like I had much of a choice. Did you see the dip in the back of that thing?" The warm gleam in Jude's eye told the reporter that yes, indeed, the tall woman had noticed and appreciated all the special effects of the Vera Wang creation. A light tension settled pleasantly over her body, contrasting nicely with the throb in her side. "Gee—" she said at last, "I guess this is why your mom tells you not to leave the house without wearing clean underwear."

"Well, yours should have told you to make sure you left the house *wearing* underwear, period." Jude laughed.

"Sure, yuk it up. I'm the wounded one here."

Immediately Jude's face sobered. "I'm so sorry, Elizabeth."

"I know that. And even though I've never been shot before—and I certainly hope it never happens again—it really doesn't hurt so bad."

"That's because the drugs are kicking in."

"Maybe so. You're beginning to look a little fuzzy around the edges."

"Before you go completely out, tell me where you live so I can send someone to fetch you some clothes. I'm sorry to say, but I'm afraid last night's true casualty was your beautiful dress."

Any effects of the sedative were immediately counteracted by the panic flooding Liz's veins at the thought of Jude in her apartment. *Talk about going down in flames....She'd probably finish off the job those guys started.* "Uh...that's probably not a good idea." The words were out before she had a chance to think. *Oh shit...*

The dark woman's brows furrowed. "Why not?" she asked, a wary edge creeping into her tone.

*Think, Liz, think...*even though it was getting increasingly difficult as the Percodan took firm root in her system. "I—I—live with someone.

But we're splitting up. In fact, he's supposed to be gone by next weekend. And it's probably best if I go myself. Or he'll assume that I'm sleeping with whoever picks up my stuff." It was an explanation directly lifted from the second novel she had written in college. *Love's Eternal Longing* had chronicled the tempestuous romance of Jake and Sonora, and its ultimate destruction because of Jake's unnatural jealously. But she didn't think she could get in trouble for plagiarizing herself. Particularly given the life-and-death circumstances.

Jude, however, had obviously only targeted one piece of her statement. "He?" she asked with a sardonic lift of her brow.

"I was kidding myself, okay?" Liz ad-libbed. That much was true. The one serious relationship she'd had with a man had been a last ditch effort to ignore the truth and had only lasted a miserable nine months. "He thought—I thought—" The drugs were kicking in full force now, and she slipped easily into the memory of the awkwardly painful six months she had tried to live a life that would never belong to her.

◻ ◻ ◻

Liz woke to a gummy taste in her mouth and a dull ache in her side. A few wildly disorienting moments ensued as she tried to figure out exactly where she was. *Jude...the beach house...gun....Oh yeah... I got it.* Slowly she swiveled her head from side to side wincing at the painful haziness. No Jude. *Hmm...*her senses prickled as her eyes caught the note taped to a glass pitcher filled with water and half-melted ice cubes. The writing was bold and solid, and Liz absently wondered what a handwriting expert would make of it.

> *"Drink plenty of water, but don't eat anything yet. There are some sweats on the chair for you. They're probably a little big, but it's the best I could do on short notice. You can take more pills if you need them at 2:00. I've got some errands to run, but should be back soon.*
> *—J."*

"Don't eat anything—Easy for her to say. I'm starving," Liz muttered, realizing that the burger she grabbed on the way home from the paper yesterday evening was long gone. She crumpled the note into a ball and tossed it on the bedside table. She chewed her lip, staring at the crumpled wad then picked it back up and smoothed it out, laying it down more gently. "Waterford, huh? Nice." She commented, running an idle finger down the pitcher. She poured herself a glass of water and drank it slowly, pleased when it didn't threaten to come back up.

"I think I may actually live." Stretching her stiff muscles gingerly, she slid off the edge of the bed and hesitantly stood. Relieved as her legs held her up fairly easily, she made her way to the chair and pulled on the promised sweats. "A little big?" They were laughably big, and she was sure she looked like some ragamuffin orphan in them, but at least she was clothed. Looking at the bed, she knew she should probably climb back in and go back to sleep, but quite frankly at the moment, her curiosity was paining her more than her side. Of course, she didn't know when Jude was due back, but the note seemed to indicate it wouldn't be until well after noon, so she had some time.

"Ooh...bad, Liz. You're being very bad..." The small woman grinned to herself as she padded across the floor towards the door.

The second floor literally curved around the first, creating sort of an open corridor that looked down upon the main living room. Saving the second floor for last, she descended the long, curving staircase to the main rooms. "Like living in the sky? Boy you weren't kidding," Liz marveled. Jude Lucien seemed to hate walls. In fact her home was a testament to light and air. There were windows everywhere that—Liz determined after quick investigation—were made of layered, leaded glass. "Seems like someone's worried about people throwing more than stones," she murmured softly. She prowled along the ground floor, discovering in addition to the living room and various bathrooms, a kitchen, a formal dining room, and a workout room. Most of the rooms had access to a large deck that ran the length of the house and offered the same beautiful view that the bedroom did. A glance outside told her that the deck circled a pool that looked cool and inviting in the warm sunlight. All the rooms were beautifully decorated in cool blues and grays with tasteful art on the walls, but somehow, it struck the reporter as remote and empty.

"Okay, I admit she doesn't come across as Ms. Warm-and-Fuzzy, but the way she talked about this place..." Narrowing her eyes, she climbed the stairs again and returned to the bedroom. "This is more like it," she murmured, taking in the vibrant colors of the room. The rich burgundy carpet was accented by the jewel tones on the comforter and sheets, and the walls were a warmer cream instead of the stark white that was everywhere downstairs. *Hmm...I wonder...*

The rooms on the second floor confirmed her suspicions. This was where Jude Lucien truly lived. A library adjacent to the bedroom was filled floor-to-ceiling with leather-bound tomes and a cozy arrangement of couches and chairs overlooking the ocean. A book, turned faced down on the arm of a worn leather easy chair, and an empty plate and mug on the ottoman in front of it testified to Jude's recent occupation. "*Anna Karenina*," she noted, reading the book's spine. "That's a surprise."

A quiet snuffling at her hands startled her into dropping the book, which landed with a muffled thud on the chair. Once she determined that her heart was indeed still beating, she regarded the four-legged sentry. The Akita stood with his head cocked and an inquiring glance in his eyes. "Aggie," she muttered. "Why do I think Clytemnestra would have snuck up and bitten me in the ass?" Aggie wagged his tail in agreement, woofing softly. He then jumped onto the couch and made himself comfortable, pulling a well-loved chew toy from somewhere in the furniture's depths. Liz chuckled at the contented picture, heartened for some reason that the dark woman had these animals. "At least she cares for something."

She left Aggie happily chewing and wandered into the next room. It was a guest bedroom in much the same style as the downstairs and held little interest for her. The next two rooms—another bedroom and the bathroom that linked them—were equally uninteresting. Reversing her steps, she entered the room on the other side of Jude's bedroom. And gasped at the sight.

"Jackpot..." A sleek computer rested on a mammoth desk, in whose clean lines Liz detected the same hand that was responsible for the beautiful house she was now in. The desk faced the ocean, and Liz was more than a little surprised that Jude would allow her back to be to any door. "But this is her haven. Nobody comes here," she realized with a start, studying the curved outer wall that provided the unobstructed panorama. In addition to the desk and file cabinets, there were several comfortable-looking easy chairs, a battered guitar that looked like it had seen better days resting in one of them. A low rumble from the other one told her she had found Clytemnestra.

"Uh...hi there." Liz grimaced, watching the dog's hackles rise. "Maybe this wasn't such a good idea." She began easing herself towards the door, but now the growling animal stood between her and that particular goal. "Easy...I'm not going to hurt you." She showed her open palms to the dog. "And hopefully you're not going to hurt me. Does that sound like a plan?" But the Akita continued to growl menacingly as Liz edged closer and closer. "What a fate. I survive a bullet only to be eaten by Cujo here." She rolled her eyes at the ridiculous dilemma she found herself in. "I must have done something horrible in a past life to deserve this. If it was so bad, why couldn't I have just been sent back as an accountant or something, huh?" Liz noticed that the dog had stopped growling and was now studying her with an arch expression. Deciding to take advantage,

Liz continued to address the animal conversationally. It seemed to be working so far. "I mean, really, what have I done here that's so bad? So I want to get to know your mistress a little more. Is that such a bad thing?"

The dog rumbled deep in her throat, but it didn't seem hostile to Liz, more like an earnest reply to her question. "I admit, my motives are mixed, but you know, I like her." Remembering the near-kiss that they had shared and the intense arousal that had preceded it, she grinned. "I really like her," she repeated.

Clytemnestra paced nearer, nostrils quivering.

"What is it?"

Now the Akita was pressed up against her legs, sniffing and wagging her tail wildly.

The small woman was perplexed as to why the dog suddenly approved of her so wholeheartedly, until it dawned on her just whose clothes she was wearing. "Oh, you like me now that I smell okay, huh?" Burying her own nose in the T-shirt she was wearing, she could detect Jude's increasingly familiar scent. The faint spiciness brought a smile to Liz's face. "I guess this means I'm not going to be lunch."

Apparently satisfied now that the reporter had passed the sniff test, Clytemnestra obligingly retreated back to her armchair. For a moment Liz contemplated fleeing from the room, but the lure of the computer was too strong. If Jude's house had told her anything, it was that the dark woman was an enthusiastic citizen of the electronic age. She suspected that the computer could tell her a great deal that casual conversation wouldn't.

Spinning the leather desk chair around, an angry bark sent her reeling back a step. It wasn't from the big dog in the corner, but rather from the soft-eyed spaniel that indignantly stood in the chair's seat.

"Oh God, another one," Liz grumbled darkly. She couldn't help the laugh that simmered in her throat at the animal in front of her. "You must be Pete."

The medium sized dog was obviously a mutt, but had unmistakable traces of spaniel and beagle in his face. His coat was a velvety black that rendered him almost invisible in the dark chair. Chocolate eyes stared out at her, assessing whether or not she intended him harm. Pete yipped quietly as Liz offered him her hand. Sniffing once, he licked it tentatively and wagged his feathery tail as she scratched his ears.

"You're an easier crowd than your buddy over there," Liz commented wryly. "Okay now, if I can just get you to move for a second, so I can sit down and plunder this drug dealer's computer, all will be right with my world."

Obediently the dog leapt down, and Liz settled into the chair in his place. "Ooh...this is nice." The chair was comfortably worn in all the right places, and she imagined the dark woman spent long hours here. "Now...where's the power switch?" The machine was a Compaq computer, similar to her own. She quickly powered up the main screen and was confronted with three possible work stations labeled "JLE," "Restaurant/Club," and "Play." Then, in the bottom right hand corner, she noticed a fourth, simply labeled "Jude." Each workstation was password protected.

"Think, Liz, think," she recited her favorite mantra aloud. Usually much pacing accompanied this activity, but her side was beginning to ache; and she didn't know how much longer she could go without some much-needed narcotic relief. "Where's the best place to hide something?" She thought for a moment. "In plain sight. So...if this is plain sight...how do I get into them? Passwords...Three stations...What do people use for passwords? Something they don't forget. Their birthday?" She typed in Jude's birthday and was immediately denied access. "What else? Familiar names?" Unfortunately none of the information she had uncovered about the drug dealer mentioned any family. A quiet *thawump* at her feet drew her attention to the black bundle of fur curled up next to the chair. "Nah..." shaking her head, "Okay, let's try it," and typed in the dogs' names in rapid succession. Clytemnestra was the key to "JLE," Agamemnon opened "Restaurant/Club," and Pete—of course—opened up "Play."

She glanced through the directories, finding only that Jude owned lots of real estate and both Monde and the Club made Jude lots and lots of legitimate money. Jude seemed to have so many above-the-line businesses that the reporter wondered why the dark woman was still engaged in her...other...pursuits. Romair Massala's presence last night had convinced her of that fact. "Play" only told Liz that Jude had a weakness for simulated shoot 'em ups. "You'd think she'd get enough of that in real life," Liz mumbled, looking at games with titles like *Postal*, *Duke Nukem*, and *Quake*. One title, *Gender Wars*, however, gave her a soft chuckle.

"Nothing, Pete, nothing," she said to the heap who had quietly edged still closer and was now resting on her feet. Her eye again caught the fourth workstation in the corner. "Jude, huh? Well, you don't have any more animals. I hope." she added. "I've done all the canine bonding I can take for the time being." She studied the one remaining closed workstation. "If my theory's right, this is where it's all hiding." She thought for a moment more, trying to think of what she knew about Jude. Then the dark woman's dry sense of humor surfaced in her mind. "No way," she grinned, typing *C-R-I-M-E* into the password slot. The computer paused a moment...then flashed the magical message: *Home base is changing workstations. Please wait...*

"Bingo!" Liz sang.

In addition to the various on-line services that were also on the other stations, there seemed to be three major directories. One looked like some sort of electronic diary, the second was marked "Communication," while the third was labeled "Documentation." Crossing her mental fingers, Liz opened up "Communication."

And felt the breath leave her body when she realized what the files contained and what their subjects meant.

Jude Lucien was still working for the DEA.

Chapter 4

The roar of Jude's tumultuous thoughts easily drowned out the combined noise of the ocean and the Boxster's purring engine. She shifted absently through the Saturday morning traffic in a meandering path that would indicate if anyone was tailing her. So far, she was clear. *Of course, it would have helped if I had been this careful last night.* The more she thought about it, however; the more she became convinced that whoever fired the shot had only been serving up a warning. A kill shot would have gone to her head, and no matter how swift her reflexes, she couldn't have gotten out of the way. Her instincts had taken over when she heard the sharp report of the rifle, but she still hadn't been able to get Elizabeth completely clear. *She got lucky...I got lucky...*

Not for a moment did she entertain the notion that the honey-haired woman had been the intended target. *Unless literary critics are putting out contracts on romance novelists these days,* she grinned to herself. Despite the unexpected depths she had sensed in Elizabeth's jade eyes, the woman was obviously an innocent when it came to umbral figures like the one who had visited them last night. Jude, however, had spent a decade living in those shadows, shrouding herself in their familiar depths and treading the dim corridors with practiced ease.

Working deep cover, Jude reflected, was like a waking schizophrenia where both personalities are agonizingly aware of the other's existence and activities. She didn't even have the luxury of forgetting for even a second the dual plane of her reality. Eventually she was no longer able to serve two masters.

They said she'd just snapped, that she'd turned rogue...seduced by the glamour, the drugs, and the aphrodisiac of illicit power. In their eyes she was the ultimate infidel. Few in the Agency knew the truth—that the madness behind her leap from grace had been motivated by a betrayal so great she could barely comprehend it. The brilliant agent that had been Jude Lucien became a relentless Fury, pursuing those who had brought about this horror. No one mentioned his name. No one mentioned the past in the vain hope it would remain buried. No one, that is, except for Jude.

Jason Childs was as fair as Jude was dark, with curling blond hair brushing his shoulders and cornflower blue eyes that reflected warmth where Jude's glittered darkly. He was the quintessential California boy, born and raised on the beaches and in the surf. His sunny looks and sweet, sweet smile however belied a shrewd mind able to juggle the myriad layers that deep cover required.

Jude was skeptical when they were first paired on a relatively tame assignment—a simple buy and bust, sort of a training mission to see how well they worked as a team. The dark woman they called the Archangel was given a wide berth at the Agency...the ease with which she garbed herself in the enemy's colors made them wary, and her presence emphasized how fine the line between "us" and "them" really was. Jude's gun and her badge marked her as a member of the team, but the restless sweep of her eyes and the ill-concealed pleasure she took in being a predator told them that she was something else altogether.

She knew Jason had heard all the rumors running rampant about her. How she had taken down this dealer or that smuggler—spectacular stunts that seemed outlandish until someone actually met Jude in the flesh. There were other, more disturbing stories about the lengths Jude had gone to in order to protect her cover—including a nasty one about beating the holy hell out of three uniformed policemen who had unknowingly stumbled into the middle of an operation. "Be grateful I didn't kill them," was the only comment Jude had ever made on the matter. Jude didn't give the rumors much thought and only hoped that her new partner would reserve judgment until he finally met Jude one chilly February night.

Wearing nothing but his smile, he stood in the center of the small hotel room watching Jude as she carefully prepared the wire. A controlled energy—almost like the energy of sexual arousal—emanated from her pores as she worked. But there was nothing sensual at all in the practiced and clinical touch taping the wire to his skin and nestling the tiny recording pack in the silk boxers that had been specially made for this purpose. "Whatever you do," she muttered wryly, sliding the cloth up his legs. "Don't get a hard-on. You might dislodge the recorder from its spot and ruin the tape."

"Is that a frequent problem your partners have?" A cheerful smile danced across his eyes, a silent invitation for her to come out and play.

Jude arched a contemplative eyebrow and shrugged. "It's been known to happen." A tiny smirk curled at the corner of her mouth as she worked, but it disappeared so quickly he almost wondered if he had imagined it. "Now look. Remember the story. You're a pothead who's trying to catch a break into the business. I'm gonna have Fortisma hook you so you can sell to your buddies on the beach. You already owe me a couple of favors and you're working them off, giving me most of what you make. In exchange for which I don't kick your ass up one side of the sand and down the other. Got it?" Watching him closely as he got dressed, she snorted and shook her head. "I can't believe that they're making me work with Polly-fuckin-ana."

"Yeah, but who's going to believe Polly-fuckin-ana's a cop?" he reasoned with a grin.

"Let's hope so," she murmured darkly.

The meet had gone down like a dream with Jason performing flawlessly the part of a slightly stoned, slightly stupid surfer. Jude sat back in silent appreciation as the weeks spun out and Jason reeled in their catch with a careful grace, never once jeopardizing her long-standing deep cover. And so, the tolerance began metamorphosing into a grudging respect, and then into genuine trust. Somewhere along the line, Jason's relentless cheerfulness began to infect Jude; and she found herself talking to the youth as they whiled away long hours in surveillance vans and filled with conversation the tedious days of waiting that often seemed the bulk of their work.

As one of the few female deep cover agents, Jude was something of an anomaly among agents. Most of the women in the DEA were support surveillance or tech crews manning the high tech gadgets that were essential to her efforts. Pursuing friendships, or even casual acquaintances, with her fellow agents seemed ludicrous to Jude.

Relationships had never come easy to the dark woman, and her life of deep ops certainly didn't foster long-term attachments. Her lovers were mostly chosen at random from the dark life where she prowled—women whose eyes weren't afraid to roam her body and whose voices weren't afraid to call to her. No... she couldn't get that from the tight-suited agents with their precisely compartmentalized lives. She had broken her rules about co-workers only once when she had fallen into a casual liaison with one of her surveillance crew members—a compact little red-head with a spectacular body and an unfortunate habit of saying "no" when she meant "yes." Wading through the heated denials of passion had been kind of exciting the first couple of times. When Sandi had finally gotten through her "No, we can't" litany, she had come at Jude like a wildcat, leaving trailing claw marks that the agent had a hell of a time explaining to others. Jude quickly tired of the whole process, however; preferring to wash her hands of the drama and take her pleasure from more...forthright...sources.

Jason didn't seem to be too disturbed by her brooding, her laconic replies, and her general dislike of all things social. His motto seemed to be "keep asking," until finally Jude found herself drifting into conversations that seemed more and more natural as they spent time together.

"Why in God's name did you join the DEA?" she asked him in exasperation one long night.

"Why not?" he replied with an easy smile.

"Because this life is fucked. That's why," she retorted bluntly.

"Then why is it okay for you to be in this life if it's so fucked?"

"Because..." she hesitated, before continuing, "I understand it." A long pause. "And it understands me."

Jason seemed unsure what to say to the statement. It was by far the most personal thing she'd ever said to him, and she could almost see him mentally hefting her words, preparing to use them as a tiny chisel to wedge his way further inside the labyrinthine passages of Jude's mind and heart. She didn't give him the chance as she continued, "Somebody like you should be living some nice, quiet life with a house and a yard and a dog. Not this..." She gestured at the cramped surroundings of the black van.

He smiled at the image. Over the months they had been partnered, Jude had developed a slightly overprotective air. They both knew that it was more than just an experienced agent looking out for a rookie. She dealt with him as she would a cherished sibling and was fiercely protective of his inexperience. "You have high hopes for me. I'm touched." They exchanged grins. "And I'm going to have all those things, Jude. A big house with a wife and kids, lots of dogs, and a barbecue so you can come over and be sullen in a social environment," he teased her gently.

She smiled back at him—a real smile that touched the remoteness of her eyes and warmed them to a pale flame. "Wife and kids, huh? Okay, hot stuff, just where do you think you're going to meet a nice girl when you're hanging out with the likes of me?"

"Well to be honest, until I meet Ms. Right, I can't think of anyone I'd rather spend the time with," he replied seriously.

Slowly, each became an indispensable thread in the tapestry of the other's life. They began spending time together outside their ops, and Jude walked tentatively in the daylight world for the first time in longer than she could remember. He called her Angel—mocking the intimidating image that dogged her throughout the agency and laughed uproariously at her intensity. "Ease down, Angel," he'd gibe. "It's only rock and roll." Sunday afternoon football became a ritual for the pair, as well as rambling walks on the beach that invariably ended at their favorite oceanfront restaurant. Jude spent more nights than she could count at what was "their" table, feet propped on the weathered wood, bourbon comfortably in her hand, telling the young man things she hadn't told anyone. She told him of the terror of her first assignment, the shock of her first kill, and the horror at how easily it all came to her. And later, witnessed only by the sand and the rushing tide, he held her—like no one ever had—cradling the dark head in his hands, softly stroking her hair, and telling her everything was going to be all right. That she was still human, that she was still whole.

Eventually Jason had found his Ms. Right—ironically courtesy of Jude—and the agent had stood by his side at the wedding, bidding a silent good-bye to their friendship. But that hadn't happened. Maria, Jason's new bride, was no fool. As much as Jason encouraged Jude's time in the sun, Maria could see the older woman plainly kept the darkness from devouring her new husband. It wasn't just a matter of protecting his life; Jude zealously guarded the young man's soul, keeping it safe for Maria's love. So Maria welcomed the dark agent—with all her rage, all her violence, and all her pain—into their home and called the predator "family." When Maria bore a daughter, it was a stunned Jude who stood on the altar once again with her friend, this time holding a cooing infant in her arms and promising to be there if the child ever needed her help...

Jude shook her head angrily to clear the memories threatening to swallow her whole. She had forsaken the illusion of being suited to anything other than the tenebrous life that she now clung to—the only thing still familiar to the tattered remnants of her soul. But something about the honey-haired woman she had met last night awakened a tentative yearning for connection. And it was shaded with a fierce physical desire that being with Jason had never evoked.

Elizabeth Peterson... She rolled the name across her thoughts, enjoying the accompanying image of the shimmering emerald dress caressing the body underneath. Less pleasant was the dress' current condition—blood-soaked and shredded by Jude's frantic hands as she searched for the wound. *What was I thinking?* she chastised herself. But her mind defiantly wandered once more to the promise of what would have happened had the shadows not interfered. An aching tendril of loneliness snaked itself loose from the iron bands of Jude's will and stroked her consciousness, eliciting a weary sigh from the dark woman. "No! I am not doing this. I am not dragging someone else down with me again. I'm going to make sure she's clear and then she's gone. Got it?" she warned herself savagely, allowing the words to be ripped from her throat as she sped through the Saturday traffic.

But an insurgent corner of her mind replied mockingly, *Yeah...right...*

▢ ▢ ▢

Kent Laird paced the length of his nondescript office in short, measured steps. Four across, turn once, four down, glance at watch, turn once, four across. Repeat. At precisely 11:00AM his phone rang.

"Laird." Already knowing who it was.

"I've got issues."

Click.

Oh shit... Kent groaned silently. He had heard the roar of the ocean in the call's background, which meant she was calling from her cell phone—never a good idea—and that she was on her way—an even worse one. *Not good, not good at all.* He clattered down the stairs to resume his pacing outside, as if his steps would bring her faster. After an interminable 10-minute wait, an unfamiliar sports car, piloted by an all-too familiar figure roared up.

"New wheels?" he inquired sardonically.

"Get in," was her curt response as she threw the car in gear and hurled them back into the sun.

Kent studied the Archangel's profile as they motored along. The steel blue of her eyes was covered by those ever-present Raybans, and her long hair fell in a neat braid down her back. His eyes patrolled her seated length—linen trousers and a matching shirt, black of course. She was inscrutable as always...*God, doesn't the woman ever sweat?* he thought, mopping his brow against the fierce Miami day. She looked for all the world like a prosperous business woman, out for a Saturday spin. If she had issues, she was damn good at concealing them. But then, he had never seen her panic, not even when her cover was blown and she was half dead...

They had been under about three months, on loan to the ATF, posing as a brother and sister team of gun runners selling arms to a group of Anti-Communist revolutionaries led by a guy named Maltos. To make matters worse, they were in some godforsaken Third World country whose name he'd never bothered to learn. Kent had been positioned as the brains, Jude the muscle. Although the reality was much different, they liked to work this way because it threw people off—no one expected the darkly beautiful woman to be such a graceful menace. It should have been simple; they were wrapping the loose ends up. Their buyers just needed to take delivery, and then the bust would go down.

Easy, right?

At the time he didn't know what hit him—hindsight later revealed his carelessness in making an inappropriate phone call from a tapped line—but none of that mattered at the moment. Kent was bound, blindfolded, and—he was convinced—about to die. It was all going to end for him in a dirty garage, the stench of grease, oil, and rubber filling his nostrils and reminding him incongruously of Saturday mornings spent with his brother in the family garage. It was an ironic way to die, he thought, but not a bad one.

Until the pain started.

Two men began working him over, demanding information that he never should have given them. But the sickening crunch of his ribs cracking under the smashing assault of iron pipes convinced him otherwise. An agonized scream rose from this throat, and the second thing out of his mouth was Jude's name and current location. Then, mercifully, he passed out.

When he awakened the blindfold had been removed, and he immediately wished to God it hadn't been.

Jude—or what was left of her—was strung up from a pair of heavy chains, the kind used to move engines. There wasn't an inch of skin that wasn't marred by some cut or bruise, and the bile rose in Kent's throat at the sight of the magnificent woman's smashed face. Maltos was directing a stream of invectives in Spanish at his partner, and Kent caught enough of the rapid fire cursing to realize that Jude had taken out four of his men before they had subdued her. "At least you took some of them down with you," he muttered softly, convinced his partner was dead. An almost hidden glint of blue caught his eye, and he realized with consuming sorrow that Jude was alive and that her torture was far from over.

Not content with simply beating the life out of her, Maltos would be satisfied only with the complete violation of this woman who to him—in wielding her body with such a combination of power, strength, and beautiful violence—was a walking abomination. Kent let out a strangled cry as he watched Jude's unresisting form released from its shackles and thrown face down over a metal workbench cluttered with tools. The thugs merely snickered at Kent's weak efforts to free himself and kicked him in his broken ribs for the effort. "NO!" he screamed and struggled all the more.

"Hey asshole, whatsamatter? Don't like sharing the raja?" one of them leered.

Kent snarled in reply, the rage filling his body and blocking out the pain of the renewed blows.

"Hey, puta!" Maltos taunted Jude's slumped form. "Te la voy a meter de mira quien viene. Huh? You like that?"

The two men working on Kent cackled with glee. "We get her next, eh?" Kent groaned and shut his eyes against the sight of Maltos tugging Jude's Levi's down over her hips. "Oh no, you gonna watch this..." They held his head and forced his eyes open. The jeans were off now in a pile at her feet. Maltos had kicked her legs apart and was fumbling with his own belt.

"Jude..." Kent whispered inaudibly, praying for whatever it was the dark woman called a soul.

Like so many others, he had underestimated the Archangel, and the howl that followed from Maltos was as much surprise as anything. Jude reared off the table, twisting her torso and swinging a heavy hammer squarely against Maltos' temple, sending fragments of skull, brain matter, and blood spraying all over her. And then the hammer was launched in the direction of one of his captors and her body was hurtling towards the other. The hammer connected with a solid thud against an arm that was reaching for a holstered weapon. Kent managed to leverage himself up and kick the stumbling man unconscious. He turned around in time to see Jude kneeling squarely on her victim's chest, crushing the back of his head repeatedly against the concrete floor. There was an evil-looking stain spreading out across the slick floor and a vicious curl of satisfaction in Jude's eyes. She heaved herself off the corpse and knelt by the one remaining suspect. Holding him by the hair, she muttered something under her breath and bent to snap his neck.

"Wait!!!!" Kent shouted and blanched at the burning pale blue that was fixed on him. "We can't.. We have to take him in..."

Jude stared at him with the same regard one would have for a particularly slow child. "Are you out of your fucking mind?" she asked calmly. "We take him in and he tells his lawyer all about the phone call that blew our cover. You'd be fucked in more ways than one. If they didn't shitcan you right away, nobody in their right mind would partner with you anymore." She looked back down at the unconscious man and then snapped his neck cleanly.

Kent closed his eyes as he realized how Maltos' people had found him. The crunch of bones—along with the understanding that he'd nearly gotten himself and Jude killed—made his stomach churn, and he felt himself gagging. Moments later, he was cut down and resting on his hands and knees, spewing up what was left of his lunch and not a little blood.

"We need to get you looked at," Jude remarked, pulling on her jeans and studying his retching form cynically. She had been beaten to a pulp, nearly raped, and responsible for seven deaths that day. And, Kent thought, staring at her composed figure, goddamned if she still didn't look better than he did. "We'll let the locals clean up the mess, okay?" He nodded silently, his tongue thick with self-reproach and guilt as they left the garage and slipped back into the night.

He later learned that Jude had saved his life by almost sacrificing hers, allowing herself to be captured to find out where he was. In the aftermath of the fiasco, they almost became friends, at least as much as his rage and humiliation at needing her rescue would let him. Jude's darkness had always bewildered and frightened him, but she had used it to protect him. Now he was beholden to her. Her defection to the other side had outraged him, but when Jude had finally called in her marker, he didn't refuse. Kent finally saw his chance to tie off the last loose threads that had been left hanging all those years ago.

Jude skillfully navigated the car out of city traffic and to an out-of-the-way dive that was an occasional rendezvous point for the pair. The Archangel had a knack for picking out the kind of places where no one asked questions and no one remembered faces—even ones as distinctive as hers. She settled them at a corner table where she could see the door and walked to the bar.

"You're kidding," he said, staring with disbelief at the beer she sat before him.

A bourbon rested in her own palm, and she arched a sardonic brow in his direction. "When you hear this, you're going to need it."

"So tell me already."

Jude sighed and tossed back half her drink. "There's another contract on me."

"Motherfuck..." he breathed, taking a long drought off the beer. A smirk darted over Jude's eyes but she remained silent. Then his forehead scrunched together in confusion. "Are you sure? I mean...I haven't heard anything from our sources. How do you know?"

"I know because somebody tried to collect on it last night at my house," she replied dryly.

"Sweet Jesus. Are you all right?"

"Yeah, I'm fine, but..." she polished off the rest of her bourbon and ran a hand over suddenly weary eyes.

"But?" he queried.

"A civilian got hit."

"How?" he asked bluntly.

Jude shrugged. "I got careless. We were out on the beach and the shot came from a sniper in the cove to the left of my property. I think it was more of a wake up call than anything, trying to make me jumpy, I guess."

"What'd you do with the civilian?"

"She's fine, just a flesh wound, recovering at my house."

Kent tried unsuccessfully to hide his surprise. "You've got a woman shacked up at your house?" He kept his voice deceptively casual. "That's a new one. I thought you didn't hang around long enough to exchange last names, let alone tell them where you lived."

"Kent..." she growled a warning.

"How did you leave it with her?"

"I told her the truth. That I was one of the bad guys. She seemed to take it okay." A Cheshire grin lit the Archangel's eyes, warming the pale blue to a smoky indigo, and Kent suddenly felt the temperature rising at the table.

"That's risky," he managed, between deep swallows of his beer.

"I thought I owed her the truth—or at least a version of it—considering she almost got killed because of me. Besides, the doc said she needed to rest for about a week or so... that should give me enough time to make sure her tail is clear. I need you to poke around, see what the rumblings about me are."

"You think the Massalas might be involved?"

Jude shook her head. "I'm not sure. I had dinner with Romair last night. He's a lot brighter than Rico ever was. I really think he doesn't want another war on his hands."

"Especially considering the last one went so badly."

The dark head nodded. "More or less."

"Still think you can bring them in?"

"That's my job, isn't it?"

"Jude...about this woman..." Kent began hesitantly. "I don't think it's such a wise idea to keep her around. I mean—"

"I don't really give a flying fuck what you think, Kent. I'm not one of your minions, remember?" The pale coldness was back in full force, glaring into him with frightening intensity. "The deal is: I bring in the rest of the Massalas and I walk away free and clear. Remember?"

Kent forced a tentative smile to his face and tried to lighten the suddenly deadly atmosphere. "Going to enjoy your illegal millions somewhere south of the border?"

She chuckled wryly. "Yeah, something like that. Maybe I'll buy a boat and sail around the world."

He studied her closely, suddenly curious. "You could do that right now, Jude. Why don't you?"

A tense silence hovered over them while Jude studied the melting ice in her glass. "Because that wasn't the deal," she said at last. "Because I owe someone."

꒔   ꒔   ꒔

By the time she finished with Kent, ran her other errands, and checked in with Sasha at the Club; it was well past three o'clock when she finally returned home. Grabbing an armful of parcels from the Boxster's tiny trunk, she entered through the deck's side door into the kitchen.

"Hey there, Carmina." She grinned cheerfully at her housekeeper. "How's our patient?"

"You coulda told me you had someone here." A rotund Mexican woman about twenty years Jude's senior complained as she bustled around the kitchen putting away the groceries. Arriving every Saturday like clockwork, the standing order at the local fresh market rarely changed, much to Carmina's chagrin. Simple was the most charitable way to describe Jude's culinary tastes, and the dark woman was usually most satisfied by hearty meals that the housekeeper disparagingly referred to as "peasant dishes." On the other hand, the years she had been in the Senora's employ had been the easiest and most lucrative of the immigrant's life, so she wasn't inclined to argue.

Discovering the petite honey-haired woman in the Senora's bed, however, had been something of a shock for her. It had been a while since there had been an overnight guest, and Carmina fervently hoped that this didn't signal a return to the days when it seemed as though she spent most of her workday changing the Senora's sheets. "She's fine. I got here a little late, cause of the traffic, but when I got here she was asleep. She woke up when I came into the room." Elizabeth had woken up because, in her surprise at discovering someone in Jude's bed, Carmina had let loose a scream that would have woken the dead—or in this case, the heavily drugged. Somehow the housekeeper didn't think it was prudent to mention this small detail to the Senora.

"Okay, I'll go check on her. Can you fix us something for lunch? I know it's late, but I'm starved," she grinned.

"You gonna ruin your dinner," Carmina warned, resting her hands on ample hips.

"Nah...I'll just eat dinner late. Fix some soup or something. Hey, what about some caldo tlalpeno?" Jude bounded up the stairs before her housekeeper could begin her usual recitation about Jude's horrible eating habits, not to mention the Senora's drinking one.

Jude laughed as she heard the grumbling Carmina begin her litany and skidded to a stop outside her bedroom door. *Damn, I'm in a good mood...Maybe I'll have to go shopping more often...Of course, I didn't really have to do all the work.* She pushed the door open softly, another smile coming to her face. "Well, well, well...ain't this a picture?" she muttered to herself. Elizabeth was sprawled across the king-size mattress, sharing the large space comfortably with all three canines. Aggie lifted his head, sleepily acknowledging his mistress' arrival, and then returned his muzzle to its warm perch on the human's leg. Clytemnestra was a bit more enthusiastic about her greeting, even going so far as to leap off the bed and pad over to Jude for a scratch behind the ears. What cracked Jude up, however, was the sight of Pete contentedly curled up in the slight woman's embrace, his head neatly tucked under her chin. "Some dogs have all the luck," she sighed. "Come on guys," she whispered softly, not sure how out-of-it Elizabeth might be. "Down," she ordered, holding the door as the obedient beasts trailed out of the room.

The movement woke Elizabeth from her nap, and she groggily regarded her surroundings. "Huh? Wha—Oh..." Her eyes registered the dark woman's arrival and sparked slightly. "Hi," she murmured, sitting up and rubbing her eyes.

"Hey there." Jude replied, grinning and seating herself on the far corner of the bed. "You seem to have won over the menagerie in my absence."

"Well, for a while Clytemnestra thought I was a doggie treat, but then she got a whiff of your T-shirt and decided I was okay." Elizabeth held a handful of the shirt she was wearing up and gestured with it. "Otherwise it would have been adios, muchacha."

Jude frowned. "I could have swore I shut the door when I left."

The honey-haired woman froze, then laughed briefly. "No, it was my fault. I was out wandering around looking for a book." Seeing Jude's continued frown, she elaborated. "My side hurt too much to sleep and I couldn't take any more happy pills yet." She shrugged. "So I wanted something to take my mind off of it." Jerking her head towards the next room, she added, "I found the library next door and grabbed a book," watching Jude carefully as her eyes drifted to the copy of *The Fountainhead* resting on the pillow beside her. "I'm sorry."

Jude shook her head. "No. I'm sorry," she assured the other woman. "I'm just not used to having someone...in my house." *Especially when I'm not home. I am really losing it.* "Decided to try it out, huh?"

"I thought it was appropriate given our conversation last night."

The rich green of Elizabeth's eyes seemed to grow warmer the longer Jude stared at them, and the dark woman had to shake her head slightly to break their mesmerizing pull. "I'm surprised you want to remember anything about last night, considering how it ended."

The light danced once more in the small woman's eyes as a puckish grin framed her face. "Oh, there's lots about last night that I want to remember."

"That so?" Jude quirked a brow. "I remember a couple of things too," she agreed. *Like the way your skin glimmered in the moonlight and the way the ocean spray haloed your hair. You smelled like the wind, or maybe the wind smelled like you, bringing your scent close just to torture me.* Aloud she said, "Like that tour I promised you. Do you think you're up for it? Might help keep some stiffness from setting in. And then we can have the late lunch Carmina is fixing."

Elizabeth's brows knitted together slightly at the turn the conversation had taken, but she nodded her assent. She allowed Jude to help her off the bed and was pleased when she was able to stand on her own. "Hey, no vertigo. I'm a happy girl," she beamed, but stopped when she heard Jude's sharp bark of laughter. "What's the matter?" she demanded.

Sobering quickly, Jude fought back the smirk that threatened to seize her mouth. "Uh...nothing..."

"What?"

"It's just...well...my sweats...on you..." She gestured at the baggy clothing that enveloped the petite blonde.

"Yeah, I know I look ridiculous," Elizabeth emitted a tiny, sad sigh.

"No. Not ridiculous," Jude corrected. "In fact, it's kinda cute. You look about twelve years old though," she snickered.

"Good thing for you I'm not," Elizabeth mumbled under her breath.

But Jude caught the statement and agreed silently. *Yeah, because I'd get arrested for some of the things I imagined us doing last night.* "Fortunately, however," she announced, triumphantly picking up the parcels she had propped by the bed, "I have something that may remedy the situation. Since you conked out before you told me where you lived, I picked up a couple of things for you." She deliberately didn't pursue the conversation they had started before she left. Jude realized there was something Elizabeth hadn't wanted to tell her, but she had also decided to let it rest. For now. "I had to guess on the size though."

"You—went shopping for me?"

Jude shifted uncomfortably at the oddly intimate question. "Uh... no. Actually I have someone who does that for me. You know...one of those...a..."

"A personal shopper?" Elizabeth offered helpfully.

"Yeah. She has my sizes and all, so I don't have to worry about it," Jude shrugged sheepishly. "I'm not really good at that girl stuff..." she trailed off, clearly embarrassed.

"Well, whatever you're doing," Elizabeth murmured appreciatively, taking in the sleek form in the tailored linen suit, "It works."

"Thanks," the dark woman replied quietly, cocking her head. Clearly Elizabeth was not overly traumatized by last night's activities, and that was more than a bit puzzling to her. Most civilians she knew would be running for the hills by now. As Jude contemplated the woman smiling back at her, she felt certain there was more to Elizabeth Peterson than met the eye. Temporarily shelving her suspicions, she sat the bags on the rumpled bed-sheets for inspection. "Let's hope she did as good a job for you." She began opening the bags, laying out the clothes gently. "I didn't really know what to get you, so I mainly got khakis and stuff. Some shorts and T-shirts. We can take it back if you don't like something or the size is wrong."

Elizabeth began softly fingering the clothes, nonchalantly flipping over the designer tags. "Khakis? Not jeans?"

"Jeans are the one thing nobody can buy for you. Or else the fit is all wrong. Don't you think?" Her blue eyes flashed in amusement as the smaller woman nodded emphatically.

"Oh yeah," she agreed. "Hey, all the sizes look right. What'd you tell her?"

"Let's see. I told her you were about this high—" Jude held a hand even with her own jaw, "And about this wide—" Holding her hands in front of her and slightly apart.

"Hmm..." Elizabeth grinned mischievously and limped into the space created by Jude's graceful hands. She curled the dark woman's elegant fingers around her waist and tucked her head neatly under Jude's chin. "Looks like you got it right." She glanced up into a pair of softly startled indigo eyes. "Thank you," she whispered, wrapping her own arms around the muscular figure.

Jude's stomach felt like it had been mule-kicked into next week, and her heart was racing to catch up with it. Elizabeth's length was warm and supple in her arms, the embrace bringing with it a curious combination of eroticism and peace to which her body didn't quite know how to respond. Her awkwardness outweighed the comfort of the lithe figure against her, and she stepped back a pace, slightly breathless from the unexpected intensity. "Um...it was the least I could do. Considering I ruined your beautiful dress." She paused, then continued, "Not to mention getting you shot."

If Elizabeth was disappointed by the loss of contact, she didn't show it. "Jude," she said, a serious look crossing her normally sunny features. "You could have just dumped me at a hospital and vanished back into the night. But you took care of me, made sure I was safe. Most people in your position wouldn't have done that." A soft smile lit her face from the inside, brightening the mossy green of her eyes into a glimmering emerald. "I'm beginning to think you're not as bad as you pretend."

"Come on, Angel...get over your big bad self," Jason's voice taunted her relentlessly as she tried to walk away. "You may have this dark and brooding thing down pat with everyone else, but I know you hurt inside. You're not as evil as you pretend..."

Jude's eyes darkened dangerously at the surfacing memory, and Elizabeth backed away instinctively from the sudden menace. "You're wrong," the tall woman growled. "I'm much, much worse," she warned, turning on her heel and fleeing, shutting the door firmly behind her.

❑ ❑ ❑

What the hell???? Liz had seen the change rush over Jude's face, hardening the bronze features into sharp planes and angles that threatened to slice her in two. *What set her off? The hug?* Liz shook her head at her mind's silent dialogue. Her embrace of the dark woman had been impulsive, and though the arms that enfolded her hadn't been unwilling, they had been accompanied by the frantic beating of a heart. *If I didn't know better I'd say she was...scared? No way.* The fleeting memory of a trembling hand from the previous evening flashed behind her eyes, setting off tiny sparks of new awareness in Liz's consciousness.

She mulled over the rapidly multiplying images she had of the dark woman. She wondered if Jude Lucien had knowingly fractured herself into millions of incomprehensible fragments. "But how on earth do they fit together?" she asked aloud. "Or do they?" Slipping a soft pair of khakis gingerly over her wound, she finished dressing, contemplating the ever-spiraling mystery she was uncovering.

She trod downstairs to find Jude comfortably ensconced on a well-padded deck chair in the sun. "Hey there," Elizabeth said softly. "I'm sorry."

Pale blue flickered over her, warming her body wherever they landed. "No," Jude replied. "I'm sorry. Again." She blew out a breath and ran a hand through her hair in a gesture Liz was coming to recognize as characteristic. "I just..." She shook her head. "I don't want you thinking that I'm some nice girl who just has a particularly exotic profession." She arched a serious brow at the reporter and steadily held her gaze. "I'm not."

The violent depths of Jude's eyes seized Liz and would not free her from their grip. It was as if she could see the blood that had permeated the dark woman's life, soaking down deep into her shuttered soul. At length, Liz took a deep breath, exhaling softly. "I understand that," she said finally.

Now the brow turned questioning, but the relentless grasp of the blue did not cease. "So...why?"

Somehow, Liz thought, two words to encompass everything that was beginning to happen between them shouldn't be enough, but there they were, falling from Jude's lips. She smiled confidently. Words were her business, and she knew better than most how to make them count. "Until you give me cause to fear you, Jude, I won't." Enjoying the sharp bite of the woman's name in her mouth. "As for the rest of it—" She gestured slightly with her hands, almost reaching out for Jude, but stopping just shy. "Something in you calls to me." She paused, allowing the dark woman to absorb the full implication of her words. "And I'd like to find out what that is."

Chapter 5

A quietly astonished silence draped itself between the two women. Finally, half a smile crept over Jude's face, and the dangerous glitter of her eyes softened. "Boy," she blew out a breath, "You really know how to put it out there, don't you?"

Yeah, and I don't even have the dress to blame this time, Liz thought wryly. Earlier this afternoon, she had accepted that her personal interest in the drug dealer far surpassed her professional interest in a story. She couldn't even begin to comprehend the diverse layers that formed the woman standing in front of her, but she had an almost overwhelming urge to try. *Oh well...I've done it now.* "I told you I wanted to get real," she said simply.

Jude regarded her soberly for a long while, and at that moment Liz would have given anything to know what was going on behind those shadowed eyes. "I'm not sure what real is anymore, Elizabeth," she stated at last. "If you want some kind of full disclosure..."

"No," Liz hastened to assure her, very much aware that she couldn't begin to do the same. "Not right now." *Not yet,* she amended mentally. "I just want to get to know you a little bit better. Is that okay?" *Can you let me do that?*

The wariness disappeared from the dark woman's face—even though Liz suspected it was only a temporary respite—and her lips curved into a genuine smile. "That I can do," she replied, unknowingly answering Liz's silent question. "Carmina's still fixing lunch, so why don't I give you that tour I've been promising you forever?"

"I love that idea," Liz grinned. "I'm dying to see what the rest of this place looks like," she added guilelessly, reasoning that of all the untruths she had told in the past twenty four hours, that one was by far the least painful.

As Liz soon discovered, however, there was a lot in the house that she hadn't seen. Because her primary interest had been in discovering a cache of Jude's secrets, she hadn't really paid attention to the downstairs. Now as she trailed behind Jude listening to the dark woman talk about the different pieces of art on the walls and the furniture in the rooms, Liz began to realize that what she had originally seen as some designer's cold air was simply a different facet of the agent's personality. *And why shouldn't she know all about contemporary art?* she thought as Jude admitted that these rooms were designed more for public consumption than her bedroom and library.

"I have to entertain sometimes," she explained. "But I keep it downstairs. People see a house like this," she shrugged, "They expect chrome and glass, abstract art. But," she grinned, unable to hide the sparkle of delight in her home, "I picked everything out myself. So..." she added mischievously, "If you hate it...it's all my fault." Leading Liz back up the stairs, she commented with a chuckle, "There's not nearly the amount of traffic up here as down there."

"Is there a message for me in that?" Liz teased, thinking about how much time she'd spent in the dark woman's bedroom during the day.

Jude stopped on the stairs and turned to contemplate the reporter fully, allowing Liz the same opportunity. The sunlight streaming through the windows was absorbed by the lean planes of Jude's face and reflected back in her skin's bronze hue. Jude seemed to radiate with some internal source of light, despite her dark predilections. Liz's heart subtly shifted into a higher gear, and she wondered if Jude could hear the low thrumming that suddenly filled her own ears. An unidentifiable expression played on the agent's face while her eyes carefully roamed over the smaller woman. "There hasn't been..." She seemed to stumble over the words, and Liz could almost swear a faint blush rose beneath her bronzed features. Jude cleared her throat and began again. "There hasn't been...anyone... in my bedroom for over a year—almost two."

The admission rested delicately in the sunlight as the weight of her own lie to Jude hit home hard with Liz. All she could do was glance helplessly at the powerful woman. Everything she had learned about the agent-turned-rogue told her that this could not be happening—that Jude could not be revealing herself so openly to a virtual stranger. "Why are you doing this?" she asked suddenly.

A rueful smile slunk onto Jude's face. "I thought you wanted to get real," she replied, eyebrow at wry attention.

"I do," Liz affirmed unhesitatingly. "But..." Her words trailed off. "Why?" she finally repeated.

What Liz failed to realize—couldn't possibly know, in fact—was that during her rambling drive home, Jude had carefully considered the few details that Liz had provided about her life. And then she had just as carefully discarded them as irrelevant. The wide gulf between what Liz presented herself to be and what Jude sensed the smaller woman actually was disturbed the ex-agent no end, but she had rationalized those doubts away by assuring herself that it really didn't matter because the honey-haired woman would be gone from her life soon enough.

Jude walked up the rest of the stairs and then back down again, stopping in front of Liz and plunging her hands into the pockets of her tailored trousers. "I don't know," she shrugged. "Why did you approach me at the Club? Why did I ask you to come back here?" She glanced out the window, and Liz could see the sharp cut of her jaw clenching and unclenching rhythmically. "I hope it wasn't just to get laid." Her gaze returned to the soft green of Liz's eyes, searching for something.

"No, it wasn't," the smaller woman agreed softly.

Jude nodded almost imperceptibly. "I didn't think so." The quiet lengthened as the two women held each other suspended in the fragile tangle of their eyes. "So..." Jude drew out the word slowly, "Can we just leave it at that for now?" She paused a beat, then added with a grin, "Because I can't take all this serious conversation on an empty stomach." As if on cue, Carmina stuck her head out of the kitchen and bellowed at them to come get their lunch before she changed her mind and decided to give it to Aggie and Pete who at least had the decency to come talk to her in the kitchen. "Why don't you go back upstairs and get comfortable? I'll bring lunch up," Jude offered. "You don't want to over-do it."

Liz couldn't think when she'd heard a better idea. Her side had been aching for a while now, but she had been so caught up in listening to Jude's resonant voice that she had ignored the pain in favor of learning more about the mysterious agent. Now, however, it had become a throb that refused to be overlooked. "Lying down sounds great right about now."

"Do you need some help?" Concern creased Jude's brow as the honey-haired woman paled, a sudden wave of pain clearly washing over her features.

"Uh...I think so." Liz awkwardly tried to slip her arm around Jude's broad shoulders, but all that accomplished was stretching the reporter's already sore side and bringing a grunt of pain to her lips.

"Not working, is it?" Jude chewed her lip momentarily before nodding. "Okay, hang on. I'm not sure I can do this, but..." She leaned down, tucked Liz's arm back around her neck, and picked the smaller woman up, cradling her gently in her arms. "Whoa..." the dark woman muttered, pausing to steady her balance. "Not exactly the way Clark Gable did it," she grinned.

Who cares? Liz thought dizzily, the warmth of Jude's body enveloping her and easily wiping awareness of the pain from her mind. They stood still a moment longer, until she was thoroughly settled in the dark woman's arms.

"Here we go," Jude murmured, taking the remaining stairs slowly, mindful of her injured cargo.

When at last Liz was situated once more in the agent's bed, Jude handed her two more pills and ran to fetch their lunch from a grumbling Carmina. "I don't know what to think, Senora," she tsked. "You keep that poor girl locked up in your bedroom all day," she reproached, but the housekeeper's eyes were twinkling. She had seen how solicitous Jude had been of the small Anglo, and—though it surprised her no end—it delighted her nonetheless.

"She's not locked up, Carmina. She's hurt," Jude replied dryly, fixing a tray laden with the aromatic soup and a plate of fresh fruit and cheese.

"That's another thing. What you doing shooting your girlfriend?"

"I did not shoot her. And she's not my girlfriend!" Jude growled. "I just met her last night."

"She's gonna be. I can tell. I gotta feel for these things," Carmina nodded knowingly.

Exasperated, Jude turned her attention from the tray and, folding her arms, regarded her housekeeper archly. "I am not sixteen. I do not have *girlfriends*...Elizabeth is not my *prom date*, understand?" she said severely, in spite of the lightheaded giddiness that had been stealthily creeping over her ever since she had been in the smaller woman's company.

"Okay, Senora. Whatever you say," the housekeeper agreed.

"She's not!" Jude insisted.

"Okay, okay, I got it." Carmina held her hands up in surrender, but the smug smile on her face belied the gesture.

Jude returned to her tray, muttering to herself. "She's not..."

Pete, ever present when food was nearby, followed close at her heels as she returned to the bedroom, wagging his tail in hopeful agreement.

Jude noticed with a frown that the pills were still in Elizabeth's hand where she had left them. "Why haven't you taken those?" she asked, a bit more harshly than she had intended. Seeing the startled expression on the small woman's features, she quickly apologized, "I'm sorry. I—" and then stopped suddenly, not wanting to explain the conversation she had just had with her housekeeper. It didn't even make sense to Jude herself. In fact, nothing about her encounter with the honey-haired woman did. Despite this, Jude had very consciously elected—as much as she could— just to go with it and enjoy their few days together. Elizabeth Peterson would be back in her nice, comfortable life soon enough, and Jude would simply be one of her more exotic memories, a time when the novelist had walked on the wild side. *She'll probably write me into one of her books...I'll be the evil drug lord who seduces the heroine into a life of crime and gets killed by the strapping blond hero,* she mocked herself. She had played the bad guy most of her life, even before she worked with the DEA, so the mental casting was easy. There had only been one person in her life who had seen Jude as something other than a malevolent and foreboding presence. *Yeah, and look at what happened,* Jude reproached herself.

"Jude?" Her silent castigation was halted by a quiet voice drifting into her consciousness, calling her back to the present. "Jude?" it repeated.

The dark woman blinked twice and focused on the slender woman in front of her. "Sorry, I guess I just wandered out of here for a minute."

"Boy, did you," Elizabeth concurred wholeheartedly. "Want to share?"

A tiny smile flickered over the ex-agent's lips, and she shook her head. "Not really worth sharing. I am sorry for snapping, though. I thought you were in pain."

"Oh, I am," Elizabeth nodded. "But those things knock me out so fast. I wanted to enjoy my soup without passing out in it."

"You do have a point. Carmina's food is definitely worth a little pain." She set the tray carefully over Elizabeth's lap and then settled herself cross-legged in the center of the bed. "Do you mind?" she asked, indicating her position.

"Not at all."

Pete looked beseechingly up at the two women on the bed, his brown eyes flickering between them. Jude glanced down at the expectant beast and narrowed her eyes. "Pete..." she warned. "Go find your play-mates," she told the now-disappointed dog, who did as his mistress bade, tail drooping. "They're all spoiled rotten," she told Elizabeth as they watched the animal depart.

"I could tell," she acknowledged, digging enthusiastically into her soup. "But that's a good thing."

"And why is that?"

"Everyone needs something to love," the honey-haired woman shrugged. She paused a moment, then added, "Pete and the others give you that. I mean...I would tend to think that your...profession...really doesn't allow you to get close to that many people."

A brow dramatically ascended of its own volition. People rarely admitted that they knew how Jude made her money, and no one ever asked her about it. Once again Jude was forced to revise her assessment of the woman in her bed. Shaking her head softly, she murmured, "I'd rather not talk about my profession, if it's okay with you." For some odd reason, she found herself not wanting Elizabeth to think badly of her; and if they spent even a moment on her livelihood, the slender woman would run screaming out of her home, injured or no.

A heated blush warmed Elizabeth's pale features. "Open mouth, insert foot, Liz," she grimaced.

"Liz?" Jude queried. *There's that panicked look again,* Jude noticed, watching Elizabeth's features momentarily freeze.

"Uh...yeah. Actually that's what most people call me." Elizabeth looked sheepishly at the taller woman.

"Do you like it? Being called Liz?"

"I never really thought about it. My mother's named Elizabeth too, so I had my choice of Beth, Liz, or Lizzy."

"You don't really look like a Beth," Jude observed.

"Not *Little Women* enough for you, ma'am?"

"I have to admit, you're not exactly the shy, retiring type." They shared an easy laugh that chased away the tiny fingers of suspicion that were prickling Jude's instincts. "And Lizzy is too..."

"Homicidal?" Elizabeth offered.

"Exactly," Jude chuckled. "I guess its Liz by default, huh?"

"Pretty much."

Jude cocked her head in appraisal. "I don't know, it kind of suits you in a breathless-Rosiland Russell-in *His-Girl-Friday* kind of way."

"What do you mean?" she looked startled.

"*His Girl Friday*...you know, that movie where Rosiland Russell plays a reporter hot on the trail of a big story..." Jude was interrupted as Liz's soup decided to make a spontaneous reappearance through her nose, shaking the slight woman with the force of her coughs.

"Are you all right?" Jude hastily shoved her own bowl of soup out of the way and grasped Liz's shoulders, pounding gently on her back.

Hacking and wheezing for a few more minutes, Liz drew a ragged breath before nodding. "Yeah, I think so. Whoa, nellie...that hurts." She wiped the tears that were streaming down her face absently with the back of her hand. "Geeze..."

"What happened?"

Liz emitted a strangled chuckle, "Oh, I think it just went down the wrong pipe."

"You sure?"

"Oh yeah." A few remaining hacks cleared her throat; and she settled back, breathing as deeply as her wounded side would allow her.

Jude painstakingly removed the tray from Liz's lap. "Let's check your stitches and make sure you didn't pull anything loose, okay? You were coughing pretty hard there." She pulled the covers back and smothered a quick grin as she noticed that Elizabeth had changed back into the ex-agent's baggy sweats. "There should be something that fits you better in the stuff I brought you," she said noncommittally.

"I know," Liz replied, grinning at her. "But I like these." She carefully studied the azure flame that was directed at her. "Is that okay?"

Jude's face relaxed into a fleeting smile before it turned serious once more. "You keep asking me that," she stated softly.

For the first time, Elizabeth seemed at a loss for words. She shrugged helplessly. "I—sometimes—" Releasing a long sigh, she gathered her scattered thoughts and returned to the gaze trained on her. "Sometimes I tend to bulldoze my way into things without thinking," she said at last, her memory drifting back to the dreadful mistakes she had made when she had promised to marry; how consumed she had been with making sure everything was fine with herself that she never bothered to ask what was going on with him. No matter how vehemently she had tried to deny the charge to him, to herself...now she had to admit that she had been using him.

Her time with Todd had been a desperate attempt to ease the truculent desires that rocked her senses, to make peace with her parents and become something they deemed respectable. Looking back, she could see how foolish her hopes had been and more than anything, she regretted the pain she had visited on both herself and Todd trying to shoehorn herself into a vision that she didn't share. Todd had never forgiven her. Her parents were somewhat more pragmatic, only requesting that she be discreet and not draw undue attention to herself. That gruff request sent her reeling from her family's home in bewildered and furious disbelief. Fortunately for all of them, she had gotten a call from the City Desk Editor at the Miami *Herald* shortly thereafter. And she had never looked back. She shook her head quietly at the memory. "And people can get hurt because of it."

"You're worried about hurting me?" the dark woman asked incredulously.

"Yeah," she answered simply. "Is that okay?"

Jude only shook her head, but Liz could see the smile tugging at the corners of her mouth. She gingerly pulled the elastic of the sweatpants over Liz's hip and uncovered the wound. "Ouch," she whispered, almost to herself—a supple finger tracing the curve of the stitches.

The agent's hands were warm from the bowl of soup she had been holding, and Liz relaxed comfortably into the touch. She had been covertly studying Jude's hands ever since they had met. Now she relished the opportunity to watch them unhindered. For a woman, Jude's hands were large; but they were graceful and sinuous, the fingers elegantly jointed and tapered. This close, Liz could see a small scar on the top of her left index finger, and—without even realizing it—she reached out and stroked the tiny mar on the skin's perfection. Abruptly, the hand stilled, resting just below Liz's wound. The reporter glanced at the bowed head whose eyes were hidden from her and took a deep breath. "Where did you get this?" she asked lightly, running the tip of her finger across the warm flesh again.

Jude swallowed hard at the rapid influx of sensation that was totally out of proportion for the touch...

"What am I going to do with you?" Jason fussed, grabbing Jude's wounded hand and reaching for the peroxide.

"OW!!" She tried jerking away, but Jason's vice-like grip held her relentlessly.

"You are worse than a child, Angel," he scolded. "Every time I turn around, you're banging the hell out of your hands." But his exasperated tone was colored with an involuntary tenderness that gentled his touch as he bandaged the scrape. "What on earth happened?"

"I don't remember," she murmured. If she closed her eyes she could almost smell the discreet fragrance of the shampoo in his hair as he bent over attending to her. But that aroma was gone now, replaced by the tantalizing essence of Liz's skin. Jude closed her eyes, concentrating on the images that the scent evoked. White light danced behind her eyes... the warmth of a summer's day... the sun's ferocity tamed by a gentle breeze sliding over her skin... clean air and unfettered freedom. *She smells like the light.* "Sunlight..." she whispered, opening her eyes to their twined fingers. "How'd that happen?" she asked, bewildered.

A gentle laugh rushing into her ears. "Um...I'm not really sure," Liz answered.

Jude reluctantly released the other woman's hand and gazed up at the shining green that hazily swam into focus. "Sorry," she said, shaking her head briskly to knock the emotional snarls loose from her thoughts. "Your stitches seem fine, doesn't look like they loosened at all."

"Stop saying that," Liz commanded quietly.

Surprised at the tone from the smaller woman, Jude cocked her head, silently waiting for further elucidation.

"Stop saying you're sorry. I'm not sorry for anything that's happened so far. And that includes getting shot."

Smiling wryly and shaking her head, Jude muttered, "You got an odd idea of fun, lady." But her eyes were teasing.

"You wouldn't be the first person to tell me that," Liz amiably agreed. Shifting and adjusting herself against the fluffy pillows at her back, she looked expectantly at Jude. "Now that we've ascertained that I'll live at least a little while longer, do you have some time to sit and talk with me, or do you have to go running off?"

Jude gazed at the petite figure tucked so snugly in her bed—at the tumble of golden hair falling haphazardly around her shoulders, the green eyes wide and smiling, the deceptively sensuous body hidden under the comforter—and something indurate and glacial shook loose from its moorings deep inside and began swirling about in the tumultuous eddies of her suddenly warm blood. "I've got time." That said, she flung herself diagonally across the remainder of the bed, propping her head on one long arm. Pete, who had been watching silently from the door, took this as his cue to bounce up on his mistress' legs and curl himself up in the *V* formed by the two women's bodies.

Seeing Jude move to evict the mutt, Liz reached out to stay her hand. "Leave him, he's sweet."

"Yeah, but wait till Aggie sees him, then he'll want to get into the act," Jude grumbled, only putting up a token resistance before easing herself back down. "So, what did you want to talk about?"

"You don't do much small talk, do you?" the smaller woman grinned.

Jude shrugged. "Nope. Never saw much need for it."

"Just tell me about you, Jude."

"I'd rather you tell me about you." Blue eyes glimmered puckishly. "Tell me how you became a romance novelist. It's not like that's a real obvious career path."

"Cool Whip," Liz answered succinctly.

"Beg pardon?"

"Cool Whip. That's how I became a romance novelist." During the last few hours they had spent together, just about any desire Liz had harbored to expose the drug dealer's life to a hungry public had drained away and been replaced with a fierce longing to understand the complex puzzle of the woman at her side. So telling the truth to Jude was easy now, and she intensely regretted the lies that had to necessarily remain between them. "I must have been about eighteen, getting ready to go off to college. One afternoon I was in the grocery store, and Cool Whip had this huge Valentine's Day display. I can still remember the heart-shaped cutout on the stand. Some promotion about giving something sweet to your sweetheart or some nonsense or other. And there was this tie-in with Avon Romance Novels. They were co-sponsoring a sweepstakes. I looked at the display and saw my first year's college tuition."

She didn't mention that she had refused her father's considerable offer to pay for tuition, an apartment, and a healthy allowance. She had long been aware that in her family, everything was a trade-off. In true political fashion, favors were granted and sought, depending on what anyone needed at a given moment. Liz turned down the offer because she was tired of currying favor. She just wanted her family to love her and—at eighteen—she was beginning to think that relatively simple thing would never happen. "Anyway..." she breathed out, pushing aside the still painful memories. "To enter you had to write a romantic story. And the winner got $25,000."

Jude smiled. "What was your story about?"

"Oh, the usual. Unrequited longing. I had a mad crush on my best friend in high school," she replied, and then went on to elaborate on her relationship with Steph, how close they had been, the things they had shared. Jude laughed at the portrait Liz painted of the antics of the two teenagers and their numerous misadventures. It seemed Liz and Steph had done everything from raiding their parents' liquor cabinets to being chased by the police for trespassing on private property. "It just all seemed so natural. So right. Unfortunately, she just didn't get it," Liz sighed wistfully.

"But you did," Jude guessed.

"I suspected. So in typical Terminator-in-the-shopping-mall fashion, I asked." Liz glanced away from the intense gaze studying her and picked idly at a loose stitch in the comforter. She looked back up and saw a quiet sympathy residing in the blue that washed over her. "Yeah, she freaked."

"It still hurts you, doesn't it?"

Liz paused a moment, considering Jude's question. Steph wasn't really someone she thought about any more. Hadn't for a long time, and she didn't know why being with Jude had brought back so vividly the memories of the girl she considered her first love. "Not really. Now I just hurt for the girl I was back then, who didn't understand why her best friend was running away from her. For opportunities missed."

An unaccustomed desire to take away the forlorn longing in Liz's face and ease the sadness enveloping the smaller woman swept through Jude, leaving her nearly breathless. "And this won a Valentine's Day contest?" she bantered, trying to lighten the suddenly oppressive atmosphere.

"Well, I changed me to Beth and Steph to Steven. I had him come back to her after his first year of college and declare that he had been a fool and would Beth please take him back. After she made him beg and plead for way too many pages, they went off and got married."

"Is that what you wanted from Steph?"

Liz ran a hand through her disordered hair. "I think more than anything, I just wanted someone to accept who I was and love me for that. Maybe even in spite of it."

The words set off a quiet explosion of recognition in Jude's soul, and she closed her eyes as the pain came sweeping back...

"Come on, Angel...what is it about you that's so terrible?" Darkness surrounded them, and it was far closer to sunrise than sunset. Long ago Jason had realized that Jude moved easier at night, as if the nocturnal cloak was comforting to her somehow. Now he tried to focus on the long form beside him, but it was about as productive as trying to study a chimera. So he gave up trying and just listened to the resonant growl of her voice.

"Oh gee, I don't know, Jase..." Her voice was thick with sarcasm. *"Is it that I can kill in the blink of an eye, or that I enjoy doing it so damn much?"*

A mostly empty bourbon bottle rested between them, and even though she had done most of the damage to it, Jason could feel the crackling energy still arcing off the woman beside him. Things had gotten very messy for Jude a few days ago on the tail end of a bust, forcing the agent to take down three suspects. And the younger agent could tell that it was finally getting to her. Throughout her life, Jude had moved in the darkness without qualm; but more and more, the things she was asked to do, and the ease with which she did them were beginning to chafe. For the first time, Jason truly feared for his friend and wondered if their relationship was such a good thing for her. He knew that he had been the only one to breach the formidable barriers that protected others—not to mention herself—from Jude's less...civilized...side. Apparently, he was at last seeing the consequences of his actions.

Each trip into the darkness and the corresponding return to the daylight was taking its toll on Jude. She had started disappearing for days between assignments, and Jason knew better than to ask where she went. Were he to be honest with himself, he'd admit that he really didn't want to know. It had gotten harder for them both since he had been married. Jude had begun pulling away from Jason, trying to leave him to his wife, his house, to all the things she knew he should have. But he held tightly to her, knowing somehow that if their tenuous grasp on each other were broken, Jude would quit trying to make that return trip into the daylight world, and he would be too afraid to plumb the adumbral depths in search of her.

"That's not you, Angel," he insisted.

"The bodies in the morgue would disagree with you." She snorted derisively and took another long pull from the bottle, settling it back into its hollowed out niche.

"It's the job, not you."

"Isn't it?" With graceful suppleness, Jude rose from her supine position in the sand and turned to face him, her blue eyes glinting faintly in the starlight. Watching her move in the shadows was like watching the night personified—her eyes were the pinpoints of some far off supernova... and he sadly mourned for the part of her that was dying tonight. She moved infinitesimally closer to him, and he could smell the faint tang of blood on her skin, mixed with the spicy odor of her sweat and something unidentifiably musky.

He didn't know where she'd been for the last two days; his increasingly frantic messages had gone unanswered until she'd finally returned his page tonight, merely confirming that she'd meet him at their old haunt. He'd found her in their cove, sprawled out in the sand that was still warm from the day's heat, making steady progress on the bourbon. "I brought dinner," was the only thing he said. They sat in silence for the longest time, until their hesitant words began to flow and they had at last reached the point they were now.

"It isn't you," he replied, shaking his head forcefully. Even as he said it, they both knew the denial to be a lie. The job wasn't the catalyst at all. Nor was the darkness that enveloped them when in deep cover. It was instead the atramentous core that Jude carried inside her all the time—and no matter how much Jason might wish otherwise, it would never change—as long as Jude lived and breathed, it would too.

A throaty chuckle wrapped itself around Jason's pulse and squeezed, eliciting a ragged breath from him. "Do you really believe that's true?"

"I believe it can be. If you want it. If you fight for it."

Jude edged nearer still, so that the harsh afterbite of bourbon was shared on the breath between them. "That's the real question, isn't it?" she murmured sensually. "Do I really want to stop being who I am? If you really think about it, nobody wants me to stop. Not the Agency, not me..." She traced a line down the slope of his cheek with the barest hint of her fingers, and a wracking shudder worked its way through Jason's body. "And certainly not you."

Before he had time to even think about what was happening, their mouths met forcefully, and the fury that ravaged Jude's soul thrust into him with brutal force. It was a kiss meant to ignite, consume, and ultimately incinerate their friendship.

And a part of him wanted it so badly that it made his marrow ache.

A breathless second later the connection ended, and Jason tumbled back, trying desperately to collect his sanity—which had been blasted apart—from the sand. Jude's eyes glittered brightly in the blackness, but she made no move towards him, and for a fleeting, senseless moment, he wondered if he had dreamed the touch.

"You need to get away from me." Her voice rang oddly hollow and fractured as it landed upon his hearing.

"Jude—"

"I mean it! Don't you see...?"

And miraculously, he did. The blackness that had enveloped his friend had been the night's last embrace before it finally relinquished its hold *upon the land. Jude's bronze skin now shimmered faintly in the rising sun, and the tide washed cleansing pink waves over the shore. "I do," he replied, understanding the darkness that was her soul and the light inside his own that would not let her go. In a single, mad instant—like a wolf trying to chew its paw loose from a hunter's trap—she had tried to destroy their connection and cut herself free from the relentless tug-of-war that now raged inside her.*

Jude looked at him for a wordless moment longer and then turned to go. With a long step Jason caught her in a fierce embrace from behind, wrapping his arms around her and burying his face in the onyx tangles of her hair. "Oh no you don't, Angel. I'm not letting you get rid of me that easy. Don't you see?"

A strangled laugh tore free from Jude's throat. "Are you crazy?"

"Maybe," he agreed. "But you're my best friend, Jude. I refuse to lose that. You're a part of me..."

Liz studied the dark woman beside her, so clearly lost to her own musings. The pain was etched in the weary slump of Jude's shoulders and the furrow of her brow. "Have you ever had that?" she asked softly, instinctively guessing that whatever held Jude in its grasp right now was very important. "Had someone who loved you in spite of yourself?"

The eyes that lifted to reply to her had paled to an almost colorless crystal. "Yeah," she said at last. "I have."

A flare of something that uncannily resembled jealousy flickered to life in the pit of Liz's stomach. "What happened?" she asked, half-fearing the answer.

Jude's eyes completed their arctic transformation, freezing solidly as Liz watched in bewilderment. Her voice rang tonelessly in the quiet room with her answer. "I killed him."

❑   ❑   ❑

Did I just dream that? Liz woke to dead silence and absolute darkness, Jude's words still ringing in her ears hours later. Groggily, she glanced at the digital display that gleamed to her right. *2:00 am...and I know it wasn't a dream.* Remembering Jude's normally bronze features turning starkly pale, and the flat harshness of her words. *That was a real conversation ender,* Liz thought ruefully. Jude had abruptly excused herself and disappeared from the house. Sensing that she wouldn't see the dark woman again that day, Liz took two painkillers and slipped gratefully into their oblivion.

Her dreams of the dark woman this night had been unlike any she had ever had before. They were filled with images of Jude wounded and in pain—the blue eyes pleading with Liz for succor—alternating with violent and bloody visions of the agent relentlessly executing a series of faceless victims that ended with Liz herself. The impact of the bullet slamming into her chest startled her upright into the night's awareness. "What the hell have I gotten myself into?" she muttered under her breath.

The shadow in her doorway shifted, drawing her attention and metamorphosing into the sleek outline of the woman in question. "I won't hurt you," came the voice from the darkness, a velvety stroke against her hearing. "I promise." The words were fleeting, delivered into the cortex of Liz's consciousness. Before she could speak, the shadow vanished, leaving the reporter alone again to wrestle with the weight of her dreams.

Chapter 6

Her second evening there, Liz insisted on moving into one of the guest-rooms, over Jude's grumbling protestations. "You like this room better," Jude pointed out flatly. "You told me."

"I'm not kicking you out of your own bed," Liz replied firmly. *Now if you want to share,* she offered mentally, but despite their earlier teasing, Jude had not pursued any further physical intimacy with the reporter. After a few more minutes of spirited debate, Jude finally gave in, moving the small woman's few things—including the laptop computer she had purchased for Liz—into the bedroom on the other side of the library.

The gift of the slender little Powerbook had been unexpected to say the least. "NO! Jude, I can't accept this," she protested when the dark woman slid the gift into her lap.

Dark brows furrowed. "Why not?"

"I—I—" Liz stuttered, trying to kick-start her brain into gear. "I thought we finished with you saying you're sorry about me getting shot."

"Well, I am sorry, but that's not what this is about," Jude smirked. "You're a writer, yes?"

"Yyeesss..." Liz drew out the word.

"So how are you going to write without something to write on? You don't strike me as the legal pad type. And this way you can sit out in the sun while you work."

"You don't have a computer?" Liz inquired innocently. Interestingly enough, Jude's tour had not included the study which was, architecturally speaking, the most stunning room in the house.

"Yes, I have a computer, but this way you have your own access," Jude answered smoothly, not dropping a beat. "And you won't have to worry about me stumbling into your files."

Or me stumbling into yours, Liz thought wryly. "This is way too expensive, I mean—"

"Liz..." Jude held out a hand to forestall any further argument. "Look around you. What I spent for the laptop is nothing to me." It was an offhand comment, meant to convey nonchalance and totally disguising the effort Jude had expended. The dark woman had prowled just about every computer store in the city, terrorizing store clerks and looking for the laptop that would suit the writer the best. "Besides," she shrugged sheepishly, muttering almost inaudibly, "I kind of liked buying something for you."

There it is again, Liz marveled. The faint blush was almost undetectable beneath Jude's tanned skin. Its appearance—the only indication Liz had discovered of a vulnerable side to the agent—reaffirmed the budding friendship that had been in doubt since Jude's surprising revelation the previous day.

Things settled into an odd, but comfortable rhythm in Jude's household. Liz learned that Carmina only came a few times a week and took care of the cleaning, preparing meals only if Jude was home— which was not nearly as much as Liz would have liked. She honestly didn't know when the tall woman slept. Liz, however, used the time alone to her advantage, calling Lucas the first chance she got.

"Are you out of your fucking mind!" Lucas bellowed after the reporter filled him in on the events that had brought her to Jude's. Liz winced, holding the phone away from her ear, thankful Carmina was nowhere to be found.

"No, Lucas, I'm not," she answered patiently.

Recognizing the resolute tone in Liz's voice, he exhaled heavily into the receiver, signaling his reconciliation to her obstinacy. "Well, have you at least gotten something interesting then?"

Liz hesitated. It was on the tip of her tongue to tell Lucas everything she had learned—that Jude was still working for the DEA and she suspected the dark woman was attempting to bring down the remnants of the Massala Cartel—but she remained silent. "Only bits and pieces, nothing concrete," she hedged, knowing that if she gave Lucas even a bare tidbit, that he would hound her until she worked the story to its fullest. Quite frankly, she didn't know if she wanted to do that anymore, although her curiosity had sent her scurrying again into the study at the next opportunity. She had stayed away from the journal and concentrated on the "Communication" folder, piecing together what she could. There were still a lot of blanks; Jude obviously didn't believe in committing much information to paper—even if it was only on the electronic variety. "Look, I don't know when I'm going to get a chance to talk to you again, so I need you to do something for me."

She could hear Lucas scrabbling around on his desk for a piece of paper. "Okay, what can I get you?"

"First of all, you need to get on-line. That way I can update you via e-mail. The *Herald* has an e-mail address for you...lucas@mherald.com." Liz was referring to the office-wide system of assigning addresses by last name, but she doubted that Lucas even knew he had one. "I'll send you periodic messages so you'll know I'm okay. Get someone to show you how to use the system, all right?"

Lucas grumbled under his breath about technology and going to hell, but he agreed. "Anything else?"

Liz paused a moment, thinking about her apartment. What were the odds that Jude would want to go there? She had bought herself a week with the boyfriend story, but she honestly didn't know where things were headed with the volatile agent. So she crossed her mental fingers and hoped for the best. "Not right now. I'll let you know if I need something else. Okay?"

"Got it. And Liz—" Lucas' gruff voice dropped an octave as he added, "Be careful."

She had e-mailed Lucas only once during the last week, just to let him know things were still fine. Her time with Jude was fast drawing to a close, and Liz was at a loss for how to propel things further between them. The intense attraction was still there, and Liz watched with growing frustration as Jude sidestepped even the mere hint of intimacy, despite their palpable connection. The dark woman didn't avoid Liz—far to the contrary—she sought the reporter out whenever she was home, listening to Liz's vivid stories of her misadventures in school and growing up. The honey-haired woman truly felt like they had become friends, but she tossed and turned restlessly in her bed at night, filled with a gnawing hunger and too aware of what she wanted to assuage it.

◻ ◻ ◻

Jude pounded down the beach in a steady, loping rhythm that ate up the ground below her. Aggie and Clytemnestra flanked her sides, tongues lolling as they kept pace with their long-legged mistress. She splashed through the surf as she ran, letting the salt water cool her heated body, enjoying the different textures brushing her skin. The scorching glare of the day had finally passed, as even the sun began to weary of its own intensity and sought relief by falling over the edge of the horizon. Jude was very content with her lot in life at this moment. The sand was gritty beneath her bare feet; the water's spray was refreshing; and her eyes were dazzled by the pastels of the sun's passing. Aggie, bless his clumsy soul, occasionally brushed against her as he gamboled down the beach with her, his fur tickling at her legs.

The sensory input inundated Jude's system, and she consciously let all the tension and stresses of the day ooze from her body. Sasha had been in a mood all week....*Sulking no doubt because I haven't been paying enough attention to her*...and that had put most everyone else in her close professional circle on edge. As a result, the cooks were throwing tantrums, the wait staff was dropping things, and the food and liquor shipments were off.

Jude's relationship with Sasha had always been a complicated one. Lover, enemy, or ally depending on the day of the week—Sasha had been a more or less permanent fixture in Jude's life since she turned from the Agency. Jude trusted the caramel woman just about as far as she trusted anyone in her life. Together they had a truculent, sensual chemistry that often left both of them breathless.

The last time she had touched Sasha had been just after the Cartel Massacre, before she had grimly decided to try and set things right as best she could. Jude had offered no explanation for the shift in their relationship, nor had Sasha sought one. The dark woman occasionally felt the burning intensity still between them, knew by looking at the smoky saffron of Sasha's eyes that she was aware of it as well. For Jude, however, a return to Sasha's bed meant a return to the darkness that she was working so hard to be rid of.

Still, Sasha was an important person in the day-to-day functioning of all Jude's businesses—both legitimate and otherwise—and the only thing Jude kept from her was the knowledge of her re-involvement with the Agency. *She's got her nose out of joint about something,* Jude thought darkly as she continued to pound down the shoreline. *And that makes life suck for everyone else....Well...*she added with a mental grin....*Everyone but me.* Whatever Sasha's problem, Jude was exempt from her wrath, treated instead with an icy calm.

At last she rounded the beachhead that brought her house into view. *Come on, Angel...one more mile....*Jason's old chant echoed in her head and brought an unexpected smile to her face. More and more these days, Jason was close to her thoughts. Much to her surprise, the memories that surged forth were the quiet ones—full of laughter and kindness—that she hadn't allowed herself to dwell on since her partner's death. It hadn't escaped her notice that the memories had returned in force about the same time that Elizabeth had entered her life. She vacillated between thinking that the memories were reminding her of the joy of letting someone in or were warning her of the consequences of such a rash act.

Trying to tell me something, Partner? she asked, talking to him in her musings the way she used to in the old days, when she was under and he was far, far away. *I think you really would have liked her....She's funny, smart as hell, beautiful... God is she beautiful.* The golden outline of the woman slowly coming into focus in the distance brought another wide smile to Jude's face, in spite of the ten miles she had just run. *And she's kind, Jase.... like you... I can see it in everything she does....Her eyes just seem to hold me when she's talking and not let me go....I know I've gotta be nuts to keep her here.* But at that moment, Jude decided she really didn't give a damn. She didn't care about all the reasons these feelings were wrong and dangerous, and instead just concentrated on why they were right.

She had spent practically every second possible in Elizabeth's company and found herself thinking about the slender woman at the oddest times. Most of all, however, her dreams for the first time in years were filled with the happy times she and Jason had spent together, instead of the horror that had ultimately befallen them. Letting go of her caution this night was the single most irresponsible act she had committed in ten years. *And damn if it doesn't feel good.* A sudden burst of energy sent her sprinting the remaining 100 yards to the deck; and she vaulted over the railing, landing softly on the other side. *Show off,* a tiny mental voice chortled. "Hey there," she greeted a slightly startled Liz.

Liz pushed her sunglasses up to better survey the woman in front of her. Skin glistening with the sheen of exertion and muscles quivering slightly from the effort of the last ten miles, Jude radiated an animal exuberance that crackled in the air around her. "Hi," she said. "Nice run?"

Jude's habits were becoming increasingly familiar to the reporter, although she had only been part of the household for a week. The ten-mile torture session was only one part of Jude's exercise routine that made Liz shudder. The small woman was in fabulous shape herself and took great pride in working fairly hard to maintain her fitness, but the agent's workouts exhausted her just by watching them.

"Great," Jude grinned, stepping behind the wet bar on the deck and retrieving a bottle of cold water. "I feel like I could do it all over again."

The reporter shivered at the thought, watching Jude as she downed half the bottle in a single gulp. "You're kidding right?" She saved the file on her computer and shut the system down. She had been making notes about what she thought Jude was up to, and it wouldn't do for the agent to see her musings.

Jude cocked her head as if considering the possibility. "Yeah, I am kidding," she said at last, grinning. "How are you doing?" she asked, throwing herself down in the chaise across from Liz. She stretched luxuriously against the comfortable pillows and fanned herself with the edge of her T-shirt, exposing a length of muscled abdomen to Liz's appreciative eyes. There was something...*different*...about Jude this evening, she immediately noticed, and the dark woman's rambunctious energy was contagious. "The doc get your stitches out okay?"

"What? Oh, right, he did," she affirmed, remembering the painfully thin man who had arrived this morning. He had cool hands and an air that was slightly hazy around the edges, but she had liked him anyway. As was her habit, she had managed to pull Stephen Ryan's entire story out of him, including Jude's own role in it.

"When you think about it," Stephen said dreamily. *"She's become something of a guardian angel for me."* Then he laughed softly. *"I guess that's sort of appropriate though."*

"What makes you say that?" Liz asked, intrigued by the light that he cast on the shadowy life Jude lived.

He seemed to focus on her for the first time since they began talking about Jude. *"You are an innocent, aren't you?"* Soft brown eyes appraised her, and a hesitant smile came to his face. *"At first I thought you were just another of her whores—she has quite a reputation in certain circles, you know—"* he rambled. Part of Liz wanted to shake the frail man to jar some sense from him, but she held back, aware that she would ultimately learn far more by letting him rattle on. *"But she was genuinely concerned about you...I could see it in her eyes....And I never thought I'd see that from the Archangel..."*

"Archangel?"

"That's what they used to call her on the streets...Back when she was with the DEA...They don't call her that anymore," he whispered, then shuddered.

Liz could plainly see that the doctor had gone to a place that was terrifying for the man. She thought about the description of Jude standing in his doorway—bloodied and enraged—and had a pretty good idea where the doctor had gone. "Stephen?" she gingerly called him back. "What do they call her now?"

He blinked rapidly, as if afraid to speak the name. But the unwavering gentleness of those verdant eyes coaxed the words from him. "El Diablo..." The name was delivered on a breath of air, and he quickly looked around to see if anyone but Liz had heard him.

"The devil..." Liz absorbed this fact for a moment longer, along with the man's increasingly distraught state, then tried one more question. "Then why do you call her your guardian angel?"

A moment of lucidity briefly passed over him, clearing his eyes. "Because she's the one who damned me. And she came back to make sure I have a comfortable ride to Hell..."

"Elizabeth?"

"Whoops! Sorry, I was just thinking about your doctor friend."

"He's not exactly a friend."

"That's sort of what he said. He was kinda fuzzy around the edges, though. He on something?" she asked idly.

Jude groaned and collapsed back onto the chaise. "Fuck..." she muttered almost inaudibly, then she sat back up. "I'm sorry. Yeah, he's a junkie, that's why they revoked his license, but I thought he'd pretty much cleaned up."

"Well, he was mostly." Liz hesitated about relating her conversation, unsure what effect it would have on Jude's euphoric mood. "He just kinda faded out; there near the end. He came in, took my stitches out, and we chatted for a little while. That's all."

"You sure?" Jude's eyes narrowed in concern. "If he was high when he got here, he might have left a stitch in there." She stood and took a tentative step towards Liz. "Would you mind if I took a look? Just to be sure?"

Liz was quite certain that Stephen had gotten the stitches out, even though he had seemed slightly spacey and had gotten downright spooky when he started talking about Jude. Liz, however, welcomed the opportunity to feel the dark woman's hands on her again. "Sure," she agreed. "No sense in worrying over it." She slid the computer off her lap and onto the deck.

Jude knelt by her side and gently lifted the edge of Liz's green polo shirt, eyes flickering briefly to the reporter's face. "Sorry if I smell a little less than fresh," she teased, a playful light flashing in her eyes.

"Since you're ministering to me, I'll let it slide for now." Actually, Liz was enjoying the musky scent that came to her faintly on the breeze, hinting at the parts of Jude that still remained forbidden to the reporter. She closed her eyes and enjoyed the delicate feel of Jude's fingers dancing over the nearly healed wound.

"Looks great. You shouldn't scar," Jude approved, glancing at Liz's shuttered gaze. Smiling softly, she let her hands linger for a moment on the lissome muscles, absorbing the warmth of the slender woman's skin. "How does it feel?" she asked. "You still sore?"

Green eyes popped back open at the question and smiled reassuringly. "A little. But you've been taking good care of me," she bantered.

"My pleasure, ma'am," Jude replied quietly. She gently brushed the rumpled tail of Liz's shirt down over the khaki shorts and straightened it. A thoughtful silence balanced precariously between them as green and blue gazes mingled hesitantly. "Um...Elizabeth..." Jude rubbed a hand absently across her still-sweaty brow. "If you're feeling up to it...um... would you like to go out tonight? We could get out of the house for a little while," she offered tentatively. "But only if you want," she added. "I mean, I don't want you to think that you have to..."

Liz fought to keep a stupid grin from running loose across her features. Jude sounded for all the world like a shy kid asking out her first date, and it was an unexpectedly endearing side to a woman who seemed to specialize in consummate control. "That sounds pretty good," she replied, managing to keep her voice casual. "Did you have anything in mind?"

"Nothing too complicated," Jude assured her. "I was just thinking— you told me you used to shoot pool in college. You up for a game or two?"

Although Liz would have agreed to anything from mud wrestling to the roller derby just to spend time with Jude, the dark woman's suggestion was truly appealing. Around the *Herald* she had something of a reputation as a little hustler and usually won enough matches to keep her in free drinks whenever they played. "I think I could manage that," she said nonchalantly, a gleam in her eye.

Jude studied her for a moment then smiled, the expression reaching into the depths of her eyes and scattering a shining blue over Liz. "Great, it's a date," Jude said lightly.

"Is it?" Liz teased.

A lazy smirk curled across Jude's lips, control firmly back in place. "You bet," she answered. "I've got a couple of errands to run first, but they shouldn't take long. "When I get back we can grab something to eat and then go play. Does that sound good?"

"I'll go you one better," Liz suggested. "Why don't I make something for dinner here while you're out and about? I'm a pretty good cook, if I do say so myself." She bounced to her feet and padded into the kitchen— Jude and the menagerie trailing behind. Carmina had the day off, so Liz plundered unharassed through the housekeeper's kitchen, her face growing more clouded the deeper she went. "Of course...having some food here is usually a prerequisite for cooking."

"What do you mean?" Jude objected. "The market didn't deliver this morning? I could have sworn I saw them here."

"Well...Jude...yes...they did..." Liz spoke, opening random cabinets as she went and glancing at the rather mundane array of pasta, bread and vegetables. "But...you don't exactly have a lot of...variety here..." A search of the refrigerator yielded similarly drab results.

Jude looked around sheepishly. "I eat in restaurants a lot."

"But what about when you want to eat at home?"

"Take out?" she offered hopefully.

The honey-haired woman clucked disapprovingly. "Drastic measures are called for here. I should have known better. Anyone who can 'phone in' her grocery order definitely would not understand."

"What does that mean?"

"Never mind." Liz turned the tall woman around, pushing her out of the kitchen and towards the stairs.

"Hey wait..." Jude spluttered at being woman-handled in her own house.

"You just run your errands," Liz commanded. "Leave dinner to me," she admonished as Jude dutifully climbed the stairs towards the shower. "How long do you think you'll be?"

Jude ran though a mental list of the things she had to do and the things she could weasel out of. "Couple hours?"

"Perfect," Liz agreed. "Hey!" she called just before Jude disappeared into her bedroom. "Is it still okay if I borrow one of the cars in the garage?" Earlier in the week, Jude—not wanting Liz to feel trapped—had placed at the reporter's disposal both her other cars, a Ford Explorer and a Jaguar XJS.

"Sure," Jude shrugged. "The keys are on the control panel by the kitchen door. Help yourself."

❏ ❏ ❏

"You're late." Kent drummed his fingers impatiently on the table's cheap Formica top as Jude slid into the seat opposite him.

"So sue me," Jude retorted, signaling the waitress. "Bourbon, neat," she ordered before turning back to Kent. "Have you got anything on the hit yet?"

"I'm fine, thank you, Jude. Yourself?" he mocked. "I swear, Lucien, your manners get worse every time I see you."

Jude sat back against the vinyl booth, an appraising cast in her eyes. "Something got your knickers in a twist, Kent?"

He waited until Jude's drink was settled in front of her then shrugged. "I'm getting a lot of heat to wind this operation up," he stated grimly.

Jude snorted derisively. "Since when? This op isn't on the books, and I'm not even supposed to exist in the eyes of the Agency. What gives?"

"The fact of the matter is, you do exist," he snapped. "To a lot of people. Did you really think the Archangel's return to the Agency would go unnoticed?"

"I'm not returning to the Agency," she replied coldly. "Got it? I get Massala and I'm gone. How many times do I have to tell you that?"

"Fine. Whatever. But they want you to do it now."

"Too fucking bad," she retorted. "I'm nowhere near ready to bring Massala in. Good God, Kent, we just sat down last week. You, above everyone else, should know that it's not going to happen overnight."

"Have you spoken with Massala since your meet?"

"No."

"Why not?"

"Enough!" she growled, the light in her eyes turning suddenly harsh as she leaned menacingly forward. "This is my game. My show. Without me, you'd have about as much chance of bringing Massala in as you'd have of getting the Pope to fuck Madonna on the altar at the Vatican. Now don't piss me off." She sat back again and smiled pleasantly. "Or I just might have to get nasty."

Kent ground his jaw together tightly, aware that everything she said was true. "There's just some...concern...with the latest hit attempt."

"Speaking of which, have you found anything?" she asked again, downing her drink in a swallow.

"Nothing. And that's got me worried. Usually we hear just about anything that's going down."

Jude considered this for a moment, silently thinking that the Agency wasn't nearly as up on everything as they thought they were. "Okay, I'll put my people on it. I don't like doing it because if they get caught, this guy's gonna know I'm coming after him. Looks like I don't have a choice this time." She beat a quiet tattoo on the tabletop, mind racing. "We done here?"

Kent's face softened. "Hey, don't run off. I'm sorry I snapped at you. It's just the pressure I'm getting..." he trailed off.

"It's not a problem," she assured him. "I worked the pressure for a lotta years, remember?"

"Yeah," he grinned. "But it never seemed to get to you."

"Oh it got to me, all right. You just didn't see it," she answered, her thoughts wandering to her lost partner, who had seen what the pressure had done to the dark agent, and how it had terrified him.

He snorted cynically, a...*yeah, right*...expression on his face. "I guess I'll have to take your word for it." He shifted in his seat. "Look, Tony and I are going over to Barrido del Mar, see Maria and have some shrimp. Why don't you come with? I know Ria'd love to see you."

"I'd love to, but I've got a date," she demurred.

Kent's brows shot up in surprise.

"Yup," she nodded. "An honest-to-goodness, no-business-I'm-just-going-out-with-her-because-I-like-her date." An oddly happy grin worked itself over her features at the thought of her plans with Elizabeth.

"Wow..." he smiled. "Can I tell Maria? She'll be thrilled."

"Sure," she replied easily. "Why not? Tell her I said 'hi' and that I'll come see her next week. Okay?"

"She'll hold you to that."

"I know. I'll be there." Jude and Maria had made their peace over a year ago, forgiven each other for all the madness that had ensued after Jason's death—finally letting go of the rage and the pain that had consumed them both. It left an aching guilt on Jude's part for the tragedy. For some reason though, tonight the thought of seeing Maria wasn't edged with the wracking sense of things lost that it usually was, and she wondered if the honey-haired woman had anything to do with that as well. Elegantly sliding from the booth, she touched Kent's arm briefly. "Thanks, I'll see you soon." Then she was gone, slipping back into the night.

❧ ❧ ❧

Jude returned to a house filled with seductive R&B rhythms pulsing softly through the stereo system, and the tantalizing smells of sizzling chicken, spices, and tangy sauce. She nodded appreciatively at the music and followed her nose into the kitchen.

"Whoa..." she whispered to herself as she pushed open the galley doors.

Most of the preparation had already been done—as the pile of pots, pans, and cutting utensils in the sink testified. A glass of wine sat on the cook's island in the center of the room, along with a platter of nachos and a spicy-smelling dip that looked liberally laced with peppers. A matched set of plates, bowls, and eating implements sat neatly in the island's corner, waiting to be set. What held Jude captivated, however, was the auric vision dancing by the stove, oblivious to any scrutiny.

Elizabeth's hair was loose, tumbling wildly about her shoulders with each enticing sway. A burgundy, long-sleeved shirt with a couple of buttons casually undone hinted at the full breasts hidden underneath the silk's softness, and it was tucked into a pair of faded blue jeans that seemed to wrap possessively around the length of the small woman's legs. Jude drank in the sight as one who had just emerged from the desert's heart might survey Shangri-La. With a simple touch, Elizabeth had turned this place—Jude's fortress—into a home thrumming with life, with heart, with desire.

Swamped by the unfamiliar sensations, Jude opened her mouth to speak, only to discover her voice was nowhere to be found. Before she had a chance to try again, Elizabeth caught sight of her, emitting a startled yelp at the tall woman framed in the doorway.

"I didn't mean to scare you," Jude apologized softly, grateful her throat had decided to open.

"S'okay," Elizabeth blushed. "I was just—"

"Dancing," Jude finished for her. "I enjoyed watching you."

Another violent blush seized the small woman's features, and her eyes burned unusually bright. "I—um—thanks."

"You went shopping," Jude observed, sliding into the kitchen and letting the door fall shut behind her.

"Yeah...You just can't play pool in khakis, you know?"

Jude glanced at her own tailored slacks, suddenly inspired by Elizabeth's example. "How long do I have before dinner?"

"Stuff's gotta bake for about 45 more minutes. I made us something to snack on in the meantime, though." She gestured to the tray on the island.

Snagging a chip and dousing it liberally in the dip, Jude moaned in delight as she swallowed. "Mmm...Those are great, Liz. How about I get changed and then make a pitcher of margaritas to go with this? I may not cook, but I'm a helluva bartender." She grinned.

"Deal," the small woman agreed, sending Jude off to change.

Once upstairs, a quick shower freshened her from the sticky drive home, and she dried her hair in record time, letting it fall just as freely as Liz's did. She then pulled a favorite pair of button-fly jeans from the closet. "Can't go wrong with 501s," she muttered to herself, relishing the feel of the worn fabric across her body. Her skin sang with awareness this evening, sensitive even to the fluttering breeze generated by the ceiling fans in her bedroom. Tapping her foot on the thickly padded carpet as she stood at the door of her closet, she perused the rows of shirts and the stack of T-shirts that Carmina had neatly organized by color until her eyes lit with sensual glee. "Perfect." Smiling to herself, she pulled the leather vest off its padded hanger and slipped it over her shoulders, buttoning it rapidly. Scuffed black boots and a matching leather belt completed her look. "Not bad," she commented, peering one last time in the mirror and running long fingers through her hair, settling a few recalcitrant strands into place. "Hope you like it, Elizabeth," she whispered.

Liz had moved to the living room while dinner finished baking and was investigating Jude's extensive CD collection when she heard the dark woman padding down the stairs. "You have the most amazing sound system," she called over her shoulder, not turning around. "I've never heard anything like it."

"Thanks," came the quiet reply. "I had the same people who wired the Club install it."

"Is that where you get all your CDs?" Liz stood, gesturing to the neatly shelved rows of discs. "I can't imagine that you have time to shop for all these." She spun around, her gaze finally landing on her date for the evening. "Oh my..." The words dropped unexpectedly from her lips, her eyes traveling up the length of Jude's long body and back down again. From booted feet to leather-clad shoulders, Jude was every bad girl fantasy Liz had ever had come to vivid, dazzling life. "This is...nice..." she breathed, stepping closer and letting her fingers brush across the black leather of Jude's vest.

"You like?" Jude murmured, eyes half-closing at the bare touch of Liz's fingers. They drifted over the leather and down her shoulder, tracing the curve of a bicep and finally coming to rest on her forearm.

"I like."

The women spent a soundless moment just absorbing the closeness between them. The resolute bands of control that kept Jude's soul bound wrenched violently—corroded by the washing of memories of her bond with Jason and by the quiet days of conversation that she and Elizabeth had already shared. Jude realized with a gut-churning clarity that her desire for this woman was rapidly surpassing want and coming precariously close to need. Despite Jude's resolve to the contrary, Elizabeth was sinking into her—skin and bone, muscle and blood.

The words made flesh, Jude thought dizzily as she realized her arms were around the honey-haired woman, and Elizabeth was nuzzling her throat, teeth nipping tenderly at the flaring pulse point. *How did this happen?* Her head instinctively fell back, opening itself to the invader's assault. Slim hands roamed the breadth of her shoulders, circling delicately as the lips found purchase on bronze skin. Her own fingers tangled in the blonde hair shimmering with the devil's highlights and guided the questing mouth to her own.

*Yes...*her mind breathed in a sibilant whisper. Elizabeth's full lips parted to meet hers, and there was a subtle pause before Jude began falling into the exquisite softness of the welcoming mouth.

Their first hesitant kiss gave way to increasingly confident ones, and a moan rippled from Jude's throat as the small woman's tongue made its way into her mouth, searching, coaxing, and teasing Jude with its sweetness. A hunger that had nothing to do with the spicy smells emanating from the kitchen roared up in Jude's body with bewildering force, jolting the dark woman into awareness of her surroundings.

She drew her mouth away gently, loathe to leave the lush warmth of Elizabeth's lips. The small woman groaned in protest and opened eyes opaque with arousal to gaze at her questioningly. Jude spoke with an unsteady voice. "Slowing down, yes. Stopping, no."

"Okay, okay," Elizabeth breathed. "I get it. I don't have to like it, but I get it," she grumbled good-naturedly. "I've wanted to do that since I laid eyes on you," she confessed, resting her head on Jude's chest and smiling at the frantic cadence of the heart underneath her ear.

"Me too," Jude admitted softly. "I just didn't think..." *It would feel like this...so terrifyingly good and right.* She glanced down the length of their bodies, arms and legs entwined so tightly that not even the tiniest molecule could pass between them.

"Didn't think what?" Elizabeth prompted.

"That it would be such a good idea for you to get involved with me," Jude covered smoothly. Just having these feelings was unsettling enough to the dark woman, but speaking of them to Elizabeth at this point was unthinkable.

"Because of your...exotic profession."

"Yeah," Jude chuckled, a low, vibrant sound that rumbled into Elizabeth's hearing. "Something like that."

"Jude?" Elizabeth looked up, the warm depths of her mossy eyes finding Jude's gaze and holding it. "Don't try and make my decisions for me." The words were soft, but there was no mistaking the resolute tone behind them. "I won't tolerate it," she continued, gaining momentum from her indignation. "The only reason for you not to get involved with me is because you don't want me. I realize that the path you've traveled has been wildly different from mine. But that doesn't make me stupid. Or naive." She leveled an intense stare at the woman in her arms. "Or ignorant of exactly what you are." Jude watched the honey-haired woman with amazement. She had expected strength from Elizabeth, but certainly not this powerful will that—she was beginning to suspect—rivaled her own. "Do you understand me?"

The final question yanked Jude from her surprise and back into the small woman's eyes. "I understand you, Elizabeth, but I can't help but... worry." Her hand ran down Elizabeth's side and pressed softly against the wound hidden beneath the jeans. "You got shot just for knowing me. Imagine what might happen if you became..." she hesitated, "Something more." *Time to fess up, Angel,* Jason's voice crooned in her ear. *She's already something more...or else you wouldn't be feeling like this....What's it like...?* his voice asked soft and low in her ear, *To finally feel yourself falling in love...?* Jude swallowed hard at the words clamoring for release that were lodged in her throat.

Liz, seeing the conflict roiling in the azure pools of Jude's eyes, sought to ease the intensity that was part raw desire and part animal fear. "Well, at least I won't have to worry about getting bored with you around." She grinned winningly. "Now that you've shown me the downside of dating you," she patted the hand that covered her wounded side. "Why don't you show me the perks? I believe you owe me at least a night on the town, Ms. Lucien."

It was an invitation to put down whatever burdens the tall woman might be shouldering and come out to play. The combination of Elizabeth's radiant smile and the warm feel of the lithe body in her arms made Jude helpless to resist. She bent down and tangled her lips sensually with Liz's for a moment. "Show me the way, lady," she whispered, breaking the kiss. "Show me the way."

⬚ ⬚ ⬚

"You are trying to sabotage me," Jude groaned two hours later as they climbed into the Boxster.

"Whatever do you mean?" Liz batted her eyelashes innocently.

"That dinner." Jude grinned, buckling her seat belt and cranking the engine to purring life. "I can't remember the last time I ate so much. When we get to the hall, I'm going to bend down to take a shot and fall over. I'm stuffed."

"Then I take it you liked my Fire-Breathing Dragon Enchiladas?"

"Loved them. Don't tell Carmina. She'll be insanely jealous. She says I don't eat enough."

Liz frowned and poked Jude in the stomach and ribs. "She's right. You're nothing but muscle and bones."

"Skin and bones," Jude corrected.

"Not in your case."

The Boxster carried them to the edge of the drive, where Jude paused momentarily before launching them into the night. The sun had taken the worst of the heat with its departure, but the earth still glowed warmly from its ministrations, and Jude was grateful for her bare arms as the wind whipped past.

"You mind if I pick out some tunes?" Liz asked, holding up the slim CD case she found resting in the Boxster's passenger seat. She was curious to see what music the dark woman kept near.

"Not at all."

Liz flipped thoughtfully through the case, taking note of the selections—which leaned heavily towards blues and jazz, with a couple of classic rock artists thrown in for good measure—but one disc brought her up short. "No way!"

Jude shot a questioning brow in her direction.

"The Bee Gees?" she asked incredulously. "You gotta be kidding me?"

The dark woman laughed ruefully. "It's a long story."

"Spill it," Liz commanded.

"Okay...about five years ago, I was stuck in this tiny Mexican village waiting on a contact who was late. Way late. So there I was...waiting on him with nothing but a paperback copy of *Wuthering Heights* and this little transistor radio that only picked up one station. KRZY—Where it's all disco, all the time!" she intoned in a faux announcer's voice. "For two weeks all I did was read Bronte and listen to 'Staying Alive' and 'Night Fever.' By the end of the first week I had memorized the book, and by the end of the second I was singing along with the radio. Enthusiastically. I've had a weakness for the stuff ever since." *Of course it was either stay in my room and sing with the radio, or start trying to make time with the putas who were the only people who would talk to me.*

"Did you say sing along?" A sly grin creased Liz's face as she slid the disc into the player and punched the select button. "I've gotta hear this."

It only took a few seconds for Jude to recognize the song before she joined in, a perfect falsetto blending with that of the Brothers Gibb. Liz laughed in delight at the revelation of this whimsical side of her companion and insisted the impromptu concert continue all the way to the pool hall.

The Boxster took them to a seedy-looking set of streets, far away from the neon and glitter that Liz associated with Jude, to a nondescript row of bars with no names on them. Liz looked around them doubtfully, glancing at her escort with a question in her eyes.

Jude laughed easily as she slid out of the car and stepped around to open Liz's door. "Don't worry. You're safe with me," she murmured close to the smaller woman's ear.

A pleasant shiver darted across her skin at the intimate promise in Jude's tone. "I'm not worried about me," she assured the dark woman. "But your car—that's another matter." Her eyes couldn't help but wander to the predatory glances of the men standing in the shadowy corners. Parked proprietarily in front of a tow zone, the Boxster was a taunting symbol of a prosperity that didn't reach these streets.

Jude waved away her concern with an elegant hand. "Nah...they know me. I grew up here." she added, ignoring the astonished look on Liz's face. "This one," she pointed to an unmarked green door, opening it for her companion to pass through.

Mick Jagger pleaded for sympathy for the devil as they entered the hall. Used to the thronging crowds of her own local yuppie pub, Liz expected the place to be teeming with boisterous people relieved that the weekend had finally arrived. What she found instead was a fairly full establishment, where the conversation was muted by the rapid click of balls rebounding off each other. They weren't the only women in the bar, but close enough so that Liz felt the wandering gaze of the bar's patrons. Jude, however, seemed oblivious to them all as she guided Liz confidently through the maze of tables to the bar.

A wizened old man whose age the reporter would have put at anywhere from 70 to ageless caught sight of them as they approached. *Of course six feet of somebody like Jude Lucien is almost impossible to miss,* Liz thought appreciatively, glancing once more at the sculpted profile of the woman beside her. The faint smell of leather and the woman's own spicy scent curled at the edge of Liz's senses, and she fought the urge to find someplace—anyplace—to rest her hands on Jude's body.

"Girlie!" the old man cackled gleefully. "Didn't think you was ever goin' to come back 'round."

"Nickie, how you doing?" Jude's voice had shifted cadences, dropping an octave, and was now tinged with a throaty growl.

"Acrk—you know these boys—punks tryin' to take what don't belong to them—" He waved his hands in a dismissive and vaguely obscene gesture. "But I'm still here!" he chortled.

"Somebody trying to hustle you, Nickie?" Jude asked, a mirthful light dancing in her eyes.

"Ain't nobody able to hustle me," Nickie objected vociferously, then he laughed knowingly. "Cept you...and you weren't nothing but a punk back then yerself. That pretty face of yours tricked me, sat's all." The pair shared a laugh, and then Nickie's eyes left Jude's imposing form to focus intently on the woman tucked neatly at her side. "Where's yer manners, girlie?" To Liz's astonishment, the old man reached out an imperious hand and smacked Jude smartly on her arm.

The dealer just looked amused. "You know, a lot of people are asking me that today," she said cryptically. "Pardon me. Nickie, this is Elizabeth Peterson."

"Hi," Liz smiled.

Nickie's eyes narrowed to slits as he appraised her, nodding to himself. "Yer a pretty one too," he nodded. "You gotta handle on this one here?" He jerked a thumb in Jude's direction.

"Hey!" Jude protested.

"I'm trying," Liz laughed at Jude's scowl. "But it's hard." She smiled at Jude, feeling a quiet jolt as their eyes met over the old man's head.

Nickie shook his head knowingly. "She's a slippery one. You watch her," he solemnly warned.

"Yeah, yeah, yeah—everybody's a critic." Jude rolled her eyes and slung a long arm comfortably around Liz's shoulders. "I don't need you giving her any pointers on how to handle me, old man. Now, you gotta table for us or do I have to move one of the punks myself?"

"I'll get you a table. I don't need you tossin' anybody else through my front windows," Nickie proclaimed, bustling from behind the counter and heading towards the rows of tables.

"Hey Nickie!" A man dressed in stained and faded work coveralls shouted. "We need another round down here!"

The old man muttered something unrecognizable and jerked his head at Jude. "Get them for me, girlie. Everything's still in the same place."

"Do I look like the help around here?" Jude retorted as the old man shuffled away.

"Close enough, apparently." Liz reached up and squeezed the hand that dangled off her shoulders.

"Uh...sorry," Jude murmured. "I wasn't thinking when I..."

"And I wasn't complaining." Green eyes caressed the smooth lines of Jude's face, absorbing its tiny details—the dark speckles in the pale blue eyes, the thickness of the lashes blinking at her—things that, until now, she had not been allowed the luxury of experiencing up close.

Jude opened her mouth to speak, but the clamoring calls of "somebody, dammit, get us another round" interrupted anything she had been about to say. Liz gritted her teeth, annoyed enough to go over and smack the owner of the offending voice, but Jude merely smiled as if to say...*next time*...and stepped behind the bar with quiet ease.

"Hey, get me a tequila shooter while you're back there!" Liz grinned impishly at her date.

Jude shook her head, drawing three beers off the tap and expertly sliding them down the length of the bar.

"That's more like it," the men grunted appreciatively, taking in Jude's sleek figure.

"You Nickie's new help?" the boldest one asked her.

Jude arched a sardonic brow, listening to their patter.

"Yeah, 'bout time he classed up the joint."

"I love a woman in leather."

"Ain't seen the likes of you around here."

A crowd was beginning to gather, drawn by the increasingly raucous group at the center of the bar. Aware of the emerald gaze upon her from the far end of the bar, Jude moved with elegant precision, racking her memory for the drinks' ingredients as more and more exotic calls came to the dark woman. *Can't fuck up now...I'll look like an idiot.*

"Come on, baby, give me a tall cool one."

"Sex on the beach, honey, can you make it?"

"A buttery nipple sounds good right about now."

Another quick glance down the bar...Elizabeth was smiling openly at her now, and Jude flashed a quick grin back. *Okay...she wants a show does she....?* A fierce grin broke across her face. She wanted to groan at the atrocious puns flying at her, but instead she began delivering the drinks with cheeky replies of her own, teasing the other customers unmercifully. Nickie's tip jar began to fill rapidly.

"Hey, bartender..." A sweet voice from the honey-haired vision watching the show caught her attention. "Can I get some service down here?"

Jude sauntered the length of the bar, a smirk meandering across her face. Propping a long arm on the edge of the counter, she crossed her legs at the ankle, providing an inspiring six-foot vision for the boys at the bar. "What can I get you, darlin'?" she drawled.

"I thought I ordered a tequila shooter," Liz replied archly, crossing her arms. She had rolled up her sleeves in the warm bar, and Jude could see the fine delineation of muscles in her forearms. She had a brief flash of those arms at work on her body, the muscles bunching and gathering as they—*Whoa right there....Too many margaritas at dinner, Angel?* "So what do I have to do around here to get a decent drink?" Liz was saying, oblivious to the private show she was giving to Jude's imagination.

Jude brought herself reluctantly back from that sweet place she had gone and smiled recklessly. "One tequila shooter...coming up." She held up a bottle. "You want Cuervo Gold? Or the house brand?"

"I only want the best," Liz shot back saucily.

An eyebrow curled upwards in amusement as Jude replied, "Then you came to the right place, querida." She long-poured the shot into a glass and reached into the cooler for a lime which she neatly sliced into quarters and placed the items in front of her customer.

"You forgot the salt."

Jude glanced down at the barren rim of the glass. *Damn...*and then back up at green eyes dancing with amusement. "No I didn't..." Thinking rapidly, she held up two fingers in front of Liz. "Open up," she softly commanded, feeling her heart pounding rapidly in its cage.

The honey-haired woman obeyed silently, and Jude slipped her fingers past Liz's lips, swallowing the groan that surged forth as their lengths were enveloped by the heat of her companion's mouth. Liz took full advantage of the invasion, brushing her tongue along the sensitive flesh and only reluctantly releasing her hold as Jude tugged them free. Jude swiftly ran the digits through the margarita salt and offered them once more to the smaller woman. "Ready?" she asked hoarsely.

Liz could only nod as she picked up the drink. Her lips parted, welcoming Jude's offering. The sting of the salt overwhelmed the sweet taste of skin as Jude's fingers abandoned her once more. She quickly downed the tequila, sitting the glass on the counter with a thump. Her eyes watered at the alcohol's bite, and her senses—already in exquisite torment—flared even more.

"You forgot the lime," Jude teased softly.

Liz's eyes flickered to the wedge resting on the bar's surface and shrugged.

"You'll remember it next time?" Jude offered.

Their eyes met for a brief, sensual moment, and Liz grinned shakily. "I don't know if I could survive a next time," she admitted.

"What's goin' on here?" Nickie came blustering back behind the bar, interrupting their rapport. "I turn my back for one second and yer puttin' on a naughty show?" Nickie shook his head reproachfully, but his eyes were grinning. "Git out from behind my bar," he shooed Jude from her perch.

"But look, Nick, I made you some money," Jude gestured to the now overflowing tip jars.

"You cost me a lotta money," Nickie snorted. "Now git. Yer at table six in the corner. Cues on the wall. Git."

Jude reached around Nickie's diminutive form and grabbed the Cuervo and two glasses from the cooler. "That way you don't have to worry about us," she assured him.

"Yer takin' my best stuff," he mock protested, hands on hips.

"Like any of these guys are gonna notice?" Jude logically pointed out. "Give 'em a beer and tell 'em to talk to me if they have a problem." Joining Liz on the other side of the bar, she nodded towards the back. "Come on, its back here."

"And I don't wanna see anymore of that kinky stuff in my bar!" he called as they sauntered over to the table.

Jude sat their stash on a convenient table as Liz strolled to the wall and weighed a number of cues in her hand before settling on one. Jude watched with ill-concealed surprise as her companion went to the table and expertly racked the balls, looking at the dark woman with an expectant gaze. "You wanna break?" she asked in a velvet voice.

Jude swallowed hard at both the sight and the sound of the honey-haired woman, wondering for the first time what the hell she had gotten herself into. "You go ahead," she managed before walking to the wall and selecting a cue for herself. A sharp smack of balls slamming together took her attention from the shapely form bent over the table to the green itself where the balls ricocheted off each other.

"You're stripes," Liz commented, before angling herself for another shot. The cue ball snicked against the red two ball, sending it neatly into the side pocket. "Oh, I forgot to ask, do you want to call our shots?" she asked innocently.

Jude's brows launched themselves skyward as she regarded her companion anew. Another player, who had been watching the pair with calculating eyes, chuckled softly. "Looks like you're about to get yourself hustled," he commented over Jude's shoulder.

Jude pursed her lips. "Seems that way, doesn't it?"

⌂ ⌂ ⌂

"Where on earth did you learn to play pool like that?" Liz asked hours later as they sprawled lazily on the deck outside Jude's home.

The pair had discovered, during the course of their evening, that they were almost evenly matched on the pool table. Whenever Liz would have a spectacular run and think she had Jude on the ropes, her companion would come back with a skillful run of her own and balance the score. Eventually they had lost count of how many games they had played and just relished the competition. Their combined skill had attracted the attention of several of the better players in the hall, but all inquiries for matches were politely declined. Neither woman was tired when Nickie eventually ran them out in the early hours of the morning; so when they arrived back at the house, Jude led them to the deck where they could watch the waves washing up on shore.

"I was going to ask you the same thing," the dark woman replied.

Liz shrugged and laughed softly. "My parents had a table in the downstairs den."

"Ah..." Jude's voice echoed in the darkness. The tall woman was swathed in shadows, sitting in the chair farthest away from the swimming pool's edge. Liz had taken off her shoes, rolled up her pant legs, and was dangling her feet in the water. Moonlight glanced off the golden light of her hair, creating a halo that—in her current condition—Jude wasn't totally convinced was illusory.

"What's that supposed to mean?" Liz arched back to peer into the shadows, only able to see the barest glint of Jude's pale eyes in the darkness.

A contralto laugh wove through the night, mixing seductively with quiet murmur of the surf. "Don't get mad. It's just a million miles away from where I learned, that's all."

"You talk like we're from different planets."

"We might as well be," Jude sighed. There was a wistful tone in the voice from the darkness that made Liz's awareness prickle. The whole night had been so sweet, and the honey-haired woman was damned if she was going to let it slip away in the agent's unspoken doubts.

"Oh no you don't," Liz warned, standing with a rolling motion and stalking into the heart of the shadows.

The dark woman had stretched her long legs out, and Liz strode right up to the edge of Jude's seat, her thighs brushing the edges of the chair. She could feel the pressure of Jude's legs between her own, and the dizzying sensation momentarily distracted her from her anger. A brutally fierce urge to know the power of those sleek muscles wrapping around her waist almost threatened to overwhelm her purpose, but she pulled herself back from the brink of the sensual purgatory. "No you don't," she repeated forcefully, feeling the hands that rose to encircle her stop abruptly at the determination in her voice.

"Don't what?" Jude asked hoarsely.

"Pull that 'I'm not good for you bullshit' out again," Liz sighed. "We've known each other seven days and you've done that three times. Twice today. And if you don't stop it, I'm going to—" Her voice ebbed in frustration. Her mind was filled with everything she had learned about the woman below her, making her aware that there were still so many things that she didn't know—couldn't know really—unless Jude decided to tell her. That meant letting her in. And, she realized with a burst of painful clarity, she really wanted in, wanted to know Jude Lucien— newspaper article or book deal be damned. The laughing, teasing woman she had glimpsed tonight only made her hunger for more, just as the tantalizing caress of the dark woman's lips and hands made her crave their full embrace. But the craving had to be mutual, or else it would never work. There was just too much to overcome for both of them for it to happen any other way. "Or I'll just have to give up," she finished softly, sadly.

Liz backed away a step before graceful hands came up to stop her. "Don't," Jude whispered. Long fingers curled tightly in the rough fabric of Liz's jeans for an endless moment before a dark head was pressed against her stomach. "Don't give up."

It wasn't a calculated tease or an overture. It was a plea—plain and simple—for Liz to have faith in something she couldn't see. So, the honey-haired woman did the only thing she could do—the only thing her heart would tolerate—she responded to that call. "I won't."

Chapter 7

For the second time in as many weeks, Jude overlooked the sun as it swaggered into the day in favor of standing in a doorway, watching Elizabeth's sleeping form. She studied the supple lines of the woman sprawled across the width of the bed, wondering what on earth it was about her that had such a devastating effect on the dark woman's defenses.

Jason had always been fond of saying that an avalanche started with just a single stone; and—Jude thought ruefully—it looked like in this case, he was right. Last night, that single, choked plea had been all that she had been able to force out through lungs suddenly constricted from lack of breath. It had been enough to set Jude's emotions into a free-fall that she seemed helpless to stop. Time had ground to a halt when she felt those small fingers running through her hair and over her back in gentling circles. Jude didn't know how long their embrace had lasted, but somehow she eventually found herself standing at her own bedroom door, Elizabeth's hands clasped in her own. "We'll talk tomorrow," the honey-haired woman had promised before depositing a sweetly chaste kiss on her lips and moving down the hall.

Although exhausted, sleep had deserted Jude at that point, and even *Anna Karenina* couldn't distract her. A hot shower had proven equally useless. Finally, in exasperation, she had thrown on a pair of sweats and a T-shirt and left the room, intent on prowling the kitchen and rescuing some leftovers. Her steps, however, had led in the opposite direction, to the open door where her guest slept, along with the canine portion of the household.

The sun flashed roseate warning lights to herald its impending arrival, but the flicker of muscles in Elizabeth's out-flung arm had captured Jude's intent gaze instead. *She must be dreaming.* The movement dislodged Pete who rose unsteadily, his legs still heavy with sleep. The small dog lost his balance on the uneven tangle of blankets and fell against Elizabeth with a muffled thump. "Wha—?" A golden head rose from its comfortable nest and surveyed the immediate surroundings. "Hi," she said softly, spying Jude's tall frame. The honey-haired woman scratched Pete's ears absently, and the dog curled up next to her again with a contented sigh.

An exultant kernel of happiness exploded in Jude's belly, bathing her soul in light that—had it been visible—would have rivaled anything the sun could have dared to offer. "You seem to have bewitched my dogs," she observed. Clytemnestra lifted a dreamy head, brown eyes flickering guiltily as she saw her mistress.

"Oops..." Elizabeth apologized, not looking repentant in the least.

"Well," Jude drawled, "I can't fault their taste, that's for sure."

That earned her a sleepy smile, as the small woman ran a hand through her tousled hair and narrowed her eyes at Jude. "Have you slept at all?"

The dark woman shrugged. "Some," she fibbed.

"What time is it?"

"A little before dawn."

Elizabeth chewed her lip for a moment. "Come here."

Jude hesitated, then covered the distance in three long strides, stopping at the edge of the bed.

"No, I said come *here*," Elizabeth commanded in a quiet voice. Pulling the covers back and sliding over, she dislodged a grumpy Pete who stumbled to the edge of the bed and flopped back down next to Aggie.

The dark woman remained still, staring dumbly at her. Green eyes sought hers, coaxing the reluctance from her body, soothing Jude with the verdant lushness of her gaze. Surrendering to the sweet promise held out to her, she shucked the sweats from her long legs and slipped into the warmth of Elizabeth's bed.

"There," the small woman murmured when Jude was settled quite snugly in her arms. "Isn't that better?"

But the dark woman was already asleep, her breathing steady and even, all awareness lost to dreams of a fair-haired man and a green-eyed woman laughing with her in the sun.

❐ ❐ ❐

Time waits for no woman, even one as exhausted as Jude, and the next time the dark woman returned to the land of the waking, the sun was industriously dousing the world in a painfully brilliant light. "Arrgghh..." she growled, narrowing her eyes to bare slits in a vain attempt to ward off the day's luminescence. Failing that, she dropped her head back to its resting-place, nestled in the dim softness between Elizabeth's shoulder and neck, burrowing close to the pliant skin.

A gentle laugh tickled her hearing, accompanied by the slight ripple of muscles underneath her hand. "You awake?" Elizabeth asked.

"Barely," Jude grunted.

Another laugh, and this time Jude raised her head far enough to see amused green eyes sparkling back at her. "Go back to sleep," the smaller woman urged. "I don't have anywhere to be."

A quick downward glance revealed that in her sleep, Jude had staked unwitting claim to the lissome body beneath her. One hand had pushed up the edge of Elizabeth's T-shirt and was now splayed lazily across an expanse of bare abdomen, while a powerful thigh draped across the smaller woman's hips, tucking them neatly against her own. "That's probably a good thing," Jude noted wryly. "Because I doubt you could move even if you wanted to."

"Do you hear me complaining?" Elizabeth snickered, her fingers playing idly in Jude's hair.

Jude knew alarm bells should be shrieking in her psyche, that she should disentangle herself from this embrace in more ways than one. But her body quite simply refused to obey, and she remained incongruously cradled by this small woman's strong arms. "What time is it, anyway?" she yawned.

Elizabeth craned her head around Jude to peek at the digital numbers on the clock. "A little past noon."

"Oh, Christ," Jude swore quietly. "Half the day's gone."

"So?"

Jude looked crossly at her bunkmate. "I have things I need to do," she replied, confused by the vaguely petulant tone in her own voice.

The honey-haired woman chuckled. "I know, I know. Bank heists to plan, jewelry stores to knock off," she teased, blithely ignoring Jude's skyrocketing brows. "Come on, Jude, it's Sunday. I thought one of the advantages of not playing by the rules was getting to make your own. And that, my bandit friend, means taking a day off when you want to."

Green eyes danced in merriment at Jude's pole-axed countenance. "I do not knock off jewelry stores," she muttered darkly. "You really do believe in living on the edge, don't you?"

"Hey, my motto is—See a bear in the woods, walk up and poke it with a stick," Elizabeth agreed cheerfully.

"What happens if you piss the bear off?"

Elizabeth half sat-up and braced on one muscular arm, twisting her torso so that she could regard Jude from above. "I run like hell." She studied the play of expressions over the dark woman's face. "Do I need to get my track shoes on?"

Cool blue silently took the measure of the woman still tangled around her—absorbing the deceptive strength of the body pressed against her, the quiet wisdom of the emerald gaze, and what both things were coming to mean to her. Her face relaxed into a disbelieving grin. "Nah...not unless you plan on joining me for a run on my 'day off,'" she replied lightly. Another iron band of will crumbled under the tender assault of emotion, and Jude absently wondered why it seemed so easy to just follow out this path—wherever it might lead. "So what exactly did you have in mind for today?"

Elizabeth looked thoughtful. "Oh, I don't know. It's supposed to be awfully hot today. I thought maybe we'd go to the movies and find some three-hour epic to while away the worst of the afternoon's heat. Then we could find some nice cool place with a couple of nice cool drinks and hole up. What do you think?"

"I think it sounds like a plan. But I do have one question." On cue, a loud complaint rumbled from Jude's stomach. "What's for breakfast?"

◻ ◻ ◻

"Huevos Rancheros."

Liz's hands were a blur as she sliced, diced, and shredded her way though what looked like most of the fresh vegetables in the Sunshine state. Huge piles of tomatoes, onions, and lettuce littered the cook's island, and pairs of eggs gently fried sunny-side up in the large, nonstick pan on the oven.

"So..." Jude nibbled on the hunk of cheddar cheese that Liz had thrust into her mouth when she returned to the kitchen after a shower. "Where did you learn to cook Mexican?" She surveyed the reporter's blonde hair and green eyes and laughed. "Since you have got to be one of the whitest girls in America."

The honey-haired woman chuckled in agreement with the description. "Truthfully? My father was in the Diplomatic Corps. And that meant that my brother and I were mostly raised by nannies and housekeepers— which changed, of course, every time he got a new assignment. I spent a lot of time in the kitchen with my keepers. We were stationed in several Latin American countries; I guess I just picked it up." Liz shrugged lightly, not sure how Jude would take the news of her privileged upbringing. From the little information available about the ex-agent's past, she knew Jude hadn't had much of a home, if any, growing up; and last night's muttered comment about being from two different worlds nagged at her. When talking about her youth, Liz had so far skirted around the circumstances of her upbringing, preferring to discuss instead her friends and life apart from the cold confines of the Gardener family. She glanced up to see thoughtful eyes studying her.

"Diplomatic Corps, huh?" Jude flicked her gaze back to the cook's island where she industriously rubbed at a non-existent stain on the wood. "Guess you got to see a lot of the world growing up." There was nothing mocking in the dark woman's words, just an inexplicably wistful tone that the reporter didn't understand.

"Guess I did," Liz agreed. Blue eyes returned to reveal a disarmingly open expression that Liz had never seen before. She fought to keep her breathing steady and even, recognizing that she was learning something about Jude Lucien that no computer file or newspaper article would ever know.

"What was that like?" Jude asked softly. The question seemed to slip out before the dark woman even noticed, but the sound of the words falling through the air sent an embarrassed flush spreading across the bronze features. "I mean," she shifted uneasily, as if caught admitting something shameful. "I never really left the state of Florida until I was twenty. Wait...that's not true," she corrected herself. "I did go to Georgia once with my sixth grade class to see Stone Mountain."

There was nothing that Jude could have said that could have possibly made her more vulnerable to Liz at that moment. With a terrifying clarity, the reporter realized that Jude was awkwardly trying to strip off the lacquered mystique that had—until now—carefully protected the brooding agent. Unsure of what she could say to acknowledge such a precious gesture, Liz brought her fingers to Jude's face and gently stroked the curve of an elegant cheek. "And here I thought you'd seen everything," she teased.

A quiet smile played over the elegant lines of Jude's mouth. "You don't need to leave Florida to do that," Jude assured the reporter. She nodded to the frying pan. "Those eggs about done?"

"Eggs?" Liz shook her head swiftly to clear it. "Oh...right...eggs... Yep, hand me those plates, will you?"

The slight tension ebbed away while they piled their plates high with Liz's breakfast concoction and settled themselves comfortably at the round oak table. Although she wanted desperately to continue down the path they had begun, the reporter instinctively knew that if she pushed Jude too hard those delicate layers that were peeling away would seal back up, and the smooth varnish of Jude's persona would conceal any evidence that they had ever existed.

Much to the honey-haired woman's surprise, the agent showed no reticence in returning to their conversation. "I pretty much grew up on the streets," Jude commented between mouthfuls of huevos rancheros.

"As if you couldn't tell," she chuckled.

"You can't," Liz replied half-truthfully. Although camouflaged by indisputably impeccable manners, the black-steel core of Jude's time on the street remained visible in every supple movement of the dark woman's form.

If Jude was aware of her friend's fib, she let it slide. "My mother would be thrilled," the agent deadpanned. "She was always after me to act like a lady. Don't know why, really. It's not as if we had two dimes to rub together, and the neighbors already considered her a whore." There was a faded bitterness in Jude's voice, as if she had just grown too tired to carry the indignation any longer.

"What about your father?"

"Never had the pleasure of meeting the man, myself." She shrugged in elaborate nonchalance, rising and pouring herself another cup of coffee. Holding the pot up in an unspoken question, she refilled the reporter's cup as well. "I never knew anything about him. How they met. Nothing." Pale blue eyes seemed suddenly very far away. "I saw a picture of them once. Standing together on the beach. He was tall—a lot taller than her, and she wasn't a small woman—and broad shouldered, with hair black as anything and ginger colored skin that seemed to glow in the sun." She shook her head. "He was a beautiful man." Her gaze found Liz's, and the dark woman smiled ruefully. The reporter wondered if her friend realized she might have been describing herself. "I got my mother's eyes, though," Jude considered absently. "When I found the picture, I couldn't believe my mother had kept it all those years. I mean, I was a walking reminder of her wrong as it was."

"Maybe she loved him," Liz tentatively offered.

Jude snorted derisively. "I never knew her to love anything except God." Then her face twisted, softening in spite of itself. "She never really had a chance, I guess. She was sixteen when she got pregnant, and her family tossed her out. Thanks to her brother the priest, she ended up at some home for unwed mothers." Her eyes hardened in memory. "From that day on, the fucking Catholic Church owned her. Convinced her that the only way she would ever atone for her grievous wrong was to prostrate herself daily at the Lord's feet. Priest's feet are more like it."

"She could have given you up, but she didn't, " Liz pointed out.

Jude ran a hand through the glossy sheaf of her hair and sighed as if tired of the discussion. "You're right. And I guess she did love me, on some level. But I was also her cross to bear on the path of atonement." She intoned mockingly, "The burden that once picked up can never be put down. The priest never let her forget that I was the issue of sin—and as I got older, I did everything in my power to live up to that title."

"A wild child, huh?" Liz teased, trying to scatter the foreboding clouds that had dotted the clear blue of Jude's eyes.

"Oh yeah," Jude sighed again with a wry smile and glanced at her watch. "Come on. I'll tell you all about it after the movie. We need to go if we're going to make it to the theater on time."

◻ ◻ ◻

If Jude had stopped to think about it, she would have realized that it was probably the most peaceful day she had spent in the last five years. Elizabeth had chosen a light-hearted, but literate, romantic comedy as their oasis from the racking July heat. Sitting in the theater, Jude fought off the desperately silly urge to put her arm around the honey-haired woman in the darkness. Throughout the movie she almost succumbed to several such ridiculous gestures, until finally as they were leaving the theater, she conceded the mental battle and clasped Elizabeth's slim hand in her own, guiding her through the large Sunday afternoon crowd.

"Where to now, o mighty planner of my day off?" Jude bantered, firing up the Boxster's engines.

"Someplace cool and dark," Elizabeth replied, falling into the game and gesturing regally with her hand. "With a view of the ocean," she added as an afterthought.

The dark woman touched a hand to the imaginary brim of a hat. "As you wish, ma'am."

As they drove in a relaxed silence, Jude allowed her mind to revel in the exuberant sensations of the last two days. The ease with which she had fallen asleep in Elizabeth's arms told her more than any amount of internal debate ever could about what she wanted from the slender woman. She wanted Elizabeth's body, her heart, her words, her kindness— anything and everything that the other woman was willing to give her.

The trouble was, she didn't know what she had to offer in return.

Well...that's the problem, isn't it, Angel? You don't think you have anything left...any heart, any light within you. And maybe you don't... But don't you think you should at least find out?

"Hell of a time to take my soul out for a test spin," Jude muttered under her breath.

"Pardon?" Elizabeth asked.

"I said, we're here," Jude smiled blithely back at her companion. "You said cool and dark with a view of the ocean. Voila!" She pulled the Boxster into a ramshackle bungalow-type structure, complete with faux thatch roof.

They entered through old-fashioned saloon doors, and their eyes were immediately soothed by a welcoming dimness. "Boy, you weren't kidding when you promised dark, huh?"

A laugh rumbled deep in Jude's throat. Adjusting her eyes after the brilliance of the day outside, she glanced around and motioned the bartender over with a wave of her hand. A swarthy man of indeterminate years ambled over, a frayed Hawaiian shirt bunched around the waist of his faded baggy trousers. His black hair was just turning gray and was a little long, barely brushing the tops of his shoulders; and the corners of his eyes bore a fine web work of lines. The entire effect was that of a sailor who, after one too many adventures, has finally come home from the sea. He surveyed them with a genuinely pleased expression.

Before leaving for the theater, Jude had changed into a long-tailed, white cotton shirt hanging loose over a light pair of white linen trousers that were now fashionably rumpled. A smooth length of tanned flesh was visible at the shirt's open collar, and her neck and ears were bare of any jewelry. Shaking her hair loose from the binding that kept it neat in the convertible, Jude cut a picture of elegant Southern decadence for the sailor's weary eyes. Immediately at her side, Liz was a golden child of redemption in a scoop-necked ochre blouse and a short, russet skirt that left her legs bare except for thin sandals. Smiling broadly at his two customers, he asked, "And how can I help you ladies this afternoon?"

Jude cocked a thoughtful brow, glancing at her watch. *Hmm...surely it's cocktail hour somewhere in the world,* she thought with an amused curl of her lip. "Give us something to fight off the day's heat," she said with a mischievous grin at her companion.

Jude's high spirits were infectious, and the sailor bantered back, "Sounds like you're wantin' my secret house brew, then."

"That depends," Liz interjected. "Just how good is this secret house brew?"

"Aye, lady, there's nothin' finer. It's as smooth as the ocean breeze caressing your hair, and it cradles you like the gentle rockin' of your ship."

"Yeah I bet, right up until the time you try to stand up," Jude commented wryly. "And then it knocks your ass back down." Her eyes were bright with a sparkle that belied her ironic comment.

"Well," the sailor allowed, "It has been known to set a lad or two back a couple of steps."

"Great!" Liz slapped her hand down on the teak bar. "We'll take a pitcher, two large glasses, and a couple of those little umbrellas if you have them." She pointed to a shady table on the outside deck. "We'll be at that table over there." She strolled away, oblivious to the fact that Jude and the sailor stood in rather bewildered surprise. Halfway through the bar, she spun on her heel and called back to the sailor, "Hey, can we get a couple of menus too? I have a feeling we're going to be staying for dinner." Not waiting for a reply before she made her way to their table.

Jude and the sailor regarded each other with bemusement. "She's a right handful, isn't she?"

The dark woman rubbed her eyes as she studied the relaxed length of her companion, now sprawled comfortably in one of the deck chairs, feet propped on the teak table. "That she is."

◻ ◻ ◻

"God, he was right, this stuff is smooth going down." Liz sat back, a satisfied smile playing over her features. They had made short work of the first pitcher and were debating the wisdom of ordering another one before dinner. Jude had filled the intervening hour with stories about growing up in Miami, how she had met Nickie and become a runner for his bar when she was twelve, and the mystery of where she learned to shoot pool with the ability of Fast Eddie Felson. Long unused to talking about herself, at first Jude's words were halting. The honey-haired woman, however, had been a patient and most-willing audience, encouraging her sometimes stumbling narrative. Most people acted as if they assumed she were the amaranthine spawn of some less-than-benevolent-deity who had come to visit His wrath upon them. Not many people stopped to realize that Jude Lucien was as much flesh and blood as they were.

It was safer, ironically, for Jude that way. The wide berth both friend and foe alike gave her made it difficult for them to perceive any weaknesses that might enable them to bring her down. Jude realized now, however, as she sat in the bewilderingly easy comfort of her new friendship with Elizabeth, it also distanced her from herself. Without the warmth of human connection, it was simple for her to start believing the same things strangers did. That she didn't feel. That she was merciless. That she was less than human.

Lost in her thoughts, Jude missed the punch line of a very long and elaborate joke that Liz had been telling. "Huh?" she asked. "I don't get it."

"That's because you weren't listening," Liz complained good-naturedly.

Jude gazed solemnly at Elizabeth, her mind noting that the slender woman's golden hair shone brightly in the sunlight, turning it into some kind of beacon for Jude's aching soul. *Uh-oh...definitely better wait until dinner for that next pitcher,* Jude cautioned herself. *When I start waxing poetic, it's definitely time for some coffee. I don't want them to have to carry me out of here.*

Jude's sometimes distant smile during their conversation hadn't gone unnoticed by the reporter, who really, really wanted to know what was going on in the dark woman's head. As far as Liz was concerned, the day couldn't possibly be going any better. Whatever had shaken loose last night seemed to have freed the agent from the worst of her reservations, and Liz had glimpsed an entirely different person from the one she had thought she was hunting down. This Jude was a laughing, gentle woman— one who had the ability to take Liz's breath away with a single, searing smile that enveloped those impossibly blue eyes. "Take off your glasses, Jude, I want to see your eyes."

Obligingly, Jude reached for the offending eyewear and tugged them off her face.

Ocean blue vistas opened to Liz at that moment, and without even pausing to check the water's temperature, the slender woman dived right in. "God, you are the most beautiful woman I've ever seen," she murmured, bringing a hand up to sketch the bold outlines of the agent's features.

Tender fingers passed over lips that stretched themselves into a self-deprecating smile. An eyebrow half-lifted and Liz expected another breezily dry comment to be tossed her way. Instead Jude only replied, "Thank you." Then she sighed softly. "I like the way you look at me, the picture of me you seem to hold in your head," she continued, as if she knew that Liz's words weren't solely about the physical package. "Even though I don't think it's terribly accurate."

"Tell me what you think I need to know to balance out the picture."

A brilliant smile broke over Jude's features, opening them far wider to Liz's disbelieving eyes than the reporter ever imagined possible. She felt her breath catch as Jude gently captured the hand that still stroked her cheek and pressed a tender kiss into the palm. "I will," she promised. "But not today. Today's not the day for it."

"Then what is today for?" Liz asked, a dawning sparkle in her eyes responding to the one in Jude's own.

"You," the dark woman replied simply.

❏   ❏   ❏

"Jude, you have got to try this. It's fabulous!" Liz moaned in delight, taking another bite of what the sailor had called his "From the Sea Salad." It was a mixture of pasta, some vegetables, and mussels, with a lemon dressing liberally sprinkled over the whole concoction. Liz held a forkful out in a vain attempt to coax Jude into trying it.

The dark woman curled a suspicious lip at the offering. "I hate to break it to you, but I'm not putting anything in my mouth that has that..." She trailed off in search of an accurate description.

"This what?" Liz examined the morsel in confusion. Looked like mussels to her.

"Consistency..." Jude finished triumphantly. "It just looks...so odd..."

"But it tastes great," the gourmand protested.

"Don't care. Can't eat it. Same reason I can't eat Rice Krispies," Jude shrugged.

"You have got to be kidding me."

"No. Have you ever really felt Rice Krispies as you've chewed them?" Jude shivered. "It's disgusting."

Liz scrunched up her face in confusion, but decided to let the comment pass. It was obviously an attempt to divert her attention from the task at hand, which was getting Jude to try her salad. If forced to answer that useless question *why* she had such a desire, the reporter would have been hard pressed to come up with a better explanation than—for some reason—at this moment in time she found the idea of feeding the dark woman incredibly erotic. "Are you sure you won't try it? I mean, you ordered grilled fish—at a seafood restaurant—how original."

Jude chuckled at the small woman's dejected expression, merely arching a wry eyebrow. "It looked like the safest thing on the menu." She nodded at the second pitcher of home brew that was fast going the way of the first. "Sailor boy there can make a mean drink, but he doesn't exactly look like Wolfgang Puck. Know what I mean?"

The reporter laughed in amiable surrender and shook her head. "Okay, okay. You win. Now, I've been meaning to ask you. What did Nickie mean last night when he said that you were the only one able to hustle him?"

"Ahh...back to my Fast Eddie days, are we?"

"It was an odd comment," Liz allowed.

"Okay...well, you know that I was a runner for Nickie when I was a kid. He had a lot of lucrative 'back door' businesses, the most profitable of which was a small gambling ring. I mean we're not talking the Mafia here or anything."

"He was a bookie?"

"Among other things. Anyway...there was this guy, I think his name was Angelo Something...I don't remember. But he had lost to Nickie big, and it was money that he didn't have."

"Don't tell me Nickie had you break his kneecaps?" Liz asked dubiously.

"Not quite. He took Angelo's prized, mint-condition 1968 TR25W Triumph motorcycle." Jude's eyes glazed over at the memory of the machine. "It was a beauty. Completely restored, all the original equipment, the works. The sucker *purred* when you kick-started it. I took one look at it and I was gone. I wanted it; boy did I want it. But of course, even if Nickie had wanted to sell it—which he didn't—I didn't have two dollars in my pocket at any given time."

"Let me guess, this is where the hustle comes in."

"More or less." Jude grinned rakishly. "I was sixteen and a bit of a hellion. Nickie was always teasing me that someday someone was going to tame me, teach me some proper manners. Same stuff my mother did, only I knew he didn't really mean it. He liked me just the way I was— behind the bar I was eye candy for the customers, gave 'em something to look at."

"Kind of the equivalent to a pin-up girl."

"Only I got to keep all my clothes on *and* all the tips. And if I couldn't handle the guys who got out of line, Nickie's big brother, Tommy, was there to back me up."

"That's how you ended up throwing someone through his front window?"

"Happened more than once," Jude commented dryly. "I didn't really like being pawed. My temper back then was even worse than it is now, and if I was in a bad mood—"

"Ouch."

"Right, but I digress. Anyway...I told Nickie I wanted the Triumph... Told him I'd work nights, weekends, whatever, but I wanted that bike... He just laughed at me and told me pretty girls like me didn't need things like that between their legs."

"Ooh—bet that pissed you off."

"That's putting it mildly. So I suggested a small wager to determine just what ended up between my legs—the bike or his cock." Liz's eyes flew wide at the statement, and Jude chuckled deep in her throat. "The expression on Nickie's face was about like yours. I could tell by the deer-in-headlights look I was getting that I had him. I had been running for Nickie for four years and had...changed...a lot in that time."

"Puberty does that to a girl."

Jude chuckled ruefully. "It did it to me in a big way. Instead of this gawky, flat-chested, clumsy girl...by the time I was sixteen, I had—as my mother so delicately put it—filled out." She spread her arms and gestured to herself in demonstration. "Into something close to this."

"No wonder he took the bet," Liz murmured.

The comment didn't go unnoticed by its subject who paused in mid-story to give Liz a warm smile.

"So that was my bet," she grinned wickedly. "One match of pool. Winner take all."

"If you won, you got the Triumph. If he won, he got you." Jude nodded. "High stakes," Liz commented.

"Not really. Nickie— to put it bluntly—sucked at pool. I half-expected him to laugh at the offer. Anyone with any sense would have," Jude snickered.

"If I had been him, I would have taken it."

"If I'd been playing you, I'm not so sure I would have offered. You cleaned my clock a couple of times last night. But Nickie knew he didn't stand a chance."

"Maybe he thought Fortune would smile on him this once."

"Well, it was close there for a while. He broke and went on this run, nearly cleaned the table. I'd never seen him play like that. But on his last ball he had ended up with a lousy set-up. He was going to have this really difficult bank off the eight ball... Fortunately for me, he missed."

"And then you wiped up the felt with him."

Jude shrugged. "Pretty much. But I'll never forget the feeling I had when he bent over to take that shot. I just kept thinking, 'Holy fuck, what have I gotten myself into...'" She laughed. "It was to become a common refrain in my life."

"So you won the bike."

"By the skin of my teeth. But, boy, was it worth it," Jude sighed wistfully. "Once I had that bike...I was free....You know? As long as I had a couple of bucks in my pocket for gas, nothing else mattered. She couldn't get to me anymore—I wasn't hostage to her piousness. Her God. My sin. Just by being born I was wrong.. but on the Triumph I just *was*. Does that make any sense?"

It made perfect sense to the woman who—as a teenager—had escaped into the nonjudgmental worlds of her own creation. Her writing had taken her far away from the chilly glares of her family. As she grew older and began to realize just what a wide gulf there was between who her family thought she should be and who she really was—that refuge had become all-important to her. It had allowed her to form an identity separate from the rest of the Gardener clan and freed her from that a stifling life of diplomacy and discreet intrigue. The identity she created for herself was something that had saved her life in more ways than one. "It makes perfect sense," she said softly, a hazy look clouding her verdant eyes. Absently she took one of Jude's hands and twined their fingers.

Sailor took their quiet moment to poke his head out of the door and ask with a questioning glance if they wanted another pitcher. Liz shook her head and simply enjoyed the tactile sensations of Jude's fingers measuring the length of her own.

"So...it didn't scare you?"

"What?"

"The thought of sleeping with Nickie."

"Are you asking if I was a stranger to the act?" Jude teased.

"Sort of," she mumbled.

Jude arched a brow in contemplation. "I don't guess I was. I mean, I knew he wouldn't hurt me, if that's what you're asking."

"Did someone?" The question tumbled out before Liz could stop it. "Hurt you, I mean."

"Why would you ask that?" Dark brows furrowed. "Because of my 'broken' and 'underprivileged' childhood?" she mocked. "Or because of my criminal past?"

"No!" Liz nearly shouted. "Because—" she hesitated, stumbling over the was about to pour forth. "Because I can't stand the idea of someone hurting you," she finished, unable to stop herself.

"Oh," Jude breathed. Their eyes met and held in a long moment of understanding that they were taking, without hesitation, the next step on the winding path that they were headed down. "Wow..." the dark woman laughed in an uneven tone. "I...thank you..."

"For what?"

"For worrying about the girl that I was. That's... nice... Elizabeth. No one's ever done that."

As she looked deep into those impossibly blue eyes, Liz wondered why no one had ever ventured far enough into Jude's soul to excavate the fragile remains of her girlhood. "Can't help it," she replied simply. Then, realizing that they were about to get far too serious for such a beautiful summer's day, she teased, "You seem to have gotten under my skin, Ms. Lucien."

They toasted the statement in silence, enjoying the falling sun, the slight breeze on their arms, the nearness of each other. It was one of those rare, utterly tranquil moments when there wasn't a single thing that could have made it more perfect.

A muffled giggle broke the hush, and Jude leaned a curving brow in the direction of her companion. "Yes?"

"So...I was just thinking...If, at sixteen 'the act' wasn't unfamiliar to you..." Green eyes danced in merriment. "Then when was it that—oh, how did my brother put it—you started 'batting for the other team?'"

Jude chuckled at the delicate euphemism. "Ah..." She paused for a moment, thinking. "I guess I've always 'batted for the other team.' I mean, there were a few men here and there, but honestly...nothing ever really compared."

"Compare to what?" Liz asked, slowly becoming hypnotized by the darkening blue of Jude's eyes. Their normally pale color seemed to take on new vibrancy, pulsing with a sensuous life all their own.

"To the feel of a woman in my arms," Jude answered without hesitation. "I love everything about making love to a woman, Elizabeth," she murmured, a husky tone edging into her voice. "The suppleness of their skin. The warmth of their bodies. The sounds they make when I touch them. There's nothing like it in the world."

Liz swallowed hard. The subject had been roiling about in the back of her mind since Jude's mouth had first tasted hers yesterday afternoon. She had no doubt that Jude Lucien was going to be a magnificent lover, and she wanted to touch the dark woman so badly it made her muscles ache from the pressure.

"Is that what it's like for you, Elizabeth?" If anything, Jude's eyes burned hotter at that moment, her desire for the reporter leaping to the front of her gaze.

"Oh, yeah..." Liz agreed. "What do you think I've been thinking about all day?"

"Tell me," the dark woman urged softly. The delicate trail of learning that the pair had embarked upon now neared its end as their minds at last acknowledged without equivocation what their bodies had been saying to them for over a week. "Tell me what you've been thinking about."

"You," the small woman managed hoarsely. "The way you feel in my arms, the way I fit in yours. I held you this morning as you slept— and I had to fight to let you go when you woke up." She nudged her chair closer to Jude's, so their knees softly brushed against each other. "I want to see you stretched out underneath me," she confided, her eyes taking on their own shimmering desire. "I want you open and wanting me as badly as I want you right now. I want to take you with my hands, my mouth, my tongue—any way you want, any way you've ever imagined. I want you helpless to do anything but respond to me—to the press of my breasts against yours, the sound of my voice in your ears. And I want to do it all knowing that as soon as you come, you're going to turn around and demand the same thing of me." The rational part of the reporter's brain that remained wondered once again where all these words were coming from. Seductions, declarations like this...they weren't something she had even done before—but something about this dark woman and her sensual menace just...inspired...her.

If there had been any doubts that this woman made her living with words, they were shattered by the rapid phrases that fell from the full lips just inches away from Jude's. A shuddering pulse visibly worked its way through the dark woman's body, and her hands twitched in a slight movement that wasn't lost on Elizabeth, who laughed throatily in response. "I suggest we get out of here first though," she added.

All Jude could do was nod wordlessly, tossing a stack of bills on the table to cover their check.

◻ ◻ ◻

The Boxster made it back to the house in record time, but even so, the sun had made its final appearance over the horizon, leaving the city to its twilight amusements. Jude opened the side door with trembling hands and punched the alarm off as if in a dream. Then Elizabeth's arms were curled around her neck, that sinfully lithe body twining about hers. *Oh god...*Jude thought incoherently. They backed their way through the house, nimble fingers that didn't belong to her trying to tug the length of her white shirt from her shoulders.

"Why'd you have to pick a shirt that had so many damn buttons?" Liz muttered inaudibly as she maneuvered Jude toward the stairs. Eventually surrendering the fight, she grasped the shirt at its open edges and ripped the joined material apart. Jude yelped in protest as buttons went flying, but Liz silenced her with a throaty growl. "I want to see you...now..."

Jude wasn't about to protest as roaming hands traced the finely delineated muscles in her abdomen. She wanted to feel Liz's own skin pressed against hers, but to do so she would have to separate from the delightful mouth skillfully invading her own. They managed to make it up the curving staircase without breaking either contact or their necks on the ascent. Jude kicked open the bedroom door with the back of her foot, sending animals flying in all directions as they entered the room. "Wait..." Jude gasped, as Elizabeth was about to free the dark woman's breasts from their surprisingly lacy confines.

Golden brows furrowed in confusion, but the hands ceased their relentless quest for skin. "Why?" she asked softly. "Are you having second thoughts?"

"God no!" Jude breathed. "I just...uh...I just...Oh hell...I just want to take it slow. I don't want us to get overwhelmed."

Liz grinned in agreement. "Okay, that I can work with."

"And...I wanted to ask you..." Jude fixed her gaze on the small hands that rested against her skin. "If...you were...I mean...we had a fair amount to drink...I don't..."

"You don't want to do anything I might regret later, right?" Liz caught Jude under the chin and focused blue eyes on her green ones.

"Something like that."

A knowing chuckle emitted from the depths of the reporter's throat. "The only thing I would regret is not making love with you right now." Then she sobered and added, "Unless you don't want this too."

"Oh, I do," Jude promised fervently.

"Then I don't think we have anything to worry about."

Mouths met again, this time in a slow, sweetly tender greeting. Jude discovered that the frantic aggressiveness had fled Liz's body, replaced by a sensual haze that enveloped both of them. Jude's tongue traced teasing paths over Elizabeth's lips and down her neck, sending sparks of delight shuddering through the small woman's body. Elegant fingers tugged the silk blouse free from the russet skirt and slipped under the material to explore the defined muscles of Liz's torso. "Oh yes..." Jude murmured, making contact with the supple skin. "You feel so good." *Just holding her feels right,* Jude thought in wonder. *And better than I had ever imagined it could be.*

They began a leisurely exploration that would have taken hours except for one simple thing: the phone rang.

"Let the machine get it," Liz muttered.

And Jude would have, but it was the shrill beeping of her private line. The line that didn't have a machine. The line that no one had the number to except Sasha. The line that meant nothing but trouble.

Groaning, she buried her face in her companion's sweet-smelling hair. "I have to get it." With a resolve she desperately wished she didn't possess, she broke their embrace and grabbed the handset from its recessed position in the nightstand. Liz's eyes grew wide as she saw that the white phone on the same table remained untouched.

"Lucien," Jude growled into the phone.

"Trouble." Sasha's clipped tones informed her. "Meet me at the office." Click.

Jude wearily replaced the handset and sat on the bed, resting her head in her hands.

"Let me guess, there's a problem?"

There was a frighteningly dead silence, and then slowly Jude lifted her head. The eyes that moments ago had been a vivid, pulsing violet were now a pale, colorless wasteland that seemed to freeze everything in its gaze. Instinctively Liz stepped back from the harshness of the stare, and Jude's head dropped again in ragged sadness. "Yeah..." she said, not meeting Liz's eyes. "I...have to go."

A glimmer of fear rose in Elizabeth's eyes, and Jude wondered if this would be the thing that finally frightened this exquisite woman away. Much to the dark woman's shock, instead of walking away, Liz placed tentative hands on Jude's. "Okay," Liz agreed calmly. "I'll be here when you get back."

"Elizabeth..." The eyes returned to the golden woman in front of her, and this time they were ringed by a faint, but unmistakable, warmth. "That might not be...such a good idea."

"My choice, remember? Unless you don't want me here."

Such gentle courage threatened to tear the breath from Jude's lungs. Her instincts told her to argue, to send Elizabeth away before she got hurt more than she already had been. But she lacked enough courage of her own to argue with this woman she wanted to make her lover. *Let her see what happens,* she thought numbly. "All right," she agreed. She glanced down at her half-dressed state and ached for things almost within reach and now lost. "I've got to get moving," she said, rising in a fluid motion as her brain finally kicked into gear. Pushing the ache to a far corner of her soul—to the place where Jason still lived—she methodically began pulling clothes from her closet and tossing them on the bed.

Liz watched in confusion as a pair of leather pants and a black silk shirt landed on the comforter, followed by a pair of boots and a sinister-looking black belt.

Jude hesitated a moment, knowing Liz was still watching, then she gave a mental shrug and pulled the Sig Sauer out of its place in the closet safe along with a spare clip. Those, too, landed on the bed.

The linen trousers fell in a heap at her feet, and she stepped out of them and began sliding the leather over her legs. She shrugged the silk across her shoulders, buttoning it with rapid precision and tucking in the tails neatly. Boots were next, followed by the belt. She saved the gun for last, sliding the clip into place with habitual precision. This last item of apparel she tucked into the back of the waistband of her pants, its weight an uncomfortable reminder of what she was.

Glancing up, she saw that Liz remained rooted to the spot Jude had left her in, a helplessly bewildered look on her face. Covering the room in long strides, she reached out a hand as if to touch the reporter, but her fingers fell short of the small woman, and she didn't try again. "I'm sorry," she whispered, then was gone, a chimera chasing down other dwellers of her adumbral realm.

A sickeningly familiar feeling blossomed in Jude's belly as she returned to the Boxster, and she shook her head savagely for thinking that ultimately things could turn out any differently. The day might have been reserved for the light, for Elizabeth, and the joy she carried within her. But Jude had made the grave error of forgetting that the day always passes, and when night falls once more, it brings the darkness with it.

Chapter 8

Sasha stared at the phone she'd hung up just a few moments ago, and a slight shudder ran through her body. *She's on her way...* It had been a long time since they had touched, and sometimes it seemed that her skin had ached every second since. Waiting, wanting more...

"I swear to God, Jude, you're worse than a tom cat." The figure in the black silk robe glared at the dark woman from the doorway. Sleep left the curly dark hair tousled, and she absently rubbed at her eyes, standing on the iron landing of her loft apartment.

In the leather pants, white silk shirt half-unbuttoned, arms braced casually behind her...Jude could have been the erotic fantasy of a million men and women. A rakish grin ignited the flame of her eyes; and with a supple motion, she left the railing and prowled closer to her quarry. "Come on, querida. Don't be difficult."

Sasha held out a hand to stop the intruder's progress, but instead found her fingers brushing across the silk and slipping underneath the fabric to the corded muscles below. Jude closed the remaining gap between them, and Sasha's arms rose of their own accord to twine about Jude's neck. "Why are you here?" she murmured before her lips were trapped by the hunter's voracious mouth.

Jude's coriander scent assaulted Sasha's rapidly awakening senses. The predator tasted of salt and sweat and heat—and the faint traces of a sex that was not her own. "God damn you..." Sasha thought to her herself, breaking free and turning back inside. Aware that Jude was following her, she used the moment's respite to settle her normally imperturbable calm firmly back in place. "Who'd you just finish fucking?" she asked lightly, watching Jude shut and lock the door behind her and noting with amusement that the dark woman obviously had no intention of leaving anytime soon.

Jude shrugged, a faint ripple of muscles across her shoulders showing in the movement. "Some blonde. I lost interest pretty quick though."

"And why was that?" She was walking away from Jude, keeping several paces between them as she headed for the kitchen. She made it as far as the dining room table before Jude caught her, wrapping long arms around her slender waist.

"Because she didn't give me what you do," Jude whispered in her ear, tracing a flickering line of kisses down Sasha's neck.

Sasha gasped involuntarily at the contact and braced her hands on the table's glass surface, letting its cool thickness steady her against the pulsing heat of Jude's body. She arched into the deft fingers that concentrated on loosening the belt holding her robe together. At last, the garment fell free, opening the warm length of her flesh to the hunter's restless search. Large hands quickly began roaming across the newly exposed territory, and Sasha mentally calculated the pros and cons of saying no or letting Jude do what they both wanted. Her refusals were rare and usually designed to make a point to the dark woman about the nature of power in their relationship. A ragged moan forced its way through her throat, and she quickly decided on a compromise.

Turning swiftly, she captured the questing hands and bent them behind Jude's back with surprising strength. "You come in here reeking of some whore and I'm supposed to let you finish off?" she mocked. "I don't think so."

A sardonic brow lifted, and Jude commented dryly. "If I had thought you were interested in joining us, I would have extended a formal invitation," she murmured, nibbling on Sasha's full lower lip. "Besides, I'm not finishing off...I'm just getting started." A startlingly swift movement freed her arms from their confines, and she lifted the slight woman onto the glass dining room table, settling herself comfortably between spread legs, which willingly circled Jude's narrow waist.

Jude grasped her prey's hips, drawing them tightly together, and the friction of the leather rubbing against an already swollen sex elicited a rasping groan from the woman in Jude's arms. "A little anxious, aren't we, querida?" Jude teased.

Sasha's mouth found hers with devouring urgency, silencing any further taunts that might have fallen from the dark woman's lips. She thrust herself against the muscular strength of Jude's body, craving contact on her aching skin. Sasha broke free only long enough to strip the silk from both their bodies, reveling in the contrast between the smooth suppleness of Jude's broad shoulders and the textured roughness of the leather between her legs.

In the tangle of their mouths, tongues and teeth warred for dominance—searching and hot, nipping, tasting, and testing. The growl rising from deep in Jude's throat sent a shiver skittering down Sasha's spine, and the dealer's skilled hands joined in the fray, finding the thick wetness already flowing from her prey's center. "So wet...God...Sasha..." Smaller hands guided Jude downwards as she obeyed, unresistingly. She kissed an incendiary path over Sasha's tawny skin, pausing over tautly puckered nipples, painting them swiftly with the brush of her tongue, then moving still lower at Sasha's ragged insistence.

Lithe thighs draped over her shoulders when Jude sank low enough to rest on her knees. The scent of their arousal was overwhelming now, and Sasha was painfully aware of her own sex throbbing tightly, anxious for the dark touch. "Is this where you want me?" her tormentor murmured, interspersing her words with slow kisses up the length of Sasha's spread legs. She parted the slender woman's glistening nether lips, slipping her fingers across the sensitive heat of Sasha's center.

The tawny woman was more than ready for Jude's touch. As the long fingers danced teasingly into her desire, she moaned on a gasping breath, "Oh Christ..."

"No..." Jude muttered, blue eyes running up the length of the shuddering woman above her. "Es el diablo," she whispered before falling easily inside the welcoming inferno...

"Not long now, Jude," she murmured softly in the darkness.

◻ ◻ ◻

The commercial district was deserted on this late Sunday evening when Jude slung her car into its spot in the underground lot. Glass and chrome rose up in industrial supplication to the deities of technology as the lift took her to the 27th floor offices of JLE Limited. She stepped into the unnatural hush of an abandoned shrine and padded noiselessly along the plush black carpeting. Her visits here were more regular than those she made to the Club, for the offices were the financial center of her legitimate operations. Accordingly, a large corner office bore her name on a silver plaque. The door was open, and she cautiously stepped inside.

Like her home, this office was a testament to its occupant's aversion to closed-in spaces. The two outside walls were floor-to-ceiling windows, the blinds opened now to allow neon-tinted moonlight to slink in and eerily splash the room's contents with a fractured glow. Immediately she knew she wasn't alone. A lithe shadow sat comfortably perched on the corner of her immense, marble-topped desk and idly played with a small Tiffany globe paperweight.

"Where's the fire?" Jude asked, fighting to keep her tone from betraying the warring impulses in her heart and in her blood. The sweet taste of Elizabeth's mouth was still on her lips, and the flaring desire that the honey-haired woman had inspired had only been intensified by Sasha's call. Her body never failed to respond to the swift and oftentimes violent measures that her life required. Though the coiled energy of action was gradually replacing the delicate sensations of arousal, there was an unmistakably sensual edge to the words that rumbled from her throat.

Saffron eyes flickered over the dark figure illuminated in the doorway. Jude felt their appraisal and the brief start of surprise in them as they surveyed her. Sasha's tone, however, was pure business as she addressed Jude. "Diego Arrgua has decided to switch teams," she said matter-of-factly.

"Diego?" Jude mentally scrolled through the myriad faces of the people who made her illicit businesses so vastly successful. "The Colombian?"

"That's the one. Seems like he didn't really like the way you had two of his culeros wasted about six months ago."

"Then they shouldn't have fucked up so badly," Jude shrugged. "He trying to dime me out?" she asked dubiously. One mention of her name to Dade County or the DEA and Arrgua would have been sent to Kent. If that were the case, the Colombian should be cooling his heels in a holding cell until Kent could talk to her.

"No, he decided to see what Romair Massala would have to offer."

Jude couldn't control the surprised flight of her brows. "Impossible," she stated flatly.

"Apparently not," Sasha retorted. Although the slender woman had been one of those who benefited by it the most, the rather loose rein Jude kept on her employees was an old bone of contention between them. Sasha was Jude's undisputed second-in-command and had become so because she had demonstrated the ability, not just to execute Jude's instructions, but also to think ahead, anticipating problems and taking care of them before they got messy.

Jude ran an agitated hand through her hair. "How did you find out?"

Sasha laughed, an oddly hollow sound in her voice. "Believe it or not, Romair came to me and told me."

Alarms reverberated throughout Jude's body, the hair on the back of her neck prickling. "Romair came to you?" she asked, a deadly calm filling her voice.

Sasha seemed unperturbed by the menacing glimmer sparking in her employer's eyes. "You haven't exactly been reachable, Jude. He and I have been trying to get you since yesterday afternoon. I've been calling the private line every thirty minutes for the last six hours."

Jude didn't like the explanation, but there was nothing out of place about it on the surface that she could put her finger on. She had blown off her second meeting with Sasha yesterday afternoon in favor of spending time with Elizabeth. The last two days had been filled with nothing but the honey-haired woman—and she found herself vainly wishing that it were still the case right now. "So what was his story?" she inquired brusquely, putting her doubts on hold for the moment.

"Diego called one of Romair's lieutenants, a guy by the name of Santiago, asking for a meet. Said he had some valuable information for the Massala family about your organization."

"What was he offering?"

"Supply routes, couriers, time tables."

"But he only has access to his own, and that's minimal," Jude objected.

"His *minimal* routes total over $10 million dollars, Jude."

"Still," Jude waved a hand. "That's nothing in the larger scheme."

"Not when you're a Cartel who's lost half its business," Sasha countered. "Besides, the Massalas don't know that all your suppliers are individualized. They probably think he has access to all the information. And there is the added little benefit of putting it to the woman who took a lot of those supply routes from them in the first place."

"True," Jude muttered thoughtfully. "So why is Romair giving that up?"

"I asked him. He said that you and he had a new understanding, and he wasn't going to betray that." Sasha studied Jude's dark form. "I guess you made more of an impression on him than you thought."

"Maybe not." Jude chewed her lip absently while strolling the length of the office. "Has Romair met with Diego yet?"

"No. That's why he's been so frantic to get in touch with you." She glanced at her watch. "The meet's in an hour. He wants you there."

"Let me guess—he wants me there so he can turn Diego over to me personally."

"That's exactly what he said."

"I bet," Jude snorted. "Doesn't this seem a little too convenient for you? I mean, here's a Cartel we've been at odds with since day one, and two weeks after we reach a 'new understanding' someone from my organization wants to defect? Something that hasn't happened—ever?"

"What are you thinking?" Sasha asked hesitantly.

"I'm thinking this whole thing reeks of a set-up, Sasha. I'm walking into an ambush." Grimly, she turned on her heel and left the office.

"If it is an ambush I'm not letting you walk into it blind," Sasha argued vehemently as Jude strode down the darkened hallway. "Or unarmed."

"I'm not walking in blind. And I have this—" She hefted the weight of the Sig in her hand.

"Yeah, a fat lot of good that's going to do you against a dozen armed men."

"I don't have to kill them all, querida. I just have to kill enough of them to get away."

"Why do it at all if you're just going to run?"

"Because I can't believe that Romair would think that I wouldn't see through this. He's testing me to see if I have the cojones to walk through the door. And there is the odd chance that Diego really is defecting, and Romair just decided to take advantage of the opportunity. He knows there's no way in hell that I'll take the chance of letting Diego give away my supply routes."

"Just how does he know that?"

"Because he wouldn't take that chance either."

The elevator doors smoothly closed behind them, lowering them to the ground with efficient ease. Sasha tapped a furious staccato with the heel of her pump and glared at her boss. "Okay, if you won't take any of the boys, I'm coming with you. You need somebody to cover that smart ass of yours."

Jude glanced at her employee with muted irritation, but couldn't suppress a quiet smile at Sasha's loyalty. "No," she said softly.

"Why not?"

"If anything does happen to me, you're going to have to take over. You know that," Jude replied, although it was only a half-truth. She had been slowly easing Sasha out of the underground work and handing more and more of the legitimate businesses over to the tawny woman's consummate expertise. Because she was surrendering the gambling, gunrunning, and drug operations to the DEA after she took Massala down; she wanted Sasha free and clear when that happened. That meant keeping her out of situations like this one.

Sasha sighed heavily in defeat, following the taller woman out to her car. "I just don't like this."

A crooked smile played over Jude's face as she regarded the smaller woman. "I've been in tougher situations. And besides, we don't necessarily know it's a set-up." There was a tiny, nagging voice in the back of Jude's head that said Romair was indeed an honorable adversary and luring someone into an ambush was unworthy of him.

Maybe I totally read him wrong, but I just don't think he'd do what it looks like he's doing....Of course that was the night I met Elizabeth, so my brain could have been completely scrambled....And after all, he could call ambushing me poetic justice...it's what I did to Enrico.

The brush of a hand on her arm shook her out of the black memories. Sasha's touch was cool through the black silk and felt good against Jude's hot skin. Briefly the dark woman was thrown back to those long, sweating nights when she had relentlessly probed the tawny woman's secrets with her hands and mouth, searching for a way to shatter that implacable calm. Oddly, the accompanying erotic surge that usually washed over her at times like this was gone, replaced only by a tantalizing echo of Elizabeth's fingers tracing flaming paths over her skin. "I'm sorry, querida, what did you say?"

"I said, I don't want to be taking anything over. So be careful. Got it?"

She clasped Sasha's hand reassuringly before sliding into the Boxster's familiar embrace. "Don't worry, okay?" Giving her employee a cocky grin, she backed the car out of its spot and roared out of the lot.

⌐ ⌐ ⌐

The meet was to be at the Marina, in the boathouse of slip #114, and Jude cautiously parked about a quarter of a mile away, confident that no one would detect the Boxster in its shadowy niche. She took a meandering path to the designated place, checking for signs of recent occupation, but the night was devoid of the usual scuffling sounds that accompanied clusters of men with time on their hands. About fifteen minutes before the meet was scheduled to go down, she slid into the boathouse, unobserved by the three men who were standing in a small pool of light cast by the streetlight outside.

Gee...does this mean I'm Goldilocks...cause damned if that doesn't look just like the Three Bears, Jude thought. Indeed the men were of three distinct sizes and she recognized the center man as Romair Massala. *The other two must be Muscle....Don't see Diego, but I am a wee bit early.* She listened to their muttered talk about Argentina's chances this year in the World Cup for a few moments before their chat was silenced by the hesitant approach of a fourth man. *Bingo...*Jude's mind sang as the familiar form of the Colombian scurried into view. *Okay...Let's see what happens next.* She watched Romair glance discreetly around for another presence, but the Muscle seemed oblivious to their employer's actions, training their eyes on Diego and the shadows where he emerged.

"I hear you have something I might be interested in," Romair began by way of introduction.

"I might," Diego acknowledged.

"About Jude Lucien's organizations?"

"Could be."

Oh, come on boys....This is the most boring round of "You show me yours..." I've ever seen, Jude groaned silently. *Time to make things a little more interesting.*

Soundlessly she slipped from the darkness and emerged behind Romair and his Muscle, appearing before Diego like some maleficent demon sweeping down to render judgment. "Is somebody taking my name in vain again?" she drawled pleasantly, a wicked smile on her face.

All the color drained from the Colombian's normally ruddy features, making him uncannily resemble the corpse he was about to become. "Ju— Ju—Jude..." he finally stammered.

The Muscle whirled around at her words, guns drawn, but Romair merely cast an amused glance behind him, folding his arms casually. "Ah, Jude...So nice you could join us. I was afraid for a moment that you had not received my message."

The Colombian recognized those words as the last nails in his coffin and, belatedly, tried to scramble free of the trap. He sprang towards the door, but Jude caught him by the collar and flung him the length of the boathouse, sending the smaller man crashing into a pair of sawhorses. "Oh no you don't," she reprimanded the now-prone man. Stalking over to her quarry with a predator's grace, she regarded the supplier coolly. "You know, I expected more of you, Diego."

He scrabbled backwards, trying to meld himself into the junk that littered the boathouse and never taking his eyes off the vengeful Fury looming over him. Stuttered incoherencies dropped from his lips faster and faster as Jude bent down and calmly lifted him by the front of his shirt. He waved his arms ineffectually in the air, afraid to touch the simmering woman who held him so carelessly.

Jude casually backhanded the whimpering man with her free arm, keeping him steady with a firm grip on his shirt. A mewling cry spewed from his lips, along with blood drawn from the blow. "Do you have anything to say for yourself?" she asked, slamming another blow into his face. There was the unnatural crunch of bones shattering in Diego's nose, and a light spray of slime and blood speckled Jude's silk shirt.

From her peripheral vision, Jude could see the Muscle nodding appreciatively at the force of her assault. Romair, however, remained placid; standing easily with his hands in his pockets, as if he were waiting for an associate to finish a phone call. She knew that this was another test of sorts, to see how she handled treachery. The Massalas prided themselves on their ruthlessness—always had—until, of course, Jude beat them at their own game.

"Haven't you been keeping up on current events?" she inquired silkily. "Romair and I are teammates now..." *SMACK!* "Which means, you miserable shit..." *SMACK!* "That what's bad for me..." *SMACK!* "Is bad for him..." *SMACK!* "Get it?" A swift knee to the Colombian's midsection doubled him over and would have returned him to the floor but for Jude's restraining hands. A familiar, ravening pleasure rushed through her blood as she studied the Colombian's bruised features. She hadn't done a tenth of the damage that she had planned, and he was already weeping piteously for mercy.

"P-p-pl-please stop..." he stuttered, holding his hands up weakly.

Jude cocked her head in contemplation. "And why should I do that?" she asked reasonably, tossing him limply to the ground. "You're here to sell me out... trade my supply routes, my time tables, my courier codes..." A sickening *crack* accompanied the muted thud of Jude's boot connecting with Diego's ribs. "And now you want me to spare your wretched hide?"

"M-m-my fa-fam-family..." he gasped.

"Yes, your family." Jude stood upright and crossed her arms like a displeased school teacher. "Let's talk about your family."

"Don't hu-hurt them."

A snarl of rage gripped Jude's chiseled features. "I'm not going to touch your family, Diego. That's not my style. You know the drill— *you* wronged me, *you* pay the price. But let's talk about what happens to them after I cut out your thieving little heart."

"Nnnooo..." he pleaded.

The very absurdity of this surreal tableau hit Jude hard, and she paused involuntarily. For the first time in her life, the pernicious clamor in her system for the blood of others seemed to flee; leaving nothing in its wake but a silent, yearning sadness. *Is this how you were going to set things right?* an all-too-familiar voice echoed in her thoughts. *You may think you've changed, Jude...but deep down...you know that turning Massala over to the DEA is simple...it's still business as usual....To really set things right...to stop this horror that is your life...you have to face some very nasty things about yourself....And you've never had reason to until now.*

"Elizabeth..." she whispered almost inaudibly.

The gossamer pull of emotions that this woman invoked in Jude was deceptively strong, almost strong enough to make her lower the burnished steel Sig Sauer that was pointed at Diego's sobbing head. Despite her feelings, she was only half-convinced that Elizabeth wasn't just a divine apparition sent from the Heavens to torment her with visions of a grace that she could never possess. Loving Elizabeth meant truly letting go of the rage that possessed her and beginning the inevitably painful road of healing. But conditioning and ten years of a life lived in the twilight overpowered this birthing sentiment, and a red veil dropped over the pale of her eyes. "I'll start healing tomorrow," she murmured savagely.

On impact, the bullet shattered Diego's head into minuscule fragments, spattering any hopes and dreams the Colombian might have had across the back of the boathouse.

To Jude it was the signal for what seemed like Armageddon. The shriek of shattering glass and the roar of automatic fire surrounded the dark woman on all sides. Instinctively she dove to the concrete floor, landing hard on one elbow, her thoughts focused solely on staying alive long enough to kill whoever was behind this. Holding up Diego's body as a shield, she inched her way into a protected position behind some haphazardly stacked crates. Looking up, she spied a window large enough to provide an escape, but it meant exposing her back to get through it. Not to mention diving through all that glass. She bounced up to answer the fire that was peppering her. *Why don't they just rush me...?* she wondered. Then she spied both Romair and the Muscle firing on four of the black-suited invaders. *What the hell...?* The sound of splintering wood on her right focused all of Jude's attention on warding off the impending assault, and she calmly pumped two bullets into her attacker's body.

Spinning at the impact, he crashed to the ground at her feet and she scooped up his discarded weapon. *Not an Uzi...that's odd,* her mind noted absently. *Okay...let's even up the odds a little bit.* Fueled by pure adrenaline, she nimbly dodged the hail of bullets and falling glass, ducking and rolling over to Romair's side.

"You sure know how to throw a hell of a party," she drawled, spraying their assailants with gunfire and dropping several of them.

"I assure you, they are strictly uninvited," Romair replied grimly, picking off an approaching gunman.

"That so?" she grunted, grabbing him by the arm and hauling him behind the flimsy cover of the crates. The Muscle was clearly outgunned, and Jude winced as both fell under the 9mm assault. "Well, looks like it's just you and me." She flicked a glance at Romair. His suit was disheveled and his tie was askew, but he showed none of the frothing fear of a man unaccustomed to the violence. "Do you trust me?" she growled.

"Why do I think I don't have a choice here?"

Jude shrugged, inching them further back in the shadows and closer to her window. "Sure you have a choice. Live or die."

The assault team had slowed their gunfire and were now surveying the area, looking for the pair.

Romair snorted. "Obviously I choose to live."

Jude patted him on the shoulder. "Good man. Okay...I'm going to cover you...on the count of three make a break for the far corner. See that window up there?" She waited until he nodded his assent, before continuing, "While I'm holding them off, make a jump for it. It probably won't be the most graceful thing you've ever done, but the fall won't kill you."

"What about you?"

"Hopefully they'll be too concerned with shooting at you and I can circle behind them and edge out through that side window over there."

"What then?"

"We run like hell. Ready?" Jude positioned herself and swiftly cast a prayer to whatever had kept her safe this long. "One—two—three—GO!" With astonishing speed, she rolled into the line of fire, drawing the attention of the searching men and managing to reduce the number of their attackers by two with a cluster of controlled bursts of gunfire. Romair sprang forward in the opposite direction, his body leaping upwards and crashing clumsily—but successfully—through the window. Automatically, the black-suits switched their fire to the fleeing man, and Jude made a break for the side window. *Of course, the one window that still isn't broken. Oh shit, this is gonna hurt,* her mind groaned as she began the leap that would take her to freedom. Flipping through the air to land feet first against the glass, the raucous shattering brought the gunfire back at her, and all she could do was pray that nothing hit her unprotected back. Bullets gouged the wooden window-frame, and one streaked by Jude's arm, grazing the flesh with a piercing sting.

Tumbling through the air, Jude knew that now her biggest adversaries were the jagged shards of glass that littered the ground. Her silk shirt was already shredded, but thankfully the leather proved a bit more durable. *I should have worn the vest,* she thought sardonically, landing with a neat tuck and roll that would have made Jackie Chan proud. *Who knew I was going to be playing stunt man?* Finding her feet, she sprinted for the protective covering of the darkness. A few dismal shots followed her, but she sensed that the men had left off any pursuit. With all their flak gear, they weren't exactly dressed for urban pursuit. Jude blessed this bit of luck as she ran a convoluted path through alleyways and squat tenement buildings. Running high on adrenaline and rage, Jude was a wrathful shade deftly traveling through the night. Finally reaching the safety of the Boxster, she slipped into its leathered comfort, breathing heavily.

The precariousness of her situation wiped any lucid thoughts from her mind. She was operating solely on instinct—an animal trying desperately to preserve itself—and all of Jude's formidable skills now bent themselves to this task. She piloted the Boxster for several blocks without lights to put just a little more space between herself and the site of the ambush. The police would be all over the scene in minutes. In fact, she could already hear the wailing approach of sirens. Deliberately taking a more circuitous route to keep her out of the emergency vehicles' pathway, she flipped the lights on and began the long drive back to safety.

Chapter 9

There was only a small hour left until daybreak by the time Jude finally made it back to the house. Ever-cognizant of the potential for further treachery, she had spent most of the night driving deserted back roads, only stopping once to gas up the Boxster at a 24-hour Mart. The pimply-faced attendant had taken one look at her ripped and blood-spattered clothing and had wisely not said a word, only accepting Jude's cash with shaking fingers. The long hours in the car had cooled the molten pulse within her, and the time had added a viscous layer of wrenching sadness that convulsed her stomach with grief.

She entered silently through the kitchen and padded through the living room, stopping at the foot of the stairs. She knew Elizabeth was waiting up there, had probably fallen asleep in her bed, and the thought of facing the beautiful young woman sent another wracking pain through her body. Wearily, she sighed and slid open the doors to the deck, breathing in the sea air's clean scent. Stopping at the wet-bar in the corner, she grabbed a mostly-full bottle of bourbon and a glass before dropping heavily into one of the deck chairs.

Images of this night merged with dozens of others just like it, all of them ending in the same way... blood, damage, death...most of it inflicted by her hands. Violence had always been a simple thing for her, her body's mindless response when thwarted or under threat. She had never questioned the coarsely erotic pleasure she took in wielding such power until she had met Jason. Throughout her life, she had been unconditionally accepted only by the denizens of life's underbelly. Her capacity for brutality and violence had marked her as one of their own and set her apart from the brightly-lit streets where people like Jason—like Elizabeth—lived. The innocents, as Jude thought of them, had always watched her with the glance of one who is not completely sure that a wild animal has been tamed. The Agency had seen a glimpse of what lurked deep inside Jude's soul and had sought to bend her malevolence to their will. Under the combined assault of the Agency's corruption and her own dark nature, the innocent in Jude Lucien never stood a chance.

Her bond with Jason's guileless soul had been the only taste of untainted acceptance she had ever known. That dizzying feeling had been the cudgel that had cracked the solid carapace that protected Jude from herself. And it had led to this...to the consuming rage and sorrow...for being who she was...for being what she was...for not having the courage to stop.

Running a blood-stained hand through her hair and wincing at the sting of the slight movements, Jude sighed deeply, wanting nothing more than to render herself oblivious to the now-eternal war waged in her soul. The sting of bourbon washing down her throat promised to dull the multitude of pains suffusing her body, and she drank fully of her own private Lethe, praying only that it would take effect soon.

◻ ◻ ◻

Liz woke with a start into complete darkness. *She's back.* Hearing a muffled boot on the first stair, she sat up in Jude's bed and waited for the inevitable ensuing footsteps.

Silence.

The sibilant hiss of rollers on metal told Liz that Jude had gone out on the deck rather than ascend the stairs to the looming darkness of her bedroom. Absently the honey-haired woman wondered how much of it had to do with her own presence there.

The stark look on Jude's face when she departed had told the reporter volumes about what that particular phone call meant. Pacing up and down the hallway hadn't made the time go any faster and had only served to aggravate the dogs. TV was insipidly annoying and not a single book in Jude's voluminous library had held her attention for more than a paragraph. Finally she had drifted off into an agitated sleep, waking at the slightest real or imagined sound. Now she slid from the warm sheets and scrambled around for something to throw on her bare skin. Her fingers found Jude's white shirt, and she slipped the soft material over her shoulders, thankful that enough buttons remained intact after the ravaging it received for her to fasten it closed.

Rolling the floppy cuffs up her forearms, she padded down the stairs in the darkness, pausing at the open door and unknowingly striking an ethereal pose before Jude's hooded eyes. The white shirt glowed otherworldly in the faint moonlight, outlining the lissome body underneath the thin cloth. Her fair hair, tangled from sleep, fell loosely around her shoulders. "Jude?" she called hesitantly, unable to see the brooding silhouette in the corner.

"Go away."

The words gave Liz direction, and now she made out the figure on the deck chair. In the brief time Liz had known the dark woman, there had always been a supple elegance in all Jude's actions, and immediately the reporter noted the graceless sprawl of Jude's legs, and the exhausted slump of her shoulders. She took a tentative step forward before Jude's voice stopped her again.

"Leave." Harsher this time, the timbre of her voice dropping dangerously.

"No." Liz's calm reply belied the sudden hammering of her heart. She moved slowly and steadily towards the dark shadow, as one might approach a trapped animal, holding her arms out loosely beside her. The glint of moonlight on expensive crystal caught Liz's eye. *Time for a different approach.* "Can I join you for a drink?" she asked, her voice as casual as if they were at a Country Club social.

A quiet sigh. "Sure. Glasses are over at the bar."

Fetching a tumbler and returning to the shadow in the chair, Liz couldn't bite back the gasp that rose in her throat at seeing Jude's shredded clothing. "Oh...Jude..." she said helplessly.

A casual hand waved her concern away. "It's nothing. Scratches mostly."

"You should have somebody look at them."

"I said they were nothing."

The harsh edge of her voice returned, and Liz backed off, busying herself with pouring a drink. Wordlessly she refilled Jude's glass, concealing her shudder when Jude downed the amber liquid in one smooth swallow.

"Do you...uh...want to talk about what happened?" Liz ventured.

"No." Jude retrieved the bottle from the smaller woman's hand to pour herself another drink. Liz's skin was warm in the cool hour before dawn, and the dark woman lingered a moment, tracing the delicate joints of Liz's fingers before pulling away.

In that fleeting gentleness, Liz saw her chance. Leaning forward, she softly captured Jude's strong chin in a trembling hand, silently urging Jude to let her in just a tiny bit. Haltingly, those blue eyes flickered up, meeting the open, verdant gaze, and then skittered away. "Hey..." Liz breathed. "Come back," she crooned.

But for some inconceivably cruel reason, the moment passed, and Jude jerked her head from Liz's tender grasp. When the blue eyes returned to the smaller woman, pale glaciers loomed at the center of her glance. Liz froze, knowing that the earth had just radically shifted under her and not certain of how dangerous her situation might be. She fought not to betray her unease.

The encroaching dawn cast a hesitant light on several small gashes peppering the dark woman's elegant features. The wounds—instead of making Jude seem more vulnerable—lent her a lawless, sinister air as she surveyed the slender woman beside her. "Why are you still here?"

Because this is where I want to be more than anyplace in the world. The unexpected reply leapt easily to her lips, but instinctively she knew Jude was in no condition to hear it—in fact, she was stunned that she was so ready to say it. Nonetheless, the words hovered there, impeding anything else she might have said. Speared by the hypnotic core of that blue gaze, Liz could only stare back and hope not to be completely eviscerated.

Restlessly Jude pushed away from Liz and rose. Whatever lethargy the reporter had sensed in the tall woman's frame seemed to evaporate as she prowled the length of the deck. "Are you having fun yet?" Jude inquired mockingly.

Nonplused by the question, Liz stood to face Jude and replied bluntly. "Not at the moment, no."

"And why not?" A silken menace wove through her contralto tone. "You must know you signed on for the Cook's Tour of Hell when you hooked up with me." She held her arms out wide, a beckoning penumbral figure.

"This is scaring me, Jude." It tumbled out before Liz could stop it, and inwardly she cursed herself for showing this deadly creature her weakness.

"I damn well ought to." The reply was soft and, surprisingly, laced with regret.

Liz covered the distance between them in a few steps, gambling that the woman she had come to know over the last two weeks was buried somewhere underneath all the rage and sadness. "I didn't say *you* scared me." She positioned herself unblinkingly in front of the other woman. "I said this scared me." Hesitantly she fingered the ruined fabric of Jude's shirt. "Seeing you in pain, not knowing what happened, or how I can help you. That scares me. Not you."

The dangerously severe coldness in Jude's eyes warmed, darkening the austere blue to a more human shade. Jude cocked her head, as if assessing the honesty of Liz's words. "The cuts don't hurt that bad," she said softly.

Liz's heart lurched violently at the quietly bewildered tone in Jude's voice. "I'm not talking about that kind of pain, Jude." An aching smile twisted itself over Liz's face. "I'm talking about this kind of pain. Here." She tapped trembling fingers against the dark woman's temple. "And here." Lowering her fingers to brush gently against Jude's thundering heart, asking for custody of a pain she had no way of fathoming.

This simple touch, so complicated in its intentions, must have pierced through the last bulwark of self-control that had kept Jude from surrendering to the small woman. A mournful howl that escaped unbidden from her lips as she slowly began crumbling. "Oh god..." she breathed.

Instinctively, Liz wrapped her arms around the larger woman and lowered them to the softness of the nearest chaise. Liz muttered shussing nonsense phrases to her, expecting tears or sobs or something other than the dry-eyed, quiet animal keening coming from Jude's shuddering form. "That's it...let it go...come on...let it go Jude...you're safe...I promise..."

"Oh, Jesus, I'm so sorry..." Jude whispered. "*I'm so goddamned sorry...*" Twining her fingers in the thin fabric of Liz's shirt, she held tightly to the woman's slender form, breathing in the warm, sleepy scent of Liz's skin, burying herself in the sheltering embrace. "I never meant for it to happen like this..."

Knowing that Jude's mind was somewhere far removed from the place where her body rested, Liz ran soothing hands over the dark head. "Tell me, Jude. Tell me what happened."

◻ ◻ ◻

Bringing down the Massala Cartel was thought to be impossible. Not a single DEA agent had managed to infiltrate their organization at any level.

Until Jude.

"It's going to be nasty and ugly," Kent warned her at the briefing. "And we don't care how you get in or what you have to do once you're there. Just get what we need to get rid of these bastards once and for all— no questions asked. Understand?"

The government had been getting their federal asses kicked in the war on drugs. Out-gunned, out-planned, and outmaneuvered, the DEA was desperate for a way to break the stranglehold the Massala Cartel had over a billion dollar drug trade through the country. With the help of the Colombian government, they had forced the Medellin Cartel out of business, but the Massalas had proven impervious to their assaults. Jude had been one of the few agents who had consistently spectacular results on her operations, and she had proven in the past that she wasn't the least bit squeamish about some of the more...unfortunate...aspects of her undercover life.

For Jude it had been the kind of assignment she had been born for... complete and unfettered freedom, so long as the agency's goals were met...and she relished the challenge. Her street sources, more thorough and reliable than any dossier the Agency could have dreamed of putting together, had told her all she needed to know about how to win the attention—and a position—within the Cartel.

A poker game...a reckless wager...a round of Russian roulette that mysteriously left one of the Cartel's network experts dead, and Jude conveniently there to fill his shoes. Enrico Massala was a bullish man, thickset with blunt features and a distinct lack of any earthly grace. He had been obviously fascinated with the preternatural elegance of his new assassin and the arrogant insouciance with which she approached life and her work with Cartel. Jude made sure he knew she was something far different from his other employees—unimpressed with the vast illicit empire he controlled and uninterested in currying favor.

"You aren't afraid to die?" he asked her casually one night as she stood to leave his office after receiving a set of instructions.

Jude turned to face him and was confronted with the open end of a Smith & Wesson .45 revolver. Arms hanging comfortably at her sides, she merely arched a contemptuous eyebrow at her employer. "Rico, when I die it certainly won't be at the hands of someone like you." Faster than his eyes could follow, she kicked the gun out of his hand, and Enrico found himself flat on his back, an irritated killer crushing the breath from his lungs. "You don't have the stomach for it," she snarled. "Or the hands." With a fluid motion she rose and extended her own lethal one to help him rise. "That's why you have people like me around." A fleeting smirk crossed her face, and then she was all business once more. "Don't ever do something like that again." She didn't say anything else, but the threat hung in the air as clearly as if she had spoken the words.

Days turned into weeks, weeks into months, and slowly the months became a year that she had passed in this life. The Agency positioned Jason as her contact source, and he floated in and out of her presence, their bond an increasingly distant memory as her star ascended within the Cartel. He tried talking to her once, trying to jar a look of recognition from those dispassionate blue eyes, but only succeeded in further alienating them.

"Look at yourself, Jude. Look at what you're becoming."

"I'm getting results, aren't I?" she asked coolly. Indeed, through her efforts the Agency was slowly weaving a net around the behemoth that it would be unable to escape.

"At what cost?" He pleaded, "I don't want to lose you."

"Lose me? Jason, you never had me. Don't you get it? This is what I am....And you don't want any part of that."

"You want me to believe—what? That you're a cold-blooded killer? I won't."

"Then you're a fool," she replied simply and walked away.

After that it was easier to let go of her cravings for the daylight world. She met a young woman named Sasha LeMontaine who proved most...distracting...when the restlessness seized her and her body ached with unnamed longings. And six more months slipped away.

⌐ ⌐ ⌐

Cursing the shrill ringing of the phone, Jude reluctantly tried to untangle the lithe form wrapped around her. "Come on, querida...I gotta get this..."

In reply, Sasha's mouth sought and found a full breast, teasing the immediately aroused nipple between her small teeth as Jude picked up the receiver.

"Oh Christ..." Jude groaned, throwing back her head and hoping whoever was on the other end wouldn't hear.

A deep chuckle through the line dashed that faint hope. "Where do you get all that energy?"

"Rico." Jude said by way of greeting as Sasha busied herself with finding more sensitive places on the dark woman's skin. Clamping down firmly on the moan that threatened to rise from her throat, Jude tangled her free hand in Sasha's curly tresses and drew the voracious mouth

slightly away from her body. "It's gotta be one in the morning." Massala was notorious for going to bed early, even though the majority of his businesses flourished in the aphonic hours before dawn, and she was more than a little surprised to hear his voice.

"Ah...yes...well I seem to have a...situation...that is in need of your expertise."

Jude shifted to a sitting position, pushing Sasha firmly away. Never in the year and half she had been with the Cartel had there been a "situation" that couldn't wait. "It has to be handled right now?" she asked, more to try and gauge Rico's mood than anything. If her employer was panicked, then it just might be the break she was needed. The one last piece that would bring the Cartel to a shattering end around his ears.

"Yes," he replied curtly. "And I want you to do it. Personally."

Because of his admiration for her ruthless efficiency, Rico had pretty much allowed Jude to roam where she wished in his organization, and she had taken on more responsibilities than just those of a hired gun. In fact, it had been months since she had executed a contract, busy instead with overseeing the arrival of most of his powdered product into the country. But now Rico's voice held the unmistakable tone of a master commanding his prize dog to attack, and Jude couldn't refuse the order. "Where?" she asked.

"The warehouse. Be there in an hour."

Sasha had known better than to protest when she saw the look on Jude's face. She simply rose with the dark woman and left for her own apartment. In the six months since they had taken to each other's bed, neither woman had broached the subject of staying over. The tenderness of waking up in someone's arms was inconceivable to the dark woman.

The scene that greeted Jude upon her arrival at the warehouse was a scene right out of her own personal Inferno.

Jason was kneeling in the center of a ring of the Cartel's goons, stripped to the waist, his arms bound behind his back.

A snarl rose in Jude's throat at the sight of her helpless partner, and only the fact that his skin was unmarred kept her from losing what rapidly fragmenting composure she had left. "This is unusual," she managed nonchalantly, sauntering into the room. Rico stood in front of Jason's prostrate form, glowering at the young agent. "Rico, you know I don't share your appetites," she drawled, referring to Massala's notorious predilection for beautiful blond boys.

A tight smile from Rico told her that her joke wasn't appreciated. "Unfortunately, my dear Jude, this is strictly business." Another tight smile. "Although you might derive some pleasure from it. Sasha's mentioned how...forceful...you can be...given the right circumstances."

"Well, I do enjoy a challenge," Jude smirked in reply to the innuendo, using the banter to buy herself time. They had Jason...which could mean a million things...but most likely someone had blown his cover. For all his apparent naïveté, Jason wasn't a fool, and he didn't make stupid mistakes. What Jude had to figure out first of all was how much Massala knew, and secondly how the hell they were going to get out of this one. She sighed theatrically. "So? Are you going to tell me what you're doing with Malibu Beach Ken here?"

"I have it on good authority that this delightfully pretty young man is a federal agent, working with someone in my organization to... how do they put it on the TV shows? Take me down."

Jason was doing a beautiful job of not giving away their connection, and she gave a silent thanks to his strength. She just prayed that it would be enough to get them through whatever came next. Now she arched a dubious brow in the direction of their captive. "That?" She jerked her head sardonically at him. "You're telling me that's supposed to be a Fed?" She threw her head back and laughed, a wonderfully throaty chuckle that worked its way through everyone in the room. "You've gotta be kidding me."

Massala shifted his bulk irritably. "I have no reason to doubt my source."

"Yeah? Just who is your source?" She doubted the ploy would work, but it was worth a shot.

Rico merely smiled tolerantly at his employee. "I do keep some counsel private, my pet."

"Well, I'm counseling you to get rid of whatever dumbfuck it was that told you this guy is a Fed."

"And why is that?"

"Cause I know this guy." She tossed the statement out casually, hoping that the bluff would work and not get them killed. Quite frankly, she couldn't think of anything else at this point that might work. "Isn't that right, Angel?" she strolled up to Jason's kneeling form and slapped him sharply across the face. His eyes gleamed murderously at her for just a moment, then the cornflower blue softened in acceptance as she used the name he had given her. It was her promise that she would get

them out alive—or die trying. In that minute gesture he told her he accepted, and that he trusted—wherever they were going.

Massala's eyebrows were dancing in surprise. "Would you care to elaborate?"

"I don't really remember when I met him....He likes the dust...and I did him a little favor once when he was short. Ever since then he's been hanging around like a tick on a dog. I can't get rid of him."

Rico's eyes narrowed suspiciously, but he didn't question her statement. There were a million and one rumors circulating about his tamed killer, each one more unusual than the next. "So?"

"So, I'm telling you that I could pound on this guy all day long, he'd probably enjoy it, and he's not gonna tell you what you want to know—because he doesn't know anything." Holding her breath, Jude knew she was close to either complete escape or something far worse.

He pursed his lips thoughtfully. "I see your point. However, if I take your word, that would mean that my source is lying to me."

"They could simply be misinformed," Jude offered. She could see where this was heading and didn't like it one bit.

"No, no...they were quite...emphatic...about this young man's guilt. If they were trying to lead me astray, it could only be to further their own ends, and that cannot go unpunished. That also means I would lose someone who's proven to be very valuable to me, and that's not something to be taken lightly." He laced his fingers together in contemplation. "No, I cannot just take your word for it."

"You were going to just take their word," Jude stated, aware that she was treading a dangerous line. She couldn't seem to be pleading for Jason's life, but she couldn't stop herself. Even though she had gone someplace he was too afraid to follow, Jason was still too important to her soul to surrender him without a fight.

"Yes, and you've shown me the error of that. So now I'm giving you the opportunity to convince me otherwise."

"How's that?" she asked skeptically.

"Simple really...just—how did you say it?—pound him. We'll see what comes out." An oily smile spread over his jowls. "And it will give me a chance to watch an...expert...at work."

Fury washed over Jude's features, nearly whiting out the arctic blue of her eyes, but she clamped down on it, knowing that disobedience was not an option. It would only get them both killed. As it was, there was still a chance—bare though it was—that Jason might escape with his life.

Walking in measured steps around her kneeling partner, she felt the fragile remnants of her humanity being sliced from her soul and laid on the altar of Massala's demand. "I'm sorry," she murmured inaudibly. Methodically she began a series of blows that quickly sent Jason to the floor writhing in pain. At her instructions, two men pulled him up by the arms. "I take it I have your attention," she commanded him icily. "Now... I promise you that this encounter won't be as...pleasant...as our usual ones are," she purred. "I also recommend that if there is any truth to what my employer is suggesting that you tell him, quickly, what it is you know."

"Don't know anything," Jason mumbled, head drooping.

Pulling him up by his thick, blond hair she backhanded him sharply across the face. Another blow opened a nasty gash on his cheek, the blood streaming evilly from the wound.

"Again...what do you know?"

"Don't know..."

Blows rained down on his fair skin, each one wrenching Jude further and further from herself until she seemed to watch the whole episode from a far corner of the warehouse. After fifteen minutes, the systematic abuse had swollen Jason's eyes shut, broken his nose, his collarbones, and most of the ribs on his right side. His increasingly incoherent denials degenerated into a single word—"Don't..." that reproached Jude every time she touched him. The stultifying atmosphere and the vicious activity had created a thin film of perspiration that trickled down Jude's face. Wiping absently at the sweat, Jude turned the ferocious blue on her employer.

"Happy now?" she snarled. The rage was etched into her features, and her muscles quivered—not from exertion—but from the suppressed desire to turn her violence upon Rico Massala himself. "He's pulverized and not a goddamned thing."

"You do seem to have proven your point." Massala nodded appreciatively. "But there's one little thing that concerns me. You seem to have quite an affection for this young lad...well, as much as you're capable of...and that's disturbing to me."

"The boy means nothing to me," Jude snorted. "I just hate having my time wasted...not to mention my plans for the evening destroyed," she added icily, reining herself in. It was almost over.

"Ah...do send my apologies to Sasha. I know she's going to be in a foul temper in the morning."

Jude managed a pleasant smile, even though she ached to throttle Massala. She was breathing a little easier now that the end was in sight. "Your own fault, Rico. You said it couldn't wait. You know how she hates to be left...hanging."

The men in the circle chuckled easily, knowing the effect that the dark woman had on their icy little executive. Jude had been the only one who had succeeded with the caramel woman; and they wished her the best, even though the combination of the two women had proven to be more than slightly...volatile...given the right circumstances.

"So can we dump the Cabana Boy here back on the beach and call it a night?" Jude moved smoothly in for the close.

"Sure," Massala waved in agreement. "But indulge me one last thing, please?"

"That would be?" Jude affected a bored tone.

"You're a gambling woman, aren't you? I believe that's how you won your place in my organization."

"So?"

"Regrettably I missed your performance that night. I'd like to see it now." Shrewd eyes focused on her, and with a sickening feeling Jude knew that her beating of Jason hadn't convinced him of a thing.

Still, she persevered, feigning amused indignation. "What the fuck are you talking about, Rico? You want me to play Russian Roulette right now? I didn't know you were that anxious to get rid of me."

"Oh no, not at all. Not you. Him." Drawing the same stainless steel Smith & Wesson that he had pulled on her over a year ago, he offered it to her, grip first. "Only one bullet and five chances to go free."

Her heart sank, and she knew she had no choice but to accept. Refusal would mean both their deaths. Jude hefted the gun experimentally. She hated .45's, with their longer barrels and flashy finishes, preferring the lighter grip of her Sig, with its more delicate lines and subdued brushed metal. "You're beginning to irritate me, Rico," she growled.

He grinned impishly. A most unattractive look for him, her mind noted idly. Glancing down at her barely conscious partner, she ran through her options and—for the first time in her life—came up empty. She certainly couldn't shoot her way out—not without leaving him behind—and that was the point, wasn't it? Sighing, she emptied the cylinder of all its bullets except one and spun it swiftly, leveling the weapon at her partner's head.

Jude had never been one for prayer...never believed in the vengeful God her mother had prostrated herself before all of Jude's life. She could *still hear the priest screaming at her, "Born in sin, wretch...and so you shall die..." and had never really questioned her accursed state. But Jason...he was someone else...she reasoned now, casting a faint prayer to whatever in the Heavens would hear her. Certainly if there were... something...up there...they wouldn't make him pay for her wrongs. In that instant, she would have gladly welcomed the worst fires of Hell if it would deliver Jason from what she was about it do. A last murmured plea...and she pulled the trigger...*

"Oh god...Jason...I'm so sorry...So sorry..." Jude murmured into the warm skin where her head rested softly, and Liz knew with horrifying certainty what had happened once Jude pulled that trigger.

The sun burned brightly in the morning sky. Jude had been talking for hours in that same position, cradled by the reporter's protective arms, and Liz had listened to the whole story of Jude's life with Jason unfold with a breaking heart. She mourned for all the pain Jude had endured, all the pain the dark woman had inflicted; but she also raged—at hazy figures in the DEA who kept Jude in their thrall, and at Jason for not having more courage in the face of Jude's darkness.

"That's not going to happen again," she promised the now-silent woman. The tensed muscles relaxed in an exhausted slumber beneath her soothing hands. "I won't let it," she vowed, closing her eyes and letting the weariness wash over her as well, carrying her into sleep.

❒ ❒ ❒

Several hours later, a burrowing movement from Jude startled her awake, and she glanced up to see Carmina's worried head peering out from the doorway. Gently she eased herself from the tangle of Jude's arms, lowering her to the soft cushions. Her limbs creaked in protest as she rose and covered the length of the deck in a few quiet strides.

"Another la noche del demonio?"

Demon night...that's one way to put it. "How often does she have these, Carmina?"

The housekeeper searched Liz's face carefully, then nodded at the genuine concern evident in the smaller woman's expression. "Come to the kitchen, senorita. We talk."

Liz padded after the rotund woman, slightly self-conscious that she wore nothing but Jude's white shirt; but Carmina seemed oblivious to her attire and bustled about the kitchen stacking dishes.

"You like the Senora, yes?" the housekeeper asked abruptly. "You— care—for her."

The reporter couldn't stop the slight smile that leapt to her face. "Yes, Carmina, I do. Very much."

The housekeeper smiled broadly back at her. "I told her. The first time I see her with you. The way she acts with you, like nobody else."

"Really?" The question bounded out, and unaccountably Liz felt her heart beat a happy tattoo at Carmina's simple sentences. Then she thought about the woman sleeping out on the deck, haunted by la noche del demonio. "Tell me about the demon nights, Carmina."

The housekeeper shook her head gravely. "Sometimes, she go out and then she comes back like that. Bleeding, hurt, evil in her eyes—like El Diablo himself," the older woman shuddered and crossed herself. "I fear for her like this. She sits, sometimes days, out there... just looking at the ocean like she wants to jump right in and not come back. Won't eat nothing...just drinks...one after another....One time I try to get her to eat, she throws the bottle at me....After that, I just stay back until it passes... She didn't hurt you, senorita?"

"No," Liz assured her. "Not at all. We—she—talked."

Carmina nodded wisely. "That one carries a lot of hurt inside. Sometimes I don't know how she stands up under it."

"I don't know either, Carmina," Liz agreed sadly. "Look, I want her to keep sleeping, but it's hot as hell out there. She's got to be burning up. And I want to look at some cuts she has. I'm going to try and wake her up and get her into a bath. Do you think you can make her some juice or something?" Then she added with a smile, "And if I promise to bring it to her, will you make her something to eat? Something she really likes?"

The housekeeper nodded briskly. "Course I can. Specially since *somebody* got some food in here." She winked conspiratorially at the reporter. "I don't know how you did it, senorita. I try and try to get her to let me do the shopping. She say, 'no no no no...let them bring it...' Glad you got her to see sense."

"Not sense, Carmina, I just took the keys to the truck and went shopping," she grinned.

"Good for you! Now go...run the Señora a bath. I make her favorite quesadilla."

▢ ▢ ▢

"Hey, Sleeping Beauty..." Liz gently brushed a matted tangle of hair from Jude's sweating brow. She hadn't been kidding when she told Carmina it was hot, and Jude's skin fairly steamed in the humid day. "Wake up," she crooned softly.

Blue eyes flickered reluctantly open, focusing woozily on the sunring-ed hair that slowly resolved itself in to Liz's tender features. "Wha—"

"Come on," she offered a hand to the larger woman. "You're roasting out here. I've run you a cool bath."

Jude's mind fought free of the cottony haze shrouding it. The night's events—culminating in her wracking confession in Liz's arms— came into sharp relief, and she regarded the gently outstretched hand with stunned disbelief. "You're still here?"

A teasing laugh rolled from the slight woman. "You keep asking me that. We've covered this. Yes, I'm still here. And no, I'm not going anywhere."

"But...but..." Jude stuttered, trying vainly to wrap her mind around the statement. "Why?"

"Because there's nowhere else I'd rather be," she said simply, bending down and brushing her lips over Jude's startled mouth in a tender greeting.

"Oh..." Jude breathed softly, not realizing how long those words had hovered on Liz's tongue.

"Now come on....You've got a bath waiting. And I hate to break it to you," she sniffed delicately. "But, boy do you need it."

Jude chuckled and allowed herself to be carefully hauled out of the chaise and guided up the stairs to the bathroom.

Once there, Liz gingerly removed the destroyed shirt and tossed it over her shoulder into the wastebasket. "You know," she muttered conversationally, "If you're going to keep wearing stuff like this, you might want to find a different line of work. One that's not quite so hard on your wardrobe." She deliberately injected a light tone into her voice, not wanting to push Jude too far, too fast.

Jude snickered as she sat down. "I can do that," she objected as Liz knelt to pull her boots off. The smaller woman pushed her hands away and resumed the task. "Right about now a new line of work doesn't sound so bad," Jude surprised herself by saying. Shocked green flew up to meet her glance and she managed a wry smile. "I...I...Oh hell," she swore gently. "I don't want to feel like this anymore."

"I don't want you to either," Liz agreed quietly. The two women exchanged wondering glances, neither quite believing what was really happening. Breaking the moment, Liz patted Jude's calf. "Stand up for me," she requested, rising fluidly. "Off," she commanded, looking pointedly at the leather pants.

Jude arched a droll eyebrow, but did as she was bade, stripping the garb efficiently from her body and kicking it to the side.

"In." Liz pointed to the water, her eyes wandering of their own volition down the magnificent length of Jude's tanned body. Angry red gashes marred the smooth perfection of her torso, but most of the wounds were shallow scrapes. A couple of them looked a bit nastier, but none seemed to require stitches. She caught a fleeting glimpse of a dark design on Jude's right hip before the tall woman sank into the cool water, sighing thankfully. She scooped a handful of water up, and poured it across the breadth of her shoulders. "I'm going to run get some antiseptic cream and check on your lunch," Liz said, a violent flush suffusing her features that they were both quite aware of.

"I get lunch?" Jude cocked her head.

"You get lunch," Liz affirmed. "I'll be back."

Jude smiled at Liz's departing form. The small woman's appreciation of her stripped down figure hadn't escaped Jude's notice, and she happily filed that information away for some not-too-distant-future reference. She felt curiously clear-headed and emotionally-cleansed, as if all the Stygian edifices that had held her soul immobile all these years had finally been shattered. Now all she had to do was clear away the debris and begin building her life anew. A frighteningly powerful wave of giddiness washed over her, and she dunked her head under the water, lest it fight its way out through her throat in a boisterous shout. Emerging sleekly from the water's surface, she busied herself washing her hair and rinsing its long length until Elizabeth returned to the room, bearing a wooden tray.

"Quesadillas?" Jude sniffed appreciatively. "Carmina's here?"

"Yup, and she made these especially for you. You can eat while I put some stuff on these cuts."

"But—"

"Humor me, okay, Jude?"

The dark woman shrugged her acceptance and obligingly leaned forward so the smaller woman could reach the cuts on her back. She noticed that Liz had put on some baggy shorts in the intervening time, but she still wore Jude's white shirt from yesterday afternoon. There were small dark stains where Jude had bled on her in the night, but the honey-haired woman didn't seem to mind. "How did you convince Carmina to stay?" she asked between huge bites of lunch. "Oh, this is good. Remind me to give her a raise."

"I didn't have to convince her to do anything. She was worried about you."

"Yeah...but...I'm not the...easiest person to deal with sometimes."

"You mean during your demon nights?" Liz asked softly.

"That what she calls it? La noche del demonio?"

"Uh-huh."

"It's pretty accurate. I think I heaved a bottle at her once."

"She told me."

"She tell you that it took ten stitches to sew it up?"

Liz couldn't control the flinch that passed through her body. "No, she didn't."

"So you see why I was a little surprised to see you this morning."

"You never raised a hand to me, Jude."

Jude's eyes turned to study her thoughtfully, the pale blue now the inviting color of a warm spring day. "I wonder if I'm capable of it," she mused aloud. "I look at you...and something just...settles right down inside me, Elizabeth." She reached a tentative hand out to stroke the fair woman's cheek. "I don't know how or why...but you just seem to fit..." She ran her fingers down the length of Liz's neck, over the increasing pulse and stopped at the center of her chest. "Here. You fit here...inside me." In her thirty-plus years on the planet, it was as close as Jude Lucien had ever come to a declaration of love, and she felt the breath flee her body with the effort of it.

In reply, Liz leaned into the caress, closing her eyes in an undeniable gesture of trust and welcome. Sensation after sensation began cascading over Jude's skin, warming places so deep inside she hadn't known they were frozen.

And then Jude was standing, the water sheeting off her muscular frame, as she stepped out of the tub on unsteady legs. Her hands gently cupped the smooth curves of Liz's face, thumbs outlining the shape of brows, eyelids, nose...waiting patiently until those verdant irises returned to her.

◻ ◻ ◻

Liz lingered in the luxuriously warm eddies swirling in her blood, loathe to leave its comfort. At last, she opened her eyes to a luminous blue, vibrant with emotion, and she found a wonderfully different kind of heat. "Jude..." she murmured before deliciously full lips found her own in a kiss brimming with tenderness, joy, and passion. Beyond anything Liz had ever known, this felt unmistakably right... but a nagging doubt colored the desire that was gathering in her core. "Jude..." she repeated, regretfully drawing back a pace. "Wait..."

Jude withdrew suddenly trembling hands with a quiet, self-accusing curse. More loudly, she said, "I—I'm sorry, Elizabeth. I thought—"

"Wait..." Liz held out her hands. "You thought right," she assured the dark woman. Just as Jude had needed to last night, now it was Liz's turn to reassure herself that this was what Jude really wanted, and not some blind reaction. "It's just that...you've been through an emotional wringer. When was the last time you let your guard down like you did last night? I don't want you do anything right now that later—after the emotions settle—you might regret."

"Like making love to you?"

Liz blushed furiously. "Yeah, like...that."

Jude chewed her lip for a moment, watching the beautiful woman standing before her. Drawing their gazes even, she reminded Elizabeth softly, "I was ready to make love to you last night. Before I got that damned phone call. Remember?" She guided them out of the bathroom, into the less-confining space of her bedroom. A ceiling fan whirled lazily overhead, sending soft puffs of air against Jude's damp skin. Hesitantly, she stroked Elizabeth's glossy hair, fiery highlights in the smaller woman's hair dancing under her hands. "Making love to you is something I could never regret," she said. "And I'd like...that is...if you want...me..." She blew out a frustrated breath and lowered her head. "I don't know how to do this," she muttered.

"You're doing just fine." Liz smiled gently, knowing that words weren't the easiest way for the dark woman to communicate. Even now, she could feel Jude's body trembling with suppressed desire. "I only want you to be sure of what you want. Who you want."

"I am sure," Jude replied without equivocation. "I want to make love to you, Elizabeth. Here...in the daylight. I need to see your face as I touch you, your body when you move against me. I want the sunlight on us... together. Do you understand?"

"With me," Liz replied softly, lifting her arms to twine about the taller woman's neck, feeling the pleasant shudders course through her body at the sensation of Jude's length pressed against her.

"Wha—what?" Jude asked, her hands automatically coming to rest on Liz's hips.

"Tell me you want to make love *with* me, not *to* me," she murmured sensually, green eyes darkening a shade in desire.

"I...I want to make love *with* you, Elizabeth..." Jude corrected, the beginnings of a smile creeping over her lips. "With you and to you and for you."

Opening her mouth to receive the tender gift of Jude's lips, Liz fell into the spicy taste of the taller woman. The kiss deepened; and leisurely, achingly, their tongues made their way across barriers of lips and teeth, mingling in the welcoming embrace of their mouths. This wasn't the frantic desire that consumed them last night, but rather long-banked embers flaring into life and beginning a slow burn that promised not to end.

Jude's warm hands slipped under the tails of Liz's shirt, playing over the smooth expanse of the smaller woman's ribs, smiling when she felt the catch in her breath. "I'm surprised you were able to button this thing closed after the damage you did to it yesterday," she teased.

A rich chuckle bubbled up in Liz's throat. "Me too," she agreed, arching into the cautious exploration.

"Poor shirt," Jude murmured. "Perhaps we should retire it. Send it to a better place."

"Oh no," Liz demurred. "This is now my favorite shirt. It's staying with me."

"Does it have to stay with you right now?"

Spying the amused arc of Jude's brow, Liz finally caught the clue lobbed at her. "Oh..." she blushed, then dissolved into gentle laughter. "Uh...no, I think...maybe...I could do...without it...for a little while. Now that you mention it."

Graceful fingers unfastened the remaining buttons on the shirt and slowly parted the folds. "You are absolutely beautiful," Jude whispered, pushing the fabric from Liz's shoulders and allowing her gaze to drift over strong shoulders, curving breasts, and a finely muscled abdomen. She slipped the khaki shorts over the gentle slope of Liz's hips, her heart pounding wildly at the beauty revealed to her.

"Funny, I was just going to say the same thing about you," Liz laughed on an uneven breath, her eyes encompassing the supple length of Jude's body as she finally allowed herself to take it all in. The dark woman's breasts were fuller than she had imagined; and her hips flared teasingly at the narrow taper of her waist, giving the muscular body an unexpectedly lush appearance. Her hands trailed up the length of Jude's arms, testing the sinewy strength of the resting muscles, over the broad shoulders, dipping the hollows of her collarbones, at last coming to rest on the swells of Jude's breasts. The dark woman groaned softly and closed her eyes at the touch, surrendering the lead of this first dance to Elizabeth.

Cupping their weight tenderly, Liz's fingers explored Jude's breasts, coaxing the nipples into blushing awareness she reveled in the contrast of her fair hands against the sun-bronzed skin. "Do you like this, Jude?" Liz teased, watching Jude's eyes flutter open with effort.

"Whatever would give you that idea?" she managed to drawl lazily, as the small fingers continued their meandering explorations. "But now that you mention it...mmm...yeah, I do like it."

The reporter's eyes sparkled at the puckish banter, relishing the connection of their minds and bodies. "Good...wouldn't want you to get bored or anything," she replied, changing the direction of her caresses just slightly, minutely increasing the intensity of her touch, smiling as Jude's breathing rose accordingly.

"I'll...uh...be sure to let you...*oh!*... know," Jude's words fractured themselves as Liz's mouth joined the fray, pressing fleeting kisses against the raging pulse in Jude's neck and along the elegant line of her shoulders.

"You know," Liz said thoughtfully. "This might go a lot easier if we weren't standing up. You wouldn't happen to know of any large, horizontal surfaces nearby would you?" she inquired innocently.

Jude cracked one blue eye and regarded Liz severely. "You. Are. A. Tease."

"So? You gonna do something about it?" Liz asked archly.

"That does it!" Jude scooped the smaller woman up in one fluid motion, covered the short distance to the bed, and flung them both down on its welcoming surface.

"This is more like it." Liz nodded approvingly, laughing. The pair tussled on the bed for a few moments, allowing the horseplay to slowly evolve into more sensual caresses and lingering kisses. Feeling her own desire reach the next level, Liz rolled the larger woman onto her back, her tongue stroking deep inside Jude's mouth—testing to see if Jude's want matched her own.

Jude moaned under the voluptuous assault, arching her back and pressing her breasts against Liz's own. "Yes," Jude murmured, as Liz slid away from her mouth to pursue points further south. Her questing tongue carved a heated trail over Jude's neck, working exquisitely delicate patterns over the bronze skin. Long fingers tangled in Liz's hair, not guiding or directing, just maintaining their tactile connection. Liz kissed her way down the swell of Jude's left breast, the hammering of the dark woman's heart clearly audible beneath the skin.

"You taste so good," she whispered, glancing briefly back at Jude's ardent face. Blue shaded to violet in passion and met her gaze with one of such open desire that it burned right through to Liz's increasingly liquid core. Her mouth found Jude's aching nipple and covered it with sweet possessiveness. Jude arched again into the contact, moaning deep in her throat. Liz lingered over Jude's breasts, feasting on their fullness with her lips, teeth, tongue... She glanced up once more to see Jude's head thrown back in abandon, offering her body up to Liz's ministrations. A blaze of falling sunlight splashed itself over their intertwined forms, and she paused just a moment to absorb the heat from the sun, their skin, and their desire. "Jude," she murmured, drawing the blue back open. "Look," she gestured with her eyes towards the open windows. "We're making love in the sunlight. Is this what you wanted?"

A guttural moan of passion twisted itself free from Jude's throat as she bent to tangle her lips with Liz's. "God, yes...it feels good. You feel so good, Liz..."

"I'm glad," she whispered, drawing away and sliding down the length of Jude's torso. "I want you to tell me, Jude, what feels good and," she grinned wickedly, "What feels better than good."

Involuntarily, Jude's hips bucked pleadingly as Liz nestled comfortably between Jude's long legs. The dark woman closed her eyes, her fingers still in Liz's hair.

"Tell me what you like," Liz crooned sensually.

"Just..." A ragged breath rasped from her lips. "Please..." she implored.

Since they had met, Liz had burned to know this woman, to know the secrets of her life, her mind, and her body. Now layer by layer, Jude Lucien fell open to her, revealing a tender heart and a frightened soul... and Liz reverently committed everything to the task before her.

Trembling fingers worked their way over the smooth flesh of one powerful thigh, feeling the answering tremors in Jude's body, and her parted lips followed the path blazed by her touch. No intoxicant in the world could have done more to dizzy Liz's senses than the clean, musky scent of Jude's center as she brushed dangerously close to her lover's need.

She traced the strong lines of Jude's waist with her fingers, grasping her hips and snugging her body more tightly in its cove. Tentatively, she pressed a soft kiss at the apex of those tantalizing legs and felt the answering arch of Jude's back in reply. Recognizing that Jude's desire was at a fevered pitch, Liz slipped two fingers between the dark woman's folds and gasped at the heated wetness that awaited her there. "Oh god..." Never imaging that she could feel so much from just the tips of her fingers, the reporter wanted to devour Jude, to wander inside her and claim the woman's need for her own. Still, Liz held back, gently working deeper and deeper—waiting for Jude to show her the rhythm, to freely offer that need to Liz. Tenderly, inevitably, hips and fingers matched in the intricate flower of consummation. As Jude spiraled up higher, Liz added another finger to the dance and dipped her mouth at last to the honey.

The taste of the dark woman was wildflower sweet, and she couldn't stop the moan that washed through her as the first wave passed her lips. An answering growl echoed in Jude's throat as she thrust herself into the caresses, implicitly trusting the small woman to lead the way. Liz reached deeper inside her lover, coaxing the need from Jude's body in molten form, wanting nothing more than to touch this woman with her hands, her mouth, her heart, her soul.

"Oh god...Liz..." Jude groaned as Liz's tongue brushed the center of her need, painting it with her own desire. A wracking shudder seized Jude's body, freezing it at the peak of its arch, and Liz felt the beginning tremors circling around her fingers. When the crest of the delivering wave came, she rode it with Jude, slowing her movements, easing her home. At last they lay still, Jude's center still pulsing gently around her hands. She proffered another tender kiss to her lover's core, smiling at the tremor that raced through Jude's quivering body, and gently slid herself up the lean form, replacing her fingers with a sleek thigh.

"Hey there..." She braced on both elbows over her new lover, a cocky self-satisfied smile running loose over her face.

An exhausted chuckle fell from Jude's lips. "Hey there yourself."

"Fancy meeting you here."

"It is a small world," Jude acknowledged with a wry smile. "Wow..." she breathed.

A delighted sparkle lit Liz's green eyes. "I guess I did okay, huh?"

"More than okay," Jude corrected, capturing Liz's head gently in her hands and drawing her down for a kiss. "Perfect," she said after long moments where their lips reacquainted themselves, flavored by Jude's wild essence.

Liz slid a little further down Jude's body to rest on her chest, the slight movement bringing Jude's thigh tightly against her own aching center. Unconsciously, she bore down on the solid pressure. The action didn't escape Jude's notice, and a rakish smile curved her lips. Deftly, she flipped the pair over, so that Liz was resting underneath her long frame. "I get the feeling there's something...I can do for you...Elizabeth," she purred sensually, the silky words sending tremors down the lithe body. "Hmm?" she arched a questioning brow.

The heat that had been kept in check by concentrating on Jude's body erupted violently, rushing through Liz's blood, suffusing her with need. "Yyess..." she murmured.

Jude was all feline grace as her hands began a prowling exploration of Liz's body, mapping out muscles, joints and nerves, marveling at the auric beauty stretched out before her. Liz was far-beyond ready for her lover's touch; and with a frightening need, she craved Jude's mouth and hands against her center. Small fingers curled in the dark hair, directing her downward, not allowing Jude time to linger over sensitized breasts, bucking hips, or flexing legs. "I want you, Jude," she gasped on ragged breath, moaning softly when she felt Jude's fingertips brush over the tight bundle of nerves. "Please..."

"Shh..." Jude crooned. "Shh...Anything for you...Elizabeth... anything...I'll take care of you...Trust me...." she promised, before bending her head to taste her lover's heat. Slipping a lithe thigh over each broad shoulder, Jude's tongue traced the slick path to Liz's center, while her hands stretched up to cup the tantalizing breasts that she had been earlier denied. Liz purred out her gratitude as her hips thrust powerfully against Jude's mouth, the adroit tongue and lips urging Liz to still another higher plane, as the women found a sinuous cadence of give and take, both moaning in delight at their discoveries.

Losing all sense of time and space, only conscious of the dark woman gliding deeper and deeper within her, Liz cried out her pleasure as each brush of Jude's tongue sent another shuddering wave through her trembling body. Reaching a peak from which there was no higher place to go, feeling as if Jude were an extension of her own body, she began the long fall into release, calling her lover's name in hoarse desire.

As the devastating tremors consumed her, she felt Jude's tongue and hands fall away, moving to gather her shivering form in the strong arms, wrapping a reassuring length around her in a sensual web. Jude kissed her forehead tenderly, brushing damp tendrils off Liz's forehead, a gloriously complete smile on her face.

They lazed in each other's eyes for a few moments longer, words utterly pointless after what their bodies had just shared. The sun was just drifting its evening's slumber, and it painted golden shadows across the sleek length of their entwined bodies.

Together, they joined the sun in its retirement, content to let the night continue on without them.

Chapter 10

Sighing contentedly in the middle of a sweet dream, Liz burrowed herself further into Jude's soft, yielding, fur-covered chest...

Fur-covered?

Green eyes reluctantly popped open, and the reporter found herself comfortably snuggled up to Aggie's obliging back. Somehow, during her sleep, Jude's smoothly muscular form had been exchanged for the furry length of the Akita stretched out against the slumbering reporter. Brows furrowing at this unfortunate turn of events, Liz sat up and rubbed a hand through her sleep-tousled hair. She surveyed the bed's rumpled landscape, looking for any sign of her new lover, slightly piqued that Jude had departed from their haven so soon. Then she spied a hastily scrawled note in a now-familiar bold hand resting on the opposite pillow.

Don't move a muscle...
I'll be right back.
—J.

"That's more like it," Liz muttered happily.

As Liz was sinking back into an inviting sleepy warmth, Jude sat in her worn leather desk chair tapping her fingers impatiently on the keyboard. A seedling thought had woken her from her contented slumber and had nagged her until she slipped away from her lover's soothing embrace. Upon hearing the muted movements of Carmina downstairs in the kitchen, Jude tugged a long, dark blue T-shirt over her head, its hem barely covering anything that might embarrass her older housekeeper's notions of propriety. She padded barefoot downstairs and hesitantly ducked her head through the galley doors. "Thought I heard you, Carmina."

"Señora!" The rotund housekeeper jumped a little at Jude's unexpected appearance, pressing a hand to her ample bosom. "You feeling better?"

Jude smiled at her way of asking if la noche del demonio had passed. "Much better, Carmina. Thank you." A broad smile ran across her face that reached up and caressed a breathtakingly deep blue into her irises, softening the austere planes of her face.

The housekeeper beamed back at her. "That little senorita...she's a special one, no?"

"That she is," Jude agreed readily.

Carmina nodded to herself, then frowned. "You not gonna hurt her, are you Senora?"

Jude's face sobered, and she shook her head gravely. "I'm going to try my best not to, Carmina."

The two women regarded each other a long moment, both knowing what Jude was capable of. The silence passed as Carmina rubbed her hands briskly together and nodded her acceptance of Jude's words. "Okay. Now what you doin' down here, half naked in my kitchen?"

"I gotta get something out of my car, Carmina." Jude grinned rakishly and dashed outside to where she had parked the Boxster. Something about the attack was bothering her, and it had finally nagged her into leaving Elizabeth's side. She leaned over the passenger door of the car and grabbed the submachine gun that she had scooped up from her dead assailant. Hefting its weight in her hand, she carried it into the house.

Carmina's eyes grew wide at the sight of the sinister-looking weapon resting casually in Jude's hand. Unconsciously the housekeeper made the sign of the cross, muttering under her breath in Spanish. "Why you bringing that trash in here?" she asked, anger at her employer overriding the common sense that told her not to anger a killer with a gun in her hand. "You said you were better."

Jude could see the worry in her employee's eyes and bit back the sharp retort that sprang to her tongue. *Two weeks ago, she never would have asked something like that,* Jude thought to herself. *Looks like Elizabeth is rubbing off on someone other than me.* A tiny, wry smile

teased the corners of her mouth. *And I don't think that's a bad thing...*
Nope, not at all. She gentled her tone deliberately. "I am, Carmina. Some
men...tried to hurt me the other day....This was one of their weapons.
Maybe I can find out something about them from it. Okay?" She waited
until the worried expression lightened a little in Carmina's deep brown
eyes. "I'm not going to use it on anyone."

"Promise?"

"I promise." She looked somberly at the housekeeper, who anxiously
rolled a tortilla flat. With one last brief smile, she padded back up the
stairs, Pete trailing at her heels. "Go see Liz, boy." She directed the small
beast into the bedroom and grinned as he obediently leapt up on the bed
and curled up at Liz's feet. Watching her lover sleep for a moment more
and resisting the urge to go join her, Jude turned in the opposite direction
and entered her study.

Logging onto the terminal, she checked her e-mail messages. She
read the one from Sasha confirming that she was sending a couple of
boys over to the scene of the ambush to try and pick up any information
about the police investigation, and then logged off. She had called her
assistant from the road shortly after the assault, letting her know that she
was fine and that Diego no longer posed a threat. Slouching down in her
chair and propping long legs on her desk, she examined the gun more
closely.

In the darkness and the haze of the attack, she hadn't registered its
make, but now looking closely at it, she saw that it was a H-KMP5— and
that knowledge made her blood run cold. H-Ks were exclusively military
and law enforcement issue, getting them on the street was almost
impossible. Even if that weren't the case, most street punks preferred the
flashier Tech 9s, while the Cartels and more organized groups used the
reliable and ever-plentiful Uzi 9mms. There was no need to go to the
expense and risk of obtaining Heckler Koches.

*Metro Dade? Nah...*she dismissed the idea almost as soon as she had
it. *There's no way in hell they would have organized something like that.*
She mused with black humor, *Of course they shot like they were county
sheriffs.* That left...*the Agency.* Jude shifted uneasily in her seat as recent
conversations with Kent played over in her head.

"Did you think the Archangel's return to the Agency would go
unnoticed?"

"They want you to bring him in now."

"Our sources haven't heard anything about a new contract out on
you."

"Motherfuck," Jude whispered to the empty room as a sinking feeling enveloped her. It was the same nauseous rage that had gripped her when she realized that Jason's cover could only have been blown by somebody in the Agency.

A number of scenarios ran themselves through her head in rapid succession.

One...cut and dried...they stumbled upon the meet independently of anyone else, didn't know of my involvement, and went for the bust. That's the best-case scenario. Even though she knew it was the least likely.

Two...Sasha sold me out. That thought left her almost as cold as the idea that the Agency was gunning for her. She turned the idea over and over in her mind, observing it from all angles, trying it on for mental size. *She's had years to do that...why now? What would be the point? Working with Romair? Nah...she hated the Massalas even when Rico was in charge....And the Cartel would never put a woman at the helm.* Although her instincts told her that Sasha wouldn't betray her this way, she kept the idea alive in her mind, realizing from past experience that betrayal most often came from the closest sources.

Three...Romair is working with the Agency...Wouldn't be too out of character for the family...But again, what's the point? The Cartel is crippled as it is; he has no leverage. Why fight your way to power only to give it away?

Four...Diego did go to the DEA to make a deal...That makes more sense than him going to Romair anyway...and the Agency used the information to set me up....It would explain why Romair looked just as spooked as I did when those guys showed up...That works.

Wearily she ran a hand through her disheveled hair, and sat up. *Okay, genius...you've figured it out...now the question is, what do you do about it?* She glanced at the computer's digital clock, surprised to realize she had been away from Liz for over an hour. *That's an hour too long, as far as I'm concerned.* She shook her head as that particular thought sank in. *Oh boy, I'm in trouble here.* She could still hear Carmina bustling about in the kitchen and decided a little preemptive strike was in order.

Soundlessly she slipped back down the stairs and stuck her head through the galley doors. "Uh...Carmina?"

"Yes, Señora?"

"Look...Elizabeth and I are gonna be... taking it easy today." A devilish grin curled her lips when she saw Carmina blush at the implication. "When you get done with what you're doing, why don't you take the day off?

What do you say? You can spend the day with your grandkids, or go shopping. On me."

A huge smile lit up Carmina's face. "Okay, Señora, but I make you two some lunch first."

"Great. Just make sure you can stick it in the refrigerator. I'm not sure when we'll make it back down here." She launched a pair of suggestive eyebrows skyward as the housekeeper tossed a dishrag at her rapidly retreating head.

"Santa Madre!"

But all Carmina heard was a throaty chuckle from her employer as she returned to her new love.

❑ ❑ ❑

Liz had returned to her pleasant dreams without missing a step, and the next time a figure nudged her from sleep it was distinctly female... distinctly human...distinctly her new lover.

"Hey there," she murmured drowsily as Jude slipped behind her, arms encircling the slender woman. Tender kisses traced lines across her shoulders, and Liz couldn't help but arch into the solid feel of the woman holding her. "Why aren't you naked?" she complained, feeling the soft cotton of a T-shirt instead of Jude's delicious skin.

"Cause it upsets Carmina when I walk around the house like that," Jude whispered, nibbling at the corner of Liz's ear.

The reporter cracked an eyelid. "Don't see her anywhere nearby."

Jude chuckled and nudged Aggie off the bed with a lazy hand, scattering the dogs who had slowly crept back after the women had fallen asleep in each other's arms. The evening had been filled with explorations of each other's bodies—sometimes gently, sometimes fiercely, always passionately and filled with a reverent air. Liz had been silently dismayed to discover a number of scars, both new and old, on Jude's bronze skin. Not because it marred the body's beautiful perfection, but rather because each mark was evidence of still more pain that the dark woman had suffered. By unspoken agreement, they had not talked of either the source of those scars or the current position Jude was in. It was a subject both knew they would have to broach soon if the marvelous discovery they had made was to last more than one night, but neither wanted to disturb the brilliant joy that consumed them.

"So?" Liz prodded.

"So what?"

"So...I don't see your housekeeper anywhere in the room." Deftly she twisted in Jude's embrace to face the dark woman who looked at her with dancing eyes. "Off." She tugged at the offending garment, indicating her desire.

"You are always trying to get me out of my clothes," Jude teased. "First yesterday afternoon and now..." She conveniently trailed off.

"Wonder why?" Liz retorted with a smug grin. "After last night, you'll be lucky if I ever let you put them back on again."

"Ooh...I could get to like that. Hey! That could be my new career—love slave. After all, a romance novelist has to get her material from somewhere, doesn't she?"

"I don't think you're exactly what Avon Books had in mind, sweetheart."

An indignant eyebrow launched itself forth. "And why not?" she demanded, full of mock-affront. "I'm not tall, dark, and mysterious enough?"

"Oh, you are all of that, and more," Liz fervently assured her. "But I think they might have a little problem with certain...other...aspects."

"My haunted past?" Jude offered helpfully.

"Ah...no..."

"My unsavory associates?"

"Uh...not quite..."

"My brooding disposition?"

"Um...not exactly..."

"Then I don't get it," Jude stated quizzically. She leaned over the side of the bed and retrieved a paperback book from the bottom shelf of the nightstand. Holding up a copy of *Love's Fevered Embrace*, she displayed it before a suddenly blushing Liz. "I read this, and the jewel-thief hero from the wrong side of the tracks had all of those characteristics. It's what drew Elana to him at first and made her want to help him redeem his thieving ways."

Liz buried her face in the cool material of Jude's blue T-shirt and tried to hide there. "I can't believe you read one of them," she moaned, feeling Jude's chest underneath her rumble in laughter. "Where on earth did you find that?" Green eyes peeked hesitantly up at her lover, who was thumbing through the book with an amused gleam in her eyes.

"Believe me, it wasn't hard," Jude assured her. "But I thought the clerk's eyes at the bookstore were going to fall out."

"Why?" Liz frowned. "The book isn't *that* bad."

Jude snickered. "No, it's not....But let's just say I've been going there for almost five years and this is a little...far afield...of my usual reading habits. He was slightly surprised when I bought four romance novels."

"You got them all?" Liz asked, incredulous.

"Sure did," Jude smiled smugly. "I've only had time to read this one, though. But there's something I don't get." Her smiled faded slightly. "The latest publication date is a little over five years ago. Why haven't you published anything since? The guy in the bookstore said that these still sold well, even after all this time."

Liz's heart began a cacophonous hammering inside her rib cage that she desperately hoped wasn't audible to the dark woman. She shifted away from Jude's embrace, but her lover's long arms gently imprisoned her.

"Hey..." Jude could easily see the panicked look in the green eyes and the sudden paleness that washed over Liz's beautiful features. "Whatever it is...it can't be that bad."

"You have no idea," Liz murmured, well aware that the truth would, at best, exile her from Jude's life forever. Willingly walking out of this woman's life was just no longer an option for her. She would have to think of something else.

"Look...Elizabeth...look at me," Jude insisted, an elegant finger catching her under the chin and holding her there. "I know what you told me when I asked you to stay here...but I also know...there's something... else. I mean...I'm not stupid. I've noticed that you haven't been in any hurry to get home."

Liz hadn't thought her heart could pound any faster, but at Jude's words, it did—so much so that she thought the muscle would burst.

"I guess I just figured you were...sort of running away from home or... I don't know," Jude continued, brushing a tentative hand over Liz's cheeks. "A husband...girlfriend...something you wanted to get away from." She shrugged lightly. "Maybe just a life that didn't fit you anymore. And somebody like me...well, I'm a good place to hide out for a little while."

Those blue eyes were gazing at her with an impossibly tender expression, and Liz wanted to cry out at the openness in that glance and the lies with which she was answering it. Her tongue, however, remained firmly lodged at the back of her painfully dry throat, unable to say a word. If there were any time to tell Jude the truth it was now...but Liz couldn't bear to add one more betrayal and loss to the agonizing list that Jude had already suffered.

She realized with a start that Jude wasn't too far from the truth. This whole escapade had stopped being about a story almost from the first moment she had met Jude Lucien. It had become instead this amazing voyage where she learned not just about the extraordinary woman lying beside her, but most surprisingly, about herself.

In a manner of speaking, she *was* running away from a life that didn't fit—one that never had and never would. Although she had moved from Arlington to Miami ostensibly so that she could live her own life, Liz never truly had done that. In the almost two years she had been down here, she hadn't taken a lover, hadn't really dated anyone, and only occasionally socialized with her office companions on the softball field or at the local pub. She had no close friends who would ask uncomfortable questions that she didn't want to answer, and she had become adept at organizing her life within the narrow boundaries of what would appear acceptable. As a result, her life had come down to her career—first, last, and only. No wonder she had become so obsessed with Jude—someone who had made a life out of not stopping at any boundary.

"I—I—" Much to her consternation, tears began to fill her eyes. She angrily tried to blink them away before Jude could see them. It was too late as a long finger caught the single drop that slipped from her eyes.

"Shh..." Jude comforted. "We don't have to talk about it now. God knows I have enough secrets myself. I just...I wanted you to know... that it was okay. I mean..." Pulling the smaller woman tightly to her and brushing a kiss across the pale hair, she released a heavy sigh, fighting for words. "I want you to know that...if you want...you can stick around as long as you need to...as long as you like." Another agonizingly long pause, and Liz could hear the rapid hammering of Jude's heart. "I'd...I'd like that."

For an eternal moment, Liz allowed herself to relax fully into the strength of that embrace, into the hesitantly loving words that flowed past her ears and sank into her heart. Jude's arms were warm and supple around her, and her hands stroked gentle caresses up and down the length of Liz's bare back, pleasantly raising tiny goose bumps in their wake. Kissing the cloth-covered surface over Jude's heart, she nuzzled a moment more and then brought her eyes back to Jude's, a clouded expression marring their green luminance. "What do you mean 'somebody like you is a good place to hide out?'" she demanded softly.

A familiar, faint telltale flush warmed Jude's bronze features. "I just meant—" She glanced at their embrace and the room that surrounded them, "I suspect that this is about as far from your regular life as you can get."

"I admit that getting shot isn't on my list of daily activities," Liz conceded wryly.

A tiny smile quirked at the corners of Jude's mouth. "I hope not. But—"

Suddenly understanding what her lover was struggling to say, Liz placed slim fingers over Jude's lips. "But nothing. I'm not here to gain *perspective* about my life. I didn't make love with you to explore my *options*." A wave of fear and anger washed through Liz's veins, and she ached to release all of her secrets to this woman. Looking into the astonished blue of Jude's eyes, she grimly determined that if she couldn't tell Jude the complete truth about the reason why she came into the mercurial woman's life, then by God she could at least be honest about her reasons for wanting to stay there. "Jude..." Loving the hard edge of the woman's name rolling off her tongue. "Jude..." she repeated, helpless to convey the force of desire, fascination, and tenderness that combined to form the tinder for the unmistakable kindling of love in her soul.

Blindly, her mouth sought Jude's, lips and tongue tracing the emotions that, for once, her words were inadequate to express. A moan rose deep in her throat, and she tangled her hands in Jude's raven locks, drawing her still closer, as if to pull the dark woman into her heart and show her its contents. Jude struggled briefly against the force of Liz's desire, but only long enough to slip her shirt off and offer the honey-haired woman unimpeded access to her skin. "Oh yes..." Liz murmured, dipping her tongue in the graceful hollow of her lover's throat. Jude still tasted of their sweat and the first mingling of their sex, of desires long forbidden and passions unexplored, and Liz felt a ravenous need seize her— a burning to know this woman inside and out and to end her own self-imposed exile from wanting things they had told her she couldn't have.

🗋 🗋 🗋

Jude saw the feverish glint in those malachite eyes, and an answering need rose inside her. Deftly, she flipped the pair over, so Liz's supple length was stretched out beneath hers. Liz groaned in protest, but Jude soothed her with expert hands roving over her glistening skin. "Please..." Jude whispered hoarsely, her own ache almost overwhelming her. She had been able to subdue the growing need in her mind and body for this slender woman by convincing herself that she could only be a transitory lover for Liz. She was convinced the small woman would never trust someone so completely consumed by violence. Liz's words, however, and the undeniable emotion splashed across her green eyes told Jude that she wasn't alone in these unfamiliar depths. Each surrender Jude had made these last two weeks—each inroad into her own troubled heart she had been helpless to prevent—had been leading her to this place where

Liz laid down her own fears and surrendered fully into the dark woman's embrace. "Please...." she repeated, her own voice sounding unfamiliar to her ears. "Let me take you..."

It was more than a request to lay her hands on the small woman's body. That she had already done a dozen times in the single day they had been lovers. This was a plea to lay claim to Elizabeth's soul with her own; an admission of need, of want, of birthing love. It was humming through her body, visible in her eyes and the quiet trembling of her hands.

A single word, a searing look that left no doubts that they were both stepping off this precipice together.

"Yes."

Jude slowly pulled herself back from their embrace, drawing herself up on her knees and gazing at Liz's glorious body, a look of reverent awe flooding the blue plains of her eyes. Then she knelt joyously to her task— at once the lover and the beloved, the supplicant and the goddess, in the intimate joining about to take place.

Could it be possible that the world does move for two people when they make love? Logic dictates the impossibility of such a tilting of the earth's axis no matter what the cause. But as Jude's mouth moved over Liz's skin in burning consummation of things as yet unsaid, the dark woman felt her existence turn itself inside out—discarding the life she had been subsisting on to make room for one in which she really lived.

Liz's legs wrapped themselves around Jude's waist, grinding her aroused center against the hard length of the dark woman's torso. "Jude..." she groaned.

Hearing the desperate plea in her lover's voice, Jude slipped her hands under the small of Liz's back and pulled her into a fierce embrace, whispering quiet reassurances in her ear. "I got you, Liz. I got you. Shh..."

Liz's arms slid around Jude's neck, her lips seeking and finding a gentle assurance in an embrace of their own. "I know," the small woman affirmed quietly.

Jude lowered their bodies once more to the soft mattress, reveling in the feel of their limbs intertwining. Long, slow moments slipped away as their mouths explored each other's skin, nipping and tasting. Jude kissed a line down Liz's neck and shoulders, lingering in the beautiful smoothness of her lover's skin. She cupped Liz's breasts in tender hands, running her thumbs along the aroused tips. Liz moaned softly in pleasure, arching her back, offering more skin for Jude's knowing touch.

Jude's hands, fingers, tongue, mouth, body were all at the service of reaching inside and making a gift of everything she felt for this remarkable woman. She guided Liz's desire through an ever-intensifying spiral until the honey-haired woman came shuddering against her, calling out Jude's name in a raw voice.

And the sun stretched out long tentacles of light towards them, placing its dappled benediction on their glimmering forms as they lay in each other's arms.

❑ ❑ ❑

"Your right ear is double-pierced," Liz accused, peering at the offending lobe.

A lazy eye opened, regarding the woman sprawled across her chest. "Yeah? So?"

"I never noticed that." Pale brows furrowed. She shifted her position on Jude's stomach, ostentatiously ignoring the dramatic "...Oof..." from her partner as she moved, and inspected Jude's left ear. "This one's not."

"Very observant," Jude teased. "OW!" She flinched as Liz dug an elbow into her side.

"You deserved it," Liz admonished, resettling herself comfortably on her lover.

"*Hhrmphf...*" Jude snorted. "I noticed right away that both your ears were double-pierced," she pronounced smugly.

"Gee, Colombo, what gave me away?" Liz mocked. "Could it have been the fact that I had earrings on at the time?"

"Well...uh...Okay, you nailed me," Jude admitted sheepishly, a grin on her face. "I like those little diamond studs on you. They're kinda sexy."

"You think?"

A wolfish smile answered her. "Oh yeah." She leaned forward and nipped an earlobe in question, then lingered a little while longer in quiet examination of the soft skin of Liz's neck.

Morning had long ago given away to afternoon, and Jude knew that she was only postponing the inevitable conversation they would have to have about what had happened to Jude at the boathouse, and where they would go—if indeed they could go anywhere—from this warm place that now sheltered them.

"So why don't you wear one?" Liz managed to ask as Jude's tongue sent delicious skitters coursing down her spine.

"One what?" Jude murmured, having lost complete track of the conversation.

In reply, Liz captured Jude's face in her hands and affixed the dark woman with a stern look.

"Oh, that." Jude fingered her earlobe absently. "I got it pierced when I was sixteen. Kind of a gang thing. It was stupid. I was stupid."

"Gang?" Liz shook her head in disbelief. "Just how rowdy were you growing up?"

The dark woman arched a sardonic brow. "You really wanna know?"

They laughed softly together for a moment, just relishing the closeness of their bodies and the pleasant lethargy invading their limbs.

"So..." A mischievous look danced in Liz's green eyes. "Was that when you got this too?" She stroked the delicate lines of the tattoo on Jude's right hip.

Jude's pulse quickened as the gentle touch threatened to rouse her somnolent desire once more. She glanced at the mark that had become such a part of her body she no longer noticed it any more. "No...that was something that happened...much later." Seeing the question in Liz's eyes, she demurred. "It's a long story. I'll tell you that one another time. Okay?"

"Deal," Liz agreed, acquiescing to the shadows flickering in Jude's pale eyes.

The pair exchanged tranquil kisses with now-familiar lips, content just to maintain contact with one another.

"You know," Jude murmured, "We are going to have to get out of bed eventually."

Liz groaned and buried her face in Jude's neck in response.

"Come on," Jude coaxed. "You going to tell me that you aren't hungry?"

"Only for this...." she nuzzled Jude's collarbone and ran a teasing hand over one of the dark woman's breasts, the nipple tightening immediately under her palm.

Jude sucked in a sharp breath at the fleeting touch. "Tease..." she grumbled. "Why do I have a feeling that if I'm going to keep up with this insatiable beast, I'm gonna have to eat?" She took another look at the sparkling eyes of her lover and added, "Lots."

⌐ ⌐ ⌐

Despite Liz's evasive tactics—which included pinning the tall woman flat on her back and tormenting her unmercifully with her fingers and hands—the pair finally made it downstairs to the kitchen where they discovered Carmina had created and left a veritable banquet in the refrigerator for the new couple.

"I gave her the day off," was Jude's comment when she saw Liz looking around for the rotund housekeeper.

"That was nice."

"Nice hell," Jude growled. "I just didn't want her to hear us," she laughed. "Besides, I can only imagine her response if you hadn't let me put some clothes on." She rolled her eyes, glancing down the length of her tanned body. "Not that this really counts."

At her lover's request, Jude was wearing the white top of her bikini and a silk wrap that Liz had tied like a sarong low on the dark woman's hips, leaving a wide expanse of smooth torso exposed for her own personal viewing pleasure. Liz was wearing a green two-piece that Jude had picked out on her initial shopping foray for the small woman, with yet another of Jude's shirt's over it. The dark woman grinned at the graceful shape of Liz's pale form moving proprietarily around the kitchen. "What are you doing?" she asked, poking her head over her lover's shoulder.

"Fixing us a tray for the deck. You go on out, I'll follow you in a minute." She slapped Jude's roving hands away from her ticklish ribs. "I thought you were hungry."

"I am," Jude grinned, "For this..." She gently lobbed Liz's own words back at her and slid her hands over the curve of the small woman's hips.

"OUT!" Liz commanded, whirling around in Jude's arms, a wide smile on her face. "Or we'll end up doing something on the kitchen table that will really embarrass Carmina." She kissed the tall woman soundly and shooed her out of the kitchen doors.

Moments later she heard the relaxed sound of Cassandra Wilson's voice flowing through the stereo speakers. The whir of the blender coming from the open deck doors told her that Jude had taken bar patrol, and she grinned in anticipation of the smooth daiquiris that awaited her. "Oh, this is turning out so well," she murmured gleefully. The click of toenails on tile alerted her to a canine presence, and she glanced down to see Pete's baleful eyes peering back at her. "What's up, buddy? You feeling left out?" The diminutive beast fanned his tail at her, and Liz tossed him a piece of steak from the fajitas she was making. "Now don't tell anyone I did that," she warned while the dog wolfed down the morsel. He wagged his tail again, but Liz shook her head at him gravely. "Don't push it," she said, shaking a finger at him. Pete sneezed in reply and trotted back out to the deck where his mistress was waiting.

"Sure," Liz grumbled. "Complain to the management." Expertly she slid the re-heated food out of the oven and arranged it on the tray Jude had obligingly retrieved from an impossibly high shelf. "Coming through..." she sang out loud, carrying the tray through the main room and out onto the deck.

A loud splash drew her attention to the pool as she sat the tray on the high bar, away from the prowling teeth of the menagerie. Jude had shed her sarong and top and was cutting a smooth line through the length of the pool. She emerged at the end of the pool closest to Liz, wringing the excess water from her inky hair. "God that feels good..." she groaned in bliss.

Liz had been paralyzed by the magnificent vision of her lover moving effortlessly through the water, and the rivulets of moisture running off Jude's tanned skin made her throat drier than she ever thought possible. She opened her mouth, but nothing came out; and she just looked helplessly at Jude's powerful form, wishing something... anything would be adequate to describe what the mere sight of this woman did to her.

"Elizabeth?" Jude's brows furrowed when she saw the expression on the honey-haired woman's face. "Liz?" She strode quickly over to her lover, cupping the pale face gently in her hands. "Are you all right?"

The sensation of Jude's water-cooled palms on her heated skin brought Liz's scattered senses back to her. "Yeah," she said, blushing furiously. "I just..." she smiled warmly. "You just looked so beautiful. Sometimes, when I look at you..." she confessed softly, "I can't breathe." She leaned up on tiptoe and captured Jude's lips with her own, rendering a sweet kiss in exchange for the exquisite gift of Jude's beauty.

Now it was Jude's turn to blush, the bronze features darkening only slightly. "Oh...I...Umm...Thank you," she finally finished, laughing with Liz at their own bashfulness. "We are a pair, aren't we?" she asked, picking up the sarong and positioning it around her hips. A quirked brow mutely asked the question, and Liz skillfully retied the knot. When Jude bent to retrieve her top, Liz put a restraining hand over the graceful fingers.

"Leave it," she requested softly. Then added, "Please?"

Jude inclined her head in acknowledgment, a sensual smile curving her features. In exchange, she slipped the shirt from Liz's shoulders and tossed it across the back of the chaise. "You ready for lunch?" she asked, peering around the small woman's shoulders to the tray behind her.

"Absolutely."

They ate as new lovers often do, curled around each other in one of the sinfully comfortable chaises, sharing tidbits and morsels. Although it seemed that they consumed more kisses than food, eventually the tray was emptied and the blender was dangerously low. Jude unfurled her length from its position and carried the tray back to its resting spot on the bar. She raised the empty blender and grinned at Liz's enthusiastic nod.

"You are a hell of a bartender, Jude. I'll give you that."

"Why thank you, ma'am." Jude tipped an imaginary hat. "It'll be nice to have a trade to fall back on when I give up my murderous ways."

Although the words were teasing and light, a glimmer in Jude's pale eyes made Liz sit up and study her companion more closely. "You're not kidding, are you?" she asked after a long moment of contemplation.

❑   ❑   ❑

Jude stared at the softly whirring blender before turning her gaze to Liz's. "It's something...I've been working on for a while now," she admitted. Pouring their drinks and returning to Liz's side, she grinned, nudging Liz's bent knee. "And besides, a murderous Drug Lord isn't exactly the kind of girl you take home to meet Mom and Dad, now is she?" she added lightly, not wanting to go into the details of her plans for Massala. The truth had simply fallen out of her mouth just now, and what she wanted was suddenly so crystal clear it was painful. And that meant ending this nightmare existence and beginning a life lived in the light inside of the shadows. Jude had no way of knowing if she stood even the slightest chance of succeeding; but after yesterday and this morning, she knew beyond any doubt that she wanted to try. "What do you think?" she inquired, sitting their drinks on the table beside the chaise and looking down at the silent form on the chaise.

"I think if I had a family that was worthy of meeting you, I'd take you there right now," Liz replied softly, a brilliant radiance seeming to pour from the golden flecks in her green eyes. Jude hesitated before the unfamiliar glint in her lover's eyes, but the honey-haired woman drew her closer. Her hands ran along the powerful length of Jude's thighs, slipping easily under the smooth silk. She slid a knee between Jude's legs, gently nudging them a little further apart. "There, that's it..." she murmured, as her fingers continued to wreak havoc along the defined muscles.

"Wha—" Jude cleared her throat, suddenly wondering where her voice had gone. "What are you doing?"

"I'm showing you how I feel." Smoky jade eyes glinted back at her. "I'm generally a talker." They exchanged grins. "You know that." Sitting up, she trailed the tip of her tongue along the edge of the low-slung sarong, relishing the ripple of stomach muscles under her touch. "But...you're changing your life...a part of the reason is to show me how you feel..." A wet kiss tormented the sensitive flesh just above Jude's hipbone, and involuntarily, the dark woman sucked in her breath at the sensation. "And I'd like to return the favor. Is that okay?" She grinned wickedly.

"Oh yyesss...." Jude hissed as Liz's fingers briefly teased the apex of the dark woman's desire to punctuate her question.

"Good," she murmured. "Lift your leg, sweetheart. That's it..." Guiding Jude's leg so that it balanced comfortably on the chaise's soft cushion, she smiled at the enticing portrait her lover made. The silk of the sarong fell open to display just a hint of the tantalizing secrets of Jude's arousal, and its white color contrasted erotically with the even bronze of Jude's tan. "You are so beautiful," she whispered, littering the inside of Jude's upraised thigh with dozens of kisses, each one slightly more intense than the last. When her teeth nipped the juncture that connected Jude's leg and abdomen, and the dark woman couldn't stop the groan slipping free from her throat. She could smell the beginnings of her own arousal, and although she longed to simply give way to the desire she felt—Jude held back, knowing her smaller lover wanted to take her on this journey.

Small hands slipped outside the silk again as Liz's mouth teased at the curly hairs protecting her lover's core. Jude felt Liz's fingers flicker over the knot of her sarong. Expecting the cloth to fall away, she looked down at her lover in surprise when it remained in place. "I like the way it feels," Liz murmured softly, with a teasing shrug. The wandering hands strayed still upwards, her fingers finding already taut nipples waiting for her attention. Another throaty growl and Jude's hips were starting a slow grind towards Liz's mouth, a wordless plea to continue.

Gliding her hands back down the length of Jude's body, she slipped them beneath the silk's surface and gently parted the glimmering folds of her lover's nether lips. A strangled groan rumbled low in Jude's throat, and she threaded trembling fingers in Liz's fiery hair. A long stroke of Liz's tongue dipped directly into the core of her desire, tasting the roiling wetness there. Jude threw her head back, closing her eyes against the sun's rays, uncertain of which heat was greater—the one beating down on her or the one rising from deep inside. She groaned again as her lover's tongue delved far within her center, seeking and finding an intense, unrelenting rhythm.

Liz's hands moved to steady the dark woman's shuddering body, clasping Jude's hips, and a lengthy moan simmered in the small woman's throat, evidence of how deeply she was enjoying her task. The sound of Liz taking her pleasure from this intimate act drove Jude to the edge, and when she felt Liz's fingers join her tongue in their leisurely exploration, she plummeted over, free falling in a whorl of sensations that emanated out from her convulsing core.

Her hands gripped Liz's shoulders now, her nails unknowingly digging into the flesh as she leaned forward, bracing her weight against the rock-steady feel of her lover. Soothing arms encircled her waist, drawing her down until she straddled an unrepentantly grinning Liz. "Oh god..." Jude breathed again, burying her face in Liz's neck and letting the pulsing in her loins overwhelm her. "Where did that come from?" she asked, missing her lover's smug gaze and the puckish light shinning in her eyes.

"Call it an overwhelming urge." Her hands never stopped roaming down Jude's back, over her shoulders, circling around to tease Jude's breasts.

"Works for me," Jude muttered, her back arching involuntarily into the caresses.

They rested in a sensual daze for a short while, before Jude reluctantly lifted herself. "I must be crushing you."

"Nope," Liz wrapped her arms around the larger woman to keep her from moving. "I like you here."

"How about a compromise?" Jude offered. "We take the cushions from those these two chaises, toss them in that shady corner there, and settle in with our drinks." She glanced at the sun, then at her lover's pale skin. "I'm afraid you'll get cooked otherwise."

Liz pursed her lips as if in deep thought. "Okay, works for me."

She gathered their supplies while Jude made a comfortable nest of the pillows, grinning when Jude sprawled lazily across them, a teasing smile on her face.

"Wish I had a camera," Liz bantered. It was an honest wish to freeze this moment and capture how completely full she felt at this instant in her life. Jude had literally added a new dimension to her existence...one where joy was possible.

"You do?" A doubtful brow was arched in her direction. "You want a picture of me? Like this?" Now the other brow joined its partner in dubiousness.

Liz paused for an instant, thinking that this impulse—to freeze, to document, to record—had been her very essence for far too long. And it had kept her from living in those moments that she so diligently reported. Everything about Jude was about the moment...she held nothing back, reserved nothing for a mythological rainy day. Trying to capture this woman's wild essence would be the same as trying to kill her. "Nah..." Liz waved her wish away with a careless hand. "I like real-time better." She sat the drinks and leftover nachos carefully out of the line of any potentially out-flung limb, and settled herself comfortably against her lover's body. "Ooh...this is nice," she grinned.

"Thought you might like it."

The view offered from their position was of the ocean rushing along the shore. An unbelievably blue sky—*almost as blue as her eyes...*Liz thought silently—stretched out across the horizon, and seagulls dotted the air and broke the silence with their calls. Aggie and Clytemnestra bounded along the sand, chasing each other with abandon, while Pete gamboled valiantly behind, trying to keep up with the bigger dogs. It could have been a scene from a movie or one of her books, but— Liz mused with awed wonder—*this is real...this is my life.* It certainly didn't erase the million and one problems that readily leapt to mind when she contemplated a relationship with the complicated woman holding her *...but, it does make me realize what we could have....* Her thoughts trailed into the darkness that surrounded her lover, and she knew it was time to ask more questions.

She twisted her body around so they were face to face. Jude looked into the solemn green gazing back out at her and asked, "You're going to get serious now, aren't you?"

Liz flushed a little and nodded ruefully. "I was thinking...wondering, really...Jude..." She fidgeted with a lock of dark hair, took a deep breath and exhaled heavily. "What happened after Jason's death?"

Jude was silent for a long while...long enough so that Liz thought she would just refuse to answer. But, finally, she pressed a gentle kiss on Liz's head and sighed. "It hurt so bad, Elizabeth...I thought...I wished...I wanted to just lie down there beside him and die too. Rico said he'd have his boys take care of the body, but I knew they'd dump it someplace and we'd never find him. I...I couldn't do that to Maria." She pressed a spot on the bridge of her nose and rubbed her eyes wearily. "So, I took him... I gathered him up in my arms...He was so light, Elizabeth....Like a little kid...and I tried not to jostle him too much... I had to... put him in my trunk...because Rico and the others were watching....He was so bruised... I couldn't look at his face...His beautiful face...Oh god...It was gone..." Tears that she had never shed for her lost soulmate now flooded her eyes, and she let them fall, unashamed at the ragged tear in her voice, at the agony visible in her face.

Liz's heart twisted at the pain her lover was feeling; and she wrapped her arms tighter around Jude, sitting up slightly, so that their bodies cradled each other's as they talked. "You don't—"

"No...this is okay...it's...good, I think..." Jude took a steadying breath and smiled shakily as Liz wiped the tears from her face. "I've never—"

"You never cried for him," Liz guessed.

"I've never really...talked about him," Jude admitted. "Maria used to try and get me too...but..."

"I'm sorry, Jude." Liz wanted to kick herself. *Of course Jude had never cried for him.* "I shouldn't have pushed—"

"You didn't." Jude ran a lingering hand down her lover's face. "I don't know why it all just...came out..." She shrugged softly. "I guess it was just time." They locked eyes for a moment, then Jude—much to the reporter's astonishment—dropped her gaze, blushing. "That's...that's not true," she confessed. "I do know why."

"Tell me."

Jude smiled unsteadily. "You," she replied. "Some part of me...just... feels safe with you. That it's okay to tell you. You'll understand."

Liz was floored by the quiet admission and gave silent thanks that she was already sitting on the floor. Otherwise, she was certain, she would have fallen down. "And...you're okay with this?"

Jude nodded, "Yeah," she answered unhesitatingly. "I am. For the first time in longer than I can remember, I really am." The statement rested quietly between them for a moment before Jude continued. "Anyway...where was I?" She ran a shaking hand through her hair. "I called Kent from my car and told him...that there was a man down. I knew I couldn't take Jason to Maria like he was...and I couldn't bear to let him go...to some hospital...that would mean..."

"I know," Liz soothed.

"As I drove all I could think about was how this had happened... How had they gotten Jason? And then when the Agency swept the investigation under the rug, I knew that somebody had to have been on the inside."

"Someone from the Agency sold him out?" Liz asked, incredulous.

"It happens," Jude shrugged. "More often than you might think. You wouldn't believe the amount of money that goes through that place. Undercover agents have to create the facade of this amazing wealth, all so they can be players in this world. We're driving Ferrari's, 'living' in penthouses, sailing around on boats...and in reality, we don't even own the clothes on our backs. It's hard not to give into that." She glanced around at her beautiful surroundings. "I did."

"Did you give in before or after Jason's death?" Liz asked, an eerie light burning intensely in her eyes.

"Does it matter?"

"It matters."

Jude sighed, shifting her weight against the smaller woman. "After," she quietly replied.

Liz nodded slightly. "I thought so."

"The Agency betrayed Jason, Rico made me kill him...I wanted them both to pay."

"So you turned. Sticking it to the Agency and the Massalas by taking the Cartel over and making it your own." It all made perfect sense to Liz now... the agent-turned-rogue for reasons no one in the press could understand. It wasn't avarice; it wasn't ambition...it was rage, fear, and pain. So many things that seemed incongruous about the dark woman... the flashes of tenderness, the skewed sense of honor—betrayal to such a woman would be the ultimate sin. A tiny shudder ran through Liz at that thought, making her uneasily aware of her own deception.

"You okay?" The tension in Liz's body was too evident to ignore. "I mean...I know this is a lot to take in. Maybe it's too much. I've done some horrible things, and I wouldn't blame you..." She tried to release herself from the strong embrace, but Liz only tightened her hold. "It's probably best if we don't..."

"Whoa! Waitaminute. Where did that come from?" Liz demanded, catching Jude by the cheek and realigning their gazes. "We've covered this—I decide what's worth my time and my worry. And you, lover, definitely are. And let me tell you something else, Jude Lucien, that you don't want to hear. I think you're an amazing, extraordinary, powerful woman. And yes, I know you've got so many kinks in you that it would tie Sigmund Freud up in knots for decades...but you know what? I don't give a damn. I'm willing to work through each and every one of them with you—no matter how long it takes, no matter what it takes. Got that? You want to meet my family...well, guess what, darlin'? I want to meet yours." Jude opened her mouth to speak, but Liz clamped a hand down firmly over it. "Stop—let me finish," she warned. "I don't know how this whole thing got started between us or why, and quite frankly I don't care. Because it is, without a doubt, the best thing that's ever happened to me in my life. Getting shot and all." Liz ran out of breath and wound down, too shocked at her own audacity to note the warmly astonished eyes of her lover. "Now there's only one thing I want to know—and I think I already know the answer—but I want to hear the words." She brushed gentle fingers down the dark woman's cheek. "Do you feel this too?"

This time Jude's eyes didn't turn away, didn't search for something else to look at, didn't flinch at the intensity of Liz's stare. A lazy grin spread over her face. "You want to meet my family, huh?" she asked by way of an answer.

Liz didn't hesitate at the non sequitur, certain that it was ultimately taking her where she wanted to go. "Absolutely," she replied, her grin matching Jude's.

"Then come on, let's go."

Chapter 11

Jude had been unfailingly tight-lipped about where they were going, saying only, "You asked for it." She had been equally resolute in her refusal to share the shower with her lover. Now, as the cool water sluiced over her still-aroused body, Liz privately conceded that showering separately was probably the only chance they would have to make it out of the house this evening. Merely contemplating the combination of pulsing water, soap, and Jude's knowing hands sent another rush of heat pounding through her veins. "Whoa...Nellie..." Liz muttered to herself, twisting the "Cold" dial even higher. Bracing herself under the now-freezing spray, she shook her head furiously to dislodge most of the decadent ideas from her thoughts. "Later, Lizzy...We'll do all that later..." she promised herself as she stepped out of the shower and began toweling off.

Briskly blowing her hair dry, she slipped on the jeans that Carmina had neatly laundered and folded and pulled a T-shirt from the stack in the dresser. She had tugged it over her head when a better idea occurred to her. Tossing the shirt onto the bed, she wandered into Jude's bedroom, a playful grin on her face.

Jude was still in the bathroom—she could hear the whine of the hair dryer and, more faintly, the dark woman's pleasant contralto singing something unidentifiable. The sound brought another smile to Liz's face as she realized that she wasn't the only one affected by the warmth curling in her belly. Spying the half-open closet door, she crossed the room and began rummaging through the rows of hanging shirts.

"Looking for something?" A voice behind her inquired dryly.

The reporter's heart lurched violently at the sound, slamming into her chest and constricting her lungs with fear. Although she had only been caught in the most mundane of activities, she realized that the potential for much worse still existed. "Geeze...knock next time, will you?" she grinned, turning around and hoping that her voice didn't crack.

"You're in my closet," Jude pointed out, a slight edge to her tone. Its harshness sent a chill spreading through her body.

"Well...yeah," Liz glanced around her. "Heh heh...It sure is. I was looking for something to wear." She gestured at her bare torso.

Jude's eyes lazily perused the figure in front of her, a finger reaching out to delicately trace the lacy material that sensually protected the swell of Liz's full breasts. Sucking in her breath sharply at the caress, Liz made a mental note to ask Jude later how she had managed to "guess" so accurately about that particular size. "I dunno," Jude drawled. "I kinda like what you've got on now." Hooking the same finger through the center of Victoria's Secret, she drew Liz out of the closet.

The safe, Liz realized, as a dull gunmetal gray caught the corner of her vision. *She's getting me away from the safe.* Then her mind was silenced by the heated feeling of Jude's palms covering her breasts, and the hungry taste of Jude's mouth descending on her own. Jude kissed her languidly, thoroughly, stroking the sweet fire that the shower had dampened back in Liz's body. The reporter moaned low in her throat, using her own hands to crush Jude's palms harder against her now fully-aroused breasts. "I thought you didn't want us to be late..." Liz managed to gasp when Jude's mouth began to slip southward across her neck.

"Then you shouldn't be torturing me like this," Jude growled, her tongue flickering over the wildly flaring pulse in her lover's neck.

"Ah...oh!..." Liz's arms twined about Jude's neck, absently noting that the dark woman had braided her hair. "Uh...I think...that...OH!...I'm the one...oh god, yes...being tortured here..." She groaned as Jude's teeth teased her painfully-aware nipples through the thin fabric of her brassiere. Jude's hands gripped the thick material of Liz's jeans and tugged the smaller woman closer.

The questing teeth and lips stopped, as Jude buried her head in the softness of the honey-haired woman's chest. "You have no idea of what just looking at you does to me," she said quietly, bringing her eyes up to meet Liz's.

"If it's anything like what looking at you does to me, then I think I've got a pretty good idea," Liz answered wryly.

"You've got a point there," Jude admitted, smirking. "Okay..." she exhaled deeply, running her hands one last time over the strong muscles in Liz's stomach. "Let's get you dressed." She stepped back a pace, folding her arms and appraising her lover. "A shirt, huh?"

"Yup."

"You out of new ones already?"

"Nope."

Dark brows furrowed in an unspoken question.

"I like yours better. They smell like...well...you."

That got her a soft blush from the tall woman who dropped her arms in surrender and motioned Liz to the closet. "Help yourself." She smiled.

Liz padded back over to the closet, noting that Jude made no move to follow her. She tugged a black shirt out and held it in front of her. She glanced questioningly at Jude who shook her head at its darkness against Liz's pale skin. Several other shirts were rejected in this silent exchange until she found a worn, white Oxford that had green stripes running through it. Seeing Jude grin when she held it up, Liz laughed and proclaimed teasingly, "We have a winner, folks!" It was a little smaller than some of the other shirts she had looked at and tucked easily into her jeans. She left it buttoned low, freeing the length of her honeyed hair from the collar. "What do you think?"

"Fabulous," Jude replied with a grin. "I feel like I should change." She looked at her own attire dubiously.

Liz surveyed her lover's dark form leisurely. Jude was wearing a white cotton tank top and faded jeans that clung familiarly to the shape of her powerful legs. Several frayed seams at the pockets and a small tear in the knee told Liz these jeans were old favorites. The reporter most definitely liked this latest incarnation of the dark woman that she was seeing. "You look absolutely beautiful."

Jude snorted derisively. "Not."

"Oh yeah..." Liz disagreed, closing the distance between them. "You look like a perfect little street hooligan—all tight jeans and surly attitude." In her mind's eye she could easily see a younger, even more defiant Jude strutting through Nickie's bar or roaring off on the Triumph, free of her mother's strangling grasp.

A dark brow arched its skepticism. "Nah...real hooligans would wear boots, not Topsiders," she bantered. "I'm not even wearing socks."

She stood only a hairsbreadth away from her lover and could feel deep in her stomach the shimmering connection of arousal that linked her to Jude. Its strength nearly left her breathless, and she marveled at how this woman affected her like nothing she had ever known. "Well, I was going to say that your outfit was missing something...but it's not the boots."

A lazy smirk spread over Jude's face. "Then what is it?"

"This—" Liz reached up and removed the diamond stud from her left ear, deftly slipping it into the empty piercing in Jude's right lobe. "Perfect," she grinned, stepping back to admire her handiwork. "Wait... one more thing." She leaned around her tall lover and freed Jude's dark mane from its confines. "Much better," she muttered, running her fingers through its inky thickness.

Jude patiently allowed herself to be fussed over, an inscrutable look in her eyes. "Finished?" she asked as her lover's ministrations tapered off and became slow caresses instead.

"Never," Liz whispered back, kissing her favorite line down Jude's collarbone.

"You're not making this easy," Jude breathed unevenly, her body responding to the sensual attention.

The kisses abruptly stopped, visibly jerking Jude back from the threshold of a delightfully warm place. She blinked her eyes open to focus on her lover who was chewing her lip thoughtfully, a bare hint of playfulness in her smile. "You're absolutely right." Liz nodded decisively. "What are you waiting for? Come on."

Much to the reporter's surprise, when they reached the kitchen, Jude had whistled for the dogs and told Pete to stay. The small beast yipped pleadingly to be included, casting baleful brown eyes at his mistress.

"Oh, come on, Jude. You can't just leave him here."

Jude cocked an eyebrow at the mutt, who fanned his tail eagerly. "Pete," she warned. "You know they'll just push you around. Remember the last time we went to see Cassandra?"

Clytemnestra woofed approvingly, and Pete's head drooped just a little.

"Uh-huh," Jude nodded. "I don't want them using you as a chew toy again," she said seriously, bending down to scratch a pair of floppy ears. Liz watched the exchange with barely concealed amusement at the earnestness in the dark woman's tone. "Now, if I promise to bring you back a big doggy bag, will you stay?" Pete yipped his agreement. "Good boy." One final scratch and Jude was standing again, rolling her eyes at the snort of laughter that escaped from Liz. "He gets upset if we leave him alone," Jude offered by way of explanation as she opened the Explorer's tailgate to let in the Akitas.

Truthfully, Liz preferred the Explorer to the powerful Porsche that Jude usually drove. The Explorer was comfortably messy, with faint remnants of dog hairs on the carpet, and some camping gear and beach towels jockeying for space in the roomy interior. The Boxster—and even the Jaguar that sat silently in the garage—were too much a part of the mystique that Jude created for people like Romair Massala. Though she knew that both the brooding drug dealer and her laughing, blue-eyed lover were merely different aspects of the whole woman Liz was falling deeply in love with, the reporter couldn't help but wish that Jude could disperse all the shadows that still shrouded her life.

⌐ ⌐ ⌐

The thirty-minute drive passed quickly, and they were soon pulling down a sandy lane that led to a ramshackle-looking restaurant directly on the beach. The sounds of laughter and music carried easily to her from the deck, and she was surprised at the number of cars parked haphazardly in the sand around the building. The dogs pranced excitedly as Jude let them out of the Explorer, but remained obediently at their mistress' side. "Okay, guys," Jude ruffled Aggie's fur. "Go find Cassandra."

The dogs woofed in approval and darted around the width of the building and out of sight. An answering bark told them the dogs had located their quarry. Moments later, Liz saw three white forms racing along the surf.

"Litter mates," Jude supplied.

"Of course—Agamemnon, Clytemnestra, and Cassandra. But wait a minute, didn't they end up killing each other?"

"Actually according to Greek myth, Clytemnestra killed the other two, and then her son killed her," Jude corrected, clasping Liz's smaller hand in her own.

"And you named your dogs after them?" Even as Liz shook her head in disbelief, a delighted smile crept over her face at the unspoken intimacy of Jude's gesture.

"It was Jason's idea," Jude shrugged, remembering the gleam in her partner's eyes as they lit upon the Akita pups squirming around in the wicker basket. He'd decided to get Maria a dog for her birthday because, growing up, she'd never had one. *"All families need dogs, Angel... I told you I was going to have it all—wife, kids, a house—gotta have the dog too.*" Dragging a hungover Jude to the breeder's house, he had talked excitedly about the finer points of the Akita; how loyal they were, how dependable, and how they made great guard dogs. Only listening with half an ear while he and the breeder haggled over the pick of the litter, Jude had sprawled her aching body out next to the basket with three pups. Their antics even brought a hint of a smile to her face as the boldest of the lot wiggled free from her brother and sister and tumbled into the dark woman's lap. Jude hesitantly scratched the pup's ears as the Akita pounced fiercely on Jude's free hand. She had sheepishly looked up to see her partner's amused glance fixed firmly upon her.

"So you got one too, huh?" Liz teased.

"I got two," Jude answered. "I got pounced by Clytemnestra. She was actually the pick of the litter, except Aggie sort of came with her. The breeder said they were inseparable. The couple of times he had tried to wean them away from each other, they both had kicked up such a fuss that it had even scared off some people who wanted to buy Clytemnestra. He didn't want to separate them, but it looked like he wasn't going to have any choice. Jason couldn't take both pups, so that's how he ended up with Cassandra."

"You took the pair so they could be together?"

Jude shrugged nonchalantly but couldn't control the beautiful flush that rose from her throat. "Well...yeah...Aggie just looked so sad sitting in the basket as I played with Clytemnestra. I figured... what the hell, they could keep each other company whenever I was gone."

"That's so sweet." Seeing Jude's scowl, Liz burst into laughter. "Oh come on, Lucien. You are soooo cold busted here....Not that this is telling me anything I didn't already know."

"And what is that?" Jude asked with a barely concealed smirk, drawing them to a halt in front of a worn driftwood sign that read *Barrido del Mar.*

Despite the thousand things she could have said to keep the banter going, Liz opted for a blunt truth that she doubted Jude had ever allowed herself to hear. "You've got a good heart. You just keep it so bricked up inside that icy demeanor so no one—including you—ever gets to see it."

At the tender words, Jude went absolutely still, amazed at how this woman could see through her so easily. It seemed that Elizabeth could see exactly what Jude had been capable of and then unearth the tenderness Jude thought she had buried away deep inside. "C'mere you," the tall woman said, tugging Liz into a fierce embrace. Settling into each other's arms, a tranquil warmth surrounded the pair, rendering them oblivious to the inquiring looks of the patrons passing in and out of the restaurant's doors.

A deep sigh ran through Jude's body as she whispered softly, "There's no way I could ever deserve the look that's in your eyes right now, so I'm just gonna thank whatever's up there that you're here with me."

Liz smiled and painted a gentle kiss across her lover's cheek. "You're wrong..." She drew Jude's head back so their eyes met. "You do deserve this. And so much more."

Their lips tangled again, a tender exchange that was a promise for this night and more to come. A low gurgle from Liz's stomach startled them apart. "Talk about a mood killer." Jude rolled her eyes.

"Hey!" The smaller woman backhanded Jude's own flat abdomen playfully. "Can I help it if you made me work up an appetite?"

"Oh, all this is my fault, huh?"

"Abso-freakin-lutely!" Liz declared. "That's my story and I'm sticking to it."

Jude laughed at the sheer joy of being in the aureate presence of the smaller woman. Without even realizing it, Liz lulled to sleep the demons who held the dark woman's soul in their grasp and showed Jude a fleeting glimpse of what her life might have been without the Agency or all the memories that scarred her sleep. The glorious sight filled the ex-agent with a burning need to feel more, and she knew without a doubt that Elizabeth Peterson was a drug more addictive than any she had ever sold. The mere idea of trying to wean herself from the small time of grace that Liz brought to her was abhorrent, and a shudder ran through her body at the concept.

"You okay?" The movement hadn't escaped the woman still resting in her arms.

"Abso-freakin-lutely," Jude echoed teasingly. "I seem to have quite an appetite myself."

⬛ ⬛ ⬛

Liz turned in the circle of their embrace so that now one of Jude's arms was draped casually across her shoulders. As far as the reporter was concerned, it was going to stay there all night—appearances be damned. She was in the company of the most beautiful, fascinating, erotic woman she had ever known; and quite frankly, Liz didn't give a good goddamn who knew it. *Mother would have a fit...Father would go into cardiac arrest.* The vision of her parents' dismayed faces brought a fiendish grin to her face, and she allowed herself a tiny chuckle at their expense.

The pair began making their way up to the wooden stairs to the main entrance when the driftwood sign caught her eye. "Barrido del mar? Swept from the sea?" she asked.

"Yep," Jude nodded. "The story goes that hundreds of years ago there was a pirate ship that wrecked here, and the loot is still buried somewhere under the dunes. The sign is supposed to be from the original ship itself."

Liz looked at the wood dubiously. "So what do they serve here?"

"Stale bread and grog," Jude answered easily, walking them up the stairs.

Liz's stomach rumbled ominously. "You better hope not," she muttered.

Ignoring her lover's frowning countenance, Jude stopped at the maitre d' stand and addressed a handsome young man clad in a gray T-shirt and comfortable-looking jeans. "Marco," she nodded with a smile. "Como estas?"

Okay...we've obviously been here before, Liz thought silently.

The youth looked delighted to see Jude, grinning broadly. "Estoy muy bein, Senora Lucien. Gracias." He flicked a look between the two women. "Table for two tonight?"

Jude nodded. "Sí. Maria around?"

The boy opened his mouth to reply, but a voice behind the women interrupted. "Of course I'm around. Aren't I around every night? Of course if you showed your face around here more than once in a blue moon, you'd probably know that." Liz turned around to see the speaker was a petite Latina with laughing eyes and a dark cascade of hair falling around her shoulders. She was dressed casually in dusky blue slacks and a cream-colored, short-sleeved blouse that set off the tawny highlights of her skin. Jude was already moving towards the tiny woman, lifting her in a huge embrace and spinning her around lightly in the foyer. "Put me down!" Maria protested half-heartedly.

Jude deposited her softly on her feet, delighted to see her friend. "I'm sorry I've been neglectful...but things..."

"Have been busy. Yeah yeah yeah..." Maria waved her excuses away. "Same story, different day. Kent mentioned you might show up this week, but I wasn't holding my breath," she said wryly. Liz noted that the banter seemed familiar to the women; as if it were an old story, and the reproaches were more a matter of teasing routine than genuine hurt. At any rate, they looked positively ecstatic to see each other again, and vaguely the reporter wondered if she should be jealous of their obvious closeness.

"When you least expect me, there I am," Jude shrugged sheepishly.

"Yes, here you are. And your manners are just as atrocious as ever." She poked Jude firmly in the arm and stepped around her tall form, looking pointedly at Liz. "Are you going to introduce us?" She glanced back at Jude and studied her appraisingly. "How many years have I known you— six, seven?—and you've never brought anyone here to meet me. Now that you finally do— you forget to introduce us."

Jude opened her mouth—perhaps to argue that Maria hadn't exactly given her a chance—but she was interrupted again.

"How do you do?" She held out a hand to an astonished Liz who was rapidly putting the pieces together. "I'm Maria."

Jason's Maria...oh Jesus...

She shook the proffered hand numbly, her thoughts a tumultuous snarl as she glanced at the wide smile on her lover's face. The disarming openness in Jude's gaze expression reached into Liz's heart and wrenched it violently in a bolt of pain-pleasure that made the smaller woman want to cry out for mercy. "Hi, I'm Liz." Aware that Maria's speculative gaze hadn't missed the stunned expression on her face, Liz quickly recovered her composure. "When Jude said she was taking me to meet her family, I thought she was kidding. I'm glad to have the chance to meet you," she said, relieved that the surprise had now visibly shifted to the woman in front of her.

Maria turned to look at Jude who remained where she was, an amused glimmer in her eyes. "Kent said something about you having a date the other night." She grinned at the dark woman. "I should have known there was more to it than that."

Jude grinned and stood between the two women, encircling each with an arm. "You should know that there's always more to it with me."

"That's the understatement of the century," Liz muttered teasingly.

Maria chuckled at Jude's indignant eyebrow, "This one seems to have your number."

Jude conceded with a graceful lift of her shoulders. She glanced down to find warm green eyes looking back at her and winked. "I think you're right, 'Ria."

As the trio strolled through the restaurant, Liz noted the relaxed faces of the patrons and enjoyed the delicious smells from the various dishes. The dining room was a little more subdued than the raucous terrace where the band, dance floor, and serious bar were located. The crowd out here was younger, but just as casually upscale as those in the main room. Several couples danced to a band that seemed to be playing mostly recognizable covers. "They're pretty good." Liz nodded at the quartet of musicians.

"They've been the house band here for about a year and half," Maria replied. Then, looking mischievously at Jude, she added, "Maybe if you ask Jude really nicely, she'll sit in with them tonight." Seeing Jude's eyes narrow and her brows furrow menacingly, she slipped out from under the tall woman's arm. "Oh look, there's Kent and Tony. Why don't you join them and I'll come over in a little while?" Throwing one last puckish glance at her friend, she scurried back to the kitchen.

Jude growled something incomprehensible and turned to look at her companion, who was regarding her appraisingly. "Oh no...no, no, no, no..." She shook her head emphatically. "Not tonight..." Seeing that Liz's expression hadn't changed, her shoulders dropped slightly. "Maybe later, okay?" she hedged. Liz remained studying her, unblinking. "Oh, Jesus, can I have a drink first?" Admitting at last that she was beaten.

"Sure," Liz agreed cheerfully now that the matter was settled. "You can even have two or three."

"Gee, thanks," Jude muttered, steering her companion over to the corner table where Kent and his partner, Tony, sat. "Hey, you boys waiting for someone in particular, or can just anybody sit here?" She grinned down at the shocked faces of the two men.

"Jude!" Tony called heartily. "It's been too long, lady."

"Who're you calling lady?" Jude growled.

"You're too good-looking to be a man, so I must be talking to you," he shot back.

Smiling slightly the dark woman only shook her head and pulled out a chair for Liz. Collapsing into the one beside her lover, she grinned. "I guess you're right. You're not too bad yourself, T. For a man, that is."

"Thank you, I think." During the short exchange, Liz had been studying the two men intently. Kent, she realized from her unauthorized snooping, was Jude's DEA contact, a former partner from what she was coming to think of as Jude's Bad Old Days. She had no idea who the other man was and took in his features with a nonchalant expression. He was a compact, well-muscled man, with dark chocolate eyes, close-cropped black curly hair, and deep bronze skin that was set off by the pale pink of his Polo shirt. "And who do we have here?" Liz realized with a flush that three pairs of eyes were on her, waiting for a response.

Jude picked up the conversational ball smoothly. "This is Elizabeth Peterson...Elizabeth, this is Tony Pinichero and Kent Laird. Be careful, Tony's Italian and thinks this makes him some kind of Great Lover by default. And Kent...he's as straight an arrow as they come. Took me three years just to get a beer down his throat."

"And look at me now," he remarked wryly, gesturing with the glass in his hand.

"You just needed somebody to knock you out of that Puritan work ethic thing you had going," Jude teased.

"Didn't work," Tony replied. "He still nags me about dotting every '*i*' and crossing every '*t*.'"

"Do you two work together?" Liz asked, an innocent tone in her voice. She was curious about how Jude would explain them.

"They're partners at the Agency," Jude answered easily, noting with a smirk Kent and Tony's stunned expressions. "When I was carrying a badge, I didn't want anyone else at my back."

It was a simple declaration, Liz mused, but one that carried such importance—because by laying bare her connection to the men, Jude told her friends that she was someone they could trust. The reporter was astonished by the admittance that Jude was granting her into this dark part of her life, and it resolved her to start clearing out the serpent's nest of lies that still rested between them. Liz gently clasped Jude's hand as it rested on the arm of her chair, entwining their fingers. She smiled back at Tony, who was grinning foolishly at them. Kent's face was shuttered, but the reporter thought she detected the faint hint of a scowl quickly concealed. Any further contemplation of the man opposite her was interrupted by Tony's rich baritone.

"So how did a nice girl like you hook up with a sullen wench like Jude?"

Jude and Liz exchanged glances, bursting into laughter simultaneously.

"What? What'd I do?" Tony asked, bewildered by their merriment.

"I'm sorry," Liz apologized between gasping breaths. "It's just that everyone seems to ask me some variation on that question."

"It's because she looks like such a nice girl," Jude explained, smirking. "Looks being the operative word."

"Hey you!" Much to the surprise of the men opposite them, Liz smacked Jude proprietarily across the arm. "Watch it," she warned playfully.

"Oh, I'm worried," Jude scoffed.

"You should be. I'm a trained kickboxer. Tick me off and I will lay you out."

"I don't know about you, Jude, but I'm worried for you," Tony offered sincerely.

Jude only rolled her eyes and shook her head mournfully. "Why did I set myself up for this? I gotta be out of my mind."

"It must be luuuuuvvvvvvvvv," Tony crooned.

"Shut up," Jude growled ferociously, but the faint blush that lit her features was visible to everyone.

"Man oh man," Tony chortled. "I can't believe this." He held up his glass in a toast. "Ladies and gentlemen...the most eligible woman in the world is now off the market. Cheers!"

Liz glanced over at her lover, a bemused smile on her face. Several curious pairs of eyes had focused on the boisterous table, and the woman who regularly faced hostile gunfire with negligent ease now squirmed uncomfortably at the scrutiny and tried to slink further down in her chair. The reporter gave Jude's hand a gentle squeeze, and the dark woman bestowed a rare, full-bodied smile upon her partner.

"You're just glad I'm off the market because you couldn't stand the competition," Jude retorted, not disputing his statement—a move that wasn't lost on the woman beside her.

"I'm not arguing with you there," Tony agreed cheerfully.

Shaking her head ruefully, Jude released Liz's hand and stood. "Well, if you're going to toast us, I suppose I'd better get us something to drink. Can I get you boys a refill?"

Both Kent and Tony nodded. "Affirmative. Sam Adams, please," the Italian agent supplied their order.

"Got it. I'll be back."

"Aren't you going to ask me what I want?" Liz asked, a faux innocent look on her face.

Jude paused a moment, then smiled sensually, determined that if she was going to go down, then it would be fighting. "I know what you want." Turning on her heel as a violent flush suffused her lover's face, she threaded a graceful path through the tables, never once looking back.

An amused silence settled over the table as Liz watched Jude's progress across the restaurant. "She is something, I'll grant you that," Tony said quietly.

"Do I have this incredibly dumb look on my face?"

He grinned back. "Let's just say that there's no doubt about the object of your affections." He leaned forward, a conspiratorial expression on his face. "If it's any consolation, she had the same expression when she was looking at you."

"She sure does," Kent drawled slowly, breaking his silence. "You know, I'm kind of surprised." He glanced at his partner. "I always thought that if the Archangel ever settled down it would be with Maria."

Incredulous, Tony's eyes widened in disbelief. "Nah..." he attempted to wave the statement away. "You know that's not the way it is between them."

Kent merely shrugged. "Maybe, maybe not. But with Jason gone..." He leveled an intense gaze at Liz. "Did she tell you about him?"

"Her partner?" Liz replied smoothly. "Yes, she did. Everything," she stated flatly.

Reading the clear annoyance in Liz's voice, Kent apologized half-heartedly, "I'm sorry. It's just that...Jude's never really been the...domestic type."

"Kent...." Tony warned.

"Oh come on, T...You know the stories as well as I do. Why should this girl get hurt because the Archangel thinks she can change?" He shook his head. "It's just not possible."

"Stop calling her that," Liz interjected softly.

"Huh?" Both men stared at her, taking in the fiercely serious look on the small woman's face.

"Her name is Jude. Not the Archangel. Not El Diablo." *Now I've got your attention.* Liz smiled grimly at their surprise. "Yeah, I know all about that one too. And let me tell you something...I know exactly who she is and what she's done. I'm not some wide-eyed little girl who's going to get hurt." Tony nodded approvingly at her, while Kent continued to stare in slack-jawed amazement at the reporter's suddenly steely demeanor. "You're right, Kent...she's not changing. She's unearthing a part of herself that people like Enrico Massala and the ones at the Agency helped bury. She's not the devil, Kent. But people like you made her think she was."

"Amen," Tony murmured as a silence fell across the trio.

Kent studied the small woman a moment longer, nodding almost imperceptibly. "I hope you're right, Elizabeth. I really do. Now if you'll excuse me, I think I need some air." He excused himself in spite of the fact that they were sitting outside with the crisp ocean breeze tousling their hair.

Liz watched him go, a thoughtful expression on her face. "I think I pissed him off," she said dryly.

"Fuggetaboutit," Tony waved her away. "Kent's..." He searched for a way to describe his partner and the uneasy relationship he had always had with the dark woman. "He's funny about the Arch...about Jude." He corrected himself with a quirky grin. "Like Jude said, he's a straight company man. The Agency above everything—even God and country, though those are next on the list."

"Sounds like Oliver North," Liz muttered.

If he heard the remark, Tony let it slide. "Jude was always a rule-breaker. But she was a rule-breaker with results, so the Agency turned a blind eye to some of her...exploits." He blew out a frustrated breath and ran a hand through his curly hair. "You gotta understand what she was like back then—"

"I've seen that too," Liz said softly, remembering that night and the pale malevolence that had gleamed in her lover's eyes. *But it must have just been a fraction of what she was,* Liz suddenly realized, shuddering at the thought.

"It scared Kent. Hell, it scared all of us... but he was her partner. For a little while anyway. Then he screwed up and nearly got them both killed. She saved his ass and covered him with the brass, but everybody knew what had gone down. I don't know what he saw that night—whatever it was, it really got to him. But after that it was like she could do no wrong. Man, and then when she turned...it fucked him up bad. He never...got... what Jason meant to her cause the Agency's always been everything to him."

"He couldn't accept that Jason was more important to her than any bust, no matter how big," Liz finished for him.

Surprise flickered over the agent's face. "Damn. She did tell you everything, didn't she?"

Liz just looked at him wordlessly.

"Yeah.. I guess." Tony shrugged wearily. "I don't understand any of it. There was something...special...about Jude's tie to Jason. But even he was afraid of her." He studied the honey-haired woman closely. "You aren't though." Shaking his head, he finished off his beer. "I guess that's why you mean so much to her, huh?"

❑ ❑ ❑

"Hey you." Jude stuck her head tentatively though the kitchen's galley doors, narrowly missing a waiter barreling past her with a heavily-laden tray.

"Get in here before someone gets knocked senseless," Maria scolded, her eyes were dancing with amusement.

Jude scooted through the doors, following Maria to her office, which was just off the corner of the large industrial kitchen where a chef and two assistants were kept busy. Normally, Maria supervised operations in the kitchen, making occasional forays onto the restaurant's floor to greet friends and make sure things were running smoothly at the bar. Sometimes, however, she just liked to putter about the kitchen, creating new dishes to try on her friends, who served as willing guinea pigs for her culinary explorations.

Barrido del Mar had been in business for almost ten years, and Maria had been its principle owner for three of them. She had been a chef's assistant when she first met the bright-eyed boy who became her husband and the brooding woman whom she recognized as his soul's mirror. Eventually she had taken over the kitchen, and then—with Jude's financial assistance—bought the place outright from the dubious figures who had owned it previously. Now the restaurant turned a healthy profit, and though Maria had offered to pay Jude back, the dark woman had recognized a good investment when she saw one and kept her silent partnership intact. The arrangement suited both women, cementing the tie between them, even though their relationship was sometimes strained at best.

"Where's Jessie?" Jude asked, looking around the office for her six-year old goddaughter. "I was hoping I'd get to see her tonight."

"She's gonna be sorry she missed her Aunt Jude," Maria commented. "It's been way too long since you came to see her."

"Mea culpa," Jude acknowledged. "Things...have been crazy." She held up her hands at Maria's exasperated glare. "I know I say that all the time, but honestly...lately, it's been for the best that I haven't been around much." *Code for it hasn't been safe to be around me.*

"I don't want to hear about that shit," Maria replied sharply, turning her back on Jude and rummaging through some papers.

Hesitantly, Jude's hands came to rest on the hunched set of Maria's slim shoulders, soothing out the anger visible there. "It's over, Maria," she whispered softly. "I've...got something worked out. If I bring in this one guy...I'm free and clear."

It was something Jude had never said aloud before, especially not to Maria—because her word to Jason's wife was a bond. Deep down, Jude had never before believed that she could really walk away—no matter how much a part of her might want it. *Things are different now,* she finally acknowledged to herself, knowing that without Elizabeth's unwavering acceptance of her, such a thing never would have been imaginable to her, much less possible.

Beneath Jude's hands, Maria took a shuddering breath and turned to confront the ocean blue of her husband's soulmate. The unflinching earnestness in Jude's gaze brought the dark woman's message home in a way that her simple words never could have. "Santa Madre... it really is," she breathed, throwing her arms around the tall figure that dwarfed her.

Jude buried her face in the fragrant tumble of Maria's hair, her heart clenching and unclenching in time to the silent sobs she could hear coming from her partner's wife. "Shh...." she crooned softly.

"What changed?" Maria asked, raising watery eyes to Jude's and studying the warm blue flame that flickered there. "Is it her?" Referring to the honey-haired woman sitting outside.

Jude couldn't keep the gentle smile from her face at the mention of Elizabeth. "Partly," she acknowledged. "It's something I've been trying to do for a long time, but..." Another brilliant smile from the brooding agent washed over Maria. "It's like she's given me my life back... and made me believe that I can walk away. I...never really thought I could before. " She thought back to all the long nights she shared with Jason when he had tried valiantly—and vainly—to convince her of that very thing. Jude didn't know why Elizabeth had been able to reach so easily inside her and hand the dark woman her soul back... but it had worked. "I don't know, Ria. What can I say? She's given me back the sunlight."

Maria laughed softly, hugging Jude tightly to her again. "I never thought I'd see this look in your eyes."

"Neither did I, Ria," Jude whispered. "Neither did I."

☐ ☐ ☐

"Why do I always end up being one of the help?" Jude grumbled, sitting the tray down at the table and rejoining her friends. Kent had returned to the table shortly before Jude and apologized for his behavior. Though her instincts crackled, Liz accepted the agent's apology gracefully, not wanting to cast a pall over the evening.

"You just have that—look—about you," Liz teased.

"And what look might that be?" Jude inquired dryly, handing out drinks. "Sam Adams, Sam Adams, bourbon for me... and something with an umbrella in it for you." She handed Liz an outrageously pink concoction with fruit tumbling out of the top and a little pink folding umbrella stuck through a maraschino cherry.

"Uh...do I want to know what this is?" Liz asked dubiously.

"Depends."

"On?"

"Why do you think I look like the help?"

"Because you look so...helpful. Like a Girl Scout." Liz blinked innocently, pausing with a razor-sharp sense of timing. "Almost," she added after a beat.

Beer shot out through Tony's nose as he took a gasping breath, hacking and wheezing as Kent pounded him furiously on the back while trying to keep the grin from his own face.

"You okay, T?" Jude asked wryly, sprawling comfortably in the chair beside her lover. "You—" She arched a menacing brow at Liz, shaking her head. "Are. Truly. Disturbed."

"No, I'm just a visionary," Liz disagreed. "I see things that..."

"Aren't there," Jude finished with a grin. "That, by definition, classifies you as disturbed," she said pointedly.

Liz knew when to cut and run, so she merely smiled regally, taking a small sip of her drink. "You never did tell me what this was."

"Does it matter? Just tell me if you like it."

"I've heard that before," Liz muttered under her breath. The comment escaped the men opposite her, but not Jude who cast a brow archly in her direction. The reporter took a tentative sip of her drink, then a more enthusiastic one. "Mmm...it's great. Tastes like Kool-Aid with a kick."

Jude smiled wickedly. "I'm glad you're enjoying it. Ria said dinner would be out shortly.

"Dinner? I haven't even seen a menu yet." The muted chuckles around her told the honey-haired woman she was missing something. "Clue me in here, gang."

"Weeellll...let's see. Being one of Ria's friends has its ups and downs. On the up side, you never have to pay for a meal..."

"And the downside?"

"You never get to pick what you have for dinner."

"Beg pardon?"

"Ria sort of likes to... experiment on us. We get sneak previews of new dishes she's working on."

"Cool!" Liz exclaimed. "What could be the problem with that?" She considered her lover thoughtfully. "Although since you're the kind of woman who orders the blandest thing on the menu, I can see where you might have a problem with this."

"Hey!" Jude objected. "Why are you giving me such a hard time?"

"Cause I can," Liz replied blithely, much to the ill-concealed delight of Tony and Kent.

Jude growled low in her throat in reply. "Actually, after I ended up in the emergency room from one of her concoctions, we sort of came to an agreement that she'd always warn me in advance."

"Who knew you were allergic to shellfish?" Maria, who had arrived during the conversation, asked. In a motion that caused Liz's brow to furrow slightly, she slipped her arms around Jude and gave the dark woman another quick hug to communicate her happiness. She directed the waiter as he set plate after plate of exotic-looking dishes in front of the quartet.

"What is this?" Tony asked, looking down at the steaming bowl and inhaling the delicious aroma. "Smells fabulous."

"I'm trying out a new Paella. It's got shrimp, mussels, chicken, clams and lots of spices. I'm thinking about making it the special one day next week, so you and Kent are my lab rats. Let me know if I need to tweak it any."

"No problem," the men enthusiastically agreed.

"You—" she indicated Jude's plate, "Get the swordfish I promised you. It's seasoned with dill, red onions, black olives, and some other stuff. Gives it a salsa type flavor."

"Cucumbers?" Jude cast a baleful glance at her friend, examining the contents of her plate. "I hate cucumbers."

"Honestly, Jude," Maria sighed. "I have less trouble getting Jessie to eat her vegetables." It was an old argument between the pair, and they fell into it with easy familiarity.

"Okay, okay..." Jude surrendered good-naturedly. "It looks great, Ria. You know I'll love it."

"You better," Maria warned playfully. "And you, Elizabeth, you get my classic Gumbo Lafayette."

"Hey!" Jude frowned, "Why doesn't she get to be a lab rat too?"

"Because anyone brave enough to get involved with you, Angel, is already living on the edge. I don't want to send her over."

Everyone at the table froze as Jason's affectionate nickname for his partner tumbled effortlessly from Maria's lips. It had been an unthinking slip, borne out of the sheer joy at realizing Jude was finally breaking free from the smothering darkness. Only Jason and his family had been close enough to her to dare use the ironic designation, and Jude hadn't heard it since the day of her partner's death. Maria had hurled the name at her like an epithet, damning her for taking his life. The dark woman closed her eyes briefly, letting the sound wash over her, waiting for the familiar sting of salt in wounds that still hadn't healed. The lashing pain, however, was gone, replaced instead by a kind warmth curling in her belly.

Maria's eyes were carefully fixed on her, her posture braced as if for a blow. Jude clasped her friend's small hand and squeezed it softly, silently reclaiming the name that had been hers all those years ago. Kent and Tony released breaths they didn't know they had been holding, not quite believing their eyes.

"Don't worry about it, Maria," Liz said cheerfully, wanting to dispel the silence that threatened to fall. "I like living on the edge."

"See a bear in the woods, walk up to it and poke it with a stick," Jude muttered.

"That's my motto, all right." The reporter flicked a glance at the four other people at the table. "Can we eat now? I'm starving."

◻ ◻ ◻

Jude insisted that Ria join them for dinner, and soon the little group was stuffed to overflowing with good food and lively conversation despite the quiet tension that existed between the Agency men and the drug dealer. While Kent and Tony still seemed to give the dark woman a respectfully wide berth, Maria showed no such restraint. It was obvious that the two women shared a strong bond, forged by their common link to Maria's dead husband. Much to Liz's surprise, as the night wore on Jude began trading agency tales with Kent and Tony, talking about some of the less hair-raising cases she and her partner had solved. Of course, this led to Ria relating her domestic misadventures with Jason—including one where they conned an unwilling Jude into painting their house.

Jude lost herself in Ria's pleasant alto, not needing to hear the details of an escapade she had lived. Dinner was long over, and the band had taken a short break before beginning their next set. The deck had grown less crowded as the evening progressed, leaving only a handful of tables still occupied with patrons lingering over their dessert. The night rested comfortably around them, ocean sounds rushing to and fro in their ears. The Akitas were faint outlines in the distance, still bounding energetically across the sand. Jude watched them bemusedly, enjoying their play. An unfamiliar peace settled across her shoulders, its point of origin the honey-haired woman beside her. As much as she had protested earlier, she knew that bringing Elizabeth here had been a good thing. She had charmed Ria and the boys effortlessly, and her presence had given Jude the courage to take the last step in healing the last wounds in her relationship with Ria. She knew Jason's wife would never completely forgive her as long as she adhered to this destructive path. Ria held firmly to the belief that Jason would never have wanted Jude to do the things that she'd done. Deep down, Jude knew she was right, and the issue remained uneasily resting between them. Now, however, she could offer Ria her friendship—free and clear—and hopefully, regain her place in the unlikely family she and Jason had formed.

Jason had been on her mind constantly this evening, and it was almost as if she could feel him near, smiling delightedly at her and saying, *"I told you so."* Her mind wandered further from the conversation, drifting in the gentle thoughts of the sweet boy she had known. *I wish you were here, partner...God, I still miss you so much...So many times I've wished I could take your place...Let you have your family, your life back...They say the dead can hear the thoughts of the living...and maybe you're listening now...I hope so...I love you, Jase...I'm sorry I couldn't keep you safe, like I promised Ria I would...Forgive me for walking away from them when we were all hurting so much, missing you...You're a part of my soul...I know that now...and I'll always carry you with me.* She bid her partner a silent good-bye—a piercing ache she had never before been able to put to rest—and returned her attention to the conversation at hand.

And found four pairs of eyes fixed firmly upon her.

"It's all her fault," Maria was saying, a teasing glint in her eye.

Jude blinked. "My fault? I'm sure you're right, but what exactly am I taking the blame for this time?"

"I was asking Ria how she and Jason met," Liz explained.

"Ah..." Jude nodded. "That was not my fault. I didn't tell you to go out with him."

"How could I not after the scene he made?"

"Explain, please?" Liz requested.

"Yeah," Tony chorused, "I haven't heard this one."

Jude started to speak, but Ria overrode her. "I was an chef's assistant then—really a waitress with very large ambitions." She grinned. "Jude and Jason used to come in here all the time. They would always sit at that corner table over there." Ria indicated a smallish table for two, far away from the band and the main lines of traffic. "They'd come in and stay for hours, usually close the place down, just talking. Somehow I'd always end up waiting on them. At first I thought they were a couple—because I never saw them with anyone else—until one night I heard Jude giving him a hard time about finding a nice to girl to settle down with. And he said, 'I'll find one if you will.' That sort of clued me in to a couple of things. After that I paid more attention to Jason. He was a charmer."

"He kept trying to work up the courage to ask her out," Jude interjected. "But at the last minute he would always lose his nerve. This from the man who could sell ice cream to Eskimos. That's how I knew it was true love. I thought I'd go nuts watching those two try to flirt with each other." Jude shook her head sorrowfully. "It was truly painful to watch."

"So they come in one night," Ria picked up the thread of the story. "In this crazy mood..."

"A bust that we had worked on for six months finally went down," Jude supplied.

"And then proceeded to get drunk as lords..."

"We were celebrating..."

"And he asked me out," Ria finished.

"That's not exactly how it went, Ria. You left out a few pertinent details," Jude commented.

"Such as?" Liz prompted.

"Well, she got the facts right. We were celebrating, and we had imbibed a few..."

"Thousand..."

"Drinks. Jason was determined to get Ria's attention in a way that would make it impossible for her not to go out with him."

"This is why it's all your fault."

"He wanted to make an impression." Jude shrugged. "So I suggested he serenade her."

Tony, Kent, and Liz all stared at her, disbelief written clearly across their faces.

"The only problem was..." Jude continued.

"Jason couldn't carry a tune in a bucket..."

"And in his inebriated condition, he could only remember the lyrics to one song."

Maria saw the demonic gleam in Jude's eye and began shaking her head rapidly. "Don't you dare, Jude Lucien."

Jude tipped her chair back slightly, leaning away from the table and closing her eyes. Then, with the bare hint of a grin playing at the corner of her mouth, she began to sing softly.

The lyrics were fairly innocuous at first, and Jude's voice was more than pleasant. However, as the dark woman continued the song, sweeping Ria up into her arms and two-stepping her lazily around the room to the band's accompaniment, the song grew progressively bawdier—until most of the patrons were laughing in merry astonishment, and Ria's entire face was flaming in embarrassment.

As the last chorus died away, Jude spun Maria a final time, giving her a jaunty salutation and bowing deeply to the applauding crowd.

"See? How could she resist?" Jude asked, flinging herself alongside Liz and grinning rakishly.

"I certainly don't think I would have been able to," Liz agreed, wiping tears of laughter from her eyes at the sight of Jude so uncharacteristically playful.

"Okay..." Maria shook her head at the dark woman. "On that note, I've got to go check on the kitchen. Now that you've made an absolute spectacle of me."

"Wouldn't be the first time," Jude cheerfully announced. She watched Maria make her way through the remaining patrons, giving and taking some good-natured ribbing for their little impromptu show. A rambunctious wave of happiness washed through Jude, leaving her light-hearted and just a little light-headed. She flicked a glance over at her lover, who was regarding her with a bemused smile. "What?"

"Nothing," Liz said. "Just looking."

"Why?" A brow arched quizzically in her direction.

"Because I want to," the honey-haired woman replied with a smile. "Gotta problem with that?"

"No ma'am," Jude assured her, leaning close. "But it is getting late. Can I interest you in looking at me someplace a little more private?"

"Absolutely," Liz grinned.

"Come on, walk with me on the beach while I round up the dogs." Jude vaulted over the low railing to the sand below and helped Liz, steadying the smaller woman as she landed unevenly on the sand. Slinging a long arm around her lover, they strolled down the beach toward the dim shapes of the Akitas playing in the distance.

"Serenade her, huh?" Liz teased. "Why didn't you do that for me?"

"I thought you would prefer a...classier...method of seduction than an obscene Country & Western tune," Jude placidly replied.

"Yeah, getting me shot is really suave..." Liz bantered, wanting to rid Jude of her remaining guilt over the incident.

To her relief, Jude snickered low in her throat. "Not one of my smoother moves, I admit. But I think everything's turning out okay."

"Really?" Liz studied her lover's dark length, mesmerized by the way the light was absorbed by the ebony sheen of her hair and reflected back in a silvery glow. Jude moved easily here among the shadows, her sure steps unerringly finding their way in the darkness. "You're really happy with the way things are going?"

Jude paused a long moment, stilling their walk. "Yeah," she said at last, turning to face her lover. The beginnings of a smile were evident in the elegant planes of her features. "I am." Jude ducked her head to capture Liz's lips in silent affirmation of her words.

The kiss was tender and lingering, hinting at the banked passion that lurked just beneath the surface. Jude's tongue led a gentle invasion of her lover's mouth, teasing a low moan from Liz's throat with its caress. The smaller woman tugged Jude still closer, wrapping strong arms around Jude's tapering waist and tracing the outline of the sleek muscles in her back. "Oh wow," the reporter breathed when Jude released her lips.

"Uh-huh," Jude nodded with a wry smile.

"How do you do that?" Liz sighed happily, tucking her head snugly beneath Jude's chin.

"I don't do it alone. That's for sure," Jude commented, enjoying the comfortable feel of the woman in her arms.

"Yeah, I guess it is kind of a joint effort, isn't it?"

"You could say that," the dark woman agreed, hugging her lover gently. "Come on, let's get the dogs and get out of here."

Aggie and Clytemnestra were reluctant to leave their playmate, but at Jude's stern command they obediently scampered up the embankment towards the Explorer, the humans meandering along behind them. An explosion of enraged barking sent Jude running uphill, huge chunks of ground speeding under her.

As she crested the rise, she saw Clytemnestra launch herself at a dark figure who had the driver's door of the Explorer open. The figure fended the Akita off with a ferocious backhand, flinging the dog backwards with a yelp. Jude didn't hesitate, taking off after the fleeing figure. She could hear Liz faintly shouting at her in the distance but paid her no heed, intent on catching her quarry. The figure was agile, hurtling over the dunes with ease. His pace, however, was no match for Jude's long stride. A final twisting leap, and Jude's hands were clenched in the fabric of his jacket, dragging them both to the ground.

He swung at her blindly, landing a sharp jab to the side of Jude's face. Snarling, she grabbed his out-flung arm, dislocating it violently with a savage *pop!* He screamed in pain as Jude slammed him on his stomach, pinning him down with a knee at the center of his back. The dark woman's expert hands found the Sig tucked into the waistband of his pants. Grinning savagely, she pressed the gun's barrel to the base of his neck.

"NO!" Liz shouted, racing to Jude's side.

"I'm not gonna kill him, Liz," Jude growled. "At least not yet," she added with a feral smile at her prey. The man squirmed underneath her—

agony clearly written on his face— yet he remained silent. She bore down on his back a little harder. "Hold still now, or I just might lose my grip on this trigger."

"Jude..." Liz pleaded with the dark woman, more terrified of the mask of rage that had descended over her lover's face than the gun she held in her hand. This was the woman they called the Archangel. "We don't know what he was doing."

"At the very least he was breaking in to my car. But I can tell you what else he was up to. A little quick surgery on our brake lines most likely." She held up the switchblade she had fished out of his back pocket. "You know," she addressed her prisoner. "I'm getting a little sick of this cat-and-mouse game."

"Fuck you," he managed.

"That's original," Jude replied dryly. She flipped the blade open and ran it lightly down the side of his face, leaving a thin red trail in its wake. "Let's try this again. You're carrying a Sig 226...which means you're law enforcement or you've got access to someone who is. Which is it?"

"Fuck you."

The butt of the gun smashed into the side of his face, fracturing his cheekbone. Liz winced at the impact, horrified by the force of this unleashed fury. "Jude..." she tried again.

"You're beginning to piss me off, asshole," she growled at the prone man, ignoring the strong pull of her lover's voice calling to her.

"Like I give a shit." He spat out a mouthful of blood.

The dark woman raised the gun once more, but her movement was blocked by a deceptively strong hand wrapping around her arm. "Jude, stop!" Liz shouted. "Don't do this." The voice was lower now, gaining strength as she saw Jude involuntarily responding. "You don't have to."

Bleak, pale eyes turned to stare hard at her, a renewed coldness burning through her. Resolutely, Liz refused to look away, willing her muscles not to tremble. The green warmth of her gaze searched Jude's face, searching for the buried remains of the tender lover she had come to know.

"Stay out of this," Jude barked.

"No! Like it or not, I am a part of this." She tightened her hold on Jude's arm, both of them knowing that at any second her grasp could easily be ripped away by the dark woman. Jude felt her close and was involuntarily reminded of their connection. It allowed her to hear the quiet words falling from her lover's lips. "I'm not going to lose you to the demon night again."

The arctic glare snapped abruptly, and Jude drew a shuddering breath at the raw entreaty in Liz's voice. A single sentence, a simple claim on Jude's bloody soul that couldn't be denied. She glanced down at her victim who bore the expression of someone who knows he's going to die—painfully. She minutely eased the pressure on his back.

Unwilling to surrender her tenuous connection to Jude, Liz shifted her stance, loosening her death grip on Jude's arm to a gentler clasp and peering over her lover's shoulder at the disabled man. "Who is he?"

"We were just covering that," Jude commented shortly. "You heard her." She prodded the man. "Who are you?"

"Go ahead and kill me, I'm not telling you anything."

Jude sighed heavily and stood up. "I'm not going to kill you." She gestured to Liz. "You have her to thank for it."

Warily the man crawled to his knees, cradling his useless arm awkwardly. "What's the catch?"

"No catch," Jude replied, unsure of who deserved her disgust more—herself or the man at her feet. "Just tell your bosses that I'm coming after them soon. Now get out of here before I change my mind."

He didn't need to be told twice, setting off at an uneven pace down the beach to where Jude was sure his support team waited. Had she been alone and in the mood for a blood bath, she would have pursued him and confirmed the answers that were beginning to take on a shadowy outline of their own. As it was, all she wanted was to bury herself in her lover's arms and wash all the rage away.

She watched him disappear into the dimness, then turned to Liz who was standing patiently beside her. Green eyes regarded her sadly. "We're in real trouble here, aren't we, Jude?"

Chapter 12

Jude had been unwilling to trust the Explorer, uncertain of what their saboteur might have done before he was interrupted. She had discreetly borrowed Ria's pickup, explaining to her friend that they were having car trouble and that her mechanics would be out in the morning. Seeing easily behind Jude's placid exterior to the ill-concealed rage in her eyes, Maria had agreed wordlessly, silently despairing of this new darkness her friend was facing.

"Okay, I know why you didn't want to give Ria all the gory details, but why didn't you want her to say anything to Kent?" Liz asked as they herded the dogs through the kitchen door. Clytemnestra favored her left foreleg slightly, but a quick check of the dog had revealed only several small cuts. Aggie hovered close by, anxiety over his hurt littermate evident in his prancing gait. "Couldn't he help you?"

Jude sighed as she trudged wearily up the stairs, the small woman tucked securely under a sheltering arm. "No, if anything he'd probably hurt me."

"Because he still thinks you're one of the bad guys?"

" I think someone is using him to get information about me."

"To do you in."

Jude chuckled dryly at the description. "That about sums it up."

"Why?"

"Why not? I mean for the last four years or so, I haven't exactly been a friend of law and order. It could be anyone in the Agency...from the people who took Jason down to a misguided white knight hoping to bring me in for my past crimes. In spite of what I'm trying to do to balance the scales."

"You said earlier that you were working on something?" Liz prodded. Reaching the bedroom, she guided her lover over to the bed, sitting her down on its welcoming surface.

Jude kicked off her topsiders and flopped backwards, exhausted by the convoluted logic she was trying to unravel. The damn thing didn't make any sense. None of it did. "I made a deal with Kent to bring in somebody the Agency wants really badly. If I do, and if I turn over all my 'off the books' operations, I can walk away free and clear. But there are a lot of people who would like to see that not happen. Who think I deserve whatever the Justice Department can throw at me. I guess they're right. Only thing is..." She laughed mirthlessly. "They don't have a damn thing on me."

She had ruthlessly instilled a code of silence in her employees, making absolutely sure they knew that extermination was the price of betrayal. She had known the DEA's methods inside and out and had easily weeded out all their ops but stopping short of shedding their blood. The Massacre had been as close as they had gotten to making any sort of case on her, and that was only because she'd had no intention of walking out of that warehouse alive. For once, however, she had underestimated her own abilities, and afterwards she was left to figure out what came next—after the acrid, empty taste of revenge had made her gag.

Liz hauled Jude upright, industriously tugging the tank top free from her waistband. "Up," she commanded. With a silent smirk, Jude obligingly lifted her arms, and Liz stripped the cotton from Jude's lean body. The smaller woman pushed her lover back down, unfastening the buttons on the worn jeans with nimble fingers. She scrambled down the length of the dark woman's long frame, tugging the fabric as she went. Jude didn't know why, but Liz seemed to have an almost frantic urge to reach her skin at this very moment. Perhaps she needed to reconnect with the flesh-and-blood warmth of her lover after her earlier encounter with the arctic plains of a killer's eyes as much as Jude needed to. The remaining silken barriers between them quickly fell by the wayside, allowing Liz to triumphantly run her hands over bronze skin. A soft kiss to the pulse of her lover's throat and a quiet sigh ended the reconnaissance.

Jude quirked a brow in unspoken question as the honey-haired woman snuggled close.

"I just needed..." Liz searched for a way to explain. "To feel you close," she finished lamely.

Jude nodded in understanding and gently pulled at Liz's shirt. "Then take this stuff off and c'mere."

"Help me."

The two women rose as one, Jude finding it hard to work the buttons free with her suddenly trembling fingers. Abandoning her task in frustration, Jude rested her head on her lover's strong shoulder, drawing a shuddering breath.

Staring at the dark head in alarm, Liz tangled her hands comfortingly in the onyx tresses. "What is it? What's wrong?"

"I'm so sorry," Jude breathed. "What happened tonight...What you saw..."

"Shh..." Liz crooned. "I'm not sorry I saw it."

"I would have killed him..."

"But you didn't."

Jude raised her head to fix on Liz's eyes. "Because of you," she murmured, unable to believe the quiet strength she saw residing in the swirling green depths.

"No," Liz corrected. "Because of you. You just needed to be reminded that there's another way." She studied the planes and angles of Jude's face, gently stroking the supple skin beneath her fingertips.

"I never...believed...that I could be any other way," Jude said haltingly.

"Believe it now," Liz whispered, capturing full lips in her own.

It was a kiss that was equal parts claiming, surrender, and accedence. Liz coaxed Jude's mouth deeper into her own with teasing caresses of her tongue. A languid dance of tenderness began in the sweet exchange, drawing a moan from deep in the dark woman's throat. The reporter tugged her lover closer, reveling in the warmth that Jude's long arms yielded.

Somehow, buttons miraculously worked loose, cloth tumbled off fair shoulders, and jeans slipped from slender hips until skin pressed against gloriously bare skin in a sensually intimate entanglement. "Need you..." Jude mumbled, her mouth working slowly over her lover, absorbing the texture of lissome muscles moving against her lips and tasting the salty heat rising from Liz's body.

The sure touch of Jude's fingers and the low growls of desire from her throat muted the clamoring in the reporter's mind for details and information about the danger that lurked outside their sanctuary. Knowing that there would be time afterwards for the talk they needed to have, Liz willingly surrendered to Jude's searching hands. Moments, hours, days could have passed as Jude slipped inside her, mouth drinking in her lover's wet essence, etching her claim into Liz's soul with the tender flame of desire.

⬭ ⬭ ⬭

"You ever going to tell me where you got this?"

Liz was kneeling comfortably between Jude's legs, idly tracing a line down the powerful muscles that loosely held her in their grip. One leg sprawled gracefully across Liz's thighs, while the other curled softly around the smaller woman's waist. The position left Jude's sex completely exposed to her lover's hands and eyes, and she was overwhelmed by the seeming ease with which Jude opened to her touch. Liz's past loves had been fraught with hesitation and fear—and a tactile inarticulateness that left the reporter fumbling for the right caresses. In stark contrast, her response to Jude had been complete and unmistakable...she *had* to know this woman's body in order to know her soul. So much of Jude was hidden in quiet motions—a discreetly quirking brow, a rhythmic clenching of her jaw—at times Liz felt as if she were learning to communicate solely through taste, touch, and smell. Jude's language was one of pure sensory explosion that Liz would gladly spend the next hundred years exploring and deciphering.

Liz's fingers danced over the small tattoo on Jude's hip, reaching over to brush the still-damp curls that protected the dark woman's center. Smiling as Jude's hips bucked gently of their own accord at the soft teasing, Liz tossed an expectant glance at her lover. "Well?"

The mark was small, but distinctive—a dark line snaked off-center through a tiny circle surrounded by shapes that looked at times like flames or the sensuous curves of a woman's body. It was clearly a unique design, something Liz had never seen before. It clearly meant something to the dark woman—and the reporter wanted to know what that something was.

Stretching her arms lazily over her head and arching subtly against Liz's fingers, Jude nodded. "I guess we do need to talk."

Liz frowned. "Why do I think this isn't just about your tattoo?"

"It is." Seeing Liz's dubious expression, she added, "Sort of."

"Let me get comfortable," Liz said, suspecting that this was going to be a long story. Jude piled two pillows behind her head and settled back on the bed, while Liz arranged herself across her lover's stomach, her chin resting on neatly folded hands. Each pair of legs twined smoothly around the other, maintaining a much-needed contact through the length of their bodies. Jude drew a ragged breath as one of Liz's full breasts pressed against her center, sending a delicious ripple of aftershocks through her body.

"Lift up a bit," she groaned, sliding Liz a little further up her body. "There, that's better." She flashed a wolfish smile at the smaller woman. "Can't have me getting distracted, now can we?"

"Absolutely not."

"Okay..." Jude ran a hand through her disordered hair. "After Jason..." she hesitated briefly. "After Jason's death...it was like the world had just turned itself inside out. Ria was in pieces...Jessie—that's their daughter—was too young to understand..."

"And what about you?"

"What about me?" Jude asked bleakly.

"Well, I can't imagine you were in much better shape than Maria was," Liz pointed out.

"*I killed him...*" Jude replied incredulously. "I didn't have a right to feel anything," she added, more softly.

"I'd argue with you over that, but I don't think it would do any good." Liz flashed an irate glare at her lover.

"Do you want to hear this or not?"

"I'm sorry...go on."

"I had a lot of time to think in the aftermath of the shooting. Because of the way they just shut everybody up and kept me away from anyone who might have some answers. And the more time I spent by myself, the more I realized that somebody sold Jase out. I mean Rico's intelligence sources just weren't that smart. And even if they were, they would have found me a helluva long time before they found Jason. I was out there by myself to keep something like this from happening." Jude sighed heavily. "But it happened anyway."

"Could someone have been using Jason to try and force you to blow your own cover? To make you sacrifice the operation?" Liz asked, her mind whirring.

Jude looked at her lover, clearly startled by Liz's incisive thinking. "I thought about that," she said slowly. "It's possible that Rico had someone on the inside...but it wouldn't make any sense for them to wait a year and a half before acting." She shrugged. "Then again, none of this ever made any damned sense."

"What if somebody wanted just to get rid of Jason? Maybe he had stumbled onto something." Liz's thoughts were racing. She was thinking aloud now, mulling over the possibilities the same way she did when considering all the angles of a story. There were several obvious questions that popped to mind—the first of which was what would someone have to gain if Jason was killed? Maybe whoever was behind this was trying to get rid of both agents. It certainly made sense if they were working for Rico.

"For a romance novelist, you sure know what questions to ask," Jude commented, studying her lover's face intently as if she were reading the reporter's tumultuous thoughts.

Liz shifted uncomfortably, aware that the shaky ground she trod was fast crumbling away beneath her feet. "Too many episodes of *Miami Vice*, I guess."

"Uh-huh..." Jude pursed her lips, her eyes narrowing suspiciously. "Anyway...I asked myself all the same questions. Trouble was, I could never find any answers. The Agency yanked me out of there and sent me on 'a psychological leave of indeterminate length.' There wasn't even a review board on the shooting. It was like they just wanted to bundle everything up and get it out of the way as quickly as possible. We were this close to bringing Rico in." She held her thumb and forefinger pressed tightly together to demonstrate. "And they just let him walk."

"That's when you started seriously suspecting someone on the inside?"

"More or less."

"So what happened?"

"I never came back from that leave," Jude answered grimly.

She spent the next hours chronicling her final immersion in the darkness, talking about her painstaking efforts to build an illicit empire to rival the Massalas and thwart at every turn the Agency that had betrayed her.

The reporter listened in bewildered amazement—here all the shattered fragments of the woman Liz was beginning to love were laid resolutely out for her inspection. Although Jude's tone was flat and even, Liz could clearly see the anguish residing behind the shuttered blue gaze. She ached to crawl inside her lover and try to heal from the inside out the wounds and scars on Jude's trembling soul. She inched further up Jude's body, bracing her elbows on the firm mattress, and cradled the dark head in her hands. "I'm so sorry," she murmured, pressing her lips against Jude's forehead.

A strangled cry caught in Jude's throat. Such tenderness was almost unbearable, and the animal that still remained deep within struggled to get free. She pushed blindly at the golden form lying on top of her. "Why are you sorry?" she asked harshly. "Sorry that you crawled in bed with a monster?"

"Stop that," Liz grasped Jude's head tightly. "You're not a monster."

"I've acted like one for too many years to think any differently."

"Is that why you did all this?" Liz demanded. "Because it's easier to believe what everyone has told you—from your mother and the fucking priests to the people like Kent who are supposedly your friends?" She paused and took a deep breath as Jude regarded her silently with a shocked expression. The small woman tapped the side of her lover's skull. "I wish I could get behind those baby blues and see what's fucked you up so badly. Why it's easier for you to kill than to love." She shrugged, dropping her gaze to rest on the crisp white sheet bunched at her side. "But I can't. Jason couldn't. Nobody can make you think your life is worth living right except you."

The words were said softly, almost inaudibly when Jude answered. "I'm trying. But Elizabeth, it's so hard. It's like everything inside me fights against it." She stumbled over her words, her eyes refusing to meet the reporter's. "I've tried to change..."

"Why?" Liz asked quietly. Jude looked at her in surprise, almost as if she had forgotten the other woman was there. "Why did you decide you had to change?"

Jude paused and took a deep breath, trying to focus on what Liz wanted to know. Finally, she began hesitantly. "Killing Rico Massala was supposed to finish everything. I had taken away most of his businesses...sticking it to the Agency in the meantime...and Rico was in no position to bargain. When he wanted a meeting, I agreed to it. Of course I expected him to try an ambush—so I set one of my own up." She shut her eyes in remembrance. "As soon as I put the bullet through his head, I expected his men to come crawling out of the woodwork. They did...but it was with their guns raised in surrender. My guys blew them all away before anybody really knew what was going on."

"You expected them to kill you," Liz stated flatly.

"Basically yeah...and when that didn't happen...I was lost." Jude looked at the small woman helplessly. "Killing him was supposed to make me feel better, goddamn it," she snarled quietly, almost to herself.

"Did fucking over the Agency make you feel better?" Liz asked.

Jude shrugged. "Not really."

"Then why did you think killing Massala would?"

Jude laughed humorlessly. "Something had to."

"But killing Massala wasn't it."

"As I discovered. And for once in my life I didn't have a backup plan."

"So what did you do?"

"Well...things were a little...hot...for me in Miami. What with the Cartel sending professionals after me every ten minutes and Metro Dade crawling all over the crime scene. The Agency wasn't stupid—they knew I was responsible, but they weren't about to send anyone else after me until they thought they might have a chance in hell of it working. Sasha and I thought it best that I take a little...vacation...until everything sort of cooled off a little."

"Sasha was with you back then?"

Jude smiled wolfishly. "She was one of the first things I took away from Rico."

Liz only nodded, not sure what unsettled her more—the continuing presence of the shadowy assistant with her undefined duties, or Jude's casual reference to her ex-lover as a 'thing' to be taken as a spoil of war. She tucked these uncomfortable thoughts away to ask her next question. "Where did you go?"

"Most of the Cartels operated out of Colombia because the government there was more...amenable...to operations like Rico's. Like mine."

Liz nodded, "That's where the Medellin Cartel was—until the Colombian government took them out."

"Right...with more than a little pressure from the Agency. Of course, the Cali's just took its place."

"Do I need to ask how you fit into all this?"

"I was the new kid on the block." She shrugged. "So I went down to introduce myself...pay my respects." Blue eyes turned distant as her thoughts drifted back over years past. "That's how I ended up in Cartagena."

⫏ ⫏ ⫏

Colombia seemed to have two types of weather: hot and hotter than hell. Even Jude's legendary cool had been shot to pieces by the lethal combination of the climate and the locals she'd had to deal with upon her arrival. Over the last few weeks she had bounced from Bogota to Cali to Buena Ventura to Medellin...and quite frankly, she'd had more than enough of the heaping helpings of machismo dished up at every meeting. Totally unused to being dismissed, Jude had been at her wits' end. As a last resort, she had seduced the mistress of one of the Cali Cartel's top lieutenants. She figured it would either earn her a seat at the table or a bullet in the head. In her state of mind, she really didn't care which it was. Either way they couldn't ignore her any longer.

Oddly, it had earned her a grudging respect from the other men. They were no longer able to categorize her as either a Madonna or a whore...and though she didn't particularly care to know what they called her when her back was turned...it allowed her a bit of maneuvering room.

She arrived in Cartagena worn out and pissed off, eager to return to the States, but unable to because of the continuing investigation into the Massacre. Sasha had told her to sit tight for at least another week and had given her a couple of contacts in Cartagena. The old city was the most "touristy" of her destinations in Colombia—indeed if anything in this godforsaken country could be called hospitable—and she fervently hoped that meant she could at least walk the streets without some pickpocket nipping at her heels. Of course, with her luck running the way it was, it probably meant that the problem was worse here than anywhere else.

She checked into the Hotel Santa Clara, listening absently to the bellhop's litany about the hotel's history as a convent. "That's appropriate," she snorted to herself cynically, thinking that the chances of her enjoying any...female...company for the rest of her stay was unlikely. Seducing Miriana had been business, not pleasure—and it had been far too long since she had enjoyed Sasha's unique talents. Random images of her assistant's naked form writhing underneath her flashed through her mind during the interminable lecture about Santa Clara de Asis. Her patience at an end, she interrupted the enthusiastic clerk. "I...Don't... Give...A...Fuck..." she said slowly and distinctly, giving his fractured comprehension of English time to decipher her meaning. "Now go away," she added, pressing an American $20 dollar bill into his hand.

The boy amiably scrambled off, leaving Jude alone again with her musings.

The room was decorated in what Jude was coming to think of as "obligatory Amazon Basin designer chic." Which meant white walls, whirring ceiling fans that barely stirred the still air, and mosquito netting draped from the four corners of the bedposts. "At least this place has clean running water," she noted, turning the shower on and stripping off her dusty travel clothes.

A long, cool shower later, Jude was feeling a bit more human as she buttoned her shirt and tucked it neatly into a pair of loose khaki shorts. "What the fuck," she muttered, braiding her long hair tightly. "I'm a tourist right? I should look like one."

She descended the winding staircase to the bar downstairs, sorely in need of a drink. Out of habit, her eyes scanned the room restlessly— noting the room's arrangement, the exits, and potential troublemakers. Early on she had learned that most men in this hellhole of a country thought a woman sitting alone at a bar had to be at the very least a woman of easy virtue, if not an outright whore. She had been called a puta more times in the last three weeks than she had in her entire life— and that was saying something. Her suitors usually only desisted after she creatively indicated her desire to be left alone. There was a string of men in each city she had visited who carried a stunning array of broken and fractured bones as evidence of her irritation.

That's why the woman in the corner caught Jude's eye immediately.

It wasn't just that she was sitting alone, unmolested. This woman seemed to bleed sunlight through every pore of her tanned skin and white-blonde hair. She was wearing a white tank dress that clung appreciatively to every leanly muscled curve of her body and exposed a length of sleek thigh where her legs crossed. A glass of something colorless sat in front of her, and she appeared entranced by the view of the gardens outside with their riot of blooms that offered the only color on the grounds.

Before she had really even thought about it, Jude found herself sliding into the booth opposite the stranger, absently signaling the bartender to come take her order.

"A lot of men have tried that seat," the stranger murmured softly. She had a perfect British public school accent, and the crisp English fell on Jude's hungry ears like manna from the heavens.

Jude's brows furrowed quizzically. "Isn't that a line from a movie?" she asked lightly.

That earned her a hint of a porcelain smile as the stranger regarded her coolly. Up close, Jude could see that she had pale, almost colorless eyes that seemed to absorb the dying sunlight around her and beam it back out at Jude, who fought from flinching at the brightness.

The bartender ambled over, looking at Jude expectantly.

"Bourbon," she told him, hoping that they'd actually have it. Tequila seemed to be the only thing they served in most places. To her surprise, the bartender nodded and glanced briefly at the blonde. "You want anything?" she asked.

"A martini, please..." the stranger replied, holding up her glass.

Their order taken, the two women were left alone again.

Jude arched a glance at the thoughtful expression on the stranger's face. "What?" she asked.

"You know...I do believe you're right. That is a line from a movie. But I can't for the life of me remember which one. I do remember, however, that the man that our heroine let sit down was up to no good."

"Maybe I'm just glad to be talking to someone who doesn't speak that fractured Banana Republic-ese the locals seem to think passes for English."

"No," the stranger disagreed. *"You look like many things, but an innocent is not one of them,"* she stated flatly.

"Oh?" Jude was intrigued. *"Just what do I look like?"*

"A pirate."

Jude chuckled at the apt description. *"So what are you supposed to be? A damsel in distress?"* she smirked.

"Oh heavens no," the blonde waved a dismissive hand and finished off her drink. *"Think of me as...a renegade heiress on a suicide mission of debauchery."*

Jude studied the sleek form opposite her. This could be fun. *"That's a helluva mouthful. You got something shorter I can call you?"* she drawled.

A throaty laugh rewarded her, its tendrils stroking the fine hair on the back of Jude's neck. *"You may call me Keir."* She bestowed the name regally. *"Short for Keirnan."*

"Keir..." Jude murmured, enjoying the feel of the name on her tongue.

"And what about you, my pirate? What sort of alias are you using to escape the notice of our fine local authorities?"

"I don't make a good first impression, do I?" Jude bantered easily. *"You're already accusing me of wrongdoing."*

"I know a predator when I see one."

The dark woman inclined her head in silent acknowledgement. *"My name is Jude,"* she said.

"Short for...?"

"Just Jude."

Keir chuckled darkly. *"Is there a reason you were named for the Patron Saint of Desperate Causes? Or is it just delicious irony for my situation?"* Seeing Jude's furrowed brow, she hastened to explain. *"Here I am, sitting in a bar alone...faced with the dreadful reality that I will spend this evening being endlessly propositioned. By the locals or by the tourists. With no relief in sight."*

"You could always go home," Jude commented dryly.

"What fun would that be?" Keir dismissed the suggestion with a roll of her eyes. *"At least here there is the possibility that something*

interesting will happen." Keir snapped her fingers. "And voila! Here you are. No more boring propositions."

"How do you know I'm not going to proposition you?"

"Oh, I most certainly hope you will. That would be a nice change of pace from all these sweaty men." Keir flashed a wicked grin in her direction. "And at least you'll let a decent interval of time pass."

"I see."

"Do you?" Keir cocked her head to one side, regarding her new companion seriously. "Do you want to get out of here? There's a little time before sunset...I could show you the sights. Such as they are."

"Lead the way."

◻ ◻ ◻

The sun was dipping below the horizon, holding on 'til the last with long tentacles of light that reached out towards the two women strolling along the city's walls. Cartagena was a city that bore its scars proudly, named La Heroica by its people during Colombia's struggle to free itself from Spain's stranglehold. Tourists still wandered through the streets freely this evening, the light granting them passage to move about in a way that would not be permitted once darkness fell. Of all the cities Jude had recently passed through, Cartagena had made the most stable peace between its daylight and nocturnal worlds. Maybe the vermin stayed relatively hidden during the light because the cruise ships made the city a port of call; or maybe the ocean vista soothed away the most violent of their impulses. Whatever the reason, Jude was grateful. She wanted to enjoy the company of this recklessly elegant creature beside her. Still, her senses were painfully aware of the predatory glances she felt raking over her body as she walked.

"A string of bastions ran along the oceanfront anchored by two larger forts—one called San Fernando and the other San Jose. Cartagena had a slight pirate problem back then." Keir flashed a grin at her dark companion. "So in the 1580s the king of Spain ordered a military engineer named Antonelli to fortify the city." She indicated a ruined tower rising above the city's streets and overlooking the ocean. "That huge tower there was the main point of defense. It's called San Felipe de Barajas. It was destroyed four times...and each time they rebuilt it. They say ghosts of dead soldiers haunt the ruins, still watching over the city. I wonder what they make of Cartagena now?"

Jude had spent the last few hours just listening to the musical wash of Keir's voice and taking in the slight, entrancing sway of the other woman's hips. She wasn't particularly paying attention to the history of the city whose streets she now walked. The blonde was almost as tall as Jude herself, but with a much leaner frame. She reminded Jude of the sleek racing hounds she had seen in Miami with their noble profiles and breathtaking speed and grace. Though her mind was occupied by musings of what the woman beside her would taste like, she answered absently, "They probably wonder what the hell happened."

Keir shook her head thoughtfully. "Somehow I doubt it...I mean, do you think human nature has really changed that much in the last four centuries? Soldiers are still soldiers...." She nodded at the military-looking uniform on the local policia standing nearby. "And pirates are still pirates," she finished, looking pointedly at Jude. There was an awareness in that cool glance as it swept over the length of the dark woman's powerful body, and Jude suddenly realized that she wasn't the only one uninterested in the light banter passing back and forth between them.

Perversely wanting the blonde to make the first overture, she ignored the look and commented instead, "You seem to know a lot about the city."

Arching a smirking brow that was an eerily pale mirror of Jude's dark one, Keir pursed her lips slightly and picked up her narrative. "I've been here a few weeks, enjoying the scenery. I've picked up some things from a couple of tour groups I ended up following around out of sheer boredom," she admitted. "I've found that the tours are much more enjoyable when you've downed a martini or six beforehand."

"Colombia's not exactly high on the list of hospitable vacation spots," Jude pointed out.

"I'm a free soul...looking for adventure," Keir proclaimed with a dramatic sweep of her arms. She walked with the casual assurance of one who has yet to confront a situation where either her charm or her money had failed to remove any unpleasantness she faced.

Jude allowed herself a small smile, enjoying the charismatic presence of the woman beside her. "They usually tell you to join the army in that case. You know... 'It's not just a job, it's an adventure.' "

"Oh god, no...I doubt the military would have someone like me." She laughed, a merry look in her eye. "Actually, I'm an escapee from a cruise ship. Hopped off here when we made the port of call. I've been hanging about, absorbing the local color. Some friends have a place over on one of the Islas del Rosario, and they've let me commandeer their sloop to come and go as I please during my stay. It's a little 32-footer down there in the harbor." Their eyes locked again—the glance

longer, more intense—and Jude felt a spark of anticipation fire in her veins. There was no mistaking the intent here. "Why don't you come back to the island with me?" *the blond murmured sensually.* "It won't take long. If we leave right now, we can be on the island before the sun is completely down."

A lazy smile crept over Jude's features. "I'd have to go back to my room first. Otherwise I wouldn't have anything to wear."

"Trust me, darling...you won't need anything."

◻ ◻ ◻

Jude couldn't remember how it started...she had helped Keir cast off and raise the mainsail...then she had walked to the vessel's small bow, enjoying the ocean breeze on her face. There were a fair number of other ships out on the water, pleasure crafts like this one, ferrying their wealthy owners to and from the coast and away from the dangers of Cartagena's nocturnal denizens and towards the safety of their island playground.

Somehow...Keir was there...behind her, lean arms encircling her and demanding that the shirt come off Jude's shoulders. Khaki shorts dropped from her hips and deck shoes were kicked to the side. It occurred briefly to Jude to protest their relative proximity to other vessels, but then she was twisted around in the blonde's arms, and red lips were finding hers with unerring accuracy.

The white dress fell away unneeded as they slithered to the cool smoothness of the teak deck, a slight spray misting their bared skin. Her scent was exotic to Jude...like some jungle wildflower whose name she would never know. Jude buried herself deep inside Keir, pulling out the other woman's desire in wrenching groans of passion, loving the feel of those long legs falling over her shoulders. Again and again Jude moved into her...hard, fast, slow, aching...until at last they broke apart, lying on their backs and staring up at the newly fallen sky.

"Oh...my..." *Keir breathed, rolling her head sideways to glance at her new lover.* "That was...extraordinary." *She ran a hand trembling from exertion over Jude's finely muscled body. The smell of sweat, sex, and heat was on their skin...and Jude resembled nothing so much as a predatory cat, sated and full from the hunt.* "Damn..." *Keir laughed unsteadily.* "I should have tried this sooner." *Her eyes drifted appreciatively over her partner.*

A blue eye appeared from under its shuttered lid. "What do you mean sooner?" *The other iris joined its twin.* "We just met a few hours ago," *she smirked.*

*"I don't mean us, darling. I mean this whole woman thing....Although
I daresay it wouldn't have been as much fun with someone else."*

*A dark brow furrowed. "You mean you'd never had sex with a woman
before?"*

*"Well...there were all the usual adolescent slumber party fumbling,
but honestly....By the time I got old enough to seriously contemplate the
possibility, all the women of a similar bent were just too much of a cliche.
Captains of the field hockey team—all of them. You know what I mean?"
She chuckled lightly. "So I put the idea out of my mind..."*

*"And meeting me put the idea back into your mind?" Jude pulled
herself up, leaning on one elbow to get a better look at the woman whose
body she had just mastered.*

*"I do confess that I was feeling a bit randy this afternoon beforehand,
but the minute I saw you—" An erotic smile drifted over the patrician
features. "—I decided I simply had to have you."*

*"That's rather...imperial...of you," Jude murmured, bending her lips
to graze the soft flesh on Keir's neck.*

*"Do you feel colonized, darling?" Keir laughed delightedly. The
warm rich sound reached out and curled firmly between Jude's legs.
"Believe me, I don't want to change one bit of your gloriously primitive
tendencies."*

*"I don't think we have to worry about that," she answered flippantly.
Jude's senses were flush with the smell of the woman on her hands, the
taste of their sex in her mouth, and the dying echoes of Keir's ragged
cries still ringing in her ears. She trailed her fingers across the elegant
line of Keir's hip. "Come here..." she ordered, her fingers digging into
the skin she found there and drawing the woman to her.*

*And so the stars spiraled up higher to flee the out-flung hands that—
reaching out in their desire—threatened to jar Heaven's lights loose from
their niches in the night sky.*

⫐ ⫐ ⫐

*"What brought you to Colombia?" The question was asked over a
breakfast of tart grapefruit and sweet skin.*

*"Business," Jude answered, preferring the latter of her two dining
options. Forsaking the grapefruit entirely, her mouth covered a puckered
nipple greedily. A low growl of satisfaction rumbled from her throat as
she tested its tautness against her tongue.*

*"Colombia...doesn't...have...any...industry..." Keir groaned. "Except
farming...and..." Her hands tangled in Jude's hair, separating the dark
woman from her self-appointed task and forcing her to look into pale*

eyes, colored gray by the rising sun. A rueful smile twisted on the blonde's face. "So you really are a pirate."

Jude shifted away from Keir's alluring skin. "Do you really care?" she taunted.

"Not really," Keir answered easily, regarding the woman anew. "But it does answer some...feelings I had about you."

"Such as?"

"You looked too...beautifully menacing...to be someone ordinary."

"You have a vivid imagination."

"I do," Keir agreed. "But that's not the point. The way you carry yourself...You fairly reek of violence..." A soft caress trailed down the side of Jude's face. "And sex...and, now that I think about it...just about any sin I could name, you would seem to inspire in me. You are a poster child for transgression," she murmured.

The words held too much of an echo of the condemnations she had received as a child. "According to the priests, even the fact that I breathed was a sin," Jude growled, still unable to quite suppress her rage at the black-cassocked men who damned her soul before she was even born.

"Do we have a problem with the Church?" Keir didn't miss a step in the odd turn the conversation had taken.

Jude's eyes paled coldly in remembrance. "Just don't have much use for it, that's all," she replied tightly.

"That's rather odd...considering what you're wearing around your neck." Long fingers dipped down to capture the cold medallion hanging between Jude's bared breasts. "Christopher...guardian of travelers and defrocked saint." She pursed her lips. "Or is that why you carry him around? Comrades in exile?"

Jason had given her the medallion at their last meeting—before the nightmare had began, claiming her existence for its own. Fearing for the blackened remnants of her soul, he had begged her to walk away from the operation. When she refused, he pulled the chain from around his neck and pressed it into her hand, curling her fingers around it tightly. "Keep this, then...Since I can't go where you're going...I know it may not mean anything to you, Jude, but it does to me. Please..." She had accepted the gift, never intending to put it on...but late that night, when darkness surrounded her and the dawn was so far away that she could easily imagine it would never reach into her adumbral realm, she slipped it over her head and let the cool metal rest against the skin covering her heart. In the ensuing chaos following Jason's death, she had yet to take it off.

"Didn't work, did it?"

The question jarred her rudely back into Keir's colorless glance. She arched a questioning brow.

"Whatever this was supposed to protect you from, whatever journey you took...it didn't work, did it?"

Jude swallowed hard, surprised at the sudden insight this stranger seemed to have. *"No, it didn't."*

A tender hand stroked her face. *"I'm sorry."*

A sharp jerk of her head shrugged off the gesture. *"Doesn't matter."* She went to turn away and was stopped abruptly, suddenly finding her shoulders gripped by strong hands.

Colorless irises met Jude's pale blue ones in an unwavering gaze. *"Something's cleaving you right down the middle, isn't it?"* she asked, her perception unnerving to the dark woman in her arms.

"Leave it," Jude warned, the cold look in her eyes at odds with the placid tone of her voice.

Keir sat back, studying the sensuously lethal woman sprawled at her side. *"Darkness falls, eh? All right then..."* In a smooth movement, she flipped Jude onto her back, straddling the tall woman's tapering waist and pressing into the hard length of muscle there. *"In that case... spend the day with me. There's an island where we can go..."*

"I'm not interested in tailgating with tour groups," Jude groaned, her hips arching into the slick smoothness between Keir's legs.

"Darling, what I have in mind is definitely not a group activity..."

⃞ ⃞ ⃞

They piloted the sloop to a tiny island, further away from the main body of the Islas de Rosario, landing in a small inlet and dropping anchor. *"We'll have to swim in,"* Keir told her matter-of-factly, tossing her a small waterproof bag. *"Put your clothes in there—they'll keep dry."* Jude cocked a dubious eyebrow at her companion, who was stripping easily out of her own shorts. *"Don't worry, we'll be quite alone. Not even the tour groups have found this place. One other thing..."* She held out a hand that contained what looked like two small, black berries. *"Take this."*

The dark woman's eyes narrowed, recognizing the peyote. *"I don't..."*

"Don't take your own medicine, do you?" Keir mocked. *"I want you relaxed this afternoon. I promise, this stuff is totally natural—and a thousand times less lethal than that crap you put out on the streets."* Jude's eyes paled dangerously at the comment, but Keir didn't back away.

"Am I wrong?" When Jude didn't answer, she smiled triumphantly. "I didn't think so." She brought the button to Jude's mouth. "Open."

Silently, Jude complied, allowing Keir's long fingers to slip past her lips and teeth, depositing their cargo. The dark woman could still faintly taste the traces of their last round of lovemaking, and she ran her tongue down the length of the retreating digits.

"Chew," the blonde commanded, smirking as she watched Jude wince at the cactus' bitterness. "I could never get used to the taste either," she remarked, disposing of her own button in a similar fashion. "Shall we?" With a graceful leap, Keir dove into the azure water, emerging moments later, water sleekly falling from her face. "Come on!" She waved an arm. "It's lovely."

Shrugging mentally, Jude tucked her own shorts and a couple of Keir's T-shirts into the bag and slipped it over her shoulder. Encumbered by the light weight on her arm, her dive was less elegant than her companion's, but equally effective. Gasping at the water's warmth, she stroked with one arm towards the woman waiting for her near the water's edge. "That was nice," she admitted, grinning at the blonde.

"Wasn't it though?" Keir smiled, running a lazy hand down Jude's wet torso. "We'll come back for a proper swim later."

The sun quickly dried the remnants of the moisture from their bodies, and soon they were clothed in shorts and light T-shirts. "So, where are we going?" Jude asked, squeezing the excess water out of her hair and hoping that it wouldn't snarl too badly.

Keir gestured to a gently winding path through the surprisingly thick foliage. "We take that trail there. It's uphill a little ways...but nothing too bad."

"Lead the way."

Walking easily along the path, Jude examined her surroundings carefully. They were indeed quite alone, and Jude found herself smiling at the lushness of the land around her. The wild cries of birds circling overhead warned other creatures of the two-woman invasion, and the rush of the ocean in the distance added rhythm to their steps.

"I can't for the life of me figure out why the tours don't come here," Keir was saying as they strolled. "I suppose it's because this island is one of the furthest out, and it's tiny. There's literally nothing to look at here but ruins. No room for postcard stops or soda stands."

They emerged from the dimness into a patch of brilliant sunlight. Much to her surprise, Jude realized they were standing on a small rise at the top tier of what looked like an amphitheater. Cracked and broken stones were all that remained of the curving benches that descended down the gentle incline until they were flush with the hard-packed earthen floor a few levels beneath them. Two stone pillars stood even with the top of Jude's head on either side of the center aisle.

"The Chibcha who lived here originally were mostly craftspeople. They were weavers, stonemasons and goldsmiths. Not warriors at all..." Keir glanced over at Jude, watching the dark woman run the palm of a hand lightly over the rough textured surface of the stones. "They really didn't stand a chance when the Spaniards came. The Europeans took the gold, destroyed the cities, and enslaved the people—all in the name of God, king, and country." Keir shook her head slowly, lost in thoughts of civilizations long past.

"What is this place?"

"As near as I can tell, it was a place of worship."

Beneath Jude's hand, the stone seemed to fairly hum with energy— a vibrant, pulsing heat that she could feel beginning to coil in her belly. She slid her palm away from the stone, flexing her hand to dispel the tingling that remained. "This is a church, huh?"

"Oh no," Keir smiled. "They didn't worship things they couldn't see. Their gods were the earth and the sky, the land around them." Watching Jude's fingers trace the faded carvings on the pillar next to her, she added, "It's said that the stones spoke to them."

Jude arched a smirking brow. "Well, if they were flying on the same shit you just gave me, I can believe that."

"They didn't use hallucinogens. Just their eyes and ears and hands," Keir replied. "Come on..."

As Keir led her down the small slope and across the earthen floor, Jude's senses exploded in a burst of awareness. Her skin absorbed the light pouring down on her, sending waves of heat soaking into her muscles. The blossoms drooped their exotic scents from nearby bushes, reminding her of the sweet essence of the woman beside her. Keir's hair shone translucent in the brilliance that surrounded them. Jude's eyes warmed, darkened, pulsed with the energy that danced to flickering life inside her.

It was a flame now...curling up from her belly, encircling the jagged remnants of a soul she believed dead. It wrapped around the muscle of her heart, squeezing painfully until each breath reminded her of her mortality. She could hear it popping and snarling in the caverns behind her eyes.

So hot...so unbearably hot...the sweat dripped down her face...and then they were in a stone enclosure, the lucent sunlight shut out by the walls, but still shining brightly in Keir's eyes. Flames surrounded them both now, curling familiarly along the length of the blonde woman's hip, reaching out with its tendrils to stroke Jude's glistening skin. And then flesh on flesh...the stone surprisingly cool beneath her back as the flame spread through her body...an open-cunt ache gripping her with its raw demand. A mouth, a hand, a flame...pressing against her...quench the fire...but it only burned higher... "More..." a voice, hers, ragged with need...hoarse with its cries... Had she been screaming? The flame...the woman...twins now...thrusting inside her, nourishing the fire until it poured out between her legs... shuddering to climax with a gut-wrenching cry...moisture, sweat....tears?...streaming from her eyes. Then...
Silence.

Had the men not stopped to watch the show, had they not taken the women's pleasure as their own, their mission would have succeeded quite easily. Two bullets. Two bodies. A handsome reward from the remaining members of the Cartel. The best laid plans...

The first bullet struck home, silencing Keir's murmured sighs of delight and shattering her skull against Jude's torso. A strangled cry tore loose from Jude's throat as her body recognized the threat, even as her mind struggled to piece together the reality. She was up and moving, flinging Keir's body in the direction of her attackers. Intended to be a kill shot, the bullet streaked by Jude's neck as she rolled away, blood and fire pouring out of the flesh wound. The men separated and began chasing her through the maze of the stone enclosure. She ducked into a blackened niche as one of her assailants edged past. She was on him before he realized it; a savage crack! Echoing through the hall as she snapped his neck. She took his gun.

The tables had turned.

"Luis?" The other man. He had obviously heard the sound of a neck snapping and was moving in her direction. "You get her?"

Flame now consumed her...rage, hate, anger...for what? Another dead at her hands, another innocent spoiled by her touch. Keir's eyes hadn't even registered what was happening. A lifetime destroyed in a moment's pleasure. The bile rose in Jude's throat, strangling her. She stood in the shadows, choking on the madness that had consumed her for these last years.

And the flame burned on...leaving in its wake the scorched ruins of Jude's soul...

*The gun fit so perfectly in her hand, its metal cold to her touch...
reassuring in the liquid inferno that surrounded her. Her assailant moved
forward, his outline clearly visible—backlit by the flame. She slipped
further into the shadows... deliberately kicking a rock to draw him out.*

*"Luis?" The man's pitch was higher, more uncertain as a silence
that promised nothing good loomed ever larger.*

*He was completely outlined to Jude's burning eyes. The gun came
up...he must have heard the quiet click of the hammer...but too late. The
bullet slammed home, destroying his frontal lobe. His last vision was of
a bloody apparition looming over him, a devil lately arrived to escort
him to Hell.*

⫐ ⫐ ⫐

"Did you love her?"

Jude gazed into the green eyes of the woman who now held her soul
and smiled softly. "No," she replied. "She was just someone...to pass the
time with...Someone looking for trouble, and thought she found it in me.
She was right." Jude shook her head. "But she didn't deserve what
happened to her either."

"That's what this is, isn't it?" Liz gently rubbed the small tattoo on
her lover's hip. The mark seemed to warm to her touch, as if it contained
a life of her own. "The vision you had when you were...making love to
her. You wanted to be reminded...of her."

Jude didn't miss the hesitation in the small woman's voice. Or the
slightly troubled look in her expression. Wrapping her arms tightly around
the Liz's shoulders, she lifted her lover across her body until they were
eye to eye. "I wanted a reminder...yes...of the last innocent to die at my
hands. I had to leave her there, you know, in the temple... or whatever it
was. I dumped the men's bodies in the ocean, got some clothes from
Keir's sloop, and took their boat back to shore. I couldn't even go back
to my hotel room. I got in touch with some people Sasha knew, and they
got me papers to get out of the country." Her eyes clouded with memory.
"And all the time I just kept thinking about all the people who had died
because of me—at my hands, because of my drugs or my guns. I was so
goddamned tired of it all." She sighed and ran an unsteady hand through
her hair. "I just wanted it to be...over. Killing Massala was supposed to
do that. I got my vengeance....And I choked on it."

"That's when you came back to the States."

"Yeah...and I learned that Brugetti had found his witness, if you can
even call him that. The reason Sasha wanted me out of the country a little
longer was because she was arranging a hit on the guy. The DEA had

thrown their lot in with the Florida State's Attorney. So with their help, Brugetti had enough to charge me."

"So you made a deal with them?" Liz asked, surprise in her voice. "The whole trial was a sham?"

"No, not at all," Jude replied. "Somehow, turning myself in just didn't seem like it was...enough. I knew that I could never make everything that I had done right, but I could try. So I went to Kent and he came up with this deal—I bring in the rest of the Massala Cartel, turn over all my ops to the Agency, and I get to ride off into the sunset. Brugetti was screwed when the Agency stopped helping him. He lost three-fourths of his case. Plus it created the perfect cover. Who's gonna believe that I'm working with the Agency after that?" Noticing her lover's thoughtful silence, Jude prodded her. "You don't seem too surprised by any of this."

"Truthfully? I'm not." Liz shrugged and sat up, sliding out of Jude's arms. "You expect me to be surprised that you keep changing the color of your hat in this never ending game of cowboys and Indians?" A harsh tone colored her words, and Jude arched an eyebrow in surprise. "Different costume, Jude...but the same character. You still kill, you still enjoy killing. Don't you?"

They locked gazes for an endless moment until Jude surrendered, looking down at her hands. "I did," she whispered. Marshalling her scattered courage, she found Liz's eyes once again. "Until tonight...when you showed me I could be something different. That I didn't have to pull the trigger." She brought a tentative hand up to stroke the length of her lover's cheek. "I never believed before..."

Liz leaned into the caress, her body naturally responding to Jude's touch. "Do you now?" she asked quietly.

"I'm trying," Jude answered honestly. "Don't..." The words lodged in the dark woman's chest, unable to free themselves from her soul's terrified grasp. "I mean... I understand if you want to walk away...I couldn't blame you...if..."

Understanding what her lover couldn't say, Liz wrapped her arms tightly around the taller woman, drawing her near. "I'm not going anywhere, Jude. I promise." Her fingers curled in the dark hair, and her eyes found Jude's own. "But I need you to promise me something too."

"Anything..." Jude whispered hoarsely, quite unaware of what she was saying, but unable to deny that hypnotic emerald gaze.

"It ends here. No more killing. We'll figure out a way to bring Massala in that doesn't involve you and a gun. Will you do that?" *Will*—not *can*...

there was no doubt in Liz's voice. She believed in her lover's ability to walk in the sun.

Liz's eyes brooked no compromise, no bargaining. If Jude wanted the honey-haired woman's love it would have to be here, in a light that threatened to commit her soul to the flames once more. A peaceful smile lit the dark woman's features, and there was no hesitation in her answer. "Yes," she replied simply. "I will."

Chapter 13

I've heard of morning breath...but this is ridiculous, Liz's slowly waking mind complained. The quiet, rhythmic panting seemed to be centered directly over her face, and the reporter cracked an eyelid to confront the source of her torment. Pete's soft brown eyes stared back at her unblinking, his mouth open in a silly, canine grin. Two paws balanced on Liz's chest as he patiently waited for the small human to open both eyes. *This is not what I had in mind for the morning after,* she thought crossly. "Off—Pete," she groaned, removing the mutt from her tender breasts. She stretched luxuriously, her body gloriously sore from the lovemaking she and Jude had shared.

Jude had completed the opening of her soul by consuming Liz again and again with her searching hands and mouth, evoking a response that Liz had honestly thought only happened in the fevered imaginations of romance novelists like her. Jude had been at turns fierce, demanding, tender and reverent—as if she considered their joining to be a consecration of this strange new life she was embarking upon. It also brought home to the reporter that her own truth had yet to be told. Though she feared what would happen when she told Jude the circumstances of their initial meeting, she knew it was something she couldn't put off any longer.

"This is not something I'm looking forward to," she told Pete. The small beast stood at the foot of the bed—head cocked, regarding her solemnly. "But I've got to, buddy," Liz continued. "She's let me in—can you believe it? She may not believe in herself, but she believes in me." Studying the black dog, the meaning of her last words finally struck home. *Oh god...she believes in me...and it's all built on a lie.* Liz closed her eyes at the thought of what might happen, the very real possibility that Jude would order her out of her life. Or worse.

"No," she said aloud, as if speaking would make the words reality. "She'll at least hear me out...and I'll make her understand..." She gave the thought voice. "I have to." Being without Jude wasn't a possibility anymore. As much as she had made the dark woman believe that she had a soul worth saving, Jude had made Liz believe she had a life that was worth living. It was a dazzling gift to the honey-haired woman...and one that Jude was completely unaware of bestowing upon her lover.

She didn't realize the shower had been running in the bathroom until the noise stopped. Moments later, Jude emerged—a towel wrapped low on her hips—rubbing vigorously at her long hair with another. "I swear to God I'm gonna cut this stuff off one day," she grumbled, flipping the unruly mass over one shoulder.

"Over my dead body," Liz grinned, her eyes wandering appreciatively over her lover's still-damp form.

"Ah...Sleeping Beauty awakens." A brilliant smile broke over Jude's face upon spying the honey-haired woman tucked neatly in the covers. "I thought you were going to sleep all day."

"All day?" Liz protested, craning her head to look at the clock. "It's barely 7:00 am. What are you doing up so early?"

"As much as I'd love to laze about with you," Jude teased, toweling still more water from her hair. "I've got places to go and people to see. Including a nine o'clock meeting for which I have stacks of reports that I've put off reading. If I don't get to the office soon, I'm not going to know what I'm talking about."

Liz glanced thoughtfully at her lover. "That sounds suspiciously like what bankers do," she said. "Besides, I would think your hours would be a bit more...irregular...than this."

The dark woman chuckled low in her throat. "You mean you thought all I did was make midnight deals in dirty alleys? It's true, there was a time when I would just be getting to bed at this hour, but somewhere along the way, I've ended up legitimately owning what seems like half of

Miami." She shook her head. "Sorting through all that mess takes more time than..."

"The other part of your business?" Liz supplied, stretching languidly again, vividly aware of her lover's gaze upon her.

Blue eyes locked on the radiant length unfurling before her, Jude swallowed convulsively—an act not lost on the woman sitting upright in her bed. "That's one way to put it," she replied hoarsely, unconsciously moving towards the intoxicating vision.

Delighted with Jude's reaction, Liz smiled smugly. "Then at least come here and give me a proper good morning kiss," she purred. Willingly, Jude closed the remaining distance between them, sitting gingerly on the edge of the mattress. "That's not here," Liz reproached the taller woman, taking her by the arm and sprawling Jude across her lap. "*This* is here." Pete yelped at the sudden movement and scampered out of the room.

"But I'm all wet," Jude cautioned, trying not to drip on the sheets.

A playful leer crept over Liz's face. "I should hope so," she teased, loving the faint flush that lit her lover's features. Her hand began to leisurely reconnoiter across Jude's shoulders, trailing slowly after stray water droplets as they trickled over her collarbone and down the swell of her breasts.

Whimpering lightly at the touch, Jude's lips met her lover's in a sweet morning exchange. "Good morning," she breathed, the pulse in her throat visibly elevating as a small hand cupped her left breast, the thumb running over a rapidly awaking nipple. "Oh..."

"Does that feel good?" Liz murmured, her lips caressing the sensitive lobe of Jude's ear. Her free hand sought out Jude's other breast and was busily coaxing it into the same tingling awareness as its mate.

Jude groaned as the tautness began coiling in her belly. Bracing her weight fully on her extended right arm, her left hand tangled itself in Liz's hair. She ran hungry kisses down the length of Liz's exposed neck. "What do you think?" she rasped.

"I asked you the question—" Liz punctuated her statement by sinking her teeth into the tender pulse in Jude's neck. The dark woman yelped softly at the contact, but her body arched into the roughness—silently asking for more. "Or should I take that as my answer?" the reporter snickered. Her hands continued to roam over the muscular expanse of Jude's torso, reveling in the shape of the woman beneath her fingertips. "Lie back, lover," she whispered.

"I...can't..." Jude sighed, burying her head in the hollow of Liz's shoulder. "I have...oh god..." she moaned as the smaller woman's hands returned to her breasts. "I've got to go..."

Liz interrupted her mouth's perusal of the warm skin on Jude's neck to regard her lover with a stern look. "You don't have to be anywhere until nine..." One hand slipped further south, caressing the smooth curve of Jude's hip with delicate strokes.

"I know...but..." The feather-light touch of Liz's fingers fractured Jude's words. With an expert flick of her hand, Liz removed the towel from her lover's waist, laying the rest of this magnificent body gloriously bare to her eyes. Each brush brought them closer to the tangle of hair that protected the tight bundle of nerves at her center. Involuntarily, her legs parted slightly, hoping to lure the maddening touch nearer.

"But nothing," Liz silenced her objections. The bright emerald sparkle of her eyes was veiled now by a smoldering arousal. The small woman needed her lover to feel the truth told by her body. She needed to speak in a language that Jude would understand without any doubts— no matter what happened later. "You're not leaving here until I have your smell on my fingers and your taste in my mouth," she murmured, her voice dropping to a sensual growl. "Do you understand me?"

Jude drew a breath to reply but found her lips covered by a voracious mouth intent on devouring her. Liz swept the arm that supported Jude from its braced position. The movement efficiently stretched the dark woman across her lap, hips poised at the edge of the mattress. "Wait—" It was more a moan than a protest, and Liz smiled at the rattled confusion in her lover's face. "I—You—"

"Yes, Jude. I. Want. You. Like this." She surrendered to the temptation of those full lips once more, leaning down and kissing Jude thoroughly, teasing a low growl from her lover's throat. "Let me have you," she whispered. "Please."

Blue eyes softened at the tender plea, then blazed bright with unreleased desire. "Yes," she answered thickly, bringing one foot up to rest flat on the mattress—an invitation for her lover to come deep inside.

Liz's heart tore painfully at the gesture, swelling in the confines of its mortal cage at the sight of this exquisite woman opening to her touch. Drawing an unsteady breath, she tucked a pillow under Jude's head with a trembling hand, letting the other tease caresses once more across her lover's breasts.

Jude's own breathing was ragged, and the cool water from the shower now mingled with the faintest traces of perspiration to form a glistening sheen on her bronze skin. To her storyteller's gaze, the dark woman glimmered sleekly in the morning sun, a golden idol the likes of which the world had yet to see. "You are so magnificent," she murmured, leaving soft kisses as offerings of her devotion across the sharp lines of Jude's face. Their mouths met, and she sucked gently on her partner's tongue, eliciting a quiet whimper from the woman spread across her. She slipped her left arm around Jude's shoulders, cradling her lover, as her other hand continued its worship of the full curves of the dark woman's breasts.

Their kiss deepened as the seedling arousal burst into blossom through Liz's body. "Oh God..." the reporter moaned, lost in the power of the sensations that just touching this woman created inside her. Breaking away vainly to try and catch the breath that had been snatched away by the heady desire pulsing through her, she brought her hand up to caress Jude's face. "So beautiful," she murmured.

"In your eyes," Jude replied quietly, kissing her lover's palm. Her long fingers entwined with Liz's small ones, drawing their clasped hands down the length of her body. "Touch me," the dark woman breathed as she pressed their fingers into the core of her need.

Both women gasped in the same instant, caught in the liquid fire they discovered together. *So wet...*Liz thought dizzily, tracing the swollen outline of Jude's sex, very aware of the elegant fingers still tangled in hers. She gasped softly at the sight of Jude's hand deep in her own wetness, glimmering with the ample desire there. "What do you feel?" she murmured.

"Sweet...Jesus..." Jude moaned. "Like touching...myself...but... not..." she ground out.

"Show me," Liz whispered intently, burning to know what story Jude's body would tell about itself. "Show me how you've touched yourself."

Jude growled incoherently, tossing her head and arching her back with need. "Please..."

"I'm here, lover...Guide me..."

Hesitantly, Jude flexed their hands against her sex, fingers instinctively searching for the spots they knew best. Another secret about the dark woman unfolded itself before Liz's awed gaze. Jude's hips bucked at the familiar yet unfamiliar touch. "Please..." she whispered again.

Lost into the immediacy of her lover's desire, Liz allowed their hands to follow the slow tempo set by Jude's body. Together, they outlined each curve and swirl of the dark woman's center, brushing lightly over her core and lingering only briefly at the tiny bud nestled there. Together, they dipped into Jude's body, the passage made easy for their entwined fingers by the flooding essence there. Together, they reached deep inside the slick walls, Jude's muscles beginning to quiver and contract around them.

"Oh...my...god...." Jude panted. "You...feel...sooo...gooooddd..."

"We..." Liz corrected with a gentle smile that Jude couldn't see. "We... feel good."

Blue eyes were shuttered to Liz, but the small woman could see the yearning need in the portrait of elegant tension painted on her lover's body. Her own muscles were taut with erotic sympathy, and a white-hot pulse beat between her own legs. Infinitesimally, she increased the rhythm of their hands, seeking to satisfy the cravings of both their bodies. Jude hissed, arching further into her lover's embrace. "Don't....stop..."

"I won't," Liz reassured her. "Not until you do..."

Moving steadily into the pattern of their thrusts, almost up the last incline before she began the freefall into release, Jude opened her eyes... to find her lover's ardent gaze focused on her. With a savage growl she took the last step, bucking fiercely into the delicious pressure; and Liz watched as the last vestiges of Jude's restraint ripped free while she surrendered to the pleasure of their combined touch. A single cry, "Elizabeth..." escaped from Jude's lips as she threw her head back, lost in that final, glorious plummet.

Jude's hand fell away, the muscles in her arm trembling from exertion and climax. Her heart pounded frantically in her chest, as if it were trying to join the rest of her body in release. Liz's fingers began to slip free as well, but Jude quickly covered the small hand with her own. "Please..." she murmured, her throat hoarse from her labored breathing. "Stay...inside me."

Liz smiled gently down at her lover. "You want me to..." She began to move tenderly over Jude's pulsing center once more.

"No," Jude answered unsteadily. "I just want...to feel you inside me." Blue eyes flickered down the length of her body to their joined hands and then returned to her lover's gaze almost shyly. "Is that okay?"

It took a moment for Liz to realize that this was the first time Jude had ever voiced a specific desire. Her body always easily communicated what she wanted, wordlessly guiding Liz to their respective releases, but not once had Jude ever said, *This is what I want from you...* "Absolutely," Liz beamed, an incandescent ray of happiness suffusing her body with warmth. She leaned down and brushed a soft kiss on Jude's forehead.

She could feel the ripples still coursing lightly through Jude's body, and every once in a while a tiny tremor would work its way through the muscles in her stomach. They floated gently in each other's eyes for a moment, until Liz quietly whispered, "Thank you."

Jude chuckled, her breath still not quite even. "I think I should be thanking you. That's a hell of a way to say good morning." She shifted easily in her lover's embrace, and Liz realized that the tall woman was still sprawled across her lap, half-on and half-off the bed. Reluctantly, her right hand left its warm haven and came to rest over Jude's heart.

"You probably aren't comfortable," she grimaced.

"I probably wouldn't be," Jude conceded with a wry grin, "If my muscles had an ounce of tension in them. Honestly, I feel like a boneless heap right now."

"Well..." Liz carefully perused her relaxed lover, a puckish light in her eyes. "You kinda look like one right now."

"Your fault," Jude accused good-naturedly.

"You helped," Liz smirked. Deftly, she tucked her right arm under Jude's legs and twisted her torso, neatly sliding the larger woman off her lap and laying Jude's length alongside her on the bed.

"Hey!" Jude yelped, startled at finding herself...positioned...so efficiently. "You're stronger than you look," she remarked.

"Piece of cake," Liz teased, making a great show of dusting her hands off. She stretched against Jude's supple form, loving the way their bodies naturally intertwined. "Now...where were we..." she murmured, kissing the perfect juncture at the base of Jude's throat where her collarbones met.

"We..." Jude groaned, "Were talking about how I need to get ready for my meeting." She captured the reporter's head in her hands and fixed a stern look at her unrepentant lover. "I'm already going to be late as it is."

"So?" The honey-haired woman blinked innocently at her. "You're the boss right?"

"You're incorrigible." She ducked her head for a quick kiss. "But I have to go." Resolutely she sat up, her body clearly communicating her reluctance.

"You don't really want to."

"Nope," Jude cheerfully admitted. "But I gotta." With a graceful, rolling movement, she was up and off the bed, strategically moving out of her love's tempting grasp.

"I know," Liz agreed with a tiny grin. "But I've got to make a fuss, or you'll think I don't care."

Jude only shook her head, laughing quietly, and disappeared into the depths of her closet. "You know..." she said, emerging a few minutes later with a cream-colored, linen suit and hanging it on the clothes rack. "If there's anything..." she hesitated, "You need to do today..."

The reporter immediately caught the drift of Jude's meaning. "Yeah," she said quietly, looking steadily at her lover. "As a matter of fact, there is."

The dark woman dropped her eyes and nodded in agreement. "Okay. Well... feel free to use the Jag or whatever..." Her voice trailed off uncertainly, and she turned away.

With her gaze fixed on anything but her lover, she didn't see Liz rise from the bed and cross the room. "There is something I need to do," the reporter acknowledged, catching her lover's chin and focusing those incredible blue eyes on her. "But I..." Now it was her turn to feel hesitant. "I want to come back tonight and tell you about it."

Jude released a breath Liz didn't know her friend had been holding. "I'd like that," she admitted, the tension ebbing from her face as her arms slipped around the smaller woman and pulled her close.

"Me too," Liz whispered, her body aching with the awareness that this might very well be the last time Jude ever looked at her with that expression. It contained so many things that the reporter never thought she would see from Jude Lucien. *No...from the woman I thought was Jude Lucien,* Liz corrected herself. *She is so much more than I thought... so much more than anyone else thinks...especially herself.*

They clung together in a perfect space, where the world consisted only of each other and the air that they breathed. Newspaper articles, business deals, and drug lords were a universe away from the gossamer existence they led at this moment.

The world, however, has a way of making itself known, and Liz reluctantly allowed it to seep through and break their embrace. A tender kiss passed lightly between their lips. "I'll tell Carmina to make something special for dinner," Jude murmured

Liz sighed contentedly, her equilibrium miraculously restored by Jude's nearness. They would survive the truth, she assured herself. *Just look at what we've survived so far...We...Huh...funny, I never thought...* Stopping her rambling musings, she glanced at her lover with a tiny grin. "Do me a favor—Let her go to the grocery store first. It'll give the lady a thrill."

Jude chuckled, shaking her head. "I don't get it. Why would anybody *want* to go to the grocery store?"

"Don't even try to understand, Jude. Just deal," she bantered.

"Okay, okay..." Jude held her hands up in surrender. "I'll cancel the order and let her do the shopping."

"Great." She patted her lover's shoulder briskly. "You won't regret it. Now..." she looked regretfully at the suit hanging nearby. "I guess you've got to get a move on."

Chewing her lip, Jude glanced at the clock. "I'm late already," she nodded, her brow furrowing slightly. "So..." A devilish gleam crept in her eye, and she scooped the smaller woman up in her arms. "I guess a few more minutes won't matter." With a wicked laugh, she bounded to the bed and flung them both down on it. "Now...I believe there were a few conditions you had to fulfill before I could leave. By my accounting, ma'am...you've only met half the requirements...."

◻ ◻ ◻

"Where the hell have you been?"

Jude cocked an inquiring brow at the indignant figure of her assistant framed in the doorway. The dark woman leaned back in her leather desk chair and propped her feet up on the desk, revealing a long length of tanned leg. The short, black skirt wasn't what she had originally picked out for the morning, but Liz had seen it hanging in the closet and asked her to put it on instead of the cream suit. Jude hadn't missed the sensual glimmer in her lover's eyes and readily agreed. *Besides,* Jude thought smugly to herself, *Never hurts to flash a little leg now and again.*

Of course, Sasha didn't seem too appreciative at the moment. "So?" She stalked through the door and leaned over the desk, glaring at Jude. "Where the hell have you been?"

Jude pursed her lips thoughtfully. "I suggest you get yourself a new line, querida," she replied archly. "Because that one sounds a wee bit... marital...for our circumstances."

Years of knowing the woman standing before her gave Jude a singular understanding of Sasha's body language. Judging from her posture, her assistant was absolutely livid and maintaining a precarious hold on her calm. Over the course of their relationship, Jude had made a game of driving her one-time lover to distraction. Rico's associates had called Sasha "Lady Ice" because—although once provoked she had a scorching temper—it was rare that she ever showed anything other than an implacably cool facade. It pleased the burly, dark-suited men, whom Sasha considered thugs and beneath her contempt, no end when she ran up against the force of nature that was Jude Lucien.

From the very start, Jude had managed to get under the executive's skin with a skill that bordered on the preternatural. She taunted and teased the smaller woman with her wit, her body, and her own unshakable exterior...until the other woman had no choice but to retaliate. Things escalated from there. As lovers, their passion had been incendiary; as business associates, they had been of a single mind in building an illicit empire. A volatile energy existed between them—no matter what the "status" of their relationship—that Jude had recognized early on in their acquaintance. Things frequently ended up broken when one of them was in a temper over the other, and they had both borne not a few bruises as a result of their intense connection. But it had served them well over the years and solidified a unique bond that mystified most.

Sasha's already irritable countenance darkened upon hearing Jude's flippant remark. She folded her arms across an impeccably creased blouse and regarded the dark woman coldly. "I'm very cognizant of our circumstances. But I am your business partner, and when you don't show up for a meeting, it tends to make us look bad."

Her morning with Liz had left Jude in high spirits, and she couldn't resist tweaking her associate just a little. "Did I miss something?" she inquired innocently. "The last time I checked you were my employee, Sasha. When did you get promoted to partner?"

She shoots...she scores!! Jude smirked silently, watching Sasha's saffron eyes narrow and a vein begin to throb faintly in her temple. "I have to maintain the appearance of at least *someone* being in charge," her assistant replied curtly. "Since you've been so...preoccupied...the last few weeks, that task has fallen to me."

Jude's recent unavailability was a first in their relationship. Even when Jude was toying with other lovers, she had always been accessible to her assistant. In no uncertain terms, the business had always come first. In the past, Sasha had shown no hesitation about pulling her out of bed with other women to deal with an emergency—and Jude was well aware that sometimes her assistant had done it just to piss her employer off. It was simply a part of the eternal power struggle between them. Over the last year, however, Jude's erotic landscape had been barren, and Sasha's 4:00 am phone calls hadn't disturbed anything other than a restless slumber. If her assistant had noticed the change, she never said anything; and Jude wasn't about to volunteer any information.

Seeing me with Elizabeth at the Club must have really thrown her, Jude mused silently, remembering that night and Sasha's disturbed expression. In fact, it looked much like the one her assistant wore right now. "Sash..." Jude sighed heavily, moving her feet off the desk and regarding her assistant squarely. "Does Miami really need one more shopping center?"

"What?" the other woman asked, nonplused by the question.

Jude smiled briefly. She knew Sasha had expected her to go off on a tangent about how her availability or lack thereof was none of her assistant's business. It was an old routine between them, and Jude decided it was time to throw a wrench into the works. "We were supposed to meet with some suits to see about selling our land to their developers so they could put more retail stores somewhere in Miami. Right?"

Sasha rolled her eyes at the gross simplification. "More or less."

"So...what difference does it really make? It's just shopping centers. Not taking this meeting isn't the end of the world. If they want the land, they'll deal. If they don't, they won't. Either way it's not going to matter in the long run to JLE one bit. It's not life or death to us." The pronoun was her peace offering to the other woman. Sasha was her employee in name only, and they both knew it.

Sasha continued to glare steadily at her boss for a long moment, then she blew out an exasperated breath and dropped elegantly into the comfortable chair across from Jude's desk. "You're right," she replied, a wry smile softening her caramel features. "The shopping center isn't life or death. But there are things going on right now that are." She looked at Jude meaningfully. "It's not like you to skip an appointment without calling. Did it ever occur to you that I might be the least bit worried about what could be keeping you? With those developers on my hands, I couldn't exactly get away to make sure you were just *amusing* yourself and not in real trouble."

Jude's eyes widened slightly with realization. "Oh," she breathed. "Sash—" She ran an agitated hand through her hair. She was used to a lot of things from her associate, but genuine concern wasn't one of them. It just wasn't in their repertoire of accepted emotions. "I'm sorry," she said finally. "I didn't even think about it."

"Don't apologize, Jude," she replied lightly. "It's just been a while since somebody's tried to blow you away. I've forgotten how to act. This is what? Twice in three weeks?"

"Yeah," Jude agreed ruefully, not mentioning the encounter at Ria's. "Just like the bad old days, huh?" *Actually,* Jude thought to herself, *It's worse than the bad old days, because the people I'm trying to help are the ones trying to kill me. But you don't know that, querida. And it's safer for you if you don't.*

Sasha nodded. "It feels like I'm having a bad case of deja vu."

"Don't worry about me," Jude shrugged. "I've got more lives than that damned Siamese cat of yours."

"Her name is Eyria," Sasha corrected, the banter moving them to more familiar turf.

"Whatever. Damned thing never liked me."

"Maybe if you didn't call her that 'damned thing' all the time, she'd like you more." The slight woman shifted comfortably in her chair, crossing her legs. "She misses you, you know."

Jude arched a skeptical brow. "That's a surprise. She never did anything but try to claw my eyes out every time she saw me."

"You were invading her domain. She was just trying to establish dominance," Sasha purred.

"She pick that up from her owner?" Jude teased, falling easily into the repartee.

"What can I say?" Sasha replied diffidently. "So, if you weren't running from some more nasty, hired assassins, what were you doing? Or do I even need to ask?" she smirked.

Jude hesitated before answering. Her randy proclivities were an old joke, and sometimes in the past the dark woman had used tales of her conquest to stroke her ex-lover's passions. Things were different now... Elizabeth was different... and she didn't want any of this new shining passion to be shaded with the ugly games she and Sasha played. To declare the subject off-limits, however, would be the worst thing she could do. An answer of some sort was required. "You know, the usual," she shrugged, hoping that Sasha would let it go.

Unfortunately, this wasn't to be the case. Sasha knew that few things could divert Jude's attention from the business of making money. "Anyone I know?"

"That blonde from the Club," she answered nonchalantly. In years past this could have meant any one of a dozen women that Jude might have encountered on her prowls. However, she had abandoned her hunting grounds in recent times—a fact that hadn't escaped her assistant's keen eye.

"You mean the one from *three weeks ago?*"

Hearing the note of incredulity in Sasha's voice, Jude realized her serious tactical error immediately. "Yeah," she said indifferently. "That one."

Sasha let out a low whistle, a mocking gleam in her eye. "That's amazing. From you, that almost qualifies as a lifetime commitment. What's the matter, Diablo, slowing down in your old age?"

Jude's eyes hardened at the old nickname, and the air between them thickened. The dark woman could see the tension rising until Sasha resembled a taut wire vibrating with suppressed motion. Jude's jaw clenched briefly in response before a lazy smile settled over her face. "Not slowing down, querida, just enjoying myself thoroughly," she taunted, knowing that Sasha's mind was now scrolling through erotic imaginings of Jude and the strange blonde woman she had seen with her employer. "Besides," Jude finished, going in for the close, "My plate has been kind of full lately, what with someone trying to kill me and all."

She let her assistant mull the idea while she walked down the hall to the commons area and poured two tall glasses of iced tea. Sash looked like she needed some cooling off. Returning to her office, she saw that Sasha was looking slightly less querulous, if a bit more flushed than when she had left. "Speaking of which..." She reseated herself and handed Sasha one of the glasses. "You come up with anything on that fiasco in the warehouse?"

"Not a thing," Sasha muttered darkly. "Massala's people cleaned up after themselves really well. The boys couldn't find anything to go on at the scene and our people in Metro Dade were pretty clueless. I'm going to put some feelers out on the street and—"

"Don't," Jude commanded sharply. The last thing she needed was Sasha stumbling into the middle of whatever scam the Agency was trying to pull. Jude had deliberately led Sasha to believe that Romair was indeed behind the assault to protect her. As she continued to edge her assistant out of the darker ends of her operations, the last thing she wanted was Sasha caught in the crossfire of the inevitable showdown. Of course, her assistant wasn't a fool, she had noticed the shift in her responsibilities and was obviously not pleased with the situation at all.

"Beg pardon?" Sasha blinked at her employer in surprise.

"I'll take care of it myself." *Drop it, Sash...drop it,* she urged silently. "Jude—I—"

"I *said* I'll take care of it." Blue eyes cooled as their gaze fixed squarely on her assistant's saffron eyes. "And that's it."

"I heard what you said," Sasha replied, just as icily. "I just don't understand."

"I'm not paying you to understand," Jude stated curtly. "Just stay out of it. Don't ask anybody anything. You get me?"

"Perfectly." Sasha stood up, rage evident in her walk as she strode across the room to the door. "Now if you'll excuse me, I'll go take care of the eight million *other* things you're too busy to take notice of."

"Fine," Jude dismissed her. "You do that."

❐ ❐ ❐

Jude spent the next few hours sorting through the mountain of paper that had accumulated during her impromptu hiatus from the office, but her mind was on something vastly different. *Something petite and blonde, with the greenest eyes imaginable.* Jude chuckled to herself. *I am losing it.* She shook her head ruefully, thinking about the morning.

As Jude had walked out the door, Elizabeth had clasped her hand and gently slid it between her slim legs, coating Jude's fingers in the ocean of honey that still flowed there. Now the scent of her lover lurked intoxicatingly near, but the woman to whom it belonged was entirely too far away for Jude's tastes. Shaking her head at the absurdity of what was happening to her, Jude swiveled her chair to face the magnificent Miami skyline spread across her windows.

She had spent most of her life in this city—a part of its haphazard potpourri existence. The powers-that-be had come dangerously close to dissolving the city altogether, carving it into little cultural fiefdoms; but honestly, she preferred Miami as it was now. She shared its mongrel heritage, had come from one of its little enclaves of the dispossessed. It always seemed to her as if people came to Miami when they somehow didn't fit the places of their origin. The only trouble was, she had been born here at the southern tip of this continent. The only place left to go was the ocean.

She had told Elizabeth she had seen it all...but really, she hadn't seen much of anything. Violence, death, cruelty—yes, and a lot of it caused by her own hand. She had seen the cities in Mexico and Colombia where the only law was strength and everyone sold their services to the blue-eyed devils who scattered their American dollars like rain across the wastelands. She had seen the darkest heart of every place she had been, and this city of her birth was no different. For most people, Miami was a fantasyland of clear skies, warm ocean waters, and brilliant sunlight. They never saw that the neon brightness could be just a cloak of mendacity giving people like Jude safe passage through its streets. The hidden sphere of alleys and back streets, of tenements and bars whose patrons had no names—this was the mother that had suckled Jude at her breast.

The dark woman held no illusions about what she was or from where she came. She was a thief and a murderer whose sense of honor was dubious at best. She had come from the twilight and traveled its realms her whole life. It was why she had never been to Paris or Rome—not because she believed she didn't deserve to see the marvels that those cities held—but because she knew that the cities she would find there would never be the places depicted in the photographic atlases she had collected for years.

Her mind wandered again to the woman she had left in her bed a few hours ago. *She's been to those places,* Jude thought to herself, smiling as she imagined Elizabeth sitting at a sidewalk cafe or walking along some scenic panorama. *And I bet they were beautiful.* She wondered what it would be like to see through her lover's emerald gaze, to be able to see the shimmering possibilities that existed along with the bleaker realities. *She's certainly seen both in me,* Jude mused. *And I can't imagine why, but she seems...okay...with that.* Jude knew that there was more to her new lover than she had been allowed to see, and her thoughts turned to what things Elizabeth might be taking care of right now.

She knew that the "boyfriend" Elizabeth had alluded to once and then conveniently forgot was a ruse, but surely there was a lover somewhere in the picture. *A real one...*someone who had rights to the honey-haired woman, who could claim this extraordinary person for their own. *Maybe she's married,* Jude considered. *She could want out. Maybe she's playing a game with him...making him pay for something he did.* Her heart constricted violently at the thought of being used by her lover. Her logic dismissed the idea—nothing she had seen had ever indicated that Elizabeth would be so coldly calculating and manipulative. But the fact remained that her lover had a secret... and that knowledge terrified Jude. *Get over yourself,* she mocked silently. *Others have done the same to you and worse. If she is using you, why should this time matter any more than those?*

The answer was so ridiculously simple that she didn't want to consider it, but her thoughts wouldn't let it rest.

You love her...

Jude stood up and walked to the window, gazing down at the vast space that separated her from the pedestrians below.

"Of course I love her..." she whispered, resting her head against the cool glass and thinking about the woman who now consumed her days and nights. *What choice do I have?*

▢ ▢ ▢

"I'm leaving, Sash..." Jude warned her rapidly approaching assistant. For hours, she had been fighting the overwhelming urge to go home and sweep Elizabeth into her arms, loving away any doubts that the honey-haired woman might have. As petrifying as the realization that she was in love with Elizabeth was, the fear didn't stand a chance against the blazing light that had warmed her soul once she had admitted it. All that remained was to tell her lover and convince that they could overcome whatever still stood between them.

If she had stopped to think about it, she would have laughed at the absurdity of finding herself in this position. A month ago it would have been unthinkable that she would allow a single person to have any influence over her—let alone this much. She only hoped she meant half as much to Elizabeth.

"Jude..." Sasha's voice intruded, unwelcome. "We have things we—"

"I don't care." The dark woman waved the handful of papers away, an uncontrollable smile on her face. "I've got to go."

"Will I be able to reach you in case of emergency?"

"No," Jude replied curtly, stepping into the elevator and pressing the "Lobby" button. As the doors closed silently behind her, she missed the cold fury that descended over her assistant's face.

The ground floor of the building that housed JLE Limited was devoted to a cache of exclusive shops, including a store called Lumac Jewels that Jude used to frequent when the population of her romantic life resembled that of a small town. Walking by the marbled glass cases holding several display items; a pair of diamond and emerald earrings caught her eye. Thinking they would look absolutely beautiful on her lover, Jude grinned to herself and absently fingered the diamond stud that still graced her right ear.

Walking into the store, a reedy man with thinning gray hair greeted her with a genuine smile. "May I show you something, Ms. Lucien?"

"Michel? Right?" Jude asked, vaguely recognizing the man.

The smile broadened as he nodded. "I'm pleased you remember me, Ms. Lucien. We haven't seen you in some time."

"It's hard to forget such great service," she replied. "Those earrings—" She gestured to the ones in the case.

"Exquisite, aren't they?" Michel quickly moved to offer the items to his customer's discerning inspection. Swiftly he laid out a black velvet cloth over the glass case and brought out the earrings in question. Ordinarily he would be well into his sales patter, but the dark woman had never been moved by such persuasion. She had an unerring eye for beauty and quality, and price was never an issue.

Jude quietly examined the jewels, pleased with their rich color and the smoothly carved facets of their pear shape. "Two carets?" she asked. He nodded briskly. "Correct."

"Okay," she grinned. "Can you wrap them up for me?"

"Of course, madam. Would you like us to put it on your account?"

"I still have one?" Jude asked. "I know it's been a while."

"You'll always have an account with us, Ms. Lucien," he assured her.

"Good to know," she replied wryly.

"Where would you like us to have this delivered?" he asked. "And would you like the usual card put with it?" His lean fingers deftly cleaned the earrings before placing them in a small black box.

"Usual card?" Jude frowned.

Michel smiled eagerly. "I know it's been a while, but we still have the card on file. You've always had us include it in the past."

"The same card?" she asked, arching a brow.

"Yes, madam," he replied, his smile dimming somewhat at the furrow forming on her brow.

"Tell me, Michel—do you keep a record of your customers' purchases?"

He seemed at a loss. "Well, Ms. Lucien...not ordinarily. But for our customers who have house accounts—like you—there's a record because everything has gone on the account."

"I see." Jude nodded. "Can I see my account?" she asked, an ugly realization beginning to surface.

"I assure you, Ms. Lucien, everything's in order."

"I'm sure it is," Jude dismissed his concern with a smile. "I'm not displeased with you or the store in any way. I'm just...curious...about my buying habits. May I see it?"

"Of course. Just a moment." He scurried away, emerging moments later with a computer printout several pages thick. "As you can see, it's been quite some time since you've come in, but here are all your purchases over the last several years."

"And the card?"

He handed it over silently.

I was just thinking about you... J.

Jude flipped through the pages, noting Sasha's address a number of times, but that was the only one repeated. She swore softly under her breath at the list of women whom she had used, discarded...paid off... with the gifts she had bought. What made it even worse—she realized with a lurch in her stomach—was that she could call up in her mind's eye the earrings and bracelets she had purchased far easier than the faces of the women to whom she had given them.

Feeling sick, Jude handed the printout back to Michel. "Will that be all, Ms. Lucien?" he asked softly.

"Yes," she nodded, swallowing hard. "I've changed my mind about the earrings. I won't be needing them."

Years of professional experience kept the thin man's face from falling in disappointment. He inclined his head in acknowledgment. "Very well, madam."

"Thank you." She turned to go, then stopped—her hand on the door. "And Michel? Cancel my account."

❡ ❡ ❡

One single question had consumed Liz since Jude had left her that morning.

How am I going to tell her?

Jude had indeed fulfilled all of the honey-haired woman's demands that morning, leaving the reporter with her wild essence painted on Liz's lips, and her scent clinging to her hands and body. They had made love until the small woman was breathless with climax and trembling with release. Still, Liz wanted more.

It was that simple. She wanted Jude. Wanted everything the dark woman had been, everything she was, and—most importantly—everything she could be. The reporter would do anything to preserve at least the possibility of a future with her lover. To that end, she considered what she had learned about Jude's attempt at atonement and the men who were trying to stop it.

That's it, she said to herself, mentally smacking herself for not recognizing it earlier. *Make it impossible for them to kill her.*

Liz picked up the phone, rapidly punching in an all-too-familiar number. "Lucas? It's me."

"Where the fuck have you been?" the roaring voice of the city desk editor demanded.

"I've been here, Lucas. And boy, do I have a story for you."

The time flew by as she sketched out for her boss only the briefest outline of the things she had learned. She wanted Jude's approval before they moved any further, but she at least needed to begin to lay the groundwork with her boss.

"Waitaminute..." he bellowed. "You're telling me that she's still working for the DEA?"

"Right..."

"How did you find this out?"

"Quit asking me questions, Lucas, and let me tell you what I know. We'll have all the documentation we need when the time comes." Well, they would if Jude agreed to her plan.

"Let me make sure I got this straight," he growled. "Lucien's still an op, but they sent her out into deep cover without backup, and now some turncoat's trying to kill her."

"More or less," Liz hedged. It was the truth. *Kind of.* And would become gospel once it went into print. The DEA couldn't deny the vast majority of the allegations, and the gaps in Liz's story—like the years where Jude really was working for the other side—would be eclipsed by the before and after parts of Jude's tale. In the public's eye, Jude would become a lone wolf hero, struggling against sinister, dark forces that surrounded her on all sides. More importantly, there would be way too much light on Jude for them to risk "removing" her from circulation.

"Why does it worry me when you say things like that, Gardener?"

"Don't worry, Lucas. Jesus, you're more nervous than an old lady."

"If you had any sense, you'd be nervous too. We're talking about the fucking government here, not to mention a woman who's cheerfully blown away dozens of people."

"She didn't do it cheerfully," Liz snapped. "She didn't have any choice."

Lucas couldn't have missed the fury in her voice. "Whoa...Liz...calm down." He paused, and Liz could almost hear the gears in his brain grinding. "Just how well have you gotten to know your subject?" he asked carefully.

The reporter took a deep breath and exhaled slowly, calming her temper. "Well enough to know that she's not a cold-blooded killer, Lucas. Well enough to know how much they've torn her up with their games." She sighed heavily. "Well enough to worry sometimes how she's survived this long."

A tense silence crackled along the phone line connecting them. She knew Lucas was fighting to ask the question, and at last he did. "What's this woman come mean to you, Liz?"

She didn't hesitate. "Everything, Lucas," she replied softly. "Everything."

They hung up shortly afterwards, Liz promising to call him later and arrange a meeting. She hoped to convince Jude to go with her idea and meet Lucas. She didn't blame her boss for worrying about her. From the outside it looked insane, but she knew in her position Lucas would have done the same thing.

What to do now? She rubbed a weary hand across her forehead, thinking about what material she would need to write the story. Carmina had merrily gone off to do the shopping an hour earlier, so she was alone with the dogs in the house. Walking by Jude's study on her way to the bedroom, she paused in the open doorway.

I'll just scan the files and refresh my memory, she thought to herself, moving towards the computer. She gently nudged Pete out of his spot on the desk chair and seated herself in his place. A tendril of Jude's leather-scented musk wound its way to her nostrils, and she closed her eyes at the essence, smiling to herself.

Rapidly booting the computer and typing in the password, she unlocked the secrets of Jude's DEA life and began working through the files.

Her attention focused on her task; she was oblivious to everything until she felt the cold barrel of a gun pressing against her neck, and the enraged presence of her lover standing over her.

"Give me one good reason why I don't kill you right now."

Chapter 14

This can't be happening...

It was the sole thought in both women's minds as they stood shocked into a frozen tableau by the unexpected confrontation. The gun was cold against the base of Liz's neck, but no colder than the fear that gripped her belly. Starting there, it worked its way rapidly through her whole body, the icy fear replacing the pulse of warm blood through her veins. By rights, her heart should have stopped beating; but it continued on, steadfastly determined to see this through. If she met her end at Jude's hands, a wildly disoriented part of her mind thought, it was somehow appropriate. She had gambled that she could make Jude love her enough so that the truth ultimately wouldn't matter. Now, it seemed, she had lost. In the surreal silence that enveloped them, she mourned. Not for the life she stood to lose, but instead for the death of this gossamer connection she had made. For the part of the dark woman's soul she was killing with this betrayal.

The barrel of the Sig nudged her, and the voice demanded again. "So? Tell me why I shouldn't kill you?"

Liz licked her suddenly dry lips, still staring at the computer screen. "It's not—" The world careened crazily as she found herself jerked from the leather chair and flung carelessly against the far wall. She landed hard against the corner of a small table that sat between the easy chairs, and the wood dug into the soft flesh between her shoulder blades. Trying to shake off the impact, she warily opened her eyes.

And saw the ruins of Jude's soul in the barren wasteland of those austere blue eyes.

The woman looming over her was every nightmare story she had heard about the Archangel personified. This was the woman whom the DEA had created, betrayed, and now wanted destroyed. The sweet lover who had offered Liz her soul in a trembling hand had vanished. She realized with a sinking heart that what was standing in its place was far, far worse than the fallen angel she loved.

"Don't," Jude warned dangerously, leaning down to fix Liz's terrified gaze on hers. "Don't tell me I didn't see you hacking into my computer, downloading the files. I'm obviously a fucking idiot, but I'm not blind."

"Let me explain." Liz's mind was frantically racing, wondering how on earth she *could* explain. She had planned this so differently—it wasn't supposed to be like this. Everything was supposed to work out between them. Her original goal had been long abandoned, and any thoughts she had entertained of writing an expose had vanished with the discovery of this extraordinary woman. A part of her heart cried out that this wasn't fair, not when they were so close...

So close to what? What did I think I could honestly build on a lie?

Jude was speaking, and Liz braced herself for the invective sure to follow. "Who are you? You're not a Fed," Jude snarled, shaking her head. "Feds don't fuck their targets." She waited a beat, then added. "At least not with such enthusiasm." She cocked her head, seeming to consider her options. "You working for Massala?" She arched an inquiring brow, pressing the Sig's muzzle solidly between Liz's eyes.

"No," Liz rasped. Although her thoughts were tumbling over each other in their haste to race across her mind, she found herself curiously unable to speak.

"Who then?"

"Nobody." Because the Sig filled her line of vision, she never saw the blow coming. Jude backhanded the smaller woman sharply across the face, splitting her lip.

"Don't you fucking lie to me!" Jude's fingers clenched themselves in the material of Liz's shirt, and she yanked the reporter painfully to her feet.

Liz shook her head woozily, vividly aware that Jude's control was shattering. If she escaped with only a split lip and some bruises, most people would consider her lucky. *"I don't know if I could ever raise a hand to you..."* Jude's words of a few days ago came flooding back to the reporter. She forced her eyes back to Jude's and saw the stunned expression in the blue.

It was as if the blow reminded Jude of those very words, for her fingers unwrapped their hold on Liz's shirtfront, and her head dropped wearily. "Just tell me," she requested dully, rubbing her forehead as if in great pain.

"I'm a reporter for the *Herald.*"

The betrayal was laid bare in those few words. She knew, to Jude's mind, a reporter from the Miami *Herald* could only want one thing from her, and it wasn't the dark woman's heart. Six words and everything that had happened between them became a lie.

A strangled laugh escaped from Jude's throat as she backed away from her lover. "A reporter?" she echoed incredulously. "You did all this for a fucking story?" As the truth sank into Jude's shattered soul, she paced away from Liz. When she turned back, the reporter noticed the graceful and predatory gleam in those pale blue eyes.

"Congratulations, querida," she murmured low in her throat. "You've done what the Feds, the networks, and the news rags couldn't. You got the whole story," she intoned tauntingly. "Sex, drugs, and rock 'n' roll. What more could you want?" she sneered. Liz was reminded of that night on the porch, when she had first seen her lover's dark heart. "So tell me—what does your public want to know?" Her voice dropped to a dangerously sensual purr. "Are you going to tell them what it felt like to be inside me? What I taste like? What I smell like?" She stalked closer to her lover, and Liz couldn't stop the shiver of fear-based arousal from running through her. Long fingers reached out to softly stroke the reporter's face. "You know, I can still smell you on my fingers." She traced the outline of the smaller woman's lips, rubbing softly over the tiny cut there. "Is that why you wouldn't let me leave this morning? You wanted to make sure you had all the details right?"

Her eyes were inches away from Liz's, and the reporter frantically searched for any hint of her lover inside. The blue gaze was cruelly devoid of any kindness, and she realized with a sinking heart that Jude's devolution was complete; the woman who touched her now was nothing more than a wildly sensual animal. "Don't..." she pleaded, still hoping for some glimmer of recognition. "Don't make it sound like that..."

"Like what, querida?" Jude asked, a mockingly innocent tone in her voice. "Like it was...research?" She frowned, the words obviously bringing home something she didn't want to hear. Shaking the moment off with a jerk of the dark head, her carnal smile returned. "I suppose that's all it was. But I have to grant you this: you were *very* thorough." She continued to stroke the smaller woman's face, her fingers occasionally brushing the honey-gold hair.

Liz sensed something desperate in the motions, as if Jude couldn't help trying to reconnect with her lover, despite the lie. Hoping there was something left inside Jude to reach, she leaned her face into the caress. "That's not what it was, Jude. Let me explain..."

The hand that had been tracing the soft curve of Liz's cheek now wrapped itself around the reporter's neck. "Don't. Say. A. Word," she warned quietly, gently squeezing the tender flesh in her hand. "Because now I know that everything that comes out of that beautiful mouth of yours is a lie."

Liz closed her eyes at the pressure, certain that it was finally all over for her. A silent fury began building—at herself for not simply telling her lover the truth earlier, and at Jude for giving in so easily to everything she claimed she wanted to be free from. Suddenly, the pressure at her throat was gone, and she opened her eyes to see Jude backing away from her again, this time towards the door.

There was a desolate sadness in the eyes that held her own, and though her mind cried out in rage that it didn't have to be this way, Liz said nothing.

"I want you out of here by the time I get back," Jude said softly in the growing dusk around them. "And if I ever see one word about any of this in print...Believe me, Elizabeth, I will kill you." Incredibly, the coldness in her eyes thawed a moment, a warm pulse of life flickering there. "No matter how much I might not want to," she added before slipping back into the shadows.

◻ ◻ ◻

Jude didn't know where she drove or how long, all she was aware of was one echoing refrain in her thoughts—*Make it stop.* She wanted it all to stop...the rage, the pain, and—most of all—the overwhelming sadness that these wonderful weeks had all been a lie. There would be no redemption now. No reason to reach down inside herself for the will to change.

As if she even could.

She knew now that Elizabeth hadn't seen anything in her worth believing in. Somehow the blonde reporter had discovered her weakness—the void aching with loneliness since Jason's death—and had exploited it with her sweet smile and accepting eyes. *Tell me, Jude...tell me why it hurts.* All the times Elizabeth had reached out for her, held her, listened to her, told her it was still okay.

It had all been a lie.

What must she really think of me?

Jude laughed aloud at the absurdity of the thought. Jude had merely been a subject—someone to be ruthlessly dissected and exposed for the benefit of the greater metropolitan area. *Of course, something like this would probably go national.* The dark woman wasn't ignorant of the market value on the inside story of her fall from grace. No matter, she'd put the fear of—if not God—then at least of the Archangel into the reporter before she had left. She didn't think Elizabeth would do anything stupid.

*Elizabeth...*Her body ached thinking of the woman who had tenderly made love to her this morning. This woman had so easily slipped past the agent's formidable defenses and captured the flag of her soul without hesitation. Did she know what she had done?

*Stop...just...stop...*her mind cried out. Savagely, she hurtled the Porsche faster into the falling sun...vainly hoping to be consumed by its dying tendrils.

◌ ◌ ◌

On the third floor of the Club, behind an entrance well-camouflaged from the paying customers and even the VIPs, was a small suite of rooms—a bedroom, a bathroom, and an office which had its own entrance. Jude had used these rooms in the past as kind of a rendezvous site for her conquests. It was an efficient set-up, and it kept her playthings from entangling themselves in her "real" life. Now she retreated there, much as a wounded animal might return to a lair long-abandoned to bleed in peace.

Beneath the roar of the shower, she didn't hear her assistant's entrance. The sudden appearance of Sasha's slender form wavily outlined by the clear shower curtain startled her. "What is it, *querida?*" she asked, standing under the spray. She had been hoping that the pounding water would ease the foggy confusion in her thoughts and wash off the remaining vestiges of her betrayer's touch. She just wanted to forget now—all of it, her brief time in the light, her birthing love, the dizzying power of Elizabeth's touch on her skin.

"Paul told me he saw you come in," Sasha replied simply. "I didn't think I'd be seeing you again tonight."

*Or for the next few days...*remained the unspoken end of Sasha's statement.

Jude arched into the spray, conscious of her assistant's lazy perusal of her muscled form through the curtain. The visual liberties that Sasha had always taken with her employer's body had been one of the things she found so appealing about the caramel woman. The defiant fearlessness in her gaze demanded respect. "I changed my mind." The Boxster had seemed to find its own way through the neon streets, leading her to the Club with its powers of distraction, to Sasha with her burning eyes and fierce hands. *Sasha can help...she always has,* her mind crooned seductively. She could make Jude forget the horrible pain slicing through her and leaving her soul in tatters.

Flicking the water off and pushing the curtain open with a sweep of her hand, she captured the saffron eyes of her assistant with a frankly sensual glance. A hunger rose in Jude's belly, long-dormant synapses firing at the remembrance of the erotic oblivion she had enjoyed at Sasha's hands. A lazy brow smirked at the slender woman. "Is that a problem?"

Sasha seemed nonplused for a moment, then smiled silkily. "Of course not. It's been a while since you've spent an evening here...for purely personal reasons."

As Jude stepped out of the shower, Sasha automatically handed her one of the thick, white towels stacked on the dressing table. "Dry my back, will you?" Jude asked in lieu of accepting the offering. She heard the sharp intake of her assistant's breath as the tall woman presented her with the bared expanse of her back. Rivulets of water trickled down the slope of her shoulders, tickling the awakening nerve-endings there. Unbidden, the memory of standing before Elizabeth, warm water running down her skin, returned to her. It was an image that rocked Jude with its resonant intensity—the honey-haired woman resting below her, that perfect mouth driving her powerfully over the edge of release.

And then the towel was blotting away the water, blotting away the memories. Jude shook her head briefly, growling softly at the firm touch of her assistant's hands. "Thanks," she said, stepping away and turning around.

"Anything else?" Sasha asked, the cloth still in her hands.

Two words...thousands of implications. She had taken Sasha like this before. Simply pushed her against the dressing table and spread the slender woman's legs, seizing her pleasure. It was part of their game—Sasha's torments, Jude's sensual brutality—each woman deriving their pleasure from the power they wielded over the other. It was an ebb and flow that had never truly gone away, merely transmuted itself into something more acceptable to their new situation. Now, the dark woman felt its seductive pull once more. It had been a long time since she had allowed herself to be so reckless; longer still since she had felt the lithe grip of those thighs draped over her shoulders. She tried to call up the memory of Sasha's taste—but her senses only responded with the honey-sweet essence of the reporter. That opened the very floodgate Jude wanted most desperately to close. The bone deep sensations of Elizabeth gently painting her scent on Jude's lips—of the kisses that were flavored by the evidence of their mutual desire—swept through her relentlessly.

The remembrances brought with them a bitter draught of betrayal, and Jude resolutely shoved the desire for things she couldn't have out of her mind. Still, a restless passion fired her eyes as she smiled sensually at her ex-lover. "Relax, querida. It's going to be long night." A light shudder rippled visibly through Sasha's body, and she realized smugly that she could still bend the icy little executive to her will. *This could be fun,* she thought, ignoring the stark truth that all her desire was reserved for someone else.

"You're in a mood tonight," Sasha observed, her eyes following Jude as she opened the tiny closet. Ever the pragmatist, Jude had little such stashes of clothing and "supplies" throughout the city. She never knew when she might just need to hole up for a while or make a hasty exit.

"A good mood," Jude corrected.

"You mean a dangerous mood," Sasha murmured, aware Jude's ears wouldn't miss the remark.

Jude tossed a smirk over her shoulder. "Dangerous for some," she replied. "Good for me."

"That's usually the way it works," Sasha agreed, a knowing look in her eye.

The dark woman chose to judiciously ignore the last comment. "What do you think?" She held up two dresses. One was an elegantly simple black dress, with a low-cut bodice and a short skirt that would fall loosely just above Jude's knee. The other was a crimson, crushed velvet number that—even on the hanger—looked like it had been conjured up out of an intensely erotic dream.

"The red one," was Sasha's unhesitating response.

Jude chuckled silently at the look in her ex-lover's eye and appraised the recommendation again. The dress was sleeveless, and the thin straps holding it up would allow the fabric to drape gracefully over her breasts, hinting at the beautiful fullness resting underneath. The whole design was a monumental tease—it would cling to the exquisite length of Jude's body and wrap around her legs with possessive familiarity, stopping just below the knees. A generous slit meandered at an angle across the fabric, allowing both freedom of movement for the wearer and a taunting glimpse of otherwise hidden secrets for those blessed enough to see. It would definitely make a statement, and the longer Jude studied the garment, the more she realized that it was just the statement she wanted to make. "You think?"

"Definitely." Sasha nodded, unknowingly licking her lips.

Jude watched the movement with an inward smile. "Then the red one it is," she decided. *Oh yeah...this is gonna be fun,* she considered, an amused gleam in her eye. It had been far too long since she had played with her subjects. Everything about tonight—from the dress that she wore to her presence in the Club and the woman at her side—would make one singular statement that not even the most ignorant observer could miss.

El Diablo was back.

◻ ◻ ◻

The evening's revelries were well underway by the time she made her first appearance. A wanton pulse coursed throughout the Club, its patrons unknowingly responding to the wild flame in Jude's blood. Sasha had discreetly advised the disc jockeys and bartenders to "crank it up tonight." So the music was a little more sensual, the drinks a little more effective, and the patrons a little more uninhibited as the night reached out its beckoning hand for them.

Jude absorbed the happenings around her with a satisfied curl of her lip. The teeming, seething, writhing masses of people below were her creatures; and she moved smoothly through them, a regal tilt to her head. Vaguely familiar faces hailed her, welcoming her back to her territory with grateful eyes. Men around her nodded, pleased to be basking in the reflected glow of her malevolent grace. Women whose bodies she had possessed—and those who wished her to do so—brushed teasingly against her, tempting her senses with their nearness.

A dance, a drink, a tease—slender arms around her neck, the taste of tequila in her mouth, smoky laughter drifting pleasantly over her ears. All those unwanted thoughts were at last mercifully crushed beneath the ruthless heel of sensory overload. Jude walked among her subjects, the gleam in her eye enticing some and warning others with its ravening strength.

And always...there was Sasha, never more than a swift glance away. The woman had an unerring sense of what Jude needed and gave her ex-lover exactly that, leaving her free to roam, but never completely unattended. The satisfied smirk in her assistant's eye bespoke of her confidence at how this night would end, but others were not so sure of the huntress' intentions. Accordingly, Jude enjoyed the sensual buffet offered—partaking of the curve of a hip or the herbal sent of a lock of hair. The occasional fleeting caress of a knowing hand brushed her skin, but none were so bold that they sought her mouth with theirs. She prowled among them constantly, looking for something that wasn't in the well-dressed, well-toned bodies on display.

People would talk about that night for months to come and the carnal recklessness that infected them all. Their dark queen had returned, and her subjects reveled in that knowledge. Maybe that's why Jude didn't see her coming at first. She was just another glorious specimen there for her to take or not, as her mood dictated. Something, though—a flash of honey, a wisp of her essence on the air—identified itself as that which the hunter had been seeking, and she turned just as Elizabeth stepped directly in front of her.

A slender arm uncoiled powerfully, and there was the harsh sound of a palm striking her face. Her head snapped back at the blow, a trickle of blood beginning from the tiny gash Elizabeth's ring had made in her cheek. The reporter snarled savagely, "First of all: don't ever hit me again." She moved as if to slap Jude again, but the tall woman caught her arm in mid-air.

"Ah-Ah," she warned, easily holding the slim wrist in her grasp. "First one's free, but the next one costs."

Jude knew that the room couldn't be silent...it was too large and there were too many people around her for all of them to have taken notice. But a deafening roar of emptiness filled her ears, and the room narrowed to only the woman in front her. Everything she had been so desperate to forget thrust itself viciously back into her consciousness. The feel of Elizabeth's skin held in hers was almost unbearable in its intensity, even though the woman in front of her was quivering with fury. She knew in that moment that she would never be free of craving this woman's touch, her voice, her body. A furious rage at her helplessness in the face of these emotions rose up inside her. An angry sneer formed on her mouth.

Elizabeth twisted out of her grip, staring at Jude with sparking eyes. "You owe me the chance to explain."

Jude studied her lover icily. "I *owe* you?"

"Yes," came the resolute answer.

She gestured mockingly. "Then by all means...Explain."

"Jude..." Elizabeth's jaw clenched, and she blinked back the shining brightness suddenly appearing in her eyes. It wasn't a plea; it wasn't a demand...but it was something the dark woman couldn't refuse.

"Follow me," Jude said hoarsely, leading her lover up the winding stairs.

❑ ❑ ❑

As soon as Liz stepped into the small bedroom, she realized the magnitude of Jude's actions the night they first met. The dark woman could have simply brought her up here in the guise of *getting real* and seduced the reporter, who knew exactly how effortless it would have been. Her body had been responding to Jude from the moment she had laid eyes on the beautiful drug dealer. Instead, Jude had taken Liz's request at face value, opening up her home—and eventually her life—to the other woman. And though Liz had not been untruthful since that first night, the lie that gave birth to their relationship was a cutting one.

The silence in these rooms was genuine, and to Liz the gulf separating them seemed unbreachable. Leaning against the heavy oak door, she watched Jude pace across the room with fiercely measured steps. The velvet dress clung to her like blood to a wound. "Jude..." she faltered.

"Why?" A guttural rasp. A question ripped from the tatters of Jude's soul.

"I...I didn't know," she replied, unable to explain that she'd had no idea that this woman would be the one to come to possess her soul.

"Know what?" Jude asked harshly. "What could you possibly *not* know?"

"That I'd fall in love with you," she whispered quietly.

Jude swayed slightly as her body absorbed the impact of those words slamming into her. "Don't say that," she ordered darkly, advancing towards Liz.

"I love you."

The words were the only thing Liz could grasp onto in the maelstrom surrounding her. As a reporter, she had learned that most truths were relative, depending on the slant of the story, the speaker, and their motivations. She had also learned, however, that there were some truths that were fundamental; truths that had formed the bedrock of individuals, of philosophies, of nations.

Somewhere along the line the knowledge that she was in love with Jude Lucien had become the foundation for everything that Elizabeth Peterson Gardener was.

Whatever happened, Jude had to know that.

"I love you."

Jude stepped closer, an angry look suffusing the patrician elegance of her features.

"I love you."

Jude was right in her face, their bodies almost...achingly...touching. "You lie."

There was genuine menace in those blue eyes...and she noted with astonishment, she could see the pale flame flickering with something that looked suspiciously like raw fear. She had gambled before and won on those unexplained expressions that played across the dark woman's eyes. Now it was time to do so again. "I love you, Jude," she repeated, bringing a barely steady hand up to caress her lover's cheek.

The sound of shattering glass surrounded them as Jude's fist smashed into the glass picture frame just to the right of the doorway. Something within Jude seemed to shatter as well, and she closed her eyes—unable to bring herself to touch her lover, but equally unable to move away.

"Shh..." Liz crooned, running her hand up the corded muscles in Jude's arm and moving it away from the damaged glass. "It's okay..." Jude's fingers were still curled into a fist, and slowly Liz pried them loose, carefully brushing away the shards of glass. Tiny cuts dotted the bronze skin, and the shallow gashes were filled with blood. "You're always hurting yourself, Jude," she murmured, clasping the hand in hers and pressing the smooth palm against her lips.

◫ ◫ ◫

"No." Jude whispered, her whole body aching from the assault of Elizabeth's simple words. "I can't do this..." She couldn't just let go of the betrayal and the fury and simply accept the waterfall of light that her lover's declaration poured over her. How could she accept this as truth, when it could be a lie as easily as the other words had been? Bewilderingly, her body persisted in naming this liquid feeling as real and the icy fury of years past as false.

The truth—she could see now—was in the infinitely tender way Elizabeth was plucking glass shards out of her hand, in the trembling pulse visible in the reporter's delicate throat and in the resolute courage needed to slap a killer in the face and demand respect. Jude tried denial one last time, knowing that to accept Elizabeth's love meant surrendering her own in return. If Elizabeth chose to betray her again, Jude knew she would not survive the devastation. "I can't do this..." She opened her eyes to the bright fields of green before her.

"Yes, you can," Liz admonished, keeping her eyes carefully fixed on Jude's. A fearful silence rested between them; and the reporter took a deep breath, hating that the next words were necessary. "I'm sorry I lied to you."

Jude's breathing hitched, the rock in her throat blocking the air's passage. She clamped down hard on the impulse to run, to strike out, to be anywhere but lost in this woman's eyes. "I'm sorry you lied too," she replied hoarsely, her throat raw with the effort of breathing.

"I don't know how to fix it. Or what else I can say."

What else is there to say, really? Jude thought.

She could either accept Liz's love or not. Walking out of the reporter's life was still possible at this point, although she knew that her soul would never recover. Either way, she knew now she could never go back to what she had known before—back to the dark heart of the life that still pumped relentlessly downstairs. The fear crested high, its viscous murkiness thrusting down her throat, seeking to drive her under. Give into the fear or fight to reach the light that was being offered.

What choice do I have?

"Tell me you love me," Jude said thickly, resting her forehead against her lover's.

"I..." Astonishment made her stumble over the words. "I love you."

"Say it again," Jude demanded.

"I love you."

"Again." Using the truth to wash the rotting scent of lies, fear, and rage from her lungs.

"I love you."

The powerful force of Jude's mouth finding Elizabeth's crushed the last declaration. She tasted the metallic tang of blood on her lover's lips, knew it was from her earlier blow. Reverently her tongue wiped away the traces of her violence and sought penitent entrance into Elizabeth's mouth. The reporter joyfully granted admittance to her dark lover, her arms wrapping around Jude's neck, clasping the woman nearer still. "I love you," she murmured, her words distorted and muffled by the kiss.

Jude's mouth was demanding, sweeping through Elizabeth as she sought to claim the love that the reporter so freely offered. She coaxed Elizabeth's tongue out of its shyness until they were exploring each other's mouths with raw abandon in a white-hot kiss that threatened to immolate them where they stood.

Then her hands were everywhere, absently noting the unfamiliar garments her lover wore and rapidly divesting her of them. She wanted

Elizabeth naked before her, as open and wanting as Jude herself had been that morning. "God, you're beautiful," Jude marveled, watching the last lace-trimmed silk drop away from the reporter's body. Elizabeth stood trapped between the cool wood of the door and the volcanic heat of her lover. "So beautiful," she repeated. She clasped Elizabeth's hands in her own, leading her to the bed. "Lie down," she commanded hoarsely.

Her eyes were a vibrant, pulsing violet as she watched her lover obey the request. Elizabeth rested expectantly on the dark expanse of the bed's comforter, waiting for the glorious sight of Jude's bronze form to emerge from its captivity. Velvet parted reluctantly from skin, hugging the length of Jude's body as it slid slowly, inexorably to the plush carpet.

"Come here," Elizabeth murmured, her slender arms reaching out in invitation.

"No," Jude replied quietly, her own hands roving across the gentle curves of Elizabeth's calves. Her strong grip testing the defined muscles of her lover's thighs, she whispered fiercely, "Mine."

Surrendering to Jude's unspoken need, Elizabeth leaned back and rested her arms easily above her head. Jude's fingers traced the outlines of Elizabeth's body in a touch of possession—over hips and stomach, breasts and shoulders. Long fingers scorched her lover's skin, searing her desire into muscle and bone. Elizabeth arched into those commanding hands, pressing her flesh into the embrace and craving the length of Jude's body against her own.

Jude's mouth followed her hands' progress across her lover's landscape, confirming with taste what touch had already communicated to her trembling body. Elizabeth was light and warmth, salt and rising musk, willingly at the mercy of the dark woman's demand. Jude straddled the smaller woman gracefully to pin Elizabeth's legs tightly together at the knees. Inclining her head to the painfully aware nipple just below her mouth, she growled low in her throat as her tongue found its tautness. Elizabeth moaned in gratitude at the contact; and her hips ground vainly against the mattress, half-mad for her lover's soothing touch.

Her own arousal flowing thickly between her legs, Jude sought to twist her lover's need higher by claiming each breast in turn. Her mouth was a ravening instrument of pleasure, bent to a single task. Elizabeth clasped the headboard seeking something to ground her as her body arched helplessly into the torment, begging for more. "Please..." she breathed.

"Yes, Elizabeth," Jude whispered. "Let me hear you...I need to hear you tonight."

The only sounds in the room became the increasingly labored rasp of their breathing, and their quiet murmurs of pleasure. In their minds and souls, the last noises of the Club had been shut away, the revelers dismissed. Now the world consisted only of their skin. Jude's touch. Elizabeth's need.

"Touch me."

It was the plea Jude had voiced to Elizabeth that morning, when she had allowed herself to be taken by the smaller woman in a final surrender of pleasure. Now it was Elizabeth's turn to strip her soul bare and lay the raw need at her lover's feet, trusting the dark woman to take her where she needed to go.

Jude slipped easily down the length of the reporter's body, gently draping a slim leg over each of her shoulders and nestling in the cove created there. She loved this place, the intimate touch of her cheek on Elizabeth's thigh, the anticipation in her body at a fevered pitch.

A low moan escaped from Elizabeth as Jude's fingers deftly found the hidden nucleus of the reporter's desire and exposed it to her questing tongue. "Oh yes..." she groaned.

For the dark woman, this touch was absolution granted to an unworthy soul. She reached far within her lover, reveling in the tight walls surrounding her fingers and tongue, searching for that one perfect spot that she could call home. A quiet gasp from above told her when she'd found it, and soon fingers and hips were moving in an inexorable rhythm. She closed her eyes to better absorb the unadulterated sensation of her lover's desire. *This was her air...this was her life...this was her home...*

This was...

Everything.

"*Oh God....Jude.........*" The climax that ripped through Elizabeth plunged into Jude with astonishing fury. She heard herself crying out in response to the powerful convulsions, felt her body trembling violently, and then...somehow... she had wrapped the smaller woman in her embrace and was murmuring hushed lover's nonsense into the honey-haired woman's ear. They held each other in the long moment of silence, both too overwhelmed by the force of their passion to say anything. Pressing a tender kiss to Jude's forehead and brushing away the damp tendrils of hair there, Elizabeth said quietly, "We need to talk."

"I guess you're right," Jude agreed reluctantly. Both women, however, remained silent, their breathing and heartbeats slowly returning to normal. She liked the way the smaller woman was sprawled across her and was loathe to leave the tenuous haven they had managed create, but there were a great many things left to say. "I thought it was another lover, you know," she said in the dimness.

"What?" Elizabeth's voice was perplexed.

"Your secret. I knew you had one you were keeping," Jude explained. "I just thought...there was someone else. Someone serious that you were trying to hurt by being with me."

The reporter took in the statement with a tilt of her head. Then she leaned across Jude, flipping on the lamp she had noticed on the bedside table. "I want to see your face." She scrutinized her lover intently. "You thought I was using you the whole time." There was an edge to her tone and a sharpness in her gaze that unsettled the larger woman, and she found herself squirming under the inquisition.

"You were." The defensive accusation leapt from her throat before she could call it back.

Liz slipped off the bed and regarded Jude wearily. "If that's what you still think then I was wrong. We don't have anything to talk about."

"Wait!" Jude gently grasped her arm. "I didn't mean it like that."

"How else could you have meant it?"

"Just sit back down, okay?" Jude released her lover's arm and ran a hand through her tousled hair. "No, wait, let me turn the bed down first."

Elizabeth couldn't stop the tiny grin that edged onto her mouth. "You're pretty sure of yourself, aren't you?"

Jude gave her a lop-sided smile. "No, I just thought if we're going to fight, we might as well be comfortable. 'Kay?"

"Fair enough," Liz agreed, allowing Jude to coax her back to her spot. Before she realized it, she was tucked neatly in her lover's arms once more, and they were both sitting with their backs propped against a generous mound of pillows at the headboard. "Now we can fight?" she asked, although Jude had effectively dismantled the anger that had begun building in them anew.

"Now we can fight." Jude nodded. "Let me start this over again. Yes, I thought you were using me...because I couldn't understand what in the world you would want with me otherwise. If I had been thinking clearly, I would have realized that you were a reporter the minute you didn't run screaming from the house after getting shot."

"So why didn't you?" Liz asked quietly.

Jude paused a long moment, wondering how to give voice to the tumultuous onslaught of feelings that had begun almost from the first moment she had seen the smaller woman. "Because I *wanted* you to want to be with me," she said finally.

Liz caught her breath sharply at the admission. "You did?"

"Oh yeah," Jude chuckled ruefully. "The morning after you were shot, I was in the car thinking about that lame-ass story you gave about some boyfriend. I remember thinking that it just didn't make sense." She leaned in for a brief taste of her lover's mouth. "And then I remember very distinctly not giving a damn." Another kiss steadied her faltering courage. "So in a way, it's my fault that the lie went on for so long. I didn't want to hear the truth."

"Stop that right now," Liz demanded. "Good God, don't you dare take responsibility for this." She faced her lover squarely. "What I did was *wrong*. Trying to manipulate you into giving me the story was *wrong*. Get it?"

Jude looked into the fierce green eyes of her lover and sighed softly. "Elizabeth, in comparison to all the wrongs that I've done to others, yours don't even register on the scale."

"Then forgive me for it." The words dropped unthinkingly from Elizabeth's mouth, and the smaller woman turned pale as she realized just what she had asked.

Forgive me...

Is it that simple? Jude mused. Thinking of all the years she had spent in an unquenched rage, the years wasted and alone...the need to have someone near who understood, accepted, and forgave...Jude's mind raced with the memories. And then the sensation of the woman wrapped in her arms sank deep inside...the joy of waking up with her, the glimmer in those green-gold eyes that soothed pains so deep she had believed they were irrevocably imprinted on her soul. "I do," she replied simply.

Elizabeth's jaw dropped. "What?"

"I do," Jude repeated, sending a cascade of kisses dancing along her lover's cheek. "I do...I do...I do..."

Their mouths tangled and danced, a lazy fire stroking into their bellies. "I can't believe it," Liz murmured. The words were more an elaborate sigh than anything, but nonetheless, they didn't escape Jude's keen hearing. "What can't you believe?" she asked, breaking off her attentions.

Liz blinked dizzily, her senses still reeling from the brush of Jude's lips. She stared deep into the gently pulsing violet of her lover's eyes and took a deep breath. "Are you sure you're not angry with me anymore?"

Jude rose and paced a few steps before turning and facing her lover. "I...I'm not...real smart about some things, Elizabeth. Most of the relationships in my past haven't lasted any longer than it took me to get my clothes back on." At Liz's snort of laughter, she smiled slightly. "I don't know how to do this..." She gestured back and forth from Liz to herself, "Talking thing." She paced a few more steps, as if trying to gather up the scattered words to make Liz understand. "When I walked into the study and saw you sitting there, I wanted to die," she said bleakly. "I didn't know I could hurt so bad and not be bleeding somewhere." Liz winced at the simple declaration, feeling it cut deep into her own heart. "And I wanted to make you hurt as much as I did. That's why I hit you. Even though all it did was make me hurt more. I just thought if I could make you feel as bad as I did, then it would be okay. I wouldn't hurt so bad." She murmured, closing her eyes as she remembered the sensation of her hand striking Elizabeth's tender skin.

"I betrayed you. I don't blame you..."

"No!" Jude's eyes flew open. "NO!" she repeated forcefully. "I had no right to hit you. Much less put a gun to your head." She shook her head. "I may be fucked up, but at least I know that much."

Liz, however, was not about to let Jude bear the brunt of their shared guilt over the horrible confrontation in the study. "I've always known that for whatever reason—violence is your first instinct. And it was a risk I took lying to you like I did." Liz wanted to reach out and hold the dark woman close, steady the gaze that threatened to turn away from her. They had to confront this last obstacle and put it behind them, because otherwise Liz knew that fear of the dark woman's violence would shatter any hopes they had of rebuilding the relationship. She studied her partner a bit longer before saying her next words. "That's not to say I enjoyed the sensation of you tossing me across the room."

Shame colored Jude's features scarlet. "I'm so sorry," she whispered.

"Don't ever do that again," Liz stated softly.

"Never." Jude shook her head emphatically. The dark woman groped for words to describe the white-hot pain that had seized her the moment that she'd seen Liz combing through her private files. She'd known then that it was more than just the rage at being lied to. It was a deeper, completely alien pain of someone who had all of their hopes and dreams reduced to ashes in a single, searing instant. Watching Elizabeth at that moment, she had been seized by the rage of the disposed—howling at being shown things infinitely precious, and then told they were not for the likes of her. Her soul had cried out in rending agony each time she had abused the smaller woman, but she been unable to stop the base instinct to annihilate anything that tried to hurt her. Pulled by a power stronger than even her formidable will, she crossed the room and wrapped the reporter in a fierce embrace, her body conveying a deeper sorrow than her words ever could.

Jude's skin against hers was salve to the reporter's battered heart. She could feel her lover's muscles trembling softly around her, and she marveled anew at the strength in Jude's darkened soul. "Where do we go from here?" she asked softly, her breath a warm puff of air against Jude's neck.

The dark woman released Liz from their embrace and sat beside her on the bed. For her, the answer was a simple one—the inescapable conclusion she had come to yesterday. Now she spoke the words out loud. "The way I see it... what other choice do I have?" Her fingers traced a lingering path over Elizabeth's features, absorbing the warm smoothness of her lover's fair cheeks. Seeing Elizabeth's brow furrowed at the rhetorical question, she tried to explain. "I can either forgive you—learn to trust you again—and we can try and figure out what we really have between us. Or I can hold on to all the anger and all the old ways that I've lived by. And honestly, Elizabeth, I realize now that's no kind of life at all."

"You can change you life without me in it," she countered.

Jude regarded the woman beside her for a long moment. "Perhaps," she acknowledged. "But the truth is...I don't want to."

"So..." Liz drew out the word, a happy anticipation building in her veins. "What do you want?"

Jude never hesitated, never blinked, never thought about it at all. "You," she said simply.

The word was sealed with an achingly sweet kiss that ignited the kindling desire that always lurked close to the surface whenever they were near one another. For now, their hesitation was gone, their regrets soothed...and there was nothing standing between them. A brilliant light that seemed to bathe the length of their bodies as Jude moved smoothly into her lover and Elizabeth responded in kind.

Liz felt Jude's hands beginning to roam her body once more. Knowing that once they began making love, all other conversation would be lost for the night, she reluctantly captured the elegant fingers in her hands, stilling their exploration. "We still have stuff..." She was interrupted by another sweetly erotic kiss. "We gotta talk about..." She gasped as Jude's mouth worked its way over her jaw to the delicate pulse in her neck. "Seriously."

It was a tone that Jude couldn't deny, and she pulled away with a roguish grin. "Then are we okay?"

"I think we're pretty damn good now," Liz replied, relieved laughter rising from deep inside. "But there's a couple more things I need to tell you." She didn't miss the rippling tension that entered her lover's body, although Jude did an admirable job of not changing her expression. The reporter smoothed the tiny furrows in Jude's brow, letting her fingers trail down the sharp cut of the woman's jaw. "Shh..." she soothed. "It's nothing bad."

The muscles relaxed under her touch, and Jude snugged the reporter a little closer in her embrace. "Then what is it?"

"I think I can help you with your problem."

Jude chuckled dryly. "And which problem is that? We've established I have dozens."

"The one that involves people pointing guns at you."

"Oh. That problem." She cocked a brow at the smaller woman. "Let's have it."

"Well..." Liz began, chewing her lip. "As odd as it might sound, me being a reporter might come in handy."

Jude already didn't like the sound of this. "What are you thinking?" she asked warily.

"We write a story. Put too much light on you for the DEA to do anything." Liz waited for the inevitable explosion, the accusation that she was still trying to use Jude, the fury...anything...

What she got was a thoughtful expression on her lover's face.

"Well?" she asked the dark woman.

"I'm waiting for you to finish explaining," Jude replied steadily, but the tension was again evident in her body.

"Okay." She could work with that. "You still work for the DEA right?"

"What do you mean?"

"Well, you said that you were on a psychiatric leave of indeterminate length, and that you simply never came back. Right?"

"Right," Jude looked skeptically at her lover. "So?"

"So... you're back now, trying to round up the rest of the Massalas. Trying to complete the assignment you were given before rogue elements in the DEA gave up your partner to the enemy."

"You think you can spin doctor the last five years of my life?" Jude snorted derisively. "That's not possible."

"Listen to me, Jude." Liz shifted her position, sitting up so that she could face her lover. "Ever since you told me about Jason, I've been thinking about why somebody in the agency would give him up like that."

"Any conclusions?" Jude asked bitterly.

"Unfortunately, yes. And they all have to do with you and your unique ability to get the job done."

"What do you mean?"

"When I was talking to Tony the other night, he described you as a 'rule-breaker who got results.' So the powers-that-be looked the other way, when in other cases they might not. Look at the Massala assignment. What did they say they wanted? Results. And they didn't care how you got them. Somebody liked having you just this side of out-of-control."

Jude opened her mouth as if to protest, then snapped it shut. "Go on," she said tightly.

"What did your relationship with Jason do? It grounded you—it made you start thinking about some of the things you were doing—it made your job harder. Made you more inefficient."

"You're saying that someone sacrificed Jason to keep me *efficient*?"

"Sort of. At first I thought they wanted to get rid of Jason and you. But the more I think about it, the more I think they wanted Jason's influence out of the way. He gets killed and you kill those responsible for this death."

"Rico and the Cartel."

"Exactly. No muss, no fuss." Liz nodded. "But the problem occurred when Rico called you to take care of Jason. Whoever sacrificed him, had no way of knowing that you'd end up being the one pulling the trigger."

Jude blanched at the raw description, a wound on her soul that would never quite heal. But Liz's gentle hands held her softly, not allowing her to slip back into the wrongs of the past. *Stay here...*those hands seemed to say.

And she did.

Taking a deep breath, she steadied her trembling heart. "So what happened then?"

"Damage control," Liz replied simply. "Who saw you when you took Jason back home?"

"Nobody." Jude shrugged. "Ria." She thought for a moment. "Kent showed up 'cause I called him." She cocked her head at her lover. "What do you mean damage control?"

"That's where they made their second mistake. They swept everything up so neatly and quickly that you started thinking and got suspicious. That's what turned you against the Agency right? I mean if you had been called onto the carpet for the events leading up to Jason's death, maybe suspended, given a vaguely plausible reason for Jason's losing his cover, and then eventually returned to duty—do you think you would have ever suspected something wasn't right?"

Jude shook her head. "I suppose you know why they want to kill me now?"

Liz shrugged. "As near as I can figure, bringing in Romair Massala has something to do with it."

The dark woman thought a moment, her mind overloaded with the all-too-plausible theory that Elizabeth had placed before her. Then it hit her. "Bringing in Romair has everything to do with it," she said quietly.

When Jude didn't immediately continue, Liz gestured with her hands. "Hello? Tell me."

The dark woman smiled wryly. "Sorry, I was just thinking there for a minute."

"Think out loud," Liz ordered.

"When Rico went down, the Massala's started throwing everything they had at me. Until word got out that Rico was working the Feds for a deal himself."

"Was he?"

"It was news to me. That's when I knew for sure that he had somebody inside the Agency, but I couldn't find out who. I'll bet you a million dollars Romair knows who it is."

"And that's why they want him in?"

"No," Jude growled. "That's why they want him dead. It's the perfect set-up...one drug lord trying to take out another, and both killed in a DEA raid. The Agency comes out looking like heroes." Jude whistled low in her throat. "That's why Kent said that they were pushing me for another meet with Romair. They were waiting for a chance to take us down."

"But you work for them."

"It's not on the books. Or at least it's not supposed to be. They'd have plausible deniability at the very least."

"Not if we go public first."

Jude smiled grimly. "That's why your plan just may work."

Chapter 15

When Liz woke that morning, she found that in their sleep they had wound seamlessly around each other, unerringly coming together to form a perfect helix. Jude was warm and supple against her, and Liz could scent musky traces of sleep and sex on her lover's skin. Sighing contentedly and snuggling closer to the larger woman, she murmured softly, "Finally."

"Finally what?" came the voice from above.

"You're awake?" Raising herself and bracing on one elbow, Liz encountered a pair of amused blue eyes regarding her.

"Yup," Jude replied succinctly. "Finally what?" she repeated.

"Oh, that." Liz chuckled softly. "Well...it's just that, this is the first time since we've...well...you know...become...well, you know...that I actually managed to wake up with you. Usually you've wandered off and one of the dogs has usurped your place. I was just thinking 'Finally I get to wake up with you.'" She studied her lover's face, feeling a faint blush suffuse her cheeks. "Stupid, huh?"

A warm smile broke over Jude's face, and she leaned up to capture the fair woman's lips with her own. "Not stupid at all," she corrected after their soft greeting. "I've never really..." she hesitated, shaking her head. "I'm not real good at the morning-after thing."

"Guess you'll have to practice, huh?" Liz teased her gently, not wanting the shadows to cloud their morning so early.

"Guess so," Jude agreed with a wry smile. "You mind?"

"Not at all," the smaller woman assured her. "I can even offer you a few tips if you want."

"I think that might be a good idea." Though Jude's words were solemn, she was unable to control the bright sparkle in her eyes.

Liz grinned rakishly at her lover, delighted that Jude wanted to play. "Okay," she said briskly. "Time for your first lesson." She shifted her position until she was sprawled completely on top of her now-grinning lover. "The most important thing is—without a doubt—the good morning kiss."

"I already kissed you this morning," Jude objected.

"Doesn't count," Liz dismissed her protest. "The official good morning kiss has to say many things. It has to say *'Good morning.'* And *'I hope you slept as well as I did.'* And, of course, *'I'm glad you're here.'*" she lectured.

Jude frowned. "All that in one kiss?"

"Trust me. It can be done." To prove her point, she leaned down and bestowed a gentle kiss on her lover, conveying not only all the prerequisites of a good morning kiss, but also love, tenderness, and her sheer joy at being with Jude.

"Mmm," Jude breathed, "I see your point." She slid her arms around Liz's neck, letting her hands trail teasingly across her lover's bare shoulders. "Can I try now?"

"Absolutely," Liz encouraged with a grin.

Their lips met again, tarrying longer still in a mutual delight. Jude nibbled delicately at Liz's lower lip, enjoying the relaxed feeling that being in the sweet woman's arms brought her. A gilded warmth swept through her soul, healing parts of herself she thought irreparably damaged and shedding light on places she had believed permanently darkened by her sins. "Like that?" she asked, her voice husky with desire.

"Oh yeah," Liz affirmed. She pressed her forehead against Jude's and grinned. "You're a quick study." Her body flexed gently against Jude's, a slim thigh nudging her lover's more heavily muscled ones apart. Jude sighed involuntarily when the smaller woman slipped casually between her legs, her body fitting there as if designed specifically for that purpose.

"So I've been told," Jude bantered. "But I have to confess, I have a little extra incentive in is case."

"You do?" Liz cocked her head skeptically.

"Yup," came the distracted answer as Jude's long legs wound their way around Liz's waist, gently centering the woman against her. Her hips began rocking subtly against the weight pressing down on her, discreetly seeking a more intense touch. Liz smiled sensually and began minutely returning the pressure. Jude's eyes fluttered shut in response, and a barely audible groan fell from her lips.

"And what incentive might that be, Jude?" she teased in a whisper.

The dark woman's eyes flickered open and gazed earnestly into the green fields before her. "I get to wake up to you every morning."

Game. Set. Match. Any lingering resisting cells in Liz's body crumbled under the tender declaration. She realized with silent wonder that she would willingly go to the depths of hell for this woman, if only she could wake up to those eyes every morning for the rest of her life.

Jude watched with growing alarm as tears streaked Liz's face. "What's wrong?" she asked softly. "What'd I do?"

"Nothing, lover." Laughing softly in spite of the emotion flooding down her face, Liz shook her head. "You didn't do anything." She paused, thinking. "Actually, that's not true. You did do something, but it was everything right."

Jude grinned hesitantly. "I did?" She tightened her hold on the smaller woman, brushing her hands tentatively though the soft golden tresses. "So I'm doing okay on this morning-after thing?"

"You're doing perfectly," Liz affirmed, inching up to capture Jude's lips with her own. Jude slowly kissed each tear that worked its way free from her lover's eyes, tasting the salt with a devout air of reverence. Liz sighed contentedly under the sweet caresses, still stunned that everything was falling into place so beautifully for them. A gentle symphony of desire played across their senses as they continued touching...and, once more, the world just fell away. Hands, mouths, tongues...all unerringly found the notes of pleasure along their skins. Quiet sighs, whispered invocations, murmured entreaties coaxed their spiraling arousal... until they climaxed with a soft breath of release and unwound slowly in each other's arms.

◻ ◻ ◻

"The second important part of the morning-after ritual is the shower," Liz proclaimed hours later, gazing across her lover's sprawled and sated form.

"I guess we do kinda smell bad," Jude conceded, a lazy eye opening to survey their tangled limbs.

"Well..." the reporter grinned, "I happen to like the way we smell, but others might disagree a little."

Jude was most content in her current position, with Liz curled snugly in her arms. As far as she was concerned, there could be no better place on earth. Unfortunately, she knew that unless they acted soon, the real world was going to intrude in a most unpleasant way, its entrance most likely proceeded by the barrel of a gun. Time enough still, however, for a little teasing. "Ah...so investing in a perfume called Eau de Brothel probably wouldn't be a good idea?" Jude bantered. "I thought there was supposed to be something in this pheromone business."

Liz released a long-suffering sigh and tugged on the dark woman's arm. "Come on, you." Obligingly, Jude allowed herself to be hauled from the comfortable bed and ushered into the bathroom. "Get some towels," her lover commanded.

When she returned, Liz was leaning over the porcelain tub, industriously adjusting the water temperature. Taking in the sight of her lover's supple form, Jude snickered approvingly. "Now this is what I call a room with a view." She molded her longer length against the reporter's smooth skin, thoroughly enjoying the musky scent that clung to their bodies. Growling low in her throat, she nipped at the tender juncture of Liz's neck and shoulder, eliciting a quiet yelp from the smaller woman. "Did I hurt you?" she murmured.

For an answer, Liz arched further back into the embrace and tilted her head back to find Jude's lips in a devouring kiss that left both women breathless.

"Guess not."

Liz flicked the shower on, and water roared against the tile. Wordlessly, she led Jude into the shower, positioning the dark woman under the spray. A seductive glow lit the green sparkle in Liz's eyes as she lathered up the soap in her hands. "I've been dying to do this with you," she confessed.

"Wash your hands?" Jude inquired, deliberately playing dumb.

Green eyes narrowed and sparked just a little bit more at the tease. "Trust me, Jude. You don't want to play this that way."

"And what way might that be?" the taller woman smirked.

"You asked for it." Liz shrugged and pushed Jude a little further away, so now the dark woman was standing behind the water.

The shower itself was generously spacious, allowing plenty of room for maneuvering; and the reporter seemed determined to use every inch of it to drive Jude to distraction. She dropped the soap onto its holder and leisurely proceeded to begin lathering her skin, ignoring the sensuous figure across from her. Aware of an intense blue gaze watching her every move hungrily, Liz nonchalantly soaped her arms and torso, deliberately ignoring her breasts—although they ached for the attentions of her lover's skilled hands. Slowly she ran her hands down her thighs, her own fingers tracing the defined muscles there. Bracing one foot on the ledge of the shower, she soaped her calves one at a time, shifting her weight from one leg to the other. When she turned her back to Jude and began sliding her hands over the curve of her hips towards her buttocks, Jude cried mercy.

"You win," Jude whispered thickly in her lover's ear, wrapping long arms around her from behind. Her hands found the soap and began running smoothly over Elizabeth slender figure.

"I already did that," the reporter objected with a throaty laugh.

"I think you missed a few spots."

They played under the water for a luxuriously long while, reveling in the slick feel of each other's body. Liz picked up the shampoo, a milky white concoction with a clean herbal scent. "Kneel," she commanded.

Jude arched a smirking brow. "I didn't know you were that kind of girl."

"You are a pervert, Jude Lucien. I want to wash your hair, and I can't reach that high."

"Bummer," Jude muttered under her breath. She knelt on the tile and allowed the smaller woman to work a thick lather into her hair.

When Liz was finished, she knelt in front of her lover, and slipped her arms around Jude's waist. "Lean back," she ordered. Jude hesitated for a moment, then flexed her thighs and leaned back into the shower spray, rinsing the soap from her hair with her hands. Liz's strong arms were locked around her waist, holding her securely. The small exercise in trust did not go unnoticed by either of them. "All done?" Liz asked after a few moments.

"Yup." Jude shifted forward and draped her arms across her lover's fair shoulders. "Now it's your turn." Liz handed over the shampoo and looked at Jude expectantly. "We gotta stand up first, though. My knees are shot." She grinned and helped the smaller woman to her feet.

They continued their play until the water began to noticeably cool. "Whoops..." Liz sputtered, ducking from under the spray. "Guess that means playtime's up, huh?"

Jude twisted the water off and stepped out of the shower. "Watch your step," she cautioned, offering a hand to her lover. Liz smiled slightly at the tender gesture and allowed Jude to help her out. "Here you go."

Jude tied one of the towels around her own waist and then softly began to dry Liz's skin.

"I can do that," the reporter protested halfheartedly.

"I know." Jude swatted her hands away. "But I like to. 'Kay?" Her hands were gentle as she squeezed the water from Liz's honeyed tresses and dabbed water droplets away from her fluttering eyes. When Jude was finished, she surveyed the lithe form of her lover with appreciative eyes. "All done." She pointed to the closed door. "There's a robe you can use."

"Thanks." The thick terrycloth robe was purple with green trim, obviously one of Jude's. She laughed as she rolled the sleeves up and wrapped the belt tightly around her waist. "I feel like a little kid in this."

Jude grinned at the sight. "Reminds me of the first morning you were at my house. My sweats swallowed you whole." Chuckling together, they emerged from the bathroom into the cooler air of the bedroom to find Sasha standing expectantly in front of them with a stack of files in hand. Because Jude was busily toweling the excess water out of her hair, Liz saw the executive first and gave a startled yelp.

Jude's head snapped up, her eyes fixing instantly on the source of her lover's alarm. Her mouth twisted into a grim smirk when she saw the look in her assistant's eyes. Sasha was clearly not a happy camper.

Her assistant was impeccably dressed, as always. A short, gray skirt and double-breasted jacket mocked the traditional banker's garb. Underneath, from what Jude could tell, she wasn't wearing a whole lot of anything else. One classic black pump tapped an incessant, silent rhythm. "I'm glad you're still here," she said without preamble. "I can get you to look over these and sign them before I head back to the office."

As if Liz weren't even there. As if Jude herself weren't naked and dripping water on the plush carpet. The dark woman cocked a dubious eyebrow at her assistant, pursing her lips slightly. She and Sasha had played this scene out dozens of times. In fact, Jude had even used it on one or two occasions to get rid of a particularly persistent conquest that had insisted on staying the night. Her assistant was daring her to treat Liz the same way. Daring her to say that this wasn't any different.

When they both knew without a doubt that it absolutely was.

"Sash—" She kept a light tone in her words, but the warning was unmistakable. "I have a guest."

The expression in the executive's eyes clearly said, *So what?*

Jude set her jaw. She was not in the mood to dance with her assistant. Turning to Liz, she asked quietly, "Elizabeth, will you excuse me for a moment? I have to see to my employee here." She re-wrapped the towel around her waist and stalked across the room to the door that led to the office. She icily gestured for Sasha to precede her. "After you."

Shutting the door forcefully enough to get her assistant's attention, Jude whirled to face her assistant. "What the fuck are you up to, Sasha?"

"Feeling a little butch today, aren't we?" Sash inquired dryly. "It's after noon," she continued. "I didn't realize you still had company."

"Bullshit." Jude batted her demurral away with an angry bark.

Saffron eyes narrowed as they studied the sleek length of their employer, obviously enjoying every second of their perusal. Jude sat on the edge of the office desk, suddenly uncomfortably aware of her near-nakedness and her assistant's close proximity. Her body had always been the battlefield where they had played out their little war games of power, and she had reveled in using it to fracture Sasha's control—taunting the other woman with things she could always look at, but only sometimes touch. Now, the tables were oddly reversed, and Sasha's eyes were seeing a thousand things Jude didn't want her to see. "Why are you so upset?" Sasha countered. "I've interrupted your little trysts before, and you've never minded."

Her assistant had always had a diabolically clever sense of timing, her interruptions often geared to drive her employer quite beyond the brink of distraction. A deep, primal growl simmered in the back of her throat as the memories pushed their way to the fore, and Jude realized that disentangling herself from the past would not be simply a matter of letting her new bright and shining love wipe everything else away. Sasha was a very tangible reminder of the dark pleasure of her life before, the life she could still have now if she could forget for one second the woman who awaited her in the other room.

All of this played itself out in a momentary flicker of her hooded blue eyes, but was not missed by the woman standing a few paces away. Involuntarily, Jude's lips parted slightly as her body warred with itself. The golden silhouette of Elizabeth's slender figure was all that stood between the dark woman and her impulse to press Sasha against the nearest hard surface, and torture away with her hands and mouth that irritatingly smug look on her face. *She'll fight,* her mind crooned, remembering the feel of Sasha against her. How one hand would tangle itself in her hair with a grip just past the edge of pleasurable, while its mate would work its way down the length of her body. *Her mouth...*Jude shuddered slightly, feeling teeth and tongue cover her skin with possessive rage. *Oh Sweet*

*Jesus...*Jude opened her eyes to find that it was not her memory wreaking havoc on her nervous system, but rather her assistant in the flesh.

She had not moved—had not even breathed, she thought—but somehow Sasha was wrapped around her, rendering the phantom-pleasure very real indeed. The hand in her hair commanded Jude to arch into the ravening mouth moving down her neck, and involuntarily Jude's body obeyed the familiar brutal touch. "Wait—" she gasped, trying to force herself to move away. Instinctively, her arms had braced themselves behind her, balancing all her weight. To move them would be to lower herself to the desk, and that would mean surrender. Unbelievably, the towel had vanished—or had at least proven no barrier between her aching sex and Sasha's inexorable quest. "Wait—" she commanded again, regaining control over at least her voice.

Not *stop...*

The difference wasn't lost on her assistant, who obligingly slowed her assault. "Jude," she purred. "Forget about all this nonsense, okay?" She nuzzled the rampaging pulse in Jude's throat with her teeth. "Let me take care of you. Like I always have."

Jude shuddered at the entreaty, her body knowing what that meant. Oblivion—plain and simple. No right. No wrong...just strength. Slick-sweat skin on skin. Reaching, grasping, taunting deep inside her—sending her down to the darkness. Where she had always belonged.

The golden silhouette dimmed, its light almost flickering out, and a part of her soul cried out in agony at its departure. "No!" Jude growled, an arm reaching out to stop it. She pried her eyes open. "Things are... different now..." she whispered.

Sasha arched a scornful brow, her fingers slipping easily across Jude's center where the evidence of the dark woman's turmoil rested. "Really?" she muttered. "I don't think so. You're just as wet for me as you ever were."

This time Jude caught the hand that tortured her. "I *said* things were different now." Her body, however, remained ambivalent.

Steel-edged saffron glared at her. "You know, Jude, I'm getting really tired of this." There was a commanding tone in Sasha's voice that Jude had never heard before this. "For almost two years I've let you have your head, waiting for this little phase to be over."

Jude laughed in complete astonishment. "You've let me have my head? What am I, some kind of animal that won't be properly trained?" *Broken, more likely.* Her body still sang with the contact between them, even as her soul clamored for its other half and her mind reeled in outrage.

"Let's talk about what you are." Sasha refused to grant Jude any quarter in this battle, forcing Jude to struggle for each centimeter she placed between them. Now she pressed closer. "I know what you're up to," she murmured, relinquishing her hold on Jude's hair and trailing a supple hand over the dark woman's broad shoulders. "All those secret meetings with Romair...how you've been easing me away from the business. Did you think I wouldn't notice? More to the point, did you think I wouldn't care?"

Jude's heart clenched painfully—both from the touch and the hushed words.

"You're going to sell me out, querida." Sasha tossed her own nickname back at Jude. "All for some prom queen and a pitiful dream of respectability." There it was...resting somehow in the infinitesimal space that separated them. "You want to prove you're just like everybody else," she continued on, her hand still stroking the bronze skin as a cool sweat broke out over it. "You're not, Jude. You are so absolutely not like everyone else. And I can't for the life of me understand why you want to be."

Why...? Her mind echoed the question. What was really there for her? Did she honestly think she could be absolved of her sins? *Why...?* Why was she fighting so hard for a peace she might never be granted?

"*I love you...*" Words she had never heard before and—if she surrendered to the icy fire in her veins—never would again. "*I love you...*" She grasped Sasha's other wrist, stopping the insidious assault on her skin. Blue eyes bore into saffron with a resolved sense of purpose. Every ounce of strength that she had poured into being an angel, a devil, a horrible figure of vengeance now shone coldly in her gaze. "I love her."

The statement stopped Sasha in a way that denial never could. She flinched lightly—more like a shiver than anything—but Jude felt it, and in that instant knew the truth. The dark woman's hands bonelessly released Sasha from their grasp as her assistant stepped back. The slightly sardonic mask settled back lightly over the tawny woman's features. "Do you now?"

"Yes."

"You sure?" She held up her hand, the glistening evidence on her fingers mocking Jude's statement.

Jude's eyes hardened even more—if that were possible. "I can fuck anybody, Sasha." Her assistant's eyes narrowed at the unspoken end of the sentence. *Even you...* Jude's eyes said. The words hung thickly in the air between them, along with the faint scent of Jude's arousal. Now she went in for the kill. "But I only love her."

Game over.

Her movements uncharacteristically graceless, Sasha nodded at the file on the desk. "I still need you to sign off on these liquor bills."

"I'll take care of it before I leave," Jude acknowledged, knowing that nothing more would be said between them.

The executive nodded and moved towards the door that led to the main corridor of the Club's third floor. Her hand on the knob, she turned to face her ex-lover. "I hope you know what you're letting yourself in for." Jude saw a bewildering array of emotions flicker over her assistant's face in that single instant. Sadness, disappointment, and fury all warred with something Jude had never seen from Sasha before—love. What was between them had always been a blood sport, and she wondered if she had at last dealt a mortal blow.

Sasha was gone before she could speak, leaving her alone in a room wondering what on earth would happen next.

◻ ◻ ◻

During Jude's absence, Liz had found the blow dryer and tamed her recalcitrant hair into a manageable pony-tail. Discovering a rust-colored polo shirt with pale green vertical stripes in the depths of the tiny closet, she pulled it over her head. She found her jeans in a pile by the door and picked them up as Jude re-entered the room. Noticing the distracted look in her lover's eyes, she placed a gentle hand on Jude's forearm. "You okay?"

"I'm not sure," Jude confessed. "I told Sasha...about us."

"I bet that went over about as well as a nun waking up in the middle of a whorehouse," the reporter muttered darkly. When Jude didn't respond, she continued, "It's obvious that your assistant feels somewhat... proprietary about you. I'm sure she wasn't thrilled about being evicted from that place in your life."

"You don't know what you're talking about," Jude replied roughly, obviously unwilling to discuss what had happened in the other room. Hoping to put an end to the conversation, she added, "Sasha and I haven't been lovers for a year, almost two. And even when we were, there were always...plenty of others." She found herself unable to control the flush that lit her features at the blunt statement.

"I'm sure there were," Liz retorted harshly, her imagination effortlessly parading the legions of women she knew Jude had taken to bed. Last night she had watched Jude for quite a while before she had approached.

The dark woman had cast a seductive glamour over everyone encompassed by her glance, and each body silently offered to Jude had wrenched a painful tear in the reporter's stomach. "But Jude, did any of them ever mean anything to you? I'm sure you told Sasha no a million times—but did you ever do it because you wanted to be with someone else instead? Or did you do it just because you wanted to control the situation?"

Jude stood silently, pinned in the cross-hairs of those green eyes. There really was no way to escape this conversation. "You're right," she said hoarsely. "It was always a game between us. She'd try to make me admit I wanted her, but I'd never let her have me completely. Those other women were a way to taunt her with it." She glanced down at the carpet, unwilling to meet Liz's intent gaze any longer.

Liz's voice was unbearably gentle. "Did you care for her, Jude?" she questioned. Not adding her unspoken one, *Do you still?*

Jude opened her mouth, closed it, then opened it again. "It's not that simple. I can't explain it in those terms. When I met Sasha, I didn't care for anything. I wasn't capable. I related to people through two things: power and sex. Sasha responds to that in me."

Liz didn't miss the present tense in Jude's last statement. "Even now?" she prompted again.

"Even now," Jude answered unflinchingly. "There's always been something between us...but it appeals to the person that I don't want to be anymore." She released a deep shuddering breath, the only evidence of her internal struggle.

"You broke it off with her when you got back from Cartagena, didn't you?" Liz asked with a sudden flash of insight.

Jude nodded almost imperceptibly and raised her eyes to meet Liz's squarely. "And there hasn't been anyone until now." She ran her hand through her rapidly drying hair. "I didn't want anyone else to...suffer... because of me." Jude's face was desolate in its sadness as she confronted with the ruins that her path had wrought of other people's lives.

Liz silently slipped Jude's arms around her shoulders and enfolded the taller woman in a comforting embrace. "All that's over now."

"Not quite," Jude replied, reminding them both of what was yet to come.

"We'll get out of this somehow." Liz lifted her head to gaze solemnly at her lover. "And when we do, you and I are going to sort all this out." She tapped Jude's temple lightly. "Okay?"

A wry smile crossed Jude's lips fleetingly. "You gonna fix me, Dr. Freud?"

"Nah," Liz waved the idea away. "You aren't broken. We both just need some...realignment."

Jude bit back a snort of laughter. "Realignment, huh? Fair enough." She ruffled Liz's honey hair and took in her attire with a smirk. "You've stolen another shirt, haven't you?"

◻ ◻ ◻

The Club staff had yet to begin arriving for their afternoon set up, so there were only two cars in the parking lot. Jude's black Porsche sat menacingly in its spot near the door, and an unfamiliar dark blue Saturn was parked at the very end of the lot. "That yours?" Jude asked, gesturing with her chin.

"Yeah," Liz affirmed. "Come on." She led the taller woman over to the car and opened the passenger door. "Get in." Jude curled an eyebrow skyward and glanced back at her car. "I want to take you somewhere," the reporter answered the unasked question quietly. Liz fell silent as she navigated their way through the traffic to the small suburban apartments where she lived. Wordlessly she guided Jude up the two flights to her home. Holding her breath, she unlocked the door and let Jude step inside ahead of her.

The place was nondescriptly expensive, but there didn't seem to be very much of the vibrant woman Jude had come to know in the last weeks. She had no way of knowing that the apartment was evidence of the life that had eluded the reporter until she met the dark woman. Jude prowled through a living room that was curiously devoid of any personal knick-knacks and the casual disorder of someone who is comfortable in their space. The bedroom was a bit warmer—the pale earth tones in the comforter and sheets reminded her of her lover's fair coloring, and a pile of books testified to a voracious reading habit. The kitchen was livelier, full of well-used cooking implements and cookbooks stained with the chef's experiments.

Walking into the study, she entered the room that would reveal the last of her lover's secrets. It was just as tidy as the others were with a computer that dominated the surface of the desk and supplies neatly arranged around it. Absently, she fingered the glass mug that held at least two dozen, identical Bic pens. A disk cache held color-coded floppies, and a pad full of meticulously written notes rested just to the left of the keyboard. Then she turned her head and saw the bulletin board that almost covered one full wall.

It was full of articles, clippings and notes about her.
Drug Lord Escapes Justice

Lucien Rising to Top of Criminal Food Chain
JLE Limited: Outlaw Corporation or Legitimate Business
Rogue: Why the DEA Can't Control Their Own
Mafia Princess: Iron Fist and Velvet Glove
And at the center of it all— a 5" x 7" index card with one word scrawled in red:

WHY?

Liz had been holding her breath, watching the play of emotions over Jude's face. When she had returned here last night, she had almost destroyed the room in her fury at having lost the only thing that now had any meaning for her. She had decided to leave it, however, as a testament to her hubris. Now it was her final attempt to rid herself of the last lies still remaining between them.

Jude turned to regard her lover with aching eyes. "Did you get your answer?" she asked hoarsely.

"Yes. But not in the way you think." Jude's silence bade her to continue; and the reporter swallowed hard, knowing their tenuously re-established connection lay in the balance. "When I started all this... No, that's not right. I don't know when I started all this consciously. When you came to trial, I was a desk jockey in the newsroom. I hadn't been in Miami that long, and the trial was everywhere."

"I remember," Jude said dryly.

"During your trial, you didn't have any of the smarmy smugness like Gotti had when he was under indictment. But at the same time you weren't pleading your innocence every time somebody shoved a microphone at you. There was something...calm and centered about you in the middle of all that circus...and I just didn't understand."

"Understand what?"

"Why," she replied simply. "Why you did what they said you had, why you turned rogue, why you orchestrated the Massacre, why you weren't bothering to deny it. Every time I looked at you, the question just screamed itself at me. Why?"

"The story of a lifetime," Jude commented bitterly.

"No," Liz contradicted. Seeing the sardonic curl of Jude's lip, she continued. "Let me tell you something about my business, Jude. News lasts approximately 30 seconds in this world. There's always something bigger and better coming down the pipeline. Your story went cold almost the minute the trial was over. You were acquitted, and you weren't talking. Brugetti knew when he was beaten and wasn't about to dwell on losing what everybody called an airtight case. There was no outraged family to cry foul on prime time or haul you into civil court. Forget about the DEA, you think they wanted to talk about the fact that their best agent now worked the other side? For all intents and purposes, the story was over."

"But you kept after it."

Liz smiled ruefully. "Not at first. It wasn't until after the trial had been over for six months—and I was still keeping my ears open for anything about your activities—that I admitted I couldn't get you out of my head." A dark brow arched dramatically in her direction. "Now you think I'm a stalker, huh? I was there the day you testified in court too. You were absolutely beautiful that day. I can still remember the suit you wore."

"Armani," Jude murmured faintly.

"Yeah, Armani." She shook her head to dislodge the memory of her first sight of the Archangel. "Anyway, I was on the crime beat anyway, so it just seemed natural to follow up my sources to try and find out what you were up to. In the meantime, I got stonewalled by the State Attorney and almost thrown in jail for trying to violate a court-ordered seal on your DEA records."

"Really?"

"Relax, I didn't get to see anything."

"You know all the important stuff now, anyway."

Liz studied her lover for a moment before reaching out and clasping a hand tentatively, half-afraid the gesture would be rebuffed. She breathed a quiet sigh of relief when Jude interlaced their fingers and tugged her over to the small couch opposite the desk. "That's what I'm trying to do now," she said quietly as they sat, curling her legs underneath her. "Tell you the important stuff. I don't want anything else between us."

Jude nodded. "I just wish you had done it earlier."

"Me too," the reporter agreed emphatically. "But honestly, I don't know if there would be any easy way to tell you that your lover is a reporter who stalked you, researched your past extensively, and insinuated herself into your life on false pretenses." At the description, Jude looked like she didn't know whether to laugh or cry. *Laugh, Jude, please,* she pled silently. *Or we don't have a chance.*

Finally a strangled chuckle escaped from the dark woman's throat. "Well...when you put it that way...I guess you're right." She studied their entwined fingers. "Why did you decide to try and find me? Especially after so long."

"Truthfully? I'm not sure, except that I knew that no file or unnamed 'source' was going to tell me what I wanted to know."

"Which was?"

She glanced into the depths of Jude's eyes, relieved to see that they were still flickering with warmth. Then she took a deep breath and said softly, "Why I couldn't get you out of my head."

The admission rested tremulously between them for a moment, until Jude asked. "What did your editor think of all this?"

"Let's see, I think his exact response was 'Are you out of your fucking mind?'" She grinned. "That's usually Lucas' response to just about anything. But he thought my scheme was particularly hare-brained."

"It was," Jude agreed bluntly. "What if I had been what everyone thought I was? What if I had—" She stopped abruptly, the rest of her sentence swallowed.

"What if you had taken me upstairs to your room at the Club and seduced me instead of taking me to your house?" Liz finished for her. "What if you had treated me like you've treated every other woman in your life?"

"Yeah," Jude said softly.

"Why didn't you?" she demanded, wanting to know why things had gone so mysteriously, strangely right when everything about their meeting should have been wrong.

Jude leaned her forehead against Liz's, closing her eyes briefly and drawing them almost unbearably close. "Because you aren't like any other woman I've ever met, Elizabeth."

"Let me see your eyes," Liz whispered hoarsely. Silently, Jude obeyed the request; and Liz found herself confronting a blue deeper and richer than any ocean vista or summer sky or sparkling jewel that she'd ever seen. In Jude's eyes she saw a raw admission of want and need and love. She answered it with one of her own, hoping that she could convey a tenth of what she felt for the woman sitting a breath away. She felt Jude's breath catch softly, knew that her lover had caught the wave she was cresting now. "Yes," she murmured, feeling Jude's lips seeking her own. "Yes..."

❑ ❑ ❑

"It's a restaurant called Barrido del Mar...yeah. I know, Lucas....No, it's not out in the middle of no-where...No...No...NO! Okay... yeah, two hours. Good. See you there." Liz dropped the phone into its cradle with a weary sigh and fell back onto the bed she hadn't slept in for almost a month.

Jude lazily stroked the fine tendrils of hair away from the reporter's face, studying the features of the woman she had come to love before anything. She still couldn't quite wrap her mind around the tumultuous events that had led her here, but she figured there would be time enough for reflection later. Provided, of course, she survived the coming explosion.

"Hey there...earth to Jude..." She focused on the gentle green in Liz's eyes, smiling at the warmth there.

"Hey...sorry, I was kinda out of it."

"Wanna share?" Liz wiggled a little further up the bed so her head rested comfortably on the flat plain of Jude's abdomen. Somehow they had ended up in the bedroom after their talk, and Jude...being Jude, and Liz... being unable to resist Jude...well, things had quickly taken their natural course. Now Jude lay stretched out comfortably across her dusky pink sheets, providing a contented pillow for Liz to recline upon.

"Just...thinking about everything that's happened." She paused. "And everything that's going to happen." She glanced down at the golden figure of her lover propped against her. "It's all going to go down quickly now. You know that, don't you?" Contrary to what she had let Elizabeth believe, she knew the minute that story hit, she would be walking around with a bulls-eye on her back. She hadn't lied when she said she thought Liz's idea would work, it was just going to work for reasons far different than her lover thought. She hoped to provoke whoever had choreographed this particular dance into coming out into the open. She couldn't shoot at something she couldn't see. It was really that simple. She knew she had promised Liz they would try and find some solution other than violence, but honestly, that eluded her. Whoever was after her wanted blood. It wasn't just something she could walk away from. Resolutely pushing the dark thoughts out of her mind she nuzzled the back of her lover's neck, nipping softly at the skin.

"Whoa there, Romeo..." Liz cautioned verbally, but her body arched into the caress. "We've got two hours before we meet up with Lucas, and we need to go by the house to pick up the documentation he's gonna ask for."

"I need to pick up my car too."

"Okay, why don't we go to the house to get the stuff, swing by the Club and pick up the Porsche and then take separate cars out to the restaurant?" she suggested, sitting up regretfully. "That way if Lucas needs me to come back to the paper I can."

Jude chewed her lip for a moment, thinking. "Sounds like a plan to me. Let's go." She stood up with a graceful motion, looking around for the shirt that seemed to have mysteriously gotten misplaced.

"Uh....Jude?" Liz caught her by the arm. "Remember the conversation we had this morning about Eau de Brothel?" A mischievous sparkle dotted the fields of green.

"You just want to get me in the shower again." Jude smirked.

"You got that right," her lover responded with a leer. "Come on, we've got time."

Chapter 16

Jude and Liz walked through the door of Barrido del Mar to find an anxious Ria standing at the maitre d' stand, a frown creasing her already-expressive features.

"What's going on?" she asked without preamble. Her arms were folded tightly across her chest, and her eyes burned intently as she studied Jude's leather-clad figure. Jude had called earlier to warn her that Lucas would be asking for her, but the dark woman hadn't offered any more detail than that. However, Maria was no fool—she hadn't been a DEA agent's wife without learning that the most important information was usually unspoken—and it didn't take much for her to realize that this tight-lipped request likely involved Jude's turn towards the light.

"I don't even get a hello?" Jude inquired dryly. "I mean—weren't you harassing me about my manners just the other day?"

Ria's expression didn't change. "Hi, Jude, it's good to see you again. Now what the hell is going on? Are you all right?"

Jude and Liz exchanged a swift glance, and Jude held her hands out in a gesture of peace. "Hang on, okay? First of all, is he even here?"

"Yeah, out on the porch. I put him at your old table, just like you asked." She motioned with a jerk of her head.

"Great." Jude turned to her lover. "You wanna go talk to him first?" she asked with a wry smile. "It might be best, since he's not exactly expecting me."

"I can do that." Liz swallowed hard, looking into the blue that had paled dangerously over the last few hours. Jude's retreat further and further into herself as they had set their plan in motion scared the smaller woman—it also didn't help that Jude had resurrected her Archangel garb when they had returned to the house. Leather pants and a dark blue silk shirt now cloaked her lover's skin with menacing intimacy, warding off even the most casual of touches from the smaller woman. When the reporter had looked at the attire questioningly, Jude had merely shrugged and replied, *"It's expected of me."* She had also removed her shoulder rig and two sinister-looking revolvers from the safe, nestling one snugly in the holster and slipping the other into the waistband of her pants as they went to pick up the Boxster. To Liz's relief, she had left both in the car when they arrived at the restaurant. Now, the reporter absently wondered where else Jude planned on going, and why she expected the place to be so inhospitable.

"Elizabeth?" Jude's voice snapped her attention back to the two women in front of her.

"Yeah, I'm here. Go talk to Lucas. I got it." She nodded, sighing heavily, and turned towards the porch.

"Hey you." Jude tugged on Liz's arm, preventing her departure. The blue softened somewhat—as though there were fissures in the frozen tundra—when she gazed at her lover. "You okay?" she murmured softly.

Liz took a deep breath, wondering how she could possibly answer that question. In the last twenty-four hours, her lover had come a hairsbreadth away from killing her; she had almost irreparably destroyed Jude's faith in her; and now—although it was the last thing she wanted to see—she was watching Jude slip deeper into her darkness as she tried to save both their lives. *How on earth can I be okay?* "Yeah, I'm fine," she replied. "Just thinking about what to tell Lucas."

Jude's eyes seemed to peer into the deepest part of her lover, and Liz felt her heart thundering within its confines. "It'll be okay soon," the dark woman whispered softly. Those eyes had missed nothing. They had read every pain, every fear, and every hope that the honey-haired woman had for the events to come. Gently she stroked the smooth curve of her lover's cheek, her fingers' soft caress offering a reassurance that her simple words couldn't. She tipped Liz's head to meet hers and tenderly brushed upon the reporter's lips a soothing kiss. "I promise."

Steadied by the familiar warmth of Jude's touch, Liz closed her eyes and allowed herself to be wrapped in her lover's embrace. She didn't care that Ria was watching with astonished eyes, or that the restaurant's patrons might be scandalized by the display. She craved the safety of those arms surrounding her and the implicit assurance that they would face whatever happened together.

"Better?" Jude murmured almost inaudibly.

"Oh yeah," Liz breathed. "I don't want to move."

"Neither do I," Jude agreed softly.

She glanced up at Jude's shuttered expression, wondering what her dark lover would choose to let her see. Jude's growing remoteness had been hard on her the last few hours, and though this small exchange gentled away the worst of her fears, Liz couldn't help but ask, "You mean that?"

Jude sighed deeply in quiet sorrow. "Of course I do." She pressed a small kiss against her lover's forehead. "When all this is over, I want us to go away for a long, long while. What do you say?"

Despite her even tone, the look in Jude's eyes told Liz that this was far more than a casual request. It was an unspoken vow that—should they get through this—Jude was willing to try, willing to trust. Again... In spite of everything.

Liz's heart responded to the appeal with simple joy. *Yes*...it replied. Yes to everything—to the present, to the future, to the pain that both would inevitably bring—but also to the overwhelming happiness that holding this woman in her arms brought her. "Yes."

"Good. It's settled then." One last squeeze and Jude released her. "You talk to Lucas first, and I'll join you in a few minutes. You want something to drink?" Ever practical, Jude was offering her something to get through the first stages of these surreal happenings that were—somehow—part of her life.

"Yeah, whatever you're having."

Jude chuckled darkly. "Why don't I bring you what you had the other night?"

Remembering her lover's fondness for bourbon, she agreed. "Yeah, that would probably be better. Thanks."

"Not a problem. I'm practically on-staff here, you know." Jude grinned ruefully, her lighter tone encouraging Liz to relax.

The reporter only shook her head with a wry smile and went off in search of her boss.

Jude turned to find Ria's gaze still fixed firmly on her. "You gonna tell me what's going on here now, Angel?" Her chocolate brown eyes swept over Jude's length once more, their look telling the agent that her transformation wasn't missed. Nor was it appreciated. "Who is that guy?"

They walked to the bar where Jude quietly placed her order. "He's the newsroom editor for the Miami *Herald*."

Ria stared at her friend in shock. "When did you start hanging around reporters?"

Jude laughed mirthlessly. "Since I starting hanging around Elizabeth." She shook her head. "But I guess I should start calling her 'Liz' now."

"Clue me in here." Ria placed a hand on the tense muscles that knotted Jude's forearm. "Elizabeth is a reporter?"

A nod.

"For the *Herald*?"

A nod.

"Why didn't you tell me this the other night?"

"Didn't know." Jude downed the bourbon in one neat swallow and nodded to the bartender for a refill. The truth of everything was sinking in fast for the ex-agent. The choices she had made in the last twenty-four hours had all been instinctive—responses to a clamoring in her heart and soul that would no longer be denied. But she knew only time would reveal if her decisions had been wise. Quickly, she sketched out the story of how Liz had come to seek out the Archangel, and the resultant confrontation the previous day.

"Son-of-a-bitch," Ria swore softly under her breath. "I can't believe it was all a lie." Her body tensed as she turned to go give the honey-haired woman a piece of her mind, but Jude's firm grasp kept her in place. "How dare she?" Outrage flared in her eyes.

"No, Maria." Blue eyes gazed steadily into brown, and told a story all their own—of anger, sorrow, and—miraculously—forgiveness. "It wasn't all a lie. It can't be."

Ria gasped softly, knowing now that Jude wasn't talking about any simple words or action. The dark woman was talking about a bone-deep truth that rested between her and the fair-haired reporter. She recognized the expression on Jude's face: it was the one her husband had always borne when talking about the dark mirror of his soul. "You love her."

Not a question.

Jude flinched slightly as if from a blow. Her mouth twisted into a grimace. "Of course I do." The admission disappeared on the breath of air that carried it. "I just wish it didn't hurt so goddamned bad right now," she muttered, looking down at the amber liquid in her glass.

Ria was as close to Jude as the dark woman ever let anyone get, but there was a lost bewilderment in the Archangel's voice that she had never heard from this woman whom she and Jason had always regarded as slightly other than human. Her heart ached now for a lost child who had never known love or safety, and at the same time it flared in murderous indignation at the one who had so sorely abused this precious gift. "She doesn't deserve your love, Angel."

Jude finished her drink and regarded Maria with a level expression. Her eyes sparked slightly at her friend's declaration, and she didn't know whether to be angered or touched at the well-meaning words. Especially since they were coming from a woman who only a few short years ago would have cheerfully committed Jude's body to the flames of whatever Hell existed. "I don't think that's for you to say, Ria."

The smaller woman ran a hand through her tousled dark hair and studied her friend in growing exasperation. "You've just stood here and told me that this woman stalked you—*stalked you, Angel*—for almost a year before contriving to meet you under false circumstances. She proceeded to get involved with you *under those same false circumstances* and only told you the truth after you caught her in the act of rifling through your private files." Her voice raised in disbelief as she finished. "What am I missing here?"

Jude's gaze had returned to her now-refilled drink. "She loves me."

It was so soft that Ria almost didn't hear it. "Loves you?" Ria repeated incredulously, stunned Jude had actually said those words. "Why should you believe her? What's to say that's not just another one of her lies?"

Blue eyes focused on her with frightening intensity. "Because I know it's the truth," Jude growled, her voice as low and menacing as Ria had ever heard it. The dark woman leaned closer to her smaller friend, so that she filled the chocolate brown gaze. "I threw her across a room, Ria. I put a gun to her head and told her that if I ever saw her again, I'd kill her." Jude leaned back slightly. "And you know what?" She paused for effect. "She came back to me. She hunted me down and demanded I listen to her." Her fingers curled themselves around the reassuring weight of the glass on the bar; and Jude shook her head slowly, still not quite believing Liz's brash actions. "Now tell me something....Even for someone you loved, would you do that? If you knew that for them, killing was easier than loving?" Unconsciously, she echoed the words Liz had spoken to her only a few days ago. This was the same monster Jason had faced, and both women knew that no matter how much he had loved Jude—he had ultimately been too afraid to face down the demons that warred with him over her soul. Their paths had parted until one last fateful encounter brought them together again, and the demons had finally won. Jude nodded slightly. "That's how I know she loves me."

"Then you've forgiven her? Just like that?" The question slipped out without her really thinking about it.

Jude laughed dryly. "Ria, I'm the last one in the world who has the right to grant forgiveness to anyone. After everything I've done—to people deserving and...not..." Failing her, the words trailed off, and she shrugged helplessly.

Ria studied her friend closely, taking in the unfamiliar light that glinted in the blue eyes when she talked of Liz, even of her betrayal. Reluctantly she shook her head. "This is a lot to take in, Angel." She clasped the dark woman's elegant fingers in her own. "If you say it's settled between you two, then I can't argue with that. But I'm furious that she hurt you, and I'm not sure if *I* can forgive her for that." Seeing Jude about to speak, she held up a warning hand. "You're my friend, and I won't give up the right to be angry on your behalf. I've never seen you like this, Jude...Never. I always knew you had an amazing capacity within you to love—your loyalty to Jason proved that. But I never thought you'd be able to let yourself be loved." She squeezed Jude's hand tightly. "That's harder for you, I think."

A deep flush warmed Jude's features, and she remembered why she had always hated talks like this. The way she felt about Elizabeth, however, wouldn't allow her to turn away either from the act of loving the reporter or—if the last 12 hours were any indication—from speaking that love aloud. In the corridors where she traveled that could prove fatal, both to her and the ones she loved. She had kept Ria and Jessie far away from the shadows by keeping herself largely away from them. This raucous, undeniable clamor in her blood for Elizabeth had destroyed any and all boundaries between them and, with that, all hope of keeping the shadows from her lover. The only option Jude had now was to wipe away the shadows, and pray to whatever gods existed that she wouldn't be burned alive by stepping into the light once and for all.

◻ ◻ ◻

Even in the rambunctious Friday night crowd, Lucas was all-too-easy to spot. Among the mostly youthful and upscale patrons, he stood in stark contrast with his wrinkled shirt, perpetually askew tie, and rumpled gray hair. It didn't help matters any that by his expression he looked like he had a cup of 6-hour old coffee in his hand and not the large mug of beer that currently sat in front of him. She wove her way gracefully through the crowd, trying to order her unruly thoughts, but unable to really concentrate on anything but the golden warmth she had felt in Jude's arms.

"Hey there," she smiled softly at her editor, taking him by surprise. She slipped easily into the seat opposite him, wondering if this was where Jude had sat all those nights with Jason or if this had been her partner's chair. Liz was no fool—she realized in many ways that she had taken Jason's place in Jude's life, filling a need in the dark woman that she could never articulate. She was also vividly aware that those very things which had driven Jason away from Jude were the things that drew her to the dark woman with a moth's unerring accuracy for the flame. To her astonishment, she had discovered the flame didn't burn...it wrapped around her tamely, entering her with an unexpected tenderness and dancing in her blood with undeniable possessiveness. That fire shone in her eyes now as she regarded her boss. "Come here often?"

"Gardener!" Lucas' head jerked up from where he had been stolidly contemplating his beer. "Where the fuck have you been?" He looked at her carefully, noting the tiny cut on the corner of her mouth and the small bruise on her jaw. "And what the fuck happened to you?"

"Lucas, you sound like my father—scratch that...he'd never say 'fuck'. Well, at any rate you still don't sound like my editor." She had first noticed the wounds herself when they were getting ready to come over here. Jude had been shamefaced until the reporter pointed out the companion gash on Jude's own cheek. *"We're even, lover...I just don't want it to happen again, okay?"*

"Good thing for you I'm not your father, or else I'd have you over my knee. I can't believe I let you talk me into this hare-brained scheme in the first place." He shook his head in agitation at his own foolishness.

"You agreed because you thought I didn't stand a snow-cone's chance in Miami of it succeeding," she replied with a chuckle. "And ordinarily, you'd have been right." The ocean, visible over Lucas' shoulder, was calming to the reporter's raw nerves with its steadiness. The continual motions of the waves reminded her of the quiet, powerful thudding of her lover's heart. She looked forward to spending long hours wrapped in Jude's arms, just listening to that sound. *When this is all over...*It was the mantra that she held to now, the one thing that was getting her through this. Knowing that she and Jude would have all the time they needed to explore each other's heart, soul, life. Knowing Jude still wanted that was all that mattered. Whatever it took, she would do her damnedest to make sure they both survived to fulfill the promise of tomorrow.

"So what went wrong? Or should I say right?" He drained most of his beer and signaled to the waiter for a refill. "You want something?"

Liz shook her head in demurral. "I've got something coming." *That's an understatement.*

"So?" He looked at her impatiently. He could smell it now—she could tell—the story that was brewing. The muscles in his neck were bunched as he unconsciously sat forward in his chair, tapping his foot in an unceasing staccato. Liz could feel the table vibrating softly in its rhythm. "What happened to you, Liz?"

She smiled serenely at her boss, knowing that her words were going to send him completely over the edge. "I fell in love, boss." Lucas drew in a lung full of air as if to begin his tirade, but Liz stopped him with an upraised palm. "Call it fate, call it kismet, call it looking across a crowded room and seeing the most beautiful woman I've ever seen in my life looking back at me. At me," she repeated softly, almost to herself. She would never know for sure what Jude had seen in that instant their eyes connected, but she believed now that it must have been something akin to the heat that had prickled her spine as she submitted to Jude's gaze. *Dark fire,* she mused to herself, forgetting her boss. *She's a flame that burns without light.* Somehow, Liz knew it was part of her destiny to give Jude back the light stolen from her years ago.

"Liz?" Lucas waved a hand in front of her. "Liz? Come back..."

She snapped her eyes to the man in front of her, staring into his worn face. The years had paid their due attention to Jack Lucas. Tiny crow's feet around his eyes created the illusion of a laughing man, but anyone who had spent time around Lucas knew those marks were the result of too many years spent squinting at news-copy. His eyes were the same gunmetal gray as his hair, and they only lost their dull hue when they spied a story on the horizon. *Like now.* "Just trying to think of a way to explain everything that's happened."

"Give me the headlines," he suggested.

"It's not that simple." Liz shook her head. Even if she had wanted to, there was no way to reduce the last weeks into a single nugget suitable for publication. For the first time in her life, her words failed her, and Liz found to her astonishment that she really didn't give a damn.

Lucas lost what little cool he had left. "Then what the hell is it, Liz? You disappear for weeks with only one phone call to tell me that you don't really know anything, can't really explain anything, but you'll keep me posted." He ran an angry hand through his hair. "I had to learn how to use fucking e-mail, Liz! Do you know what a pain in the ass that was for me? And what do I get? Nothing. Abso-fucking-lutely nothing."

Liz objected, "That's not true. I sent you e-mails—"

"Saying basically 'Having fun. Wish you were here.' Only I didn't know where the fuck 'here' was. I knew you had managed to almost get yourself killed after less than three hours in this woman's company. And you weren't spending your nights at home anymore. Then you call me yesterday and say that Lucien's still working for the D-fucking-E-fucking-A. Now you show up looking like you've gone three rounds with Joe Louis."

"Hardly," the reporter scoffed.

"Liz...you're missing the point. Who the fuck are you messing with that's putting bruises on your face?"

"I am," was the low reply coming from behind the reporter's back.

Lucas' attention flew to the imposing woman standing behind Liz, his eyes widening involuntarily as they took in the imposing vision of Jude Lucien. There was nothing subtle about the waves of intimidation that seemed to emanate from her skin. Liz cocked her head back to give Jude a tiny grin. She could faintly detect the warm traces of her lover's spicy scent mixed with the leather, and it reminded her of the softer, suppler side of the woman behind her. Eyeing the two drinks in Jude's hand, she asked, "One of those for me?"

"Yeah. Here you go." An almost imperceptible smile intended for Liz alone flickered across the dark woman's face as she handed the drink over. Negligently, she hooked her boot in the rungs of a nearby chair and dragged it over. Sprawling beside her lover with the alert grace of a predator, she turned a piercing blue gaze to the man across from her. "You're Lucas." Her voice had dropped an octave in its register, and Liz watched in amazement as Jude's features seemed to reconfigure themselves into the hard planes that she recognized as belonging to the Archangel. While she worried for her lover's sanity, a part of her storyteller's instinct reveled in the opportunity to watch the dark hunter at work.

"And you're the bitch who beats up on women." He nodded at Liz's bruised face.

Liz's eyes flew open as Lucas revealed cojones she never dreamed he had. Then again, she remembered, he had tangled with corrupt unions in his prime. She flicked a glance over at her lover, who was smiling slightly and showed no trace of insult. *Thank god she left the guns in the car.*

"You going to defend her honor?" Jude inquired mildly. "Very noble of you. However..." Her fingers underscored the dark gash across her own cheek. "Elizabeth is more than capable of defending herself." She grinned at her lover and then returned her gaze to Lucas. "She said we were even, but if you don't think so..." Her words trailed off lightly, the implication clear. Liz watched in amazement as everything about Jude seemed to change—from her speech patterns to the way her body rippled with quiet menace, every muscle attuned to her surroundings.

Lucas looked from Jude to Liz and back again. "Even, huh?" That the two women were together was unmistakable. Liz's body leaned slightly towards Jude's, while the dark woman had by her choice of seats clearly aligned herself with the smaller woman.

"Although I daresay the whole episode would have never happened had I not found her in the rather compromising position of raiding my computer files." She arched a dubious brow at the newsroom editor. "Tell me, Mr. Lucas, are you in the habit of allowing your reporters to fraternize with murderous drug lords? All for the sake of a story? Even to me, a life seems too high a price to pay for a simple headline."

"You're not a murderous drug lord," Liz protested, instinctively defending Jude, even to herself.

A soft smile broke over the dark woman's face, but she covered it with a skeptically arched brow as she glanced at the editor across from her. "Ah, but that's what Mr. Lucas called me in the editorial he wrote during my trial. Isn't it, Mr. Lucas?"

Lucas opened his mouth, then closed it in astonishment.

"Research works both ways, you see."

"Jude—" Liz warned in a tone of voice that clearly told her to stop playing with her food.

The dark woman smirked at the reporter, but nodded her head slightly in acknowledgment. "Fortunately—as Elizabeth is fond of saying—I am both less and more than that description implies."

"Meaning?" Lucas asked.

"Meaning that I have no interest in killing an innocent woman." She paused, taking a deep breath and hesitating over the words she was about to say. "Much less one that I love as much as I love Elizabeth."

The hastily choked-off gasp came not from Lucas but from Liz herself, who had not expected the declaration. *She does...?* She reached over and carefully interlaced her fingers with Jude's, managing to contain the rest of her reaction in a happy death grip that threatened to break the dark woman's hand.

Jude's countenance remained unchanged, but she return the pressure with her fingers, acknowledging the importance of what she had just said. "So you see, Mr. Lucas. I think we can help each other."

▢ ▢ ▢

Jude and Liz spent the next hours filling in the details of not just what had happened over the last few weeks, but indeed of the last few years of Jude's life. Lucas listened with growing amazement as Liz told the real story behind Jude's fall from grace, her subsequent rise to illicit power, and her more recent attempts at atonement.

"No fucking way," was all he could say when they were finished.

"Beg pardon?" Jude asked blankly.

"He means he can't believe we're sitting on a story this big," Liz translated.

The agent arched a wry brow. "Thanks."

"Spin?" He looked at Liz.

Jude turned to her lover for a translation.

"How am I going to write it," Liz muttered under her breath. To Lucas, she replied. "I was thinking of going hard on the present day. How she's working her ass off to bring the rest of the Cartel in while the real rogue tries to get her killed."

He nodded. The reporter's convenient glossing over of recent history didn't escape anyone at the table. He looked shrewdly at Jude. "I hope you know this is going to make you a walking target." He hadn't spent years busting the asses of corrupt unions in print for nothing. Whistle-blowers—particularly in dirty games like this one—were always the first to fall.

"I know that," Jude replied evenly, even though she was cursing Lucas silently for making her say so in front of Elizabeth.

"What are you talking about?" Liz flicked a glance from her lover to her editor. Lucas was looking at Jude with compassion and respect—mixed with a very healthy dose of fear for the things she had been and still was. "No, Lucas, we're doing this to throw *too* much light on her. See? So she'll be too high profile to kill." She looked back at Jude who was studiously examining the bottom of her bourbon glass. "Jude?"

No reply.

"Jude..." She grasped Jude's chin and forced their eyes to meet. "Look at me."

Lucas couldn't hide his shock at seeing the Archangel so easily handled by the smaller reporter. He hastily stood up and excused himself from something he knew he shouldn't see. "Why don't I get us some refills?"

Neither woman acknowledged him as he slipped gratefully away from the table.

"What is he talking about?" Liz's eyes were half-frantic, half-furious as they searched the shuttered expression of the woman by her side. "What are you planning?"

Jude gently extricated her jaw from Liz's grasp and clasped the hand in her own, bringing it to her mouth and softly kissing the palm. "C'mere." She led Liz by the hand over to the far end of the patio railing, far away from the prying eyes of the exuberant crowd. Evening's cloak protected them here, allowing Jude a freedom of expression she didn't otherwise have. "I love you," she said quietly, her gaze never wavering from the warm green richness of her lover's eyes. "I'm sorry I didn't tell you before...I said that...to him." She gestured at the empty chair where Lucas had been sitting.

"I love you too, Jude." She stroked the graceful line of Jude's cheek, the tip of her finger tracing the wound that she had put there. The dark woman sighed deeply, dropping her head and closing her eyes when she felt the tender caress of her lover's hands running through the thick fullness of her hair. "But I need to know what you're planning. Please."

Jude returned to the worried green of her lover's eyes. "He's right, Liz. When this story gets out, they're going to come after me."

"Then why the hell are we doing it? Why did you say you thought my plan would work?" Anger flared deep within the reporter, born more from the desperate worry over what would happen to her lover than from being misled.

"Your plan will work," Jude contradicted her. "Just not for the reasons you think it will."

Liz gestured impatiently, as if to say, "Explain..."

"I can't shoot what I can't see, Liz," Jude said simply.

Involuntarily, the honey-haired woman's thoughts flickered to the hardware Jude had left in her car. "I thought we were going to try and settle this some way that didn't involve you and a gun."

Jude ran a weary hand through her hair and stepped back a pace. "If I knew any other way, I would. But the fact of the matter is...no matter what kind of 'spin' you put on this...there will always be more people who will be just as happy to see me dead as alive. It's not like I'm an innocent in all this. When you get right down to it, I don't think the

Agency really wants me dead. I know it's not saying much, but they'd rather have me than the Medellins or the Callis. And I did essentially get rid of the Massalas for them."

"So you think it's just the one guy or group?"

"Yeah. But if that story comes out...splashing the Agency's dirty linen all over the front pages, they will want me dead."

The reporter shook her head. "I'm confused. Then why do the story at all?"

"I'm betting that the rogue finds out about the story before it goes to press and that provokes him into making a move. If he thinks we know who he is, he'll try and stop me." She paused and then added. "Kent's on his way."

Liz's eyes grew wide with alarm. "You think he's involved?" She gripped her lover's forearm tightly.

Jude gently stroked Liz's hand, prying the fingers from their painful grip on her muscles. "I think he's a conduit for information. That's all." *I hope.* In talking over the past with Elizabeth, she had realized that Kent had been involved in some way through every step of her nightmare journey. While she didn't think he was smart enough to have masterminded the whole thing, the speed with which Jason's death had been covered up had—as Elizabeth had pointed out—reeked of panic and fear. *That has Kent written all over it,* she thought grimly, remembering the ease with which he had given her up before.

The press of Elizabeth's skin against hers refocused her attention. "So this whole thing with Lucas was just a cover?"

Jude shook her head. "No. I want you to write the story. But hold it. If I'm right, this whole thing is gonna go down tonight or tomorrow. And if things go bad..."

"Don't say that," Liz pleaded.

"I have to say it," Jude insisted, staring intently at her lover. "Listen to me...If things go bad, I want you to run the story. It will protect you. While the Agency doesn't mind taking out the odd civilian or ten, they'd hate to do it in the middle of a spotlight. Breaking the real story behind the Archangel will give you a plenty big spotlight. Trust me." She reached out and gently traced the outlines of her lover's face. "Even if I can't come back to you, I can still protect you. Let me do that." Jude leaned in for a sweet kiss, letting their lips tangle gently for a few moments before breaking away. "Please."

"You better come back to me, Jude Lucien," Liz murmured, burying her head in the crook of Jude's shoulder and surrendering to the gentle embrace of her lover's arms.

"Believe me, I have every intention of coming back to you." Jude could feel the shape of Elizabeth's smile against her neck. "You and me, we've got a vacation to plan." That got her a gentle kiss pressed into the warm skin there. "Deal?"

The discreet clearing of a throat behind them interrupted Liz's answer. Jude glanced over her lover's honey hair to see Kent's broad form outlined by the restaurant's brilliant lights.

She had never considered him a friend...when they met she hadn't had any concept of what friendship was...and his cowardice had lodged a wedge between them that would always remain. She didn't hold his actions against him personally: some people, most people, were simply not made for deep cover work. What she did hold against him was his not admitting it and getting out before the catastrophe had happened. Had he been partnered with anyone other than the Archangel, there would have been two dead agents and months of work destroyed by his carelessness.

Fortunately, Kent had survived to see the error of his ways.

He had proven to be a very talented administrator, keeping track of multiple agents and providing background information. Jude had gladly let him supervise her support teams, relying on his administrative expertise to get her what she needed and when. The stench of cowardice, however, had always clung to him. She could see it in his eyes when he looked at her. She hadn't been kidding when she told Liz that Kent was a company man. He had been Agency—first, last, and always—and his failure in the field had dealt him a hard blow. Others called him a fanatic—of course, those same people called her an Archangel—so she paid their assessments no heed, preferring her own judgment.

Now as she stared at his silhouetted form, she was wondering if she shouldn't have paid more attention to the whispers that had always trailed after him.

"Sorry to...uh...interrupt." He flashed them an easy smile. "But your call sounded kind of important."

"Not a problem," Jude replied just as easily, an arm resting casually around Liz's shoulders. "We were just...taking a moment."

"Can't blame you there." His gaze encompassed Liz's lithe figure appreciatively, and Jude's eyes involuntarily narrowed at the scrutiny. "You're a very lucky woman, Jude."

The dark woman's muscles relaxed just a little at the respectful note in Kent's voice. "Yes I am," she agreed simply. "Come on, let's sit down. We have a lot to talk about."

⫐ ⫐ ⫐

Liz excused herself from the pair as discreetly as possible, half-afraid that if she remained any longer she would betray their suspicions to Kent. She found Lucas still at the bar inside. "A lot to take in, huh?" she asked ruefully, standing easily at the corner of the bar where he sat.

He shook his head. "I still can't believe half of the things she's done."

"She's not an evil person, Lucas," Liz retorted heatedly, still ready to defend her lover.

"I didn't say she was." He held up his hand in surrender. "I think she's done some evil things...but then again, I can't imagine what it would be like to be forced to kill the only person in my life that meant anything to me."

Liz blew out a deep breath. "I know...I don't know how she's survived."

"Most people wouldn't." Lucas replied bluntly. "And in a way you can't blame her for losing her way. But Liz, that doesn't absolve her of the horrible things she's done since. Do you know—"

"Yes, Lucas, I know," the reporter interrupted. "I know exactly what she's done. Remember, I was the one obsessed with her for months. Who pulled all the files, who talked to all the people too afraid to talk, who looked at all the crime scene photos of the Massacre." She rubbed the bridge of her nose tiredly, and then ran a hand through her hair. It was a gesture that mirrored Jude's own habit exactly, and if the reporter could have seen herself she would have laughed. But her mind was filled with the memory of her lover, covered in blood that wasn't her own. "I know," she repeated softly.

"And you love her?" Lucas asked softly.

She met the concerned gaze of her boss, wondering how in the world she could explain why loving Jude Lucien wasn't something she had to think about...it was simply a part of who she was now. How could she explain the days and nights of conversation as Jude tentatively opened herself, revealing the decades of pain buried there. As Jude had surrendered the fragments of her shattered soul to the fair-haired reporter's care, together they had begun to repair the damage, replacing Jason's lost bond with a warm, golden love the likes of which neither woman had ever dreamed of feeling. Liz had seen firsthand the scars upon her lover's psyche, and she knew there was no way to express to Lucas what Jude's darkness had cost her. She loved Jude for all these reasons.

She also loved Jude because of the infinitely precious gift she had given Liz. For the first time in her life, she felt like she lived and breathed, not just functioned to tell other people's stories. The gauzy distance between her and the rest of the world that had allowed her to understand without empathizing was gone...and she was thrust headlong into the dizzying world of emotion—passion, anger, violence mixed their dark colors with the lighter ones of love, tenderness, and joy on the canvas of her life. She knew now what drove people to love...and to kill...and a part of her wondered what would happen to her should Jude not return from this last journey below.

"How?" he repeated softly, drawing her from her introspection. "How can you love her?"

No, there was no way to explain, she realized. "I just do."

Out of the corner of her eye, she caught Kent walking hurriedly through the tables, pausing at the maitre d' stand to speak to Ria and kiss her on the cheek. His normally ruddy features seemed pale to the reporter, but it could have been just a trick of the light. A warm presence at her back announced itself as her lover. "Hi," she said without turning around.

"Hey," Jude murmured softly, nodding at Lucas. Her arms wound themselves around Liz's waist of their own accord, wanting the comfort of her lover's lithe body pressed against her for just a few moments longer before she had to go.

Liz tilted her head slightly to study Jude's closed expression. "What did he say?"

"About what you'd expect," Jude answered cryptically.

"Where's he going?"

"He said that he was supposed to meet Tony at the office for a debriefing on a case they'd been working. My guess is he's calling his boss."

Lucas' alert ears had missed none of the exchange. "Are you expecting trouble?"

Jude chuckled darkly. "I'm always expecting trouble, Mr. Lucas."

The older man studied the pair closely as their bodies seemed to intertwine naturally—two halves of a long-sundered whole. "Jude..." He seemed to stumble over her name. "Call me Lucas. Everyone else does."

Liz's fair brows flew up dramatically at her boss' tacit acknowledgment of Jude's place in her life. The dark woman felt the ripple of surprise running through her lover's body and accepted the overture gracefully. "Thanks."

"Okay..." Lucas downed the last of his beer and reached for his wallet. Throwing a couple of bills on the bar, he nodded to them both. "I think I've got enough to get started on the sidebar pieces to the main story. I was thinking maybe a timeline, other ops that she pulled out. Stuff like that."

"Sounds good," Liz agreed, her muscles tensing as they returned to the reasons that brought them together. Tightening her arms, Jude silently offered her comfort. The reporter relaxed gratefully into the embrace, drawing renewed strength from the powerful body behind her. "I'll start working on the lead. There are some files in my car that should provide us with all the deep background we need."

"Good. We'll need that documentation." Lucas nodded. "You want to come with me to the paper? Get started there?"

Liz felt a sudden wariness in the set of the arms around her. *Trust.* The word flickered across the reporter's thoughts. "I think I'll stay here instead," she demurred, tacitly agreeing to stay under Ria's watchful eye. The dark looks that her lover's friend had been tossing her from across the restaurant hadn't been missed by the reporter. She knew Jude must have told Maria at least some—probably all—of what had happened between them. "There are some last minute things that may develop. I've got a PowerBook in my car, so I can work just as easily from the restaurant."

Lucas narrowed his eyes at his employee, but wisely didn't say anything. "Suit yourself." He shrugged. "Jude, it's been an experience." He held out a hand that Jude immediately accepted from her position behind Liz. Her fingers were warm and supple, her grip firm and confident as she shook hands with the newsman. Slate gray eyes regarded the woman in front of him with new respect. "I hope I'll get a chance to see you again when this is all over."

"I'd like that, Lucas." She offered him a genuine smile, and the editor saw a totally different woman. The austere lines of her features softened, and the menacing exquisiteness of the predator was replaced by a warm, pulsing beauty that shimmered in her eyes and threatened to take his breath away.

Liz Gardener was a very lucky woman indeed.

He grinned back at her, shaking his head. "Fuck me...if anybody'd said two days ago that I'd be socializing with the Archangel, I'd have told them they were outta their fucking minds."

"She isn't the Archangel," Liz irritably reminded him.

Jude interrupted before Lucas could offer his apologies. "Yes I am," she said softly, turning her lover around to face her. "I have to be." Her tone—though gentle—brooked no argument. "At least until this whole thing is over."

The vice that gripped Liz's heart slowly eased, allowing the reporter to breathe normally once more. "I understand," she murmured, looking into the blue that had almost completely thawed. She knew, however, that one word would bring the twilight's angel back from wherever she had temporarily retreated. "I don't have to like it though."

Realizing that he was once more intruding where he had no business being, Lucas discreetly excused himself to the two women who had forgotten his presence.

Nodding her good-byes to the departing editor, Jude returned a solemn gaze to her lover. "I hope you don't like it. God knows, I don't."

"I'm just afraid of losing you." She buried her face in the warm silk of Jude's shirt.

"Look at me." She tilted green eyes to meet her blue eyes. "I promise you, if you lose me it won't be to that." Her eyes gleamed eerily in the restaurant's gentle lighting. "I'm never going back to what I was before, Elizabeth. Never. They'll have to kill me first."

In that brief instant she could see Jude's broken and battered body sprawled across the floor of an empty room, the flimsy silk and leather she wore no barrier to the life's blood pouring from her body. Liz shivered, icy tentacles reaching through the warm room and clutching at her soul.

Chapter 17

The night cradled its favorite subject in its arms once more as the humid darkness wrapped around Jude, snapping sharply at her face and hair. She could smell the faint hint of moisture on the wind's breath and knew Miami was probably in for a nasty thunderstorm later. *Great... that's all I need,* she thought grimly. *God putting in His two cents' worth... What's next? Hellfire and brimstone?*

A sweat that had nothing to do with the 100-plus degree heat wave currently gripping the city slid down the angular planes of her face. *Fear...* she realized with surprise. For the first time in her life, she was absolutely terrified. Her fear wasn't cold and stark...no, it was warm and insidious... working its way easily through her body, down deep into the very synapses that carried her will from her brain to her muscles. It encircled her heart and squeezed gently to remind her grimly of her mortality. It danced on the wind and whispered in her ear, coaxing her to abandon her mission and to forget the path she sought to forge through the darkness.

It told her that her life would be forfeit if she failed. That much had always been true. This time, however, her failure would carry with it too high a price—it would mean leaving Elizabeth forever.

That was simply not acceptable.

Of course, on the other hand, success meant trying to make a life with Elizabeth. Trying to blend the darkness that had been her habitat for so long with the natural brilliance in which her lover dwelt was not something Jude looked forward to doing. A great part of her doubted that it could ever be done. But she could no more stop trying than she could stop living.

Which brought her right back to where she had started—face to face with a fear that gripped her no matter how she tried to twist out of its grasp.

I gotta stop thinking so much.

Fortunately her musings were brought to an abrupt halt as she found herself reaching the locked gate that guarded Romair Massala's home. The wrought iron extravagance of the fence was de rigeur for the discreet area in which he lived, its bolted gate and sinister-looking gatehouse the only outward indications of its owner's illicit vocation. A dark-clad sentry shifted within the gatehouse, his eyes sweeping suspiciously along the length of the Porsche and coming to a halt on the woman piloting it. "You lost?" he asked, the musical lilt of his accent unintentionally removing any menace from the question.

Jude didn't blink. "I'm here to see your boss," she replied curtly.

"Mr. Massala's not receiving visitors this evening," the sentry informed her.

"I think he'll see me." When the sentry made no move for the sleek cell phone she could see sitting on the desk, she growled low in her throat. Negotiating with a little piss-ant employee was the last thing she had time for. A single agile leap had her standing in the Boxster's seat, her Sig pressed up against the guard's nose before he could move for his own piece. "Get on the fucking phone and tell your fucking boss that the Archangel is here to see him. Comprehende?"

The sentry's eyes widened as the dark woman revealed her identity. The Archangel's assassination of Rico Massala was the stuff of legend, even now, within the Cartel. The story was whispered through the Cartel's ranks like a child's ghost story, terrifying everyone who heard it. There had been two survivors of the Massacre, and their descriptions hadn't done justice to the beautiful, terrible visage that was now staring him down. The gun in her hand meant nothing—it was Jude's eyes that sent his trembling hand to the phone.

As soon as he punched Romair's code, Jude snatched the phone out of his hand, too irritated to wait a minute longer. "Romair? It's Jude. We need to talk."

Romair's voice—though clearly startled to hear her voice on his intercom line—was calm. "Certainly. When would you like to meet?"

"Now. I'm sitting outside your gate."

There was a long pause on the other end of the connection, and Jude could almost hear the thoughts tumbling through Romair's brain as he examined all his options. Romair wasn't an idiot...he would have to know something big was going down to bring her to his door. Finally, he spoke. "All right. Have Miguel buzz you in." He cleared his throat delicately. "That is...if you haven't..."

"Your guard is fine, Romair," Jude assured him, grinning at the youth who was still eyeing her—and her Sig—warily. She had never seen an Argentinean turn quite that shade of pale before. "I just got a little impatient."

A deep, rolling laugh echoed through their connection. "I can imagine. Well, if he's not too petrified, he can send you in. I'll let my people on the door know, so they don't get a...similar greeting."

"Thanks, Romair. I'll be through in a minute." She broke their connection and handed the sentry back his phone. "See? That wasn't so bad, now was it?" she asked him conversationally. "Your boss says to let me through." The sentry nodded shakily and reached for the automatic latch. Jude slid back down into the leather seat, tucking her gun snugly back in her shoulder rig. Its weight was a reassuring pressure against her side, a familiar companion as she traveled the shadows once more.

Once granted admission, the Porsche purred smoothly along the winding path. She threw the car into park at the head of the circular drive in front of the brick mansion's impressive front door. Two men wearing identical dark suits stood between her and the entrance.

Should I call them the Men in Black? Jude snickered to herself as she approached them.

"No weapons," the larger of the pair informed her, looking pointedly at the shoulder rig.

I hate Muscle. "If I were going to kill your boss, you dumb sonofabitch, I wouldn't have called and announced myself."

"No weapons," he repeated.

Good Lord...I wonder what else this guy says if you pull his string.

She opened her mouth to fire off a sardonic reply but was interrupted by Romair's smooth voice. "A bit belligerent today, aren't we?" He stood framed in the doorway, an easy smile stretched over his features that reached into his brown eyes. He was dressed casually, in cream-colored, linen trousers and a pale peach shirt that complemented his dark good looks. His shirtsleeves were rolled up over his muscular forearms, and—Jude noted with surprise—he was barefoot.

"Too much coffee I guess," she replied with a smirk, confirming her internal suspicion that she liked this man, despite her ostensible mission to bring him down. It had been easy to dislike Rico—he had been a loathsome little toady with a penchant for treating his employees as if they were circus animals available solely for his entertainment. Jude had been his prized panther, sleek and glistening with brutality, and he had enjoyed watching her jump on his command. But as wild animals are wont to do, Jude had proven that she would not be tamed to his call.

Bringing in Romair was supposed to be the price of her redemption, but as the Argentinean waved the guards away with a casual hand and invited the panther into his home, Jude finally understood that redemption—the kind she wanted and craved—could not be bought by betraying another. She would have to live with her sins for the rest of her days. No one else—no agency, no church, no one —would be able to grant her peace. Whatever grace she managed to achieve would only be what she granted herself...and that left her precious little hope indeed. Elizabeth's face drifted through her thoughts, and unconsciously the dark woman remembered the tender embrace they had shared before she left. The quietly whispered, *"I love you..."* still shimmered through her hearing and bolstered her courage with its strength.

Maybe there's hope for me yet.

"I must say, Jude, that your unexpected arrival is a little... disconcerting," Romair was saying as he led her through the house to his study. She caught fleeting glimpses of tasteful furniture, plush rugs, and subdued lighting as she trailed behind him. A small boy peeked around the corner from the far end of the corridor, regarding the intruder with undisguised curiosity. She grinned at him, and he squeaked softly in surprise, his small head ducking back out of sight. "I don't usually do business in my home." This last was said with an almost imperceptible tightening in his voice as he eyed Jude's leather-clad form carefully. "It's bad enough that I have to have armed guards protecting my family...but I insure they are as...discreet...as possible."

"In other words, you don't like the boogey man showing up at your house because it scares the kids," Jude interpreted dryly. "Look...I'm not happy about this either. I assure you, I have no interest in terrorizing your family and I don't have time to spar with you. We have a problem."

She watched him sit down behind a massive mahogany desk littered with the tasks that had occupied him before her untimely interruption.

Behind him was a matching cabinet that ran the length of the broad window under which it rested. That surface was crowded with pictures of Romair, a woman she assumed to be his wife, and a number of small children who closely resembled the man in front of her. *They look happy,* she noted almost wistfully, suddenly hating her own menacing intrusion into what was obviously Romair's haven. "I'm sorry," she said quietly.

Romair pursed his lips and motioned her to the chair opposite him. "Sorry for what?" he asked softly, although it seemed he already knew. His eyes were warming with regard as he gazed at her.

"Barging in here." She glanced down at her own attire and the gun that often seemed as if it were an extension of her very body. "Like this." She smiled wryly. "I'm not exactly the kind of person you'd normally invite home for dinner."

"Nonsense, Jude." Now he, too, was smiling. "You're always welcome in my home for dinner. Just leave the gun behind." He studied the pants that clung to her sleek length appreciatively. "And the leather too," he added with a regretful sigh that Jude didn't miss.

"Paola the jealous type?" she asked lightly.

He laughed delightedly. "Not at all. However, you might prove too tempting for my eldest." He gestured to a silver framed photograph of an exquisite young girl who stared challengingly into the camera. "Ariana seems to have inherited not only her father's eye for beautiful women but also his headstrong will." He laughed self-deprecatingly. "Someone like you...would prove an irresistible challenge to her."

To Jude's discerning eyes, Ariana seemed to be about 18 years old, and she studied the picture with surprise. She could have sworn that he had told her that he had only been married for ten years. Glancing at the array of other photographs scattered along the cabinet, she noticed that none of Romair's other children had yet reached adolescence. He followed her eyes as she studied the pictures. "She seems...older than your other children," Jude said carefully.

He chuckled at her inference. "Ariana was the result of a...youthful indiscretion...on my part. I wasn't any older than she is now when Ariana's mother found herself expecting." He looked solemnly into Jude's eyes. "I am a man who takes his responsibilities seriously. I proposed marriage to Julia and was rejected." His mouth twisted in a grimace, the wound still tender after all these years. "My family wasn't...appropriate...enough for hers. Despite Julia's condition, I was turned away from her door and Julia was sent away to have the child in secret."

"Then how did...?" In spite of the urgency of her mission, Jude was pulled into his tale. Romair was unmistakably a man of strength, resolution, and honor—despite his illegal empire. Her own resolve not to buy her freedom at the cost of his grew.

"I found the place where they sent her, and my family arranged for the 'adoption' of my own child. Ariana has been in my family's care from the day she was born. And when I married Paola, Ariana was acknowledged as my daughter and has lived with us ever since." He smiled fondly at the picture of his eldest child, who was indeed a distaff version of her father. "She is intelligent, wild, and completely tempestuous. And you—my dear Jude—are exactly the kind of trouble she craves finding." He looked carefully at the woman opposite him. "Although I don't think a dance or two with you would do her any harm at all. She is entirely too used to getting her own way with everyone." He nodded, a small smile playing across his features.

Jude had the grace to blush at Romair's frank assessment of her appeal, never mind the fact that he was talking about his own daughter. "Uh... well..." She was completely at a loss, and it delighted the man opposite her.

"Oh this is *wonderful*..." he laughed. Romair had a rich, deep voice and his laugh was no exception. It was warm and kind, expressing a happiness that Jude had never associated with people in their line of work. "The notorious Archangel caught flat-footed. Too bad no one would believe me."

"You got that right," Jude agreed dryly. "As...intriguing...as this line of conversation is, it's not the reason I'm here."

His face immediately sobered, and the warm brown of his eyes took on a calculating glint. "There's something you want from me."

"Yes," Jude replied unhesitatingly. "But there's something I can give you for it in return."

"And what might that be?"

"Your life."

The Argentinean frowned, studying the sleek length before him again. "You've already done that, Jude. I haven't forgotten that you're the one who got me out of that boathouse when the DEA decided to pay us an unexpected call."

Jude's eyes sparked. "You knew they were Agency?"

"Not at the time, no. I dispatched several of my men to the site afterwards. They found..."

"Heckler-Kochs shells." Jude nodded grimly. "I figured it out once I got home and looked at the weapon I took from one of them."

"Are you here to tell me I have a mole in my organization?"

"It's a little more complicated than that. How in the loop were you when Rico ran the Cartel?"

Romair sat back in the comfortable leather chair and linked his hands together in front of him. His brow furrowed in thought as Jude sat silently, mentally urging him to hurry up. After a long pause, he spoke, "You want to know the name of the man who betrayed your partner to my cousin, don't you?"

For the second time in as many minutes, Jude was caught thoroughly flat-footed. "You've known all this time?" Her blue eyes paled violently, the muscles in her body instinctively coiling. "Why didn't you tell me sooner?"

"Let's just say it was my ace-in-the-hole." Romair held out a cautioning hand. "Before we met, I thought perhaps I could use it as a bargaining chip. To make you come to the table with me." He shifted in his chair and eyed the Archangel shrewdly. "But you agreed without question. That's always confused me, Jude. You had no reason to sit down with me." He laughed mirthlessly. "My charming daughter aside, I have nothing to offer you. The Cartel will never be what it was...It won't even be a fraction of that. And you know it."

"Perhaps I was tired of having to worry about freelancers trying to bring you my head on a pike as a greeting card."

"I seriously doubt there is anybody—affiliated or no—that could bring your head anywhere it didn't want to go."

"Doesn't stop them from trying," Jude commented wryly. She shifted in her chair and stood, her muscles clamoring for activity. The muted roar in her ears was growing as she felt herself inching closer and closer to the answers that had eluded her these long years. She paced the long length of Romair's office, her booted feet leaving soft indentations in the plush gray carpet. Spinning on her heel, she confronted him squarely. "You're right. I had my own reasons for sitting down with you."

"Which are?"

"I had a deal with the DEA—strike that, I had a deal with a man who was collaborating with Jason's betrayer, to bring you in and take down the rest of the Cartel." She paced away again, deliberately turning her back on him.

Romair's face hardened into a mask of fury, and his body trembled with the effort of remaining seated as he gently eased his Glock from its recessed ledge under the desk.

"Put the gun down, Romair. I'm not going through with it," she said without turning around. Her pacing brought her to his eyes once more. "The thing is, there never was a 'real' deal. It was all a scam to get us both killed. It was actually a very nice set-up. Two drug dealers haggling over territory get killed in a DEA raid." She smiled in grim admiration of the plan's beauty. "The rogue's name dies with you, and the one loose end—namely me—finally gets tied off."

Romair thought for a moment, considering Jude's words. "So why haven't they done this before?"

"Two reasons. One—power was only recently re-consolidated in the Cartel. They had no way of knowing who in your organization to hit until now. Two—they could never get close enough to me. As long as I was still in business, nobody could get near me."

"But if you thought they were your allies, your guard would go down."

Jude shrugged. "At least enough to let them get closer than they ever have."

Romair looked shrewdly at her. "You certainly have to have more than one contact there. You could go to them with your suspicions with my head as a peace offering. So why have you decided not to follow through with your end of the bargain?"

Blue eyes met brown, each taking the measure of the other. Each gaze was equal parts strength, resolve, and suspicion as they studied one another. Finally Jude gestured to the cluster of pictures sitting behind the Argentinean. "Because of them," she said at last. "Because you seem to be the person of honor that I'd like to be—despite what we both do for a living. After everything I've done, I've no right to trade your freedom for mine." She shrugged softly. "Recently, my...priorities...have changed. Going on the way I have for the last few years...just isn't enough anymore." Jude ran an agitated hand through her hair, uncertain of why exactly she was opening herself to Romair's penetrating gaze, but unable to stop herself.

The expression on Romair's face was inscrutable, but at last his tense muscles visibly relaxed, and his eyes warmed again to the woman standing across from him. "Do your remember when we met? I said that I hoped to one day be able to tell you what I saw in you."

"I'm not sure I want to know."

He smiled broadly at her. "Think about what you just said. About why you won't deal with the Agency," he replied gently. "That's what I see. You are a woman of honor, Jude. And strength. And compassion. Whatever darkness you've walked in has only blinded you to those qualities—not taken them away." He paused then carefully added, "I'm just glad something has helped you begin to see your way clear again." Jude winced as a blush began to softly warm her features, and Romair's smile grew. "Or should I say someone?" The blush deepened, and he chuckled happily. Rising from his seat, he crossed the room to her, placing his hands on her shoulders and drawing their eyes level. "I like this side of you, Jude. I like it very much."

Jude glanced away from the taller man, unable to take the kindness in his glance. "I'm glad you like it, but it's not gonna do us much good if it gets us both killed." With the wry words, Jude gathered up the emotions of the last few hours and tucked them neatly away in the back of her mind. She needed to concentrate fully, and thinking about Elizabeth would only distract her from the ruthless tasks she had ahead of her.

Romair nodded slightly and stepped away in understanding. "So what's your plan? I give you the name and you go have a showdown at high noon?"

Jude shrugged. "Something like that. I've already got something in motion that will hopefully draw them out, but I want to know who and what to expect when that happens."

"I see. Well, it's not as simple as one man's name."

"It never is, Romair. But we can start with that name. Who is it?"

Without hesitation, Romair supplied it. "Kent Laird."

"Kent." Jude paused, the muscles in her jaw clenching rhythmically. She shook her head. "He's an accomplice. I knew that already. Who's he working for?"

"Back then—no one. He supplied Rico with your partner's name. But he must have been, what do you call it? A double-agent. Because he never said a word about you."

Jude's mind was racing frantically as she realized that every one of Liz's theories were playing out. Kent hadn't been on Rico's payroll, he was trying to force her hand by eliminating the "distraction" that was her relationship with Jason. Now he was trying to clean up his mess. Something occurred to her. "What do you mean back then?"

"Jude, how did he know about the meeting you and I had scheduled at the marina? The only person I shared that with was—"

"Sasha." Jude closed her eyes in realization. *Oh my god.*

❏ ❏ ❏

"So are you actually going to talk to me, or are you just going to keep glaring at me from across the room?" Liz braced both hands on the table where Ria sat and looked at the other woman expectantly. Jude had been gone about an hour, explaining that she had to see Romair. During that time. Liz had struggled over the first paragraphs of the "Archangel Expose." Years of training had taught her never to bury her lead, but for Liz, being in love with Jude was the lead.

That was something the people of Miami really didn't need to know.

However, it shone through in every word she wrote about the dark woman. It was in each paragraph she typed, deleted, and retyped. The laughing, blue-eyed lover was the woman she wanted to capture on her screen and, through this, wipe out the Archangel's spectral presence in their lives.

She knew it was probably a foolish hope. Jude's darkness would remain with them always, she suspected, creeping into the wonderful light that they shared together. *I can deal with this,* she told herself, not wanting to think about the sinister guns that Jude had lovingly handled, or the ease with which she had disabled that man on the beach. She had felt that wrath turned upon her and was very grateful for whatever impulse had stilled Jude's finger on the gun's trigger that night.

Liz had been conscious of Ria's scrutiny during her mental gyrations, and she really wished that the other would just yell at her and get it over with. Ria was an important person to her lover, and Liz was going to be damned if Ria's disapproval was going to be one more thing that was standing between them. With an unusual lack of rhetorical grace, she had confronted the restaurateur.

"So?" she prompted again. "If you have something you need to say to me, say it. Because I don't have all night."

Ria's brow darkened even more, if that was possible, as she studied the honey-haired woman across from her. "You don't want to start this, Liz. Trust me."

The reporter pursed her lips, then relaxed into the chair opposite Maria. "She told you everything, right?"

"Yes," came the curt reply.

"She tell you that I'll cut my own tongue out before I ever lie to her like that again?"

Ria absorbed these words with no change in her expression. "That's a very noble sentiment, but forgive me if I'm a little skeptical. Especially considering recent events."

A wave of anger washed through the reporter. "Look—"

"NO!" Jason's wife interrupted. "*You* look. Jude said she forgave you—and I honestly believe she has. I've never seen an expression in her eyes like I saw tonight. But it's not that easy for me. Whether she knows it or not, that woman is incredibly dear to me. And you walk in out of nowhere and turn her life upside down."

Liz wanted to defend herself, wanted to excuse her actions, but she knew deep inside that Ria was right. However, it didn't make it any easier to hear.

"Two days ago I thought you were the best thing to ever happen to her." The expression in Maria's eyes was steady and unwavering. "Today I'm worried that you're the worst."

The honey-haired woman mulled those words and the stark trail of fear they blazed through her body. "Maybe I'm both."

"Maybe," Ria agreed. "That's what I'm most afraid of."

Knowing there was no way she could explain her actions, but wanting to anyway, Liz took a deep breath. "Look, Ria. What I did was terrible. And if I'd had any sense I would have told her that first day. I realized even then that what was happening between us was like nothing I'd ever felt. But I didn't say a word." She ran a hand through her hair and blew out an exasperated breath. "I just thought...I don't know what I thought. That maybe the lie would go away...that something would happen to make it not matter." She shook her head and added softly, "I just didn't want to stop the miracle that was happening to me."

Ria regarded her silently for a moment, then spoke quietly. "Watching you two together is like watching a lion play with a child. Knowing that disaster could happen at any second."

Liz bristled at the analogy. "Look, I know she's dangerous and everything, but I'm not a child."

"Oh no, you're not," Ria agreed. "Jude is." Seeing Liz's stunned expression, she continued. "I'm serious, Liz. She has no frame of reference for what's happening between you two. Even what she had with Jason doesn't begin to compare. For as long as I've known her, she's kept everything locked carefully away, so no one can touch what is essentially her. And now you've just plowed right through all that. I'm not kidding when I say that you hold her life in your hands, Liz. Do you know what kind of power you have over her?" Ria held Liz's green eyes in an almost-hypnotic gaze. "She has no defense against you."

Liz swallowed hard, a thousand rushing sensations crashing haphazardly through her. Visions assaulted her mind of how easily Jude had curled her long body into Liz's smaller one, how tightly the dark woman had held on during the demon night they had shared, how anguished Jude's eyes had been when she had realized her betrayal. *"What choice do I have?"* Jude had said to her that morning. Feeling as though someone had reached inside her chest and snatched her lungs from her body, Liz gasped softly for breath—finally understanding the depth of the dark woman's feelings for her. "Oh god..." she choked, bracing her elbows on the table and holding her head in her hands. She drew another shuddering breath and brought her eyes back to Ria's. "It works both ways, you know," she realized softly, knowing that her fearlessness in the face of Jude's rage was propelled by the same out-of-control need to have the dark woman close to her.

"I hope so, Liz. I truly hope so. Because God help you both if it's not."

The women sat in silence, contemplating both the past and the future, until a hearty voice interrupted them. "What are two of the most beautiful women in Miami doing sitting here alone? I can't believe Jude would leave you alone for a moment. I know I wouldn't."

Liz felt a tiny tremor of fear ripple its way through her body as she glanced up at the man beaming down at them. "Kent..." she said, forcing a smile to her face.

◻ ◻ ◻

As Jude careened through the city streets, a quick phone call told her that Sasha hadn't been to the Club that night and wasn't expected. An ominous bank of clouds, obscuring the moon and stars, rolled in and reflected back the neon glow of the city. Miami was painted in an oddly pulsing gold and rose light, and people on the streets seemed to welcome the coming storm. Lightning broke the sheen occasionally with piercing white bolts, while thunder echoed distantly. The wind had picked up noticeably in the time she had been with Romair, and though raindrops had begun to dot her windshield, she hadn't taken the time to pull the Boxster's top up.

Her body piloted the car automatically towards Sasha's loft, her subconscious reminding her of the twists and turns down dark alleys that it took to get there. The Porsche roared to a stop, and she took the steep stairs three at a time, knowing all the while that this wasn't the smartest thing she had ever done. *"Sasha!"* She pounded the metal door ferociously, the pain running from her fist down her arm. *"God damn you! Open the fucking door!"* She paused for a minute, listening for any remote sounds from inside, until her memory dredged up where her ex-lover kept a spare key. Swinging by her legs from the landing, Jude twisted her body under the metal structure, long arms reaching for the tiny, magnetic box underneath it. When Sasha had first told her the key's location, Jude had complained about how difficult it was to reach. *"Anything worth taking is worth working for...don't you think, Jude?"*

"Worth taking, huh, Sash?" Jude muttered as she grabbed the key and twisted her torso back up. "What are you trying to take from me, *querida?*" A few swift moments later, Jude was in the darkened loft. She drew her gun carefully from its holster and proceeded in cautiously. *Like caution's gonna do me a lot of good now after that ruckus I just made... Shit...Angel, you're losing it.* She prowled swiftly through the area, noting that it looked like Sasha had indeed been home earlier. She glanced into the kitchen, noting the cordless phone sitting beside the remains of a salad and a pile of spread-out papers. Jude rifled through them, grimacing when she recognized the coded spreadsheets detailing the organizational structure of her Colombian routes and the money they brought in. She grabbed the phone and hit *69. When Kent's recorded voice told her that he wasn't able to take her call right now, Jude swore loudly and hurled the instrument across the room. It landed with a crash against a framed print, shattering the glass into thousands of pieces.

"Think, Angel, where would they meet?" She scrolled through the possibilities in her head, before the answer came clear. "The office," she growled. Not only would they have total privacy on a Friday night, but Sasha would have access to everything she needed to set up their plans. "That's gotta be it."

The rain had begun in earnest now, but Jude felt nothing as she ripped along the slick pavement in the Porsche. As she neared the office district, she paid careful attention to the cars she passed, recognizing none of them as belonging to any of her employees. It was possible that Sasha would bring in freelancers to help her take control, but not probable. *Why rock an already smoothly running boat? Once I'm out of the picture, she just steps in and everything stays the same. The middlemen respect strength, and if she gives them no reason to doubt her, they'll stay with her.* "Motherfuck..." she muttered, easing her car into the underground garage. That was the only entrance any of them could use, the only one keyed to after-hours access. "One way in, one way out. Question is—are they expecting me?"

Still no sign of Sasha's car. Or Kent's. Jude left the Porsche parked near the elevator and punched in a request for the 14th floor, just in case anybody was monitoring the comings and goings on the elevator. She'd climb the stairwell the rest of the way, just to be safe. Slipping the Sig free once more, she also pulled the other one from its resting place at the small of her back. "I look like something out of a fucking episode of *Miami Vice*," she complained to her reflection in the elevator's mirrored surfaces. She checked the clips in both guns and then slid the second one back behind her back. Jude wasn't usually the type to go in guns blazing. Her theory was, the more guns you had, the more chances you had of blowing your own head off. When necessary, however, she would shoot whoever and whatever stood in her way.

The adrenaline kicked in, endorphins rushing through her blood now with abandon. This was the part of the hunt her body always responded to, and her muscles quivered in anticipation. She took to the stairs silently, cautiously...her mind cataloging the pain she was going to inflict on the man who had delivered Jason to his enemies. Her eyes were almost white as the rage consumed her, the blue disappearing almost completely. Somewhere in the far recess of her mind, the warmth of Liz's love cowered in the face of so much ice, hiding itself away in fear of being extinguished.

18...19...20....

The floors fell away as she continued her steady ascent towards her quarry. She was focused on one thing now. Finding Kent and making him pay. Sasha would be dealt with harshly as well, but she was far from committed to killing her ex-lover. Maybe some renegade carnal impulses from the morning remained, maybe she simply didn't want to kill a body that she had possessed so thoroughly. Whatever it was, Sasha's fate was still undecided.

23...24...25...

She reached the 27th floor and soundlessly opened the fire exit door, her gaze sweeping the corridor both ways before she emerged. Every nerve ending awake, every instinct attuned to noises that could indicate trouble, she crept down the hall towards her office. Stopping at the door, she readied herself to go in, but a trickle of light leaking from the boardroom down the hall caught her eye.

What the fuck...?

Stealthily changing directions, she continued down the corridor and drew closer to the half-open door. Catching sight of a honey-blonde flash of hair, Jude let out a strangled roar and kicked the door open.

"Hello, Jude. Welcome to your nightmare. Again."

Kent was sitting easily at the head of the table in one of the leather, wingback chairs. Liz was beside him, tied to one of the cubicle desk chairs. Her face was bruised viciously, her hair matted with blood from an unseen wound. She was slumped over, and Jude couldn't tell for sure, but she thought her lover was still breathing. *He'd better hope she is.*

The Sig came up and pointed unwaveringly at Kent's head. "You're going to die, motherfucker," she said calmly.

"Jude, we're all going to die. The question is, who's going to die today? Not me, I assure you." His own Glock was pointed at Liz's head. "Now, put the gun down or she dies right now."

"How do I know she's not already dead?" Jude deliberately played dumb. "More to the point, how do I know you're going to let her go if I put my gun down?"

"I never said a thing about letting her go," Kent replied. "But she is still alive, I promise." He kicked the chair roughly. "Rise and shine, baby. Your sweetheart's here to see you."

Liz groaned softly and lifted her head, her green eyes slowly focusing on her lover. "Ju...Jude," she rasped.

It was all Jude could do to stay motionless, her heart screaming at her to run to her lover's bleeding form. But that would mean death for them both. Obediently she dropped the gun to the floor.

This can't be happening again...God no.

As if he could read her mind, Kent cackled with glee. "Deja vu all over again, huh? Tell me, how is the Archangel going to get herself out of this one? I'm sure you'll think of a way. You seem to have nine lives. Of course, your partners usually aren't so lucky, are they?"

"I saved your miserable little hide, didn't I?" Jude growled. "I should have just let you die in that garage."

"Yes, you should have," Kent agreed amiably. "Because afterwards I was branded a worthless coward who gave his partner up."

"That pretty much sums up what you did," she mocked him, wanting to get under his skin. *If I can get him to turn the gun on me, she might have a chance.*

His face darkened with fury. "They took me off the streets because of you and put me in a fucking office where I couldn't do any good. Or so they thought."

"Good? You call betraying one of your own good?" Jude was incredulous.

"Jason was an unfortunate casualty, but you needed a reminder of your mission. You were getting too good at being bad."

"And I needed a reminder of who the bad guys were?"

"Yes." He beamed at her as if she were a prized pupil. "Jason's death served that purpose."

Jude's composure was rapidly fragmenting, and she felt her muscles trembling with rage. "You made me kill my partner, you crazy sonofabitch. Don't you get that? *The only good thing in my life and you made me kill it...*" she roared.

Kent paled a little at the barely controlled violence directed at him. "You're not meant for things like that. Like this beautiful young thing here. You used to know that."

"Remind me, Kent," Jude purred, her voice dripping with menace. "Remind me of what I'm meant for."

"Don't you see, Jude? You have a gift...you were born like them. You can wallow in their filth—drink their booze, take their drugs, fuck their women—in a way that I can't. And then you can bring them to justice...where they belong." His face hardened. "The Agency saved you, Jude...they gave you a purpose, a reason for living, and you repaid them by turning on them and spitting on everything they gave you."

Jude closed her eyes at the ranting litany. It could be her mother or her childhood priest screaming at her just as easily. The words were the same. They were all people who thought they had a claim to her soul to serve their ends.

They were all the same—people like her mother, like the priests, like Kent—believing her fundamentally born into sin. For so long she had believed they were right, that she belonged to the shadows where she had fled to avoid their contemptuous eyes. Only the shadows, which had once seemed so accepting, tried to make their own claim on the darkness within her, and now she turned from them as well.

She opened her eyes, a blazing determination burning deep within her. No one owned her soul...she would belong to no one except the woman who had seen her darkness and her light, who had accepted it all. The woman to whom she had entrusted her heart. She glanced over at the slumped form of her lover in the chair. "You're wrong, Kent. You betrayed the Agency." Her words gained momentum as she spoke. "You were the coward. You were the one who let everyone else do the dirty work because you didn't have the balls for it. I saved your worthless hide. Jason, Tony, and I covered for you because you couldn't cut it. You sold Jason out to Rico because you couldn't control the operation. I was so close to bringing them in, Kent. But you were too stupid to realize that." She laughed tauntingly. "Let's face it, Kent, you're just too fucking dumb to do the Agency any good. That's why they benched you. You're not just a coward—you're a fool."

Kent's face, which had been growing progressively darker as she tormented him, contorted itself with a bellow of outrage, and he turned the gun on her. Jude had been anticipating the motion and hurled herself out of the way as he fired at her. She tucked and rolled, launching herself at Kent. They collided in a tangle just in front of Liz's bound form, and the gun went off again with a loud report.

Jude felt the bullet tear through her right shoulder with searing heat, but she continued towards him relentlessly. She caught him squarely in the jaw with her left fist, but he retaliated by punching her wounded shoulder. With a scream of pain, Jude fell back, and Kent landed squarely on top of her, straddling her muscled abdomen in a mockery of a lover's embrace. Holding her by the throat, he began backhanding her rhythmically across the face, enlarging the cut on her face into a gouge that poured blood, and opening up several new wounds.

Jude felt the second Sig grinding into the muscles of her back and tried frantically to think of a way to get to the weapon. *At least his attention's distracted from Elizabeth.* Gathering her scattered wits, Jude grimly struck out at Kent's gray eyes. An injured howl told her she had made contact, and the agent's grip lessened a fraction. Taking advantage, Jude heaved herself upwards, marshaling the remaining strength in her right arm to land a punch to his larynx.

Kent fell backwards, and Jude tumbled over with him, her knee grinding solidly into his groin. "That's gotta hurt," she chortled, gasping for breath. "Let's see how you like this," she snarled, back-handing him across the face. "Hurts, don't it?" With her left hand, she reached behind her and pulled the second Sig out. "Now you get to die, motherfucker..."

"I'm afraid I can't let you do that."

Jude froze on the trigger, recognizing the voice behind her. The Sig's nose still resting between Kent's eyes, she glanced over her shoulder to see Sasha calmly regarding them from the doorway, her own gun trained on Liz.

"As tiresome as he is, Jude, I can't let you kill him just yet." She strolled the length of the boardroom and gently helped Jude to her feet. When Kent made a motion to rise, a minute gesture from Sasha's gun kept him down. She took in Jude's bloody form with a grimace. "I can't believe you let yourself get shot."

"He got lucky," Jude muttered, not quite believing they were having this conversation. However, Sasha made a point of being civil at the most uncivilized times, and Jude was not about to disrupt the equilibrium that was keeping both her and Liz alive at this point.

"He must have. Hurts, though, huh?"

"Like a bitch," Jude agreed.

"I'll call Stephen afterwards. He's the one that takes care of you, no?" She arched a questioning brow.

"Sure," Jude answered uncertainly.

Sasha indicated Liz with a jerk of her head, "Untie the reporter and get her to her feet. We're going for a ride." She looked with disdain at Kent's still-prone form. "Get up now, you fool." She shook her head at the bloodied federal agent. "You've unbearably complicated things, you know. Bringing *her* into it." She pointed at the softly moaning reporter.

Jude tried to ignore the uneasy gnawing in the pit of her stomach, hoping to all the gods that what she thought was about to happen wasn't. "Hey there..." She swiftly freed Liz from her restraints and caught the slender form in her arms, wincing at the pressure on her injured shoulder. "Can you walk?"

Liz opened swollen eyes to focus hazily on her lover. "You look like shit, Jude."

The dark woman managed an uneven chuckle. "Tell me about it. Can you walk?" she repeated.

"Yeah...as soon as somebody tells the room to stop spinning." She slipped her arm around Jude's waist and let herself be enfolded in a half-embrace. The blood rushing down Jude's arm and over the Sig she still clutched in her hand made the reporter start in alarm. "You're hurt."

"So are you, love. Come on, we've got to get moving."

"Is it over?" Green eyes pleaded softly with blue.

Jude glanced up at the two figures waiting by the door. "Not just yet."

▢ ▢ ▢

To her surprise, Sasha allowed Jude to keep the Sig and disarmed Kent who stood almost sulkily beside the tawny woman. He obviously had not registered the fact that wherever they were all going now, he would not be one of the ones making the return journey. Jude was a little more uncertain of what her assistant had in store for her and Elizabeth. But she suspected that it bode ill for the small woman. Her mind began racing through various scenarios until it hit upon a likely one. "We're going to go see Romair, aren't we?" she asked Sasha as they stepped into the elevator.

Sasha smiled in acknowledgment. "That's why you get the big bucks, querida. You're always one step ahead of the competition."

"Except this time."

The tawny woman shrugged gracefully. "You were a little... distracted." Her eyes narrowed as they took in the honey-haired woman resting under the shelter of Jude's good arm. "Anyway...the boys are waiting in the garage. I've set up a little meeting with Romair where we're going to settle things down. Can you keep the bleeding down long enough for the ride over there?"

"Yeah," Jude muttered, even though her arm was already going numb with pain. "Where exactly are we going?"

Sasha offered her a mysterious little smile. "You'll see when we get there."

And no doubt that's where you'll kill Kent and Elizabeth. A part of her still wondered if that was Sasha's real intention. The tawny woman had to know that the one way to bring all of Jude's fury crashing upon her was to injure Liz. Her optimism rose several notches with this thought. Sasha also had no way of knowing that Jude and Romair had met that evening, and that they had pooled their knowledge—including their suspicions about Sasha. *So what are you going to do, Romair? Do you not show? Or do you—*

As the elevator doors opened, they were greeted by the roar and scream of a gunfight. *Oh...that's what you do.* Romair had apparently decided to take the initiative and bring the meeting to Sasha. Jude recognized several of the Argentinean's man firing on her own people.

Tightening her hold on Liz, she ducked them down and rolled them towards the cover of the nearby Porsche, managing to fire a few shots to back her attackers off. Already the expensive car was riddled with bullets, so she reasoned a few more wouldn't hurt. She saw Sasha raise her gun and fire on an approaching Argentinean, then tuck and roll out of the way. Kent wasn't so lucky, however, as he leapt for the safety of a nearby pillar he was caught by a stray bullet that tore through the top of his skull, exposing the vulnerable remains of his cerebral cortex.

As Jude watched her old partner die, her only regret was that she hadn't been the one to fire the bullet.

"This is not good, Jude. This is not good." Liz groaned as she slumped against the wall.

"And you said you had a way with words." Jude grinned. This was what she knew best. How to get out of impossible situations. Without Liz as a bargaining chip, no one had any hold over her. She could concentrate on getting them both out safely and let Romair's people and her own shoot it out. Of course, the police were probably going to be here any minute.

She saw Sasha's sleek form pop up and take down two more Argentineans. The tawny woman shouted for her men to regroup, and the dark suits began falling back towards her and away from Jude and Liz. "Where did Kent park?" she asked her lover.

The honey-haired woman frowned. "I wasn't exactly paying attention at the time."

"I know, but think. We can't drive the Porsche out of here."

Liz regarded the expensive machine that was acting as their shield. "I never liked this car."

Jude's brow furrowed. "Really? Why not?" A bullet streaked by her head. "Fuck...that was too close. Think Liz, where'd he park?" Bullets flew thickly over their heads, the booming reports of gun making hearing impossible. "Oh never mind...we're gonna just have to run for it and hope we make it out of the garage." Even as she said the words she knew that in the shape they were in, they wouldn't get far. Her right arm was numb now, and she suspected that the nerves had been damaged. With only one good arm, she was going to have to shoot and hope that Elizabeth could keep up. Judging from the contusions on Liz's face, she figured her lover probably had a concussion and was in no condition to run.

A gentle hand caught her arm and tugged her into a fierce embrace. "I love you, Jude." Jude buried her head in the honey hair, now matted with blood. It still smelled faintly of the clean-scented shampoo she had lovingly rubbed into it, and Jude just let herself drift for a precious moment in the sensation of resting in her lover's arms once more.

She forced herself to look into the deepest green eyes she'd ever seen. They were shining with a love so powerful, if Jude hadn't already been on her knees, she would have fallen to them. "I love you too, Elizabeth." Using time they didn't have, her lips found her lover's and captured them in a painfully sweet kiss that threatened to tear her soul from its moorings. Everything she had been, was, and would be resonated in that kiss. And it promised an eternity to them both.

Time seemed to stop for the dark woman, and she could hear each distinct sound—the thunder booming out-of-sync with the flashes of lightning that still streaked through the jagged sky, the wail of sirens closer than she had expected, and highlighting it all the rapid fire *boom-boom* of Sigs and Glocks answering each other in a symphony of bloodshed. Men littered the ground, pouring out their life-force on uncaring concrete, and Jude realized in this frantic instant that she didn't want to die.

Not here...

Not like this...

Not anymore.

With a last embrace, Jude asked unsteadily. "You ready?"

"As I'll ever be." Liz managed a smile for her lover, her thoughts unerringly paralleling the dark woman.

"You decided on where we'll be taking that vacation?"

A strangled sound that was part laugh, part cry at the question. "Why don't we just decide when we get to the airport?"

"Well...I'm warning you, I wanna go someplace really cool..." she tried to tease.

Slender fingers stretched out and caressed Jude's wounded face softly. "Jude..." Acceptance reflected deep in the reporter's eyes. "It's time to go..."

The dark woman took a steadying breath and nodded. "Count of three...ready..." She checked the clip in her Sig one last time and flexed her fingers around the grip. "Three...two...Go!"

Ducking as they ran, Jude and Liz cut a zigzagging path towards the door. Jude dropped a man that appeared suddenly in front of them, but it distracted her attention from her lover by her side. She had taken a few more steps ahead when she realized that Liz wasn't with her. With a yowl of rage, she whirled around to see her lover lying on the floor, blood flowing from her leg and neck. She dove towards the reporter, Liz's name ripping from her throat. Just as she reached the honey-haired woman she felt an ugly heat blossoming from her back and leg as she fell over her lover's body.

And then mercifully...everything went black.

Epilogue

Six weeks later...

"You have a minute?" Lucas was uncharacteristically shy as he peered around the fabricated gray wall of Liz's cubicle.

She had only been back in the office for a few days and everyone was still treading very carefully around her. She had written her article, "Rising to Grace," from a hospital bed. Now Bantam Books was offering her an obscenely large amount of money to tell the whole story from start to finish.

Trouble was, there were some parts of the story she desperately wanted to forget.

She remembered kissing Jude fiercely and running alongside her until a searing pain cut her down...and even though her mind was screaming at her to get up, to run, to join her partner...she fell, another agonizing burn gripped her, this time in her neck....She couldn't see Jude's face, but she could hear the anguished cry that was her name tearing from the dark woman's throat. She forced her eyes open...willing her arms to raise... and then she saw Jude falling...so far...so hard...how could the ground be so far away? Jude fell bonelessly against her, evil red tendrils of her life pouring from the wounds in her body....She tried to scream, tried to cradle her lover's still form...but every breath cost her energy and her eyes fell shut against the welcoming black tide....Her last thought was of Jude...and her last hope was that wherever she ended up, Jude would be waiting for her there...

When she woke up in the hospital, they told her three days had passed. Jude was nowhere to be found. The police had questioned her almost as ruthlessly as she questioned them... but nobody knew where Jude was. The SWAT team found no trace of her or Sasha among the dozen or so bodies they recovered. Kent had been among the corpses, and slowly the story had unfolded.

The doctors told her she had been lucky. A bullet that should have been fatal only grazed her neck. She would have a nasty scar on the right side of her neck, but she was alive. The bullet in her leg was more problematic, but after a few weeks of physical therapy it was well on the way to returning to normal. As soon as she could sit up, she called Lucas and had him bring her PowerBook to the hospital. She had been surprised when Maria had delivered it. They had shared an awkward exchange, both wracked with grief and still uneasy over everything that had happened. Maria had pounded on the doors of all the DEA agents she knew, including Tony's, to try and find out what had happened to Jude. They knew nothing.

Or so they claimed.

She had tried going to the house, but the DEA had cordoned it off and prevented her from getting inside. She had managed to speak to Carmina for a few moments, and found the rotund housekeeper as distraught as she was. She had promised the older woman that she wouldn't rest until they both knew what had happened to Jude.

That was six weeks ago, and the faint hopes that she had clung to were fading hard. It showed in her eyes, their usually vibrant green now dulled to a lusterless gray. Dark shadows attested to the sleepless nights she spent, her body longing for the comfort of her lover's sleek form. She shifted back in her seat with a weary sigh and waved her boss in. "What's up, Lucas?"

"I guess it would be kind of stupid to ask you how you are. You look like shit." He perched on the edge of her desk, her tidy area visibly unsettling him.

Liz managed a half-hearted chuckle. "You really know how to make a girl feel special, boss-man." She shrugged. "I'm going home in a few anyway."

"Good." Lucas nodded, scratching his head and looking anywhere but at his employee.

She really wasn't in the mood for his tiptoeing around anymore. The entire staff, which was generally being very supportive, was nonetheless regarding her uneasily. Liz didn't know if it was because of her ordeal, or because of the blunt honestly with which she had written about her lover and the events leading up to the shooting. She knew she had broken the cardinal rule of reporting, but quite frankly, she really didn't give a damn. To be honest, she didn't feel much like being a reporter anymore either. It required a detachment she no longer possessed. If all of Jude that remained was that legacy—Liz's resolute refusal to be a bystander in her own life— then, by God, Liz was going to honor that. "Something you need to say to me?" Liz prodded.

"Yeah...that book deal. You gonna take it?"

She sighed again and ran a hand through her hair. More and more, Liz noticed she had been appropriating habits that had been her lover's. It was one of the small things that made her feel close to Jude still. It was just about all that she had left of the dark woman. "I don't know, Lucas. Probably. They'll give me a nice fat advance, and I can go somewhere far away."

"That might do you some good." He latched onto the idea eagerly. "Put all this behind you."

Liz regarded him with a cold stare that made him blanch. "I don't want to forget, Lucas. Ever." She wanted to scream at him, *Don't you get it? Everything that meant anything to me disappeared with her....Memory is all I have left.* No, she wouldn't go away to forget. She would go away and remember, and, with loving detail, record everything that they had been to each other. She closed her eyes and exhaled softly. "I'm sorry, Lucas. I'm just really tired," she apologized lamely.

"Still not sleeping?"

"No." She shook her head. "And I hate that stuff the doctor gave me. It makes me feel all fuzzy, even when I'm awake." *I'd rather have the pain...and remember...than sleep and forget.*

"Well...go home and try and take it easy." He stood awkwardly as if to leave.

"I thought there was something you wanted to tell me?"

"Nah..." He seemed to think better of why he had wanted to talk to her and instead edged over to the corridor and turned back to her. "Go home, Liz. See you Monday."

"Thanks, Boss." She waved at him and bent to gather up her things. Several other people nodded as she left the office and absent-mindedly punched the lobby button in the elevator.

After the chilly climate-controlled hallways of the office, the searing late summer heat felt good on her skin. Blinded by the sun's brilliance, she dug in her bag for her sunglasses, slipping them gratefully over her eyes. Zipping the shoulder bag closed she turned towards the parking garage across the street to her right.

"You want a ride, querida?"

Liz froze in mid-step, afraid to turn around. She knew that voice. It had whispered its secrets to her at night, called out her name in passion, and tormented her with its absence these endless weeks.

"Turn around, love." It coaxed her suddenly trembling muscles. "Elizabeth..." Her name—a breath, a whisper, a plea. "Turn around."

Somehow, with strength she didn't know she possessed, Liz slowly pivoted on one foot, ready to flee lest the voice prove that of a phantom.

She gasped at the sight before her.

It was Jude, thin and drawn—her bronze skin paler than Liz had ever imagined it could be, white linen trousers and a blue T-shirt hanging loosely on her long frame. She leaned heavily on a mahogany cane, and her right arm was bound carefully in a sling. The injuries to her face seemed to have healed, but there was a light scar across her cheek. Instinctively, she took a step forward, a bitten-off sob in her throat. "Oh god..." she whispered. "Is it...Is it really you?"

Jude gave her a lopsided grin, the halting movement the only indication of her pain. "C'mere."

Liz erased the distance between them with quick strides, her arms reaching out for Jude. Hesitatingly, with fingers trembling so badly she could barely control them, she caressed her lover's face, drawing soft lines across her cheeks and jaw. "Can I?" *Can I touch you? Can I love you? Are you real?*

The brilliant smile on Jude's face answered all three unspoken questions with a resounding, *YES*...and Liz placed tender arms around her lover's waist. They both gasped softly at the touch, both having feared that it was something to be forever denied them. Jude silently cursed the cane she had to grasp and the wounded arm that kept her from returning the embrace, but she pressed her body against the reporter's as firmly as she could, pouring all her love into that fleeting contact.

"How? What? What happened to you, Jude? Where did you go?" All the questions tumbled out, along with tears that Liz thought she had already cried.

"Shh..." Jude soothed her, pressing gentle kisses to the top of her lover's head. They swayed precariously as Liz tightened her hold, never wanting to let the dark woman out of her sight again.

"Careful there," Jude warned unsteadily. "Don't let my tough act fool you. A stiff breeze will knock me down."

"Then let's sit down." Liz was full of questions, but she was loathe to let her newly-resurrected lover go. "How did you get here?

Jude gestured to the green Explorer illegally parked next to the curb. "We could go somewhere..." Her voice trailed off uncertainly, and Liz beamed.

The next few minutes were spent getting Jude settled into the passenger seat of the Explorer. Liz couldn't believe that the woman had managed to get it this far, she seemed so pale and exhausted by the effort. "Why don't I drive us to the beach house?" She smiled tentatively at her lover. "I haven't been able to see the menagerie. I miss them."

"I'm sure they miss you too," Jude grinned. "I hope they remember who I am."

"You haven't been home? Where have you been? And why haven't you gotten in touch with anyone? Ria and Carmina are about to go out of their minds with worry. Why?"

"WHOA!" Jude squeezed her hand pleadingly. "One thing at a time. 'Kay?"

"Sorry." Liz smiled sheepishly. "You were gonna give me the short version while I got us home." Jude didn't comment on the reporter's choice of pronouns, but the quiet smile that flickered across her lips said more than enough for them both.

Jude took a deep breath, trying to settle her racing pulse. With a start, Liz realized the dark woman was trembling violently. Leaving the truck in park, she softly clasped Jude's left hand, and was pleased to see that her touch seemed to settle the worst of the dark woman's uncertainty. "After you..." she stumbled over the words, "Went down, I tried to get to you."

"You got shot too."

"Yeah. I remember falling, thinking that it was all over for both of us, until I woke up a week later in a private room at some triage center that I don't want to know anything about. I don't know where Romair found him, but Stephen was there. Turns out he had spent the better part of a day picking bullet fragments and other assorted stuff-- including a kidney—out of my body."

"Jude—a kidney? Oh my god...Are you...?"

"Don't worry, the other one works just fine. I'm just going to hurt like a mother for another month or so. The bullet in my leg fucked up the muscle, but that'll be okay too."

"Your arm?"

"Nerve damage." Jude shrugged. "They tell me I'll have a hell of a thunderstorm detector, and some of the mobility will be permanently restricted...but all in all it's not too bad of a trade-off. Fortunately it was my right arm and not my left. I'd hate having to learn to write with my other hand."

"So...I don't understand. Romair's people got you out?" Liz kept one eye on the road, the other on Jude's thin profile.

"Yeah, he was there himself. Although I didn't know it at the time. They grabbed me and were going back for you when the cops arrived. Since they knew you'd be free and clear legally speaking, they let the EMT's take care of you and they hustled me off to this triage place that apparently Romair has stashed for shit exactly like this." She smiled in appreciation of the Argentinean's planning. "That guy knows what he's doing, Liz."

"Sasha?"

Jude shrugged. "Disappeared. Permanently if she has any sense. I have no idea what she was planning. She could have killed you." Her grip on the smaller woman's hand tightened. "If I ever see her again..."

"Shh..." Liz quieted her with a tender gesture. "Don't think about that right now, okay?"

"Anyway...I was pretty much out of it for almost three weeks, not doing much of anything except sleeping. I wasn't conscious for more than a few minutes at a time."

"I still don't understand why Romair didn't get in touch with me."

"He didn't want to get you involved, Liz."

"*Involved?*" Involuntarily, her voice rose three octaves. "I love you, goddamn it. I *am* involved."

Jude shifted so that she could see her lover as she drove and squeezed their entertwined fingers. "Legally speaking, love. He didn't know exactly where I stood with the DEA, not to mention the state. There was a distinct possibility I was going to have to leave the country permanently. If that were the case, I didn't want you to know anything until I was settled. That way the Feds couldn't harass you."

"I am assuming since you're here and not in Tijuana that you're clear."

Jude chuckled lightly at the understatement. "Mostly," she agreed. "The Agency's got their underwear in a collective wad over what Kent did. That and the rose-tinted portrait you painted of me convinced them that pursuing anything further against me would be a waste of time."

"It wasn't rose-tinted," Liz protested. Beneath the fragile skin of Jude's wrist, Liz could feel the strong and steady pulse of the dark woman's heart, and it brought home the message that still hadn't quite sunk in. "You're really here," she choked, the tears beginning to stream once more down her face.

"I'm here," Jude crooned softly, stroking the golden head and sighing softly. "I'm not going anywhere else. I promise."

They rode in a comforting silence the rest of the way home.

▯ ▯ ▯

The house was a cacophony of barking dogs as Jude allowed her smaller lover to help her into the house. Finally released from the kennel where Ria had been keeping them during Jude's absence; Clytemnestra, Aggie, and Pete danced around their mistress and the smaller human doing a sort of canine shuffle, each one competing for attention. Pete got stepped on one too many times, and let out a mournful yelp that startled the other two larger dogs into silence. Jude and Liz laughed at their antics, lavishing attention on all three until Liz opened the patio gate and left them to run off their excess energy on the beach.

Jude limped after her and quietly shut the sliding glass doors. "Hi there," she said quietly, standing behind the honey-haired woman.

"Hi yourself," Liz breathed, soaking in the warm scent of the woman she loved. The tears had been cathartic, wringing out the last of her sorrow and her joy at seeing Jude again and knowing their connection still existed.

"I'm kinda gimpy," Jude apologized. "I can't hug you properly."

Liz spun around to gaze upon the bluest eyes she had ever seen. "Then kiss me."

The tiny beginnings of a smile curled Jude's lips as she bent down to capture the honey-haired woman's mouth with her own. They were tentative at first, their lips barely touching. The familiar flame soon overcame any reticence, and Liz's mouth opened in joyful welcome. Her arms slid around her lover's broad shoulders, careful of her many injuries as she tried to communicate every once of love she felt for the woman in her arms.

Neither woman was conscious of time passing as they indulged in a lingering reintroduction. Their kisses grew progressively more playful as both women realized that the events that had nearly killed them both had not destroyed their feeling for each other. Desperate for breath, Jude regretfully broke away. "Have I told you how good you are at that?" she smiled.

"It takes two, lover," Liz replied, her eyes glimmering brightly.

Jude leaned in for another kiss, "Mmm...I think you're right." She grinned but couldn't quite conceal a flinch as she stood straight.

"Let's sit you down, okay?" Liz suggested, not missing the flash of pain in Jude's eyes.

"That's probably a good idea," Jude concurred, allowing herself to be seated on a nearby chaise. "We need to talk anyway."

"Sounds serious," Liz tried to banter.

The warm blue of Jude's eyes remained earnest. "It is," she replied.

Liz settled herself comfortably within arms' reach of the dark woman, not quite willing to sever their physical connection so soon. "Okay, shoot." She winced at the pun. "Sorry. Forget I said that."

A wry smile graced Jude's features. "Not a problem. I read your article. Elizabeth...if that's the way you truly see me..."

"It is," Liz assured her, quite willing to defend the portrait of her lover that she had painted for the world.

"Then I'm the luckiest woman on earth. I don't deserve it...I don't deserve you..." Jude fought for words. "You should be with someone who doesn't nearly get you killed on a regular basis..."

"Hey!" Liz's green eyes darkened dangerously. "I thought we established I decided what was best for me."

Jude held her hand up in supplication. "You do, and believe me, I'm not arguing with your choices." She dropped her eyes, suddenly intent on the fabric covering the chaise cushions. "In fact...." A blush softly warmed her features. "That's kinda what I want to talk to you about."

A giddiness Liz thought had been destroyed by the bullet that ripped through Jude's back began to simmer deep within her belly. "You do?"

Jude fidgeted as much as her wounds would allow her. She raised a trembling hand to trace the line of her lover's fair cheek. "Yeah...I...uh... Damn this is hard." She narrowed her eyes at Elizabeth. "I thought you were supposed to be the talker."

"Nu-uh..." Liz shook her head with a grin. "This is your show." Her face softened as she added, "I need to hear this, Jude. I need to hear you."

The dark woman swallowed hard and nodded. "I never expected to be in this place. To be free and clear with no one lurking over my shoulder. I...don't know what kind of partner I'll be." She glanced at the waves rolling against the sand and the dogs playing there. "I've told you that before. I've never tried living a...normal life."

"Is that what you're going to live, Jude?" Liz looked at her lover intently. "A normal life?"

Jude nodded. "Yeah. I've...divested...all the holdings that would tend to make people want to blow me away." She chuckled. "Although I hear those real estate developers can be pretty ruthless." She clasped Liz's hand softly in her own. "I'd like to try to make that life with you..." She dropped her eyes again. "That is...if you...well...if you want to try."

Liz brought their entwined hands to her lips, pressing a soft kiss into each of her lover's elegant fingers. "Are you sure about this, Jude?" She steadied the blue eyes with her own. "After everything that happened?"

Jude looked at her somberly. "I don't know. But the only thing I am sure about is that I can't walk away from you. I have to try this..." She leaned towards her lover...her partner...her soulmate, ignoring all the aches and pains until they were in one another's arms, their lips and tongues communicating what their words could not. Liz sighed deeply, opening herself to the dark woman's embrace, an indescribable joy surrounding her with warmth, laughter, and love.

Liz had discovered the secret to Jude Lucien...this extraordinary woman who had been gifted with a formidable intelligence and a heart stalwart enough to endure a brutality that no man or woman should ever have to face. She had left the light and walked in the darkness. She had met evil and made it serve her. But despite all that—or maybe because of it—she had retained an essential purity of soul that no blackness—no matter how ugly or vile—had been able to destroy.

Jude would say that she was no saint...just as surely as Elizabeth would say that her lover was no devil...but to the honey-haired reporter this woman whom she called her soulmate was a unique angel—granted a grace that only those who have fallen may know.

She didn't know what would happen to them now that things were changing. Jude's darkness would not be dispersed by the simple dissolution of her illicit empire. What she carried within her, she would carry always— more than one night would be lost to the demons that clamored for her all the more violently now that they were denied. But they both faced it with a lightness of spirit that would have to be experienced to be understood. For neither woman stood alone any longer—they had found in each other the component that their souls had been lacking.

Through Jude, Elizabeth had known the darkness...and now, through her, Jude would know the light. Simple? Perhaps...but she firmly believed it would be enough to carry them through the days and nights to come.

It would have to be.

FINIS

JHP

VISIT OUR WEB SITE AT
www.justicehouse.com
JHP@justicehouse.com

AND OUR SITE DESIGNED
ESPECIALLY FOR WRITERS
www.houseofbards.com

JUSTICE HOUSE PUBLISHING

INCREDIBLE BOOKS
INCREDIBLE AUTHORS
INCREDIBLE WOMEN

Justice House Publishing, Inc.
books are available
wherever fine books are sold